K-D

A Season to Lie

Center Point
Large Print

Also by Emily Littlejohn and available from
Center Point Large Print:

Inherit the Bones

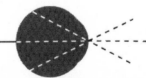

**This Large Print Book carries the
Seal of Approval of N.A.V.H.**

A Season to Lie

Emily Littlejohn

CENTER POINT LARGE PRINT
THORNDIKE, MAINE

The text of this Large Print edition is unabridged.
In other aspects, this book may vary
from the original edition.
Printed in the United States of America
on permanent paper.
Set in 16-point Times New Roman type.

ISBN: 978-1-64358-152-1

Library of Congress Cataloging-in-Publication Data

Names: Littlejohn, Emily, author.
Title: A season to lie / Emily Littlejohn.
Description: Center Point Large Print edition. | Thorndike, Maine :
    Center Point Large Print, 2019.
Identifiers: LCCN 2019001276 | ISBN 9781643581521 (hardcover :
    alk. paper)
Subjects: LCSH: Women detectives—Colorado—Fiction. | Murder—
    Investigation—Fiction. | Large type books.
Classification: LCC PS3612.I8823 S43 2019 | DDC 813/.6—dc23
LC record available at https://lccn.loc.gov/2019001276

For the loves of my life,
Chris and Claire

Acknowledgments

First thanks go to my patient and loving husband, Chris. Pam Ahearn and Elizabeth Lacks, your critical eyes and supportive words are, as always, invaluable. And to the readers who asked for a second Gemma story, I hope you enjoy.

A Season to Lie

Prologue

On a cold and bitter night in February, twelve weeks after giving birth, I returned to what I know best: death.

I follow death into black woods. I chase death across deserted meadows. I seek death in the faces of strangers.

Death is a son of a bitch and I study his plotted moves and sly maneuvers, the way he sneaks in and strikes when least expected. As a cop, I tell myself that I am the hunter and death is my prey.

But I'm starting to think that's a lie.

The truth is, it's death that's following me.

It has followed me all my life.

Death stalks me like a Colorado summertime thunderstorm—after noon, it's always there, past the horizon, an hour still out of sight. I can't yet see the iron-shaded clouds building beyond the mountains or smell the wetness in the air, but it's coming nonetheless.

Death is coming, and there's nothing I can do to stop it.

Chapter One

I stepped into the central squad room of the Cedar Valley Police Department and then stood still a moment, taking in the familiar sights and smells. In contrast to the freezing, frenetic energy of the blizzard outside, the room was warm and calm.

Christmas had come and gone more than a month ago, yet tinsel and evergreen boughs were still draped high on the walls. I have been inside enough law enforcement centers around the state to know how common that is; holiday cleanup always seems to take a backseat to crime.

The room smelled as I remembered: fresh coffee, burnt microwave dinners, and paper, so much paper. There were folders and files stacked high on the desks. Post-it notes in every shade of the rainbow were tacked to the edges of computer monitors, on the handsets of the telephones at each desk, and across the bulletin board that ran the length of the back wall. Much of our day-to-day business had gone electronic, but old habits are hard to break.

Photographs of haunted, hunted men and women stared out from that same bulletin board. At one time, their stories may have been unique, but the moment their picture hit that board, they became one and the same: criminal, thug, wanted.

In front of me, a doll from the popular holiday game Elf on the Shelf hung from the ceiling in a noose fashioned from a dirty shoelace, her small arms twisted up to grip the sides of her head as though in shock at her fate. I gave her foot a gentle push and she swung in the air, her coy smirk unchanging even in death.

In the corner, the radio was tuned to an oldies station. Elvis Presley sang softly about a boy, born in a snowstorm, to a mother all too aware that his was to be a hard life, short-lived in the ghettos of Chicago. The song breaks my heart every time I hear it.

" 'Well, the world turns,' " a deep voice crooned along with the King. I turned to see Finn Nowlin, mostly a decent cop and generally a pain in the ass, strike a classic Elvis pose. He shimmied his hips and then swung his arm up and held the move.

I rolled my eyes and turned away before he could see me smile.

I was home.

Grinning, I went to my desk, expecting a bare surface. Before I had gone on maternity leave in November, I'd cleaned house. Stained mugs and a few long-forgotten spoons went home with me to be deep cleaned. Files were returned to the records room, outstanding cases were handed over to my colleagues, and pens went into hibernation in my desk drawers.

To my surprise, though, a stack of file folders sat in a tidy pile waiting for me. A purple note on the top folder read "Ask Finn." They were coded for local, recent misdemeanors; they belonged in the records room, not on my desk.

The rest of the space was still clean, and I dropped my bag and pulled off my heavy parka.

"It's warm in here, isn't it?"

Finn shrugged. He rubbed his hands together. "Feels good to me. The thermostat was busted all week. They finally sent someone to fix it yesterday. We've been freezing our balls off."

I snorted. "Don't you first have to have them, before they can freeze off?"

Finn grinned. "You know you missed us, Gem. Your baby is pretty cute but you're not exactly June Cleaver. Tell me you haven't been getting antsy."

"Yeah, I missed you guys like I miss dysentery." I tapped the files on my desk. "What's happening? I hope I didn't get dolled up to watch you channel Elvis the Pelvis and read week-old files."

"Chavez wants you to get up to speed on all the work the rest of us have been doing while you've been sitting around playing Betty Crocker," Finn said with another flash of his wolfish grin. The smile faded as he snatched up the top file folder and flipped through it.

"What is it?"

He scowled. "Ever heard of Black Hound Construction?"

Thinking hard, I shook my head slowly. "I don't think so. Should I know them? Are they local?"

"No. They're new in town. They arrived a few months ago, from New York. Alistair Campbell and his seven dwarfs. More like seven assholes. They're a hotshot construction crew. Campbell's got a thing for ex-convicts, most of his crew have records. I've been keeping an eye on the group."

"Why? We have other people in town with records, probably more than we know. Most of them are harmless."

Finn said, "I don't know, call it a hunch. There's something off about them. They travel together like a pack of wolves; you see one, there's another one around the corner. Anyway, it's been par for the course the last few months. A couple of robberies, hotel rooms ransacked. It's mostly tourists getting hit. Armstrong and Moriarty believe it's a gang of employees, from the different hotels, working together. They'll catch them eventually. Christmas was quiet, New Year's Eve was a disaster as usual. Drunks all over town, on the road, in the bars. Some clown decided it was a good idea to climb the old water tower after drinking a bottle of champagne. He made it to the top and then panicked. The fire department had to climb up after him. They brought him down, and his date, some hot little ski bunny in town from Denver, finished her night with the deputy fire chief."

"Sounds exciting. What else did I miss?"

Finn shrugged. "Like I said, the usual. We do have our own little Banksy up at the Valley Academy. Someone's spray-painting graffiti on the campus after hours. So far, no one's been able to catch him. Or her. The little goon is spraying the Grim Reaper. He's actually very talented, whoever it is. Hey, did you hear the one about the priest, the rabbi, and the Grim Reaper in Las Vegas? So they walk into a bar . . ."

I tuned out the rest of Finn's joke and stared down at my desk, running a hand across the surface of it, feeling the coolness of the old wood, the pits and scars where countless other officers had scratched the surface with their pens and paper clips. I could smell the citrus furniture polish the custodial service used.

It was good to be back.

Before Grace was born, I worked a day shift that often had me chasing leads into the evening and on the weekends. There were long hours and too many nights spent far from home, far from Brody. That kind of time away, especially the evenings that dragged into early mornings, has a way of changing the dynamics of your life and your relationships. Like the tide on a sand castle, it ebbs away the very things that make up the foundation of what's important.

I was back on a part-time basis but I've been a cop long enough to know that sooner or later part-time turns into full-time, and then into overtime, and suddenly you realize it's been days since you thought about anything but the case at hand. Tonight's shift was only a few hours— seven to midnight. Not quite the graveyard shift but close enough.

There's a certain kind of tension that lives in those hours, an anticipation of one day's ending and another's beginning. I didn't mind it, though. The last few months had seen me up at all sorts of strange hours. If I wasn't nursing Grace, then I was lying in bed, worrying about things beyond my control. Would she grow up good, and strong, and kind? Would my baby find her way in this world, this world that will beat you down, chew you up, and spit you out faster than you can say "pretty please"?

I sat back as a Tina Turner song ended and a commercial began. It was quiet, especially for a Friday night. The bone-chilling blizzard might have one saving grace, if it kept folks home and off the roads. I should have known better than to even think the words *quiet night,* for in the next minute, one of our dispatchers poked her head in the room.

Chloe Parker waved. "Welcome back, Gemma.

18

Guys, I got a call about a suspicious man, a prowler, at Valley Academy. The caller wouldn't leave a name and the number came through with a New York area code. You two want to check it out? Twenty bucks says it's a prankster. I can radio patrol if you'd rather stay here. It's terrible weather."

I looked at Finn and stood, then began shrugging back into my heavy parka. "No, save patrol for the roads. There will be at least a few accidents for them to respond to before tonight is over. Maybe it's your Reaper artist, Finn."

Chloe added, "I'll call campus security and have someone meet you at the school. They'll need to open that front gate if you want to get on the property."

Across the aisle, Finn stood, too, and reached for his jacket. On the radio, the commercial for acne cream ended and the Temptations came on, wishing for rain. Finn danced along with an imaginary partner. Chloe giggled and retreated back into the tiny room that was the dispatch call center.

"Oh, but I wish it would stop snowing," Finn muttered along to the song.

I joined in, " 'But everyone knows that a man ain't supposed to cry.' "

Finn rolled his eyes and made a gagging sound. I know I'll never win *American Idol* but I'm not that bad. I've heard worse.

I rounded up my hat, gloves, and flashlight and followed Finn down the short hallway that led from the squad room to the front door. He paused so I could button up my parka, then he opened the door. The storm had picked up in intensity and the screaming wind seemed to tear the oxygen from the air.

"Jesus," I muttered. No one in their right mind would be out in a blizzard like this. I was sorry I'd returned to work, tonight of all nights. I should have been home, with Grace and Brody, in front of a roaring fire with a hot cup of cocoa and a gossip magazine in my hands.

I thought I was ready to be back, but all of a sudden, I didn't feel so sure.

Chapter Two

In early February, at the peak of winter, darkness comes early to the Rockies. A particular coldness takes hold and the wind blows in hard, gathering speed and strength as it races down from the high peaks and crosses the continental divide before hitting the Great Plains and dispersing its energy like seeds tumbling from a farmer's hands.

It was that same dark, cold, hard wind that fed the snowstorm we found ourselves in. We drove to the Valley Academy in whiteout conditions on roads that were slick with low to no visibility. The air smelled of wet steel. The scar that curved around my neck like a comma felt tight, as though it was made of piano string, tuned just past the right key.

Some people feel the weather in their bones, or in the acting up of old injuries. I felt it in the one physical reminder I have of the car accident that left my parents dead.

Finn drove in silence.

He was hunched over the steering wheel, peering through the windshield, while I controlled the heat, letting the defroster run for a few minutes and then spinning the dial over to warm our feet and hands. We sat in his personal car, a heavy Suburban. The big truck crept along like a tank, and I felt a hell of a lot safer than I would have felt in any of the department Jeeps or sedans.

Finn muttered something underneath his breath.

I pulled the hood of my parka to the side. "What was that?"

"Who the hell is out on a night like tonight, able to spot a prowler?" he said, slowing down and carefully pulling around a thick tree branch that lay in the middle of the road. "Let's drag that thing out of the road on the way back."

I nodded absentmindedly. "I bet it's some busybody that lives in that tiny trailer park across from the school, Shady Acres."

Finn barked a laugh and then swore as his breath fogged up the window.

I sighed and changed the heat back to the defroster. I leaned over and wiped the windshield with the sleeve of my parka. "Is that what it's called? That doesn't sound right. . . ."

Finn said, "Shaded Acres. Shady Acres would be something out of a comic book, like a suburb outside Gotham."

"It's the perfect name for a villain's estate," I said, humming the theme song to *Green Acres*.

Finn flinched and then punched my shoulder. "You know, you have the worst singing voice I've ever heard. It's terrible. You could skin a cat with a voice like that."

I rolled my eyes and rubbed my shoulder. I tried to think of a biting comeback but nothing came to mind. I watched him out of the corner of my eye and remembered how infuriating he could be.

He returned my side-eye with a look of his own. "What?"

"Nothing. We're here."

Finn pulled into the private school's parking lot and stopped at the heavy, locked front gate. Beneath a streetlight, the falling snow was caught in the light's beam and I watched, mesmerized, as the wind blew the flakes sideways.

He put the car in park and shut off the engine but left the heat running. Almost immediately the snow began to collect on the windshield. We stared out into the storm through the rapidly narrowing view and took stock of the situation.

The lot was deserted.

The school was deserted.

I felt the skin on the back of my neck crawl. A cramp, sudden and intense, hit me in the gut, a primordial punch of unease.

Finn spoke first. "Something's wrong. It's too . . . quiet."

Quiet was an odd choice of words, given the howling wind on the other side of the window, but I knew what Finn meant.

Something was wrong.

Dim headlights swept over us. Finn and

I watched as a big, rumbling truck with the words KASPERSKY SECURITY printed on its side slowly drove past us. The truck stopped a few feet ahead of our car and sat in park, its red taillights glowing back at us like the eyes of some prehistoric creature.

I lifted my chin in the direction of the truck. "Do you know them? Kaspersky?"

Finn nodded. "I've met the owner, Dan or Daryl or something like that. Devon maybe. I think he's got five or six different guys running security for him."

After another moment, the driver turned off the truck and slid out from the front seat. He slowly walked back to our car and Finn rolled down his window.

"Sir, ma'am," the driver said as he leaned into Finn's open window. "I'm Bowie Childs. I'm in charge of campus security."

He was blond and heavily bearded, with light, intense eyes and a chipped front tooth. We introduced ourselves and he shook Finn's hand. He peered in at me and after a long moment said, "That's a nice jacket. I like it."

"Um, thanks," I said. "We'd like to drive through campus. I think our dispatch told you we got a call about a prowler?"

Childs nodded and said, "Yes, a prowler. It's probably a damn kid. I'll open the gates for you and wait here. Watch your rear, so to speak. Keep

24

your radios on Channel 2 and let me know if you need anything. You'll have to walk, though. It's all sidewalks from here on out."

Childs leaned back and motioned for Finn to roll his window up. The guard walked over to the gate and entered a code into a pad on the side, then the gate swung slowly open.

"Are you kidding me? I don't want to get out of the car. As in, I *really* do not want to get out of this car."

Finn shook his head and gently patted his cheeks, talking himself into it. "You can wait here if you want. I'm sure Childs could use the conversation. Listen, the campus isn't that big. Didn't you go to school here for a few years?"

"Just one year," I said, staring out the window. The falling snowflakes were mesmerizing, totally and completely at the wind's mercy. "It was the second worst year of my life."

"Well, you can wait here but I'm going."

Finn put a hand on the door and gave me a devil-may-care grin.

Ah, hell. I knew what that grin meant. I groaned and gripped the passenger's side door handle.

He said, "Come on, let's do this. You take right and I'll go left. We'll meet somewhere in the middle. Keep your radio on. This'll take ten minutes. Welcome back, baby, welcome back."

Welcome back, my ass. It wouldn't surprise me in the least if Finn had arranged this

25

whole thing as a nasty little welcome-back prank.

I took a deep breath and pushed my way out of the car, into the wild of the blizzard. The blizzard, with its blowing snow that hung before me like a living veil. The blizzard, with its frigid air that made my teeth hurt when I inhaled. The scar on my neck felt as though it would snap in half.

I went right while Finn veered left. After a few steps, I turned around and scanned the parking lot. I could hardly see the grape-colored Suburban, let alone Finn or the security guard.

They had disappeared into the darkness. I was alone.

My heart skipped a beat and it took more effort than it should have to turn away and continue walking. My legs, normally sturdy and muscular, felt weak and foreign.

"Get it together," I whispered to myself. "You've been out of the game too long, Gemma."

All around me, a manic performance played out for an audience of one. The wind shrieked as it blew through the trees, making their limbs dance and their few remaining leaves jump like marionettes.

Anything was possible on a night like this.

I kept that in mind as I walked the school's perimeter, wary, thinking of the anonymous caller who'd phoned in the report. Callers stay anonymous for four reasons: they're scared because they know the perpetrator or they've got a rap sheet themselves; they don't want to deal with the hassle of filling out an official report; or they're punks pulling a prank and there is no real danger.

"Shit!"

I stumbled in a knee-high snowdrift and barely managed to catch myself from falling. Angry at my clumsiness, I regained my balance and swore again. I was out of shape, for the first time in years. Everything seemed off: my balance, my sense of direction. Even my hearing seemed dulled. Twelve weeks at home with a newborn, doing little more than feeding, sleeping, and eating, had left me out of practice, soft both literally and figuratively.

I caught my breath and kept moving forward, trying to keep my senses on high alert, aware that in this weather, with the wind covering all sounds, anyone could come up behind me and get within kissing distance before I ever had any idea they were there.

As I walked, though, the Valley Academy slept. All seemed secure on the campus and, slowly, I got my sea legs back and my uneasiness faded.

The private school hadn't changed much in the years since I'd been a student. The main structure on campus, McKinley Hall, was a two-story building with a sloped roof and a basic redbrick exterior. Students walked five steps up to McKinley's front entrance and then wrestled with a pair of heavy, oversized doors that were notorious for pinching fingers and bruising shoulders. A handicap ramp ran parallel to the step, leading to another, smaller set of doors. Along the perimeter of McKinley, on the ground floor, were windows set high in the walls and exterior classroom doors and emergency exits.

A handful of smaller buildings spread out from McKinley like petals on a flower. One was the library, another a science lab, and still others were new, and I didn't know what studies went on in them. I tugged on the handle of each door as I passed by, testing the locks, making sure the prowler, if there was one, hadn't crept into the school proper. The doors held fast and the walking kept me warm. I swung my arms and took large, exaggerated steps to keep the blood flowing from my core to my extremities.

I stopped at what was in my day the freshman algebra classroom; Mr. Turpin was the teacher. We called him Turnip. He died a few years ago in a rock-climbing accident in California. He'd waited until retirement to tackle his bucket list, never knowing he'd die checking off the first item on that list.

I thought about that sometimes. I didn't have a bucket list. They seemed made for dreamers and planners; maybe I'm too much of a realist. In my line of work, you learn rather quickly how short and precious life is, how no single moment can be taken for granted. Futures are hard-won and reserved for the lucky few.

Hell, every day should be a bucket list kind of day.

Snow covered Turpin's old window. I brushed it away and made binoculars with my hands but it was too dark to see inside. I knew, though, what lay beyond the closed doors, beyond all the doors, in these quiet classrooms: pink and scarlet hearts, cut carefully with kid-sized scissors, lining the edges of the dry-erase board, flirting with paper snowflakes that still hung from the ceiling. The nurses at St. Agatha's made them every year, without fail, working with sick children in the local hospitals. They donated them to the schools, hundreds of paper hearts.

Valentine's Day would be here soon. I thought of the hanged elf back in the squad room, and the Christmas decorations at my own house that had yet to make their way from the corner of the living room up to the attic. The days were coming too fast for me to keep up.

I could see the daily changes in Grace. When she was born, and they handed her to me, I felt like handing her right back to the doctors. That's a hard thing to admit, but she looked like every other screaming, red-faced infant I'd ever seen.

I couldn't find a single thing in her that felt familiar.

Now, though, just eighty-four days later, I could see in her features pieces of Brody and pieces of myself and a third piece, a piece that was all Grace. In the days to come, I hoped the Grace piece would grow and grow, until it was strong enough to overshadow the Brody and Gemma pieces. There were dark places in the two of us, and I wanted Grace to have more light than dark.

But in my heart I know all too well that without the dark, the light is just as much a void. It's the contrast that adds any color, any richness, to life.

Coldness crept back into my bones and I pushed back from the window to continue walking. I thought of Bowie Childs, the security guard, sitting in the parking lot in his warm truck. At least I hoped he was still there. The thought of turning a corner and running into him gave me a fresh set of chills.

A sudden burst of noise startled me. Finn, on the walkie-talkie, was saying something. I'd missed it. "Ten-nine, Finn, come again?"

"North and west sides are clear. Not so much as a footprint, but then with this wind, there wouldn't be. How are things on your end?"

His voice came over the radio the way a fire crackles in the fireplace, bursts of noise and then nothing.

"Ten-four. South side is good, too. I'm heading to the east," I replied.

His garbled reply was incoherent. I struck the

walkie-talkie against the palm of my hand and then brought it to my mouth again. "Finn?"

There was no response. I jammed the radio back into my jacket pocket. Finn would continue his circle and we would meet up somewhere around the perimeter, just as he'd promised back at the Suburban.

I walked a few more minutes and came to the old footpath that runs between the school and the forest. The trees of the forest, evergreens and pines and aspens, rimmed the footpath. The screaming wind quieted down, the snowflakes seemed to pause in mid-flight, and for a moment it was as though the blizzard itself needed a rest.

The respite was so brief I could almost tell myself I imagined it, but it was long enough for me to see what stood against an aspen a few feet away.

I froze and stared at the man before me.

He was tall and dressed poorly for the weather. No hat adorned his round head; no gloves cloaked his hands. Not even so much as a scarf around his pudgy, pale neck.

He stared back at me with cloudy eyes fringed by delicate snowflakes.

The mascara of the dead . . .

I swallowed and slowly took a step toward him and then another. I stopped. I retrieved the walkie-talkie out of my pocket and without taking my eyes off the man, depressed the largest button on it. I spoke, cupping a gloved hand over the mouthpiece to block out the noise of the wind.

"Finn? I've got something. We're on the east side, somewhere between the gym and the library."

There was no response from my partner.

I knew I should move away, get my back to a building, and try to maintain a line of sight. I knew that's what I should do but instead I replaced the walkie-talkie, drew my service weapon from my hip holster and checked the safety, then kept it in my right hand, forcing myself to keep the grip loose and relaxed.

I turned around in a slow circle, scanning the blackness at the edge of the forest, seeking out light that looked out of place, or movement that didn't belong. There was nothing, though, only a nervous cop and a dead man, skewered to a rotting aspen tree. A large hunting knife protruded from his belly, the final, culminating exclamation point to his life.

We tell ourselves that we, as sworn officers of the law, control the crime scene. We take charge when we arrive. We make order from chaos and apply rules to havoc. In this manner, we uncover secrets, find evidence, and move in pursuit of the guilty.

The truth is that's all a bunch of lies.

I knew forces mightier than me were in charge, and those forces would dictate our next steps, here at this elite private school, and in the days to come.

Death ruled this night now, death and the blizzard.

Chapter Three

I couldn't stop turning, scanning, watching. The wind continued to beat the forest, smacking the tops of the trees, shaking limbs, moving violently through and circling back again, relentless.

Somewhere out there, in those woods, was a person who had taken a life. He might be running from here as fast as he could, making his way through knee-deep snow. Out of breath, stumbling, clawing at the snow-laden branches that hung level with his face.

His face. Her face? Eyes bright with adrenaline, mouth agape, nose red from the bitter cold. His first kill. Nauseated at what he'd found himself capable of, shocked he could commit such a heinous act. He was a thief, a robber of life, a stopper of time.

I liked to think he was running. The alternative was much, much worse; that maybe he was standing still, just beyond the pines and aspens, watching me, waiting to see if he would need to kill again on this terrible night. Watchful, calm, ready. One killing had not broken him. Surely another would not, either.

Waiting.

I spun around again, aware my breath was coming in fast, catching up with my racing heart.

Incredibly, in spite of the cold, a damp sweat broke out across my body and with it came the sense that I was slowly losing control.

Breathe, Gemma . . .

I went scuba diving once, in Mexico. Thirty feet down, face-to-face with a parrot fish, and I had a panic attack. It felt as though all the oxygen in the whole world was suddenly gone. I would have shot up to the surface had the class instructor not been so skilled. She calmed me, nearly held me down, and likely saved my life.

I'd never had an attack before or since.

Tonight, though, it felt like I was thirty feet down again and losing my mind.

Drowning on dry land.

One day back on the job and I was lost.

"Stop it," I whispered to myself. I stopped spinning around and forced myself to stand still. "There's no one out there."

I took a deep breath and then another. "Stop it."

I made a fist with my left glove and gave my thigh a whack, and then another. A dull ache flooded my leg but that was enough to shake me out of the panic I'd been stuck in.

Then Finn was at my side. He leaned in and spoke loudly, over the screeching wind. "Did you get any closer?"

His dark puffy parka and brimmed winter cap were familiar, instantly grounding. I gripped his shoulder and put my mouth to his ear. For a moment, my lips brushed his skin and the warmth was enough to flood my cheeks and thaw my face.

"No. I was waiting for you."

Finn took a few steps closer to the body and because he did, I did, too. I'd never be able to explain it to him, but he made me brave in a way that didn't come naturally. That's what partners are supposed to do, make us stronger than we are alone. Jackass or not, I've never doubted that he had my back.

We stood before the dead man and took a moment to compose our thoughts. It was quieter under the shelter of the trees. In the grim presence of death, a whisper of something sacred swept by us. Death asks for forever, after all. That's a serious thing, when you're staring it down as we were.

Finn pulled out his phone and took a series of pictures. "Man, what a way to go."

The dead man was just on the other side of middle-aged and clean-shaven. His mouth was slightly open and his tongue filled the space we could see. His left eye was glass. His right eye stared out at us but saw nothing. His bloodied, bare hands gripped the knife that protruded from a slit in his belly.

I closed my eyes but the images remained, one after another, quick snapshots of the terrible scene: Open eyes that could not see. White snow stained red. The wooden handle of the hunting knife, elaborately carved, gnarled like an old man's finger.

He was a stranger to me, and for that, I was grateful. In a small town like Cedar Valley, that's not always the case. I opened my eyes to see Finn photographing the blood, and other vital things, that ran down from the man's stomach and legs in slushy, near-frozen streams, pooling at his feet.

"Skewered like a marshmallow," Finn murmured. "It looks like he was trying to remove the knife, doesn't it? Pull it out?"

I agreed. "That handle . . . see the carvings, the design? It looks unique, maybe an heirloom piece."

Finn nodded, moving for a close-up shot of the knife and its distinct carved handle.

Spooked, I said, "This didn't happen very long ago. The rate the snow is coming down, this was recent, Finn."

Finn removed his glove and laid the back of his hand near the man's neck. "There's no warmth. It took us twenty minutes to get here after the call came in. Was it a man or a woman?"

"Who?"

"The anonymous caller."

I shook my head. "I don't know, we didn't ask. That was stupid of us."

"Sometimes it doesn't matter. Other times, it does," Finn said and replaced his glove. "In this case, what I want to know is, was this guy the prowler or the anonymous caller?"

"Well, if he was the prowler, then we have both a prowler and a murderer out here. And if he was the caller, well, what the hell was he doing out here, dressed like that? He'd have died from exposure even if someone didn't kill him. Let's phone it in, we're losing evidence every minute with the storm."

Finn took another step forward. He was less than a foot from the man and he peered at the man's face. Then he moved back, and then forward again as though gauging something.

I asked, "What is it?"

Finn clasped his hands and put them on the top of his head. He exhaled in one long, deep breath. "The shit is about to hit the fan, Gemma. I hope you're ready."

"What are you talking about?"

"You don't recognize him?"

I took another look, reluctant to get as close to him as Finn had. The man had a dark complexion. His shoes, sweater, and jeans were expensive but not luxury. His build was on the heavier side of average.

"I suppose there's something familiar about him. . . ."

Finn leaned forward and held his hand over the dead man's left glass eye. "Picture a black patch over this eye and a thick salt-and-pepper

37

beard. Hair a few inches longer and covering the forehead and ears."

I did, and then it came to me.

I gasped. "No! What's he doing in Cedar Valley?"

Finn shook his head. "I don't know. Delaware Fuente. What a loss. This is the most depressing thing I ever saw."

"I had no idea you were such a fan. Finn, we've got to make the call. We need to preserve what evidence we can. Especially now, given who our victim is."

"That's going to be a losing battle, Gemma, and you know it. This?" he said, motioning bleakly to the wind and the snow. "This junk destroys a crime scene like nothing else."

I thought of something. "Do you have a tarp in your truck?"

Finn shook his head. "No, it's in my garage with all my camping gear."

"I knew we should have taken the station's Jeep. We would have had tarps, rope, and crime scene tape. . . ."

I trailed off and pointed to a garbage can near one of the locked classroom doors. "See if there's an extra liner in there. We could at least cover him up, maybe save something."

Finn jogged to the barrel and pulled out a half-full bag of trash, which he promptly tossed to the side. I watched as he reached back down into the barrel, felt around, and then smiled as he pulled out a large empty black bag. With a pocketknife, he sliced it lengthwise, creating a shroud that would protect the man's face and stomach wound.

Before we draped the body, Finn emptied Fuente's pockets. A wallet and a few smaller things were all I saw fall into the clear plastic evidence bag that Finn pulled from his own coat pocket. We tucked the black bag around Fuente as best we could. It wasn't great but it would hold until the crime scene team arrived.

"There's no cell phone. And he's not dressed for this weather. Where's his hat, his scarf? No gloves . . . we didn't see any other cars in the lot. How did he get here? He didn't walk in from town, no way, not dressed like that."

Finn wiped his nose with his sleeve. "Someone drove him here. Someone drove him here, and then killed him. Nothing about this seems random."

"Or he drove his killer here, and then the killer took his car. God, this is going to be messy. Bestselling author found dead in the middle of a blizzard, in the middle of a private school, in the middle of nowhere."

"I wouldn't say we're the middle of nowhere. That's, like, Kansas."

"Well, Cedar Valley isn't exactly in the national spotlight. After tonight, though . . . what does a man do to get himself stabbed like that? Why here, at the academy? The knife, the rotted tree . . . it's like a sick piece of art."

Finn shrugged. "A murder like this, all we've got is questions."

Finn peered again at the man's face. He shone the light from his phone at the man's mouth. "There's something in his mouth."

"What?"

Finn shook his head. "I can't tell. It looks like a piece of paper. Like a crumpled ball of paper."

"In his mouth?" I asked, moving closer. "Don't touch it. There might be prints on it. We'll let the crime scene techs retrieve it."

We watched the black plastic shroud flap wildly in the wind. "What an awful first day back."

"You love it," Finn said. "Admit it. Not the fact that someone's dead, of course, but you love being back in the game. I saw you, watching him, watching the woods. Watching is in your blood, Gemma. It's all you know."

"Sure, I missed it," I said, not bothering to clarify that I wasn't watching, I was panicking. "It's good to know I can do both, you know, be a mom and a cop. I don't have to choose one or the other."

"Not yet, anyway," Finn muttered. "Call it in, would you? My phone's about to die."

Chloe Parker, the same woman who had

dispatched us to the scene, answered. I knew she would call out the usual cast of characters in this production we call a crime scene: the techs; the medical examiner; and Chief Angel Chavez. Standard protocol was an immediate alert to him in the case of any suspicious death. I asked Chloe to keep Fuente's name off the public airways and only use it with Chavez and the medical examiner when she called their personal numbers.

As I was about to hang up with Chloe, Finn waved his arms to get my attention.

"What?" I mouthed to him.

He mimicked putting a phone to his ear and dialing. "The caller."

"Oh, Chloe, hang on a sec," I said. "That anonymous call that came in, was it a man or a woman?"

"Well, Gemma, I'm not sure. A woman, I think, but it was hard to tell. She had a real deep voice, like a smoker's," Chloe answered. "I'll queue up the tape and leave it on your desk; you can listen to it when you get back. You know, now that you're asking, I'm really not sure. Certainly could have been a man. And that New York area code, too. Rough first day, huh? Bet you need to pump soon."

Oh, damn.

I pulled the phone from my ear and checked the time. As I did, my breasts began to throb, right on cue. I hung up the phone. This was going to be awkward.

"Uh, Finn? I'm going to need to get back to the station. As soon as the techs arrive."

Finn looked at me funny. "You got to pee? Go around the corner. Jesus, Gemma, you've worked crime scenes before. Go do what you have to do. I won't sneak a peek. There isn't anything new there, anyway; once you've seen one, you've seen them all."

I sighed and shook my head. "I have to pump, Finn. You know, for the milk? I have to do it every couple of hours. It's the only way I could come back to work, since I'm breastfeeding Grace. Chavez got a small, empty office cleared out for me at the station. I wasn't expecting to be out in the field tonight."

Finn's gaze slid to the right. "Oh. Yeah, okay, we'll leave when they get here. No problem," he replied. "Does that . . ."

"What?"

He shook his head. "Never mind, I don't want to know."

We left the dead man where he was and waited for the rest of our team under the protective shelter of a low-hanging eave that jutted from the school like the prow of a ship. From where we stood, we could keep an eye on Fuente—although he wasn't going anywhere—and stay out of the worst of the blizzard. The wind remained too loud for conversation. Finn and I were quiet, each lost in our own thoughts.

Delaware Fuente.

I whispered the man's name to myself twice more, a chant of sorts.

Delaware Fuente.

Delaware Fuente.

I, along with countless other college students, first read Fuente during my freshman year literature class. He wrote *The Slave Trader's Son* when he was in his early twenties. The book followed the journey of a South American family from the jungles of Colombia to the streets of New York, in pursuit of their father, a minor drug lord in the cocaine-frenzied days of the early 1980s.

The Slave Trader's Son won the Pulitzer Prize and made Fuente an overnight literary darling. His second novel, *Call the Locusts*, was an even bigger hit. He was one of those public figures that everyone loves, with his Santa Claus beard and his refusal to be put in a box. After his first two novels, he turned to writing horror for a while, then tried his hand at a historical trilogy. All were bestsellers.

My thoughts ran dry and I realized that was all I knew about the man. Did he have a family and children? Was there a wife, or a husband, somewhere, expecting him back? What the hell was he doing in Cedar Valley?

And most important, what had Delaware Fuente done in his fifty years of living to earn this end?

"He was born, he lived, and somewhere along the line, he did something to cause this. What did you do to call down this death upon yourself?"

I said it softly, thinking the wind would carry my words away, but Finn heard them. He reached over and patted me on the back. "We'll figure out the in-betweens, we always do."

I nodded. We always do, but at what price? The last case I worked nearly cost me my sanity. It also cost a good man his leg and exposed dark, deep secrets that had lain buried in this town for over thirty years.

I wondered what secrets would float to the surface with Delaware Fuente's death.

An eerie blue light filled the sky, coming in over the trees, and it was a testament to the strength of the wind that I didn't hear the sirens until the crew was nearly upon us. They filed in, one after another, moving slowly on the wide footpath, their vehicles parked at the same lot where we'd had to leave the Suburban.

I saw that Bowie Childs, the security guard, led the group. He lit the way with a powerful flashlight, moving it slowly back and forth across the ground as though searching for clues.

At the rear, behind our department's crime

scene technicians, was Dr. Ravi Hussen, accompanied by her own techs, two brothers named Lars and Jeff, who moved as they always did, in silent tandem. Ravi was the only person I knew who could appear glamorous at a crime scene in the middle of a damn blizzard. Her pale blue parka was fitted and expensive looking, with fur trim and sleek silver accessories.

"Doc, you look like a Bond girl," Finn said. He whistled appreciatively and shook his head. "You sure know how to warm up these bones."

Ravi smiled sweetly back and quoted, " 'For never-resting time leads summer on/To hideous winter and confounds him there/Sap cheque'd with frost and lusty leaves quite gone/Beauty o'ersnow'd and bareness every where.' "

Finn groaned. "I forgot you're such a nerd. I'll save the Bond girl comparisons for those who deserve them."

"*Macbeth*?" I asked Ravi.

The medical examiner shook her head. "Not a bad guess, but no. 'Sonnets.' Is that really Delaware Fuente?"

I nodded. "Unfortunately, yes."

Finn said, "Listen, I have to take Mom here back to the station. The Milk Machine is about to blow. I took pictures of Fuente, before we covered him, and cleared his pockets. Have your guys preserve what they can. We know it's a losing battle out here. The cause of death seems obvious to us but hey, you're the experts, maybe there's something else going on."

Finn left to go speak to the techs. Ravi smirked at me. "Milk Machine? Honey, those things are fantastic. You look great. Welcome back, I know it's got to be excruciating to leave her."

I nodded slowly. "Yes, hard . . . actually, I'll be honest. Why not? Here's the thing. It's not that difficult. I feel . . . I feel like I don't know what I'm doing half the time when I'm with Grace. I mean, I hold her and I feed her and I love her, but there's not much else happening. Sometimes . . . sometimes I'm so bored I could scream."

Finn was on his way back. I didn't want him to overhear our conversation, so I quickly added, "I'm okay, really. It's . . . nothing prepares you for it."

I thought Ravi was going to respond with another wise and relevant quote, but to my surprise she hugged me and whispered, "Hang in there. It will get better. At least, that's what all my girlfriends tell me. You have to pay the piper before he starts playing, Gemma. Grace will grow into herself. So will you."

I thanked Ravi as Finn said, "Doc, before we go . . . come check this out."

We followed Finn back to the body and Finn borrowed a strong flashlight from one of the techs. The black shroud had been removed and Lars—or maybe it was Jeff—was carefully folding it and stuffing it into an evidence bag. Finn aimed the beam at Fuente's mouth.

"See it?"

Ravi nodded. "I do. One moment."

She removed her thick ski gloves and replaced them with a thin latex pair, then gently pried Fuente's mouth all the way open. His jaw hung down like an open nutcracker doll.

Ravi reached in and pulled out the object that had been stuffed in Fuente's mouth. Or perhaps he had done it to himself? Maybe he was trying to hide something from his killer?

Ravi carefully unfurled the ball of paper and then held it up to Finn's flashlight. It was small and lined, the kind of sheet you might find in a small notebook or diary. One sentence was scrawled across it with what looked like a black Sharpie.

"This is only the beginning," I read aloud.

A chill that had nothing to do with the blizzard ran across the back of my neck. I thought of the minutes I'd stood here, before Finn reached me, wondering if the killer was running away from the scene or standing in the woods somewhere, watching me.

Finn, Ravi, and I looked at one another in silence. We didn't need words; I knew the same question was running through each of our minds.

The beginning of what?

"Ah, man, that is messed up," said Childs. "You found that paper in his *mouth?* That is some real *Silence of the Lambs* shit. Is there blood in it, on the note?"

The security guard stood behind me, breathing heavily, stroking his thick blond beard with one gloved hand.

I shook my head. "No, Mr. Childs, there's no blood on the note. Listen, this is a crime scene and I think it's best for everyone involved if you stay back by the building and let our guys do their job."

Childs stopped rubbing his beard. "Where did you buy that jacket? It looks expensive. Being a cop must pay a lot more these days than when my daddy was a cop."

I shrugged. "I wouldn't know about that. There, by that trash can . . . please wait at least that far from the scene."

Childs looked pensive until he noticed Ravi. He stared at her silently.

Ravi introduced herself, then grew uncomfortable with Childs's attention and moved away. I hated to leave her but the ache in my breasts was becoming unbearable.

I did make Finn wait, though, until Childs turned and walked from the crime scene.

Back at the front of the school, Finn's Suburban looked like a humpbacked dinosaur. I began wiping the snow off the front windshield with the sleeve of my jacket. Finn unlocked the car, ducked in to start the engine, and then yelled something at me over the howling wind.

"What?" I screamed back.

He waved his arms dramatically. "Get in the damn car, Gemma. Turn the heat on."

"Are you sure? I can help!"

Finn shook his head. "Get inside. Your cheeks are turning blue."

He didn't have to tell me a third time. I climbed in and turned the heater as high as it would go. Though the heat began to flow from the Suburban's vents in a steady stream of warmth, it did little to thaw the chill that had settled into my very core. I thought about the paper in Fuente's mouth; was it a promise from a killer or a message from Fuente?

This is only the beginning. . . .

Finn jumped in the car, his hands shaking as he put the car into park, and drove us away from the school toward the station. I felt as though I'd never get warm, and one thought kept running through my head: it was a cold night to kill.

Chapter Four

Back at the station, I slid off my jacket and gloves, then set a hot cup of tea to brew. My limbs were frozen, my nose swollen. My socks and boots were soaked, so I pulled them off, as well, and set them to dry by the creaking radiator along the north wall. In the bottom drawer of my desk, I found an old pair of wool socks. They were threadbare and holey but better than nothing. As I slipped them on, I realized that it had been months since my last pedicure. My toenails were short and clipped, but the remaining polish looked like purple freckles on the nail beds.

I cringed. I hoped motherhood wasn't going to be me giving up personal hygiene in exchange for raising a tiny human. I pulled the wool socks on quickly, before anyone could see my feet. Across the aisle, Finn, too, was removing his damp socks, only his spares turned out to be fur-lined slippers. I watched out of the corner of my eye as he carefully counted out ten mini-marshmallows and added them to his own hot drink, a cup of cocoa.

Once the feeling came back to my toes and fingers, I grabbed my black bag and locked myself in the spare office that Chavez had set up for me. I had told him I could easily use the women's locker room in the basement, but he wouldn't hear of it. Chavez has four kids and a strong wife and prides himself on being a modern man.

"Nothing but the best for the breasts," he'd said, and immediately horrified, apologized. "God, listen to me, I don't know where that came from. Gemma, I'm so sorry, I didn't mean . . . well, I mean, I . . ."

It wasn't until I had locked the door and settled into the chair that I saw what he had done. There was a stack of *People* magazines, an unopened bottle of Perrier, and a framed picture of Grace at six weeks old, a photo that I'd emailed to the crew. A bright yellow Post-it note stuck to the frame read, "Feed me, Momma, feed me."

The man didn't know when to quit. I flipped through one of the *People* magazines, appreciating the thoughtful touches, but I was in no mood for Hollywood gossip. I couldn't get Delaware Fuente's frozen stare out of my mind.

I didn't know Fuente personally. But I did know that no man deserves to die like that; cold, alone in the dark save for his executioner. I also knew that sooner or later, like Cedar Valley's secrets, Fuente's secrets would rise to the surface.

And when that happened, we would find his killer.

After I finished pumping, I returned to my

desk. The night's murder was going to extend my shift so I texted Brody and let him know I'd be home late, sometime in the early morning, so he wouldn't worry. My tea had grown cold and I reheated it. Finn was nowhere to be seen. But he'd left me the evidence bag with the contents of Delaware Fuente's pockets. I slid on a pair of latex gloves, opened the top of the bag, and upended it on the desk.

Three things slid out: a worn black leather wallet; a few coins; and a single key on a plastic red fob with a bottle opener on one end and a lobster tail on the other. There was no paper or pen. If the note in Fuente's mouth was written by him, then it was written somewhere else, before he was outside, before he was stabbed. And that in and of itself made little sense.

What made more sense was that the killer wrote the note and stuffed it into Fuente's mouth.

I wondered once again where Fuente's cell phone was. There was a chance, of course, that he didn't own a phone, or carry it with him, or had forgotten it somewhere. But the reality was I could count on one hand the number of people I knew who didn't carry their phones with them at all times.

I set aside thoughts of the phone and stared at the three items. They would tell me a story, if I was willing to listen. The coins told me Fuente carried cash; the fact that he kept his change told me he was frugal. The key appeared to be a house key, and I'd bet money that he was renting a cabin or an apartment somewhere. All the hotels in town used electronic key cards.

It was the wallet that interested me most. The contents of a wallet can often tell you all you need to know about the man who owns it. Some men are practical: driver's license, one or two credit cards, and a handful of their own business cards. Some men are sexy: driver's license, credit cards, cash, and a dozen or so receipts from old purchases, kept for the hastily scribbled phone numbers on the backs of them.

Most men fall somewhere in the middle. Delaware Fuente was no exception.

He had a New Jersey driver's license that pegged him as slightly overweight for his height and generous: he was an organ donor. There was a loyalty card for a gas station I had never heard of, and another for a grocery store chain that I knew was found primarily on the East Coast. An American Express card, a Visa debit card, and a fifty-dollar bill rounded out the contents.

Behind the cash was a single index card, and I silently thanked Delaware Fuente for having the kind of foresight not too many people have.

Fuente was a man prepared for the worst.

The index card, white and unlined, was worn from being handled time and again. Maybe Fuente was a melancholy man; perhaps when he was lonely he pulled the index card from his wallet and unfolded it to stare at the single name written there.

I keep a similar piece of paper in my purse, laminated, with a half-dozen names and numbers: Brody; my grandparents, Bull and Julia Weston; Chief Chavez. All the people I've designated to be the unlucky winner of a terrible lottery with a single prize: the phone call that something has happened to me.

Did the fact that I had five more names on my list make me more loved than Fuente? I didn't know. Maybe it's enough these days to have one person on your list.

On Fuente's card was written, under the heading "Emergency Contact," a name—Bradley Choi—and a phone number with a New York area code.

New York area code . . . Chloe Parker, the dispatch operator, had twice mentioned that the night's anonymous caller had a New York area code. Her shift had ended, but she'd left me the recording of the 911 call and a note with the number that had called in. It would be something to follow up on.

I pulled up the internet and did a keyword search using the terms Bradley Choi, New York, and Delaware Fuente. A few dozen results appeared and I skimmed them, quickly putting two and two together. Bradley Choi was Fuente's literary agent. Choi's firm, The Choi Agency, was based out of New York with a satellite office in Miami. I opened a few of the links and scanned the articles. One included a grainy photograph of Choi arm-in-arm with Delaware Fuente. The picture was taken five years ago at an awards show. Choi and Fuente were both smiling. They held cocktails, and when I zoomed in on the image, I saw Fuente was sauced. Choi, a thin, petite man, was burdened by the much larger Fuente, holding him up.

I skimmed another article, an interview between Choi and a Harvard journalism graduate student. Straight out of college, Choi took a massive loan from his parents and opened his agency. One of his first clients was Fuente, then a struggling writer without so much as a magazine article with his byline. But Choi saw something in that first draft of *The Slave Trader's Son*, and the rest, as they say, is history. It hadn't been a smooth ride, though. Choi had ruffled quite a few feathers over the years. He had been sued seven times in the last ten years by clients and other literary agencies for various issues. All of the cases were settled out of court.

Sitting back, I finished the rest of my tea. I'd learned a lot but I wasn't sure what it all meant. I checked the time and decided to wait until eight in the morning, his time, before calling

Choi. It would be Saturday, and I hoped to catch him at home.

At some point during my research, Finn returned to the squad room. I caught him up on what I'd found. We spent the next few hours putting together a rough dossier on Delaware Fuente and writing up our reports of the night's events. Then we started tossing ideas around. It seemed to me that someone local must have killed Fuente; the academy was too random a place for a murder. And who but a local would have known about the footpath that ran on the side of the school?

Finn argued that anyone could have killed Fuente, including perhaps someone who followed him from the East Coast specifically to kill him and stage the gruesome scene. The New York area code on the anonymous call seemed to justify Finn's train of thought.

At eight, I phoned the number that I'd found in Fuente's wallet. As it rang, I suddenly wished that I'd given more thought to what I was going to say. Before I could hang up, though, a man answered. His voice was high-pitched and breathless. The image of a ferret crawled across my mind.

"This is Brad."

I took a deep breath. "Good morning. My name is Gemma Monroe, out of the Cedar Valley Police Department, here in Colorado.

Mr. Choi, I'm sorry to call so early but I'm afraid I have some bad news."

"Oh, God, what has Del done now? Has he been drinking again? I can be there in . . . uh . . . give me six hours and I can get on a flight," Choi said. "I swear, that man is not worth fifteen percent."

"Mr. Choi, I'm afraid it's much more serious than that. Mr. Fuente passed away this morning."

I heard a gasp on the other end of the line and again wished I had thought this through better. NYPD could have sent someone to deliver the news in person. But that might have taken hours. I had a trail, born in the snow, which was growing colder by the minute.

"Sir? Mr. Choi, are you still there?"

I waited. After another half minute, his sobbing voice was back on the line. "Yes, yes, I'm here. This is terrible. What happened? It was his heart, wasn't it? Del lived like he was twenty-two."

"We're not sure what happened. The circumstances are suspicious," I said.

Another sob came through the line.

"Mr. Choi, we need to understand what Mr. Fuente was doing here in Colorado. Can you help us with that?"

"Yes, yes, this is just such a shock. I'm sorry, I . . . Del was a friend."

I nodded into the phone. "Brad, can I call you Brad? Brad, we didn't have any idea that

Mr. Fuente was in town. Now, for someone of Fuente's fame, that's unusual for us not to be aware. I see on his driver's license a New Jersey address. Was that his main residence?"

Choi took a deep breath, then another. When he spoke again, he sounded calmer. "Yes, Del lived in New Jersey. He was sick of being in Los Angeles. He had his house custom-built, a brand-new place made to look like an old authentic brownstone. He paid a fortune for it, and the land. It's beautiful, right on the edge of a nature preserve, birds as far as you can see. He also keeps an apartment in New York. Del was in Colorado at the request of an old friend, Lily, Lila, something like that. She works at a private school there. He was giving a series of guest lectures for an English class. Maybe it was creative writing. I don't know all the details."

"Did Mr. Fuente do that sort of thing often? Lectures, teach classes?"

A laugh, and that was somehow worse than the sobs.

Choi said, "Have you ever seen Del do an interview on television? What you see is what you get. He's a lovable teddy bear. Generous to a fault. He's probably given away more than he's kept. I tease him that he's atoning for some sin in a prior life. He was my friend, and I loved him. When the news of his death breaks, there will be a lot of tears shed for both the man and for the loss of future works."

I leaned back in the chair. "You're describing the same impression I had of him, granted mine was formed from the perspective of a fan, not a friend. Can you think of anyone who might have had reason to harm Mr. Fuente?"

The agent sniffled. "I don't know. There were certainly a lot of people who didn't like him, of course, but that's the nature of any public figure. Del was outspoken. The Jews thought he was too soft on the Middle East. The Catholics hated his liberal stance on social issues. The Democrats didn't like his outspoken investments in big oil, and the Republicans couldn't stand his freewheeling allegiance to whatever caught his fancy. As is usual in the publishing world, it was his readers that showed him the most love. Del was okay with all of it. He loved the ridiculousness of it all. He was truly a force of nature."

"Was he ever married? Did he have a girl-friend? A boyfriend?"

"Nothing serious. Listen, he had no wife, no living relatives. He'd bring tail around some-times, but even that didn't seem to interest him much. For all he did, the writing, the philanthropy, I could never quite put my finger on what made him happy. I mean, truly happy. I asked him, just once, and you know what he said?"

Brad waited for me to respond. I said I had no idea what made a man like that happy.

"The hamster wheel. He said what made him happy was the sheer idiocy of our little hamster lives, spinning away on our hamster wheels. What was the point of life? You're born; you spin, spin, and spin some more. Then you die. You fall off the wheel, and someone else gets on. Depressing, huh? And yet he was one of the greatest writers of our generation."

"Aren't all the good writers tortured souls? Hemingway, Faulkner. . . ?"

Brad laughed again. He laughed so hard he started coughing and it took him a minute to get back on the line.

"Tortured, yes. Crazy? Some. Del wasn't tortured and he wasn't crazy. I think he was searching for something, some pure truth that he could lose himself in. I need to go now. I have to start making some calls, before the press gets wind of this."

I promised Choi we would keep news of Fuente's death out of the media as long as we could. I also promised to let him know as soon we got word that the body could be released. He agreed in the meantime to make all the necessary arrangements, starting with contacting Fuente's attorneys.

"Oh, Brad?"

"Yes?"

"Hang on a sec," I said as I reached for the recording and note that Chloe Parker had left on my desk. "Any chance you recognize this number?"

I read him the phone number of the anonymous caller. When I finished, I waited for a response but the agent was silent.

"Brad? Are you still there?"

"Is this some kind of joke?"

Taken aback by the sudden sharpness in his voice, I replied, "No, not a joke."

Brad breathed into the phone. "That's Delaware's number. I should know, I've only had to call it about a thousand times over the years."

After we hung up, I dialed Fuente's number. It went straight to voice mail.

"Damn it, Finn, the anonymous call came from Fuente's own cell phone," I said. "It's been turned off."

Finn stood and came over to my desk. "You're kidding. Play the tape."

I brought up the recording Chloe Parker had left and hit play.

A low, gravelly voice filled the air. We listened to the recording three times and by the end of the third time, were in agreement about only one thing: we couldn't tell if it was a man or woman's voice.

" 'There's a prowler at the Valley Academy.

He looks suspicious. Come quickly,' " Finn read the words he'd jotted down.

This is only the beginning. . . .

I rubbed my eyes. "So, Fuente calls in the prowler and then confronts him. He's murdered and the killer steals his phone."

Finn looked troubled. "What if the killer stabbed Fuente, then used Fuente's own phone to call us in?"

"That makes no sense. Calling us guarantees the body is found, tonight. Don't call us and Fuente wouldn't have been found until Monday when everyone's back in school."

Finn paced, his hands jammed in his pockets. "It makes sense if you consider that the note we found in Fuente's mouth was a taunt. 'This is only the beginning.' The killer wanted us to find the body, and the note. Gemma, we have to consider that there may be more murders to come."

"Jesus. I'm going to put a trace on Fuente's cell phone. I want to know the minute it gets turned on," I said and set about filling out the form online that would make its way up the chain and land as a request with the phone companies. "If it gets turned on."

Finn continued pacing. "What I don't understand is why the school?"

"I don't know but Fuente did know a woman who works there," I said, recalling my conversation with Brad Choi. "Her name wasn't familiar to me. Lila or Lily Conway."

"Lila." Finn nodded. "I know her. She does administrative work. She might be a secretary. I've met her a few times at different events. She's about Fuente's age, I suppose, real quiet. I think she's a cat lady."

"What the hell is a cat lady?"

Finn nodded. "You know, a widow with thirty cats and a husband buried in the backyard. The kind of woman that ends up on *Dateline* or *60 Minutes*."

"On behalf of widowed cat owners everywhere, I'm offended. Choi said Conway and Fuente were old friends," I said. "Listen, I'm worried. A killing like this . . . at the academy . . . what if the students are in danger? I think they ought to beef up security. Didn't you say someone's been spray-painting the Grim Reaper on campus?"

"I'll call Director Silverstein." Finn stopped pacing and glanced up at the clock. "In the meantime, go home and get some sleep. You look terrible. We'll touch base in a couple of hours."

I started to protest and say I wasn't tired, but a huge yawn swallowed my words. I realized with a guilty start that this was the longest I'd been away from Grace since she was born. Aside from pumping, and a few minutes at the high school, I'd barely thought about my baby.

Mother of the year, right here, folks.

"What's wrong? You look flushed."

"Nothing. You're right, I'm tired." I packed up my bag, then checked the master schedule on the wall and was disappointed to see that Sam Birdshead wasn't due to come on shift for a few more hours. I hadn't seen him since I went on maternity leave. And before that, he was in the hospital. I was eager to see him back on the job, but a part of me realized he was in a different place now, emotionally, mentally, and physically.

I knew things would never be the same as they were before the accident. They couldn't be, for any of us. During the course of a murder investigation the previous September, a hit-and-run accident had nearly cost Sam his life. He'd lived but lost his right leg at the knee. He had been on the job only a few months and it was a tragic way to begin a career in law enforcement.

Chief Chavez was more optimistic than the rest of us. He said that no cop worth his badge thought with his legs anyway. Chavez hoped Sam's skills in research would lend themselves to an expertise in cyberspace, working internet cases.

"How's Sam doing?"

Finn shrugged. He sat down and started rearranging his pens and pencils, lining them up one by one along the edge of his desk. "It's hard to say. He's . . . different. I know they've got him on antidepressants and counseling, in addition to therapy or rehab or whatever you call it. He's on desk duty and he's got a prosthetic that he wears sometimes. He's still getting used to it. We've been calling him Old Stumpy. He says he's still longer than any two of us in his . . . uh, never mind."

"Nice," I muttered. "At least he's kept his sense of humor."

I grabbed my bags and the files on my desk and started to pull on my parka. The coat was halfway on when my desk phone rang. I didn't recognize the local number, but I set my bags back down anyway.

"Monroe."

"Good morning, this is Denise Harvey, executive assistant for Missy Matherson. We've heard multiple reports of a homicide at the Valley Academy last night. Can you confirm or deny?"

Inwardly, I groaned. In general the press was a pain in my ass. Especially press like Missy Matherson. She was a bulldog in heels, a stubborn broad with ambition as big as her blond Texas-born hair.

"I can confirm there was a suspicious death at the school, yes."

In the background, I heard furious typing. "And the victim's name?"

I replied, "Pending notification of next of kin,

the victim's name has not been released. And that's about all I can give you, Denise. You can contact our public information officer if you want any more information than that."

In the background, furious whispering, then a new voice came on the line. "Gemma? Is that you? Missy Matherson. How the hell have you been?"

"Oh, just fine, Missy, and you?"

She said, "Enough with the pleasantries. Who's the corpse? You know I'll find out sooner or later and if it's sooner, like right now, I can give you a nice quote in the paper."

"What happened to your television gig, Missy? Last time I saw you, you were gracing my television with your lovely face."

She was heated. "Cut the bullshit. There's no love lost between us, Gemma. My station manager was a prick with one hand on my ass and the other on my career. I'm back to print. It's the last frontier; or rather, the first frontier. There's a drought of morals in journalism and I'm ready to flood the scene."

"Missy, you always were one for the dramatic. But you're wasting your breath. You'll get the identity when everyone else does."

She hung up without another word.

Finn looked at me. "Matherson?"

I nodded. "She's left her anchor job, back to print. Must have been a pretty big pay cut."

Finn grunted and returned to his computer. "She doesn't do it for the money. She could work for free if she wants."

He looked at me again. "Don't you know who her mother is?"

"No, why would I?"

"Her mother is Birdie Matherson."

I stared at him blankly. "And I should know who that is because why?"

"Come on, Gemma, didn't you play with dolls when you were little? Ever have a Birdie Baby? The family is worth millions."

I sat back. "No way. I loved my Birdie Baby! You could feed it real water and it wet the diaper. It even squealed as it peed. I had no idea Missy had ties to Ruby Jane. That was my Birdie Baby's name, Ruby Jane."

"So Matherson is back to her old haunts. That's great. You can't trust a word she prints; she's doing the nasty with half the elected officials in this town. Wait, scratch that, this state."

"Yup. And let me guess, she turned you down for a date?"

Finn looked disgusted. "I wouldn't touch that cockroach with a ten-foot pole. She's bad for business, no two ways about it. She probably has syphilis. And gonorrhea."

A few cops walked into the squad room, ready to begin their shifts. That was the last cue I needed that it was time to leave and head home.

Exhaustion hit me like a ton of bricks. I told Finn I'd call him in a few hours.

I wondered if I was ready, really ready, to be back. There's nothing the press likes better than blood in the water. Things would blow up, big time, once Missy Matherson and her ilk got wind of Fuente's murder. If he wasn't already headed there, Fuente's killer would go deeper, even further underground, and we might not ever catch him.

With a chill, I realized that ready or not, I *was* back. I was already slipping into the killer's mind, anticipating his thought processes and his next moves. If Finn was right, and the note in Fuente's mouth was a promise from the killer, then there would be another death. Maybe not today, maybe not this week . . . but soon enough, we'd be face-to-face with another victim.

Somewhere out there, a man or woman walked through life, blissfully unaware that a killer had him or her in his sights. They could move through a crowd, pause, turn around, and never know that the killer was right there, all along. Because right now, his face was a shadowy image, a blur of features, as masked as a bank robber behind a mesh of beige panty hose.

It was our job to peel away that mask.

I said a silent prayer that we'd do just that, and soon.

Chapter Five

Outside the station, the early morning sun was trapped behind the storm but at least the wind and snow had stopped their violent assault on the valley. The sky was a shade of dull steel that seemed to press down on everything around me. Under ten inches of snow, the cars in the parking lot all looked identical. I cleared the license plates on three before I found mine. It was another thirty minutes of steady digging and shoveling before I had the car and tires freed.

I took a moment to rest, breathing heavily, my back against the driver's side door.

The employee parking lot of the Cedar Valley Police Department is located in the rear of the building. There are two houses across the alley, an older Victorian model that belongs to an elderly widow, and a more modern Craftsman bungalow that I think is owned by a young family with a couple of kids. At least, there are usually a few tricycles and children's bicycles abandoned in the front yard. I'd seen the mother once. We'd waved, but I hadn't seen her since.

Both houses were dark now. The widow was rumored to be a busybody and I wondered if she was at her window, watching me. I gave a little wave in her direction, just in case.

Finn had called me a watcher, at the crime scene.

He was right.

I am a watcher.

That's how I do my job. I'm always watching, looking, seeking. Searching. I think I've been like that my whole life.

Somewhere, on the other side of the station, a car backfired. The noise jerked me out of my daydreaming. Shivering, I hustled into the front seat and sat there, with the heat blaring, as I waited for the windows to defrost. I leaned forward to pick up a CD that had fallen to the floor, and as I sat back up, something moved in the rearview mirror.

I froze.

Slowly, I turned around. Shifting caused the thing to move again and I swore and smacked at it. It was the mobile of small, fuzzy stuffed safari animals that slipped onto the handle of Grace's car seat and supposedly kept her entertained.

The expressions on the animals' faces were a little too smug for my liking, especially on the lion, but the mobile had been a gift, and I felt guilty not using it. The car seat took up one half of the backseat and a gym bag with toiletries and a change of clothes took up the other half.

A single solitary sock, pink and impossibly tiny, lay between the car seat and my gym bag. I picked it up and slipped it over two of my fingers like a miniature glove. Its size took my breath away. How could something so small keep anybody warm?

I tucked the sock in my purse and put the car into drive. As I pulled out of the lot and eased down the alley, my thoughts again turned to Delaware Fuente. For me, cases don't exist in a vacuum. I knew that Fuente, and his killer, would start appearing in my dreams. The two of them would keep me distracted, unable to carry on trivial conversations, competing for my attention like needy children. Soon enough, they would be my whole world. The scary thing was I looked forward to that. I'm comfortable in that world, obsessive, driven, with a singular goal.

Delaware Fuente didn't have children. He wrote books, raised them, and then like parents have done since the beginning of time, he released them into the world. I wondered if his books were raised to hurt or to heal. Judging from his fan base, they'd clearly brought a lot of joy to a lot of people. But things are not always as they appear on the surface.

Perhaps his books were independent little monsters and they led lives out of his control.

Did one of Fuente's books hurt someone? Did that person take revenge? Sooner or later, I'd know. Each step of the investigation would bring questions and then answers, and then more questions, and more answers, until finally something would break. It always did.

The roads were slick and for the most part, empty of traffic. For a while, a large truck followed me, then it turned off on a side road and I was alone again for the rest of the drive.

I arrived home to a small house on the hillside of a canyon, across the street from a river that twisted down to town. Now, in the dead of winter, the river traveled under a skin of thin ice that crackled and hissed as it melted and refroze. The water never looked the same from day to day, and there was solace in that, a daily reminder that life keeps moving.

Our closest neighbors were a quarter mile away, and our internet was slower than molasses, but we loved our home; the stillness of the road at night, the majestic beauty of the forest as it grew down the canyon, inch by inch, impatient to reclaim the land as its own.

Grace was awake when I walked into the nursery. She looked up at me with steel-blue eyes that held more wisdom than they should have.

She scared me.

She scared me more than all the murderers and rapists and thieves in the whole world.

She, at thirteen pounds, could do more damage to my being than anyone else ever could or would.

We went to the living room to nurse. I sat in

an armchair by the window and pulled a worn, handmade quilt over us. I was still cold; it felt as though winter had touched my bones and ice water had seeped into my veins.

The curtains were open and I scanned the backyard, hoping to see some brightness in the form of a jay or cardinal. The bird feeder was empty, though, and I waited but the backyard remained silent and still and white.

From upstairs inside our bedroom, Brody coughed. Then came the heavy thud on the floor as his feet moved from bed to ground. A few minutes later, he was there beside me, kissing my forehead and nudging Seamus, our basset hound, out of the way with his toe.

"Coffee?" Brody called back over his shoulder as he headed into the kitchen.

I said no. "I need to catch a few hours of sleep, then get more work done. I'm sorry. There's been a murder. Do you know who Delaware Fuente is?"

In the kitchen, which I could see from my spot in the living room corner, Brody scratched the back of his neck and then his hand moved lowe, to his backside. His pajama pants were navy blue with white snowflakes, and his gray T-shirt was an old Denver Broncos championship souvenir. He looked ten years younger than he was, a college kid living a grown-up's life.

I waited patiently.

He stared at the coffee machine a few seconds and then he shook himself. "The author? Sure. He had a program on the public radio station for a few years when I was in college. He's brilliant. Why?"

At my breast, Grace finished. She fell back asleep and I held her even closer. "I know you'll keep this confidential. He's dead. He was killed last night."

My words had Brody fully awake now. He stood in the doorway with a bag of coffee from my favorite local café, Four and Twenty Blackbirds, in his hand. "No kidding? He always seemed larger than life. What happened?"

"We're not sure yet. Finn and I went to the Valley Academy after an anonymous call came in about a suspicious person, a prowler. We found Fuente, stabbed to death with a hunting knife. The call came from his own cell phone. It's complicated. I'm going to be tied up for a while, Brody. I'm sorry. I wish it wasn't so soon after my return to work. I thought I'd be able to ease back into this stuff. Do we have any cinnamon rolls from the Blackbird?"

Brody shook his head. "No, only the coffee. I thought we were dieting. Or do we have different health goals this month? Perhaps no sugar? Or gluten elimination? Want me to make an omelet with egg whites and veggies?"

"Sure, an omelet would be good. These last

five pounds are making a home on my ass and I hate them. Do we have any strawberries?"

"I'll check," he said and headed back into the kitchen. Then he yelled, "I like your ass."

It felt strange to be waited on. For a good portion of my pregnancy, Brody had been in Alaska on a geology expedition. I'd had to spend most of the second trimester by myself. Brody was back by the time I delivered, and while the man had some deep faults, I would not have survived the last few months without him. I truly don't know how single parents do it, especially on two or three hours of sleep a night.

I was also happy to be able to keep an eye on him, at least for a while. Those faults of his had a way of creeping to the surface when he was out of sight. The biggest one, of course, was his cheating. Although it had happened early in our relationship, years before a baby was even a glimmer in our eyes, I couldn't seem to move past it. It was the number-one reason why we weren't married yet, to the disappointment of Brody, my grandparents, practically everyone who knew me.

Except for Finn. Finn thought it was the wisest decision I'd ever made. That alone made me overlook a lot of Finn's more grating personality defects.

I couldn't shake the sense that marriage would somehow snag on the trust that we'd built up over the last few years. I was sure that over time, like a bracelet caught on a knit sweater, it would slowly unravel our lives. And things were good right now.

Brody had received a prestigious grant to write a geology textbook. The stipend would allow him to work from home for the next six months, if we were careful with our finances and didn't take any big vacations or have any expensive home repairs. Between my somewhat flexible schedule and his working from home, one of us would be with the baby for most of her first year.

In the kitchen, Brody started gathering omelet ingredients. I shifted my legs, careful not to wake Grace, and eased back into the chair. Finally warm, feeling cozy with the baby in my lap and breakfast on its way, my eyes grew heavy. Once more, though, my thoughts drifted to Delaware Fuente.

The start of any murder investigation is with the victim. But in the background the killer is always there, lurking, hovering in the shadows. As the investigation progresses, it becomes more and more difficult to keep the victim in the forefront. You're on the hunt, chasing the bad guy, and it's easy to focus on him.

But the best cops remember one thing above all else: it starts and ends with the victim. The blame doesn't fall on the victim; but something he said or did triggered the actions that ended his life—choosing a less trafficked road to take home late at night, wearing flashy jewelry. There's always an action, a cause that leads to the murder.

What path had Delaware Fuente's life taken him on?

The trouble, of course, is thinking there's an answer to that question. Sometimes, though more rarely than the mainstream media would have you think, murder truly is the result of a madman's actions. It cannot be explained in any way other than a misfiring of the synapses.

This is only the beginning. . . .

I looked to the snow in the backyard once more, chilled by the thought of someone out there capable of killing again. Serial killers are notoriously difficult to track; in the dead of winter, isolated by the weather, that was the last thing we needed right now in the valley.

Chapter Six

While I slept, the blizzard moved out of the Rockies and headed east, toward the Great Plains. It clobbered Kansas and Nebraska, and petered out somewhere over Ohio, sparing the East Coast.

When I woke, it was after noon. At the bedroom window, I watched as a weak ray of sun struggled to break through the cloud layer. I dressed quietly and checked in on Grace. She was asleep in her crib, one tiny arm stretched over her head. Downstairs, I threw a load of laundry in the washing machine, then found Brody in his office, staring at his computer, typing, then stopping, then starting again. He looked frustrated.

"How's the book coming?" I asked.

Brody looked at me, then back at his computer and turned the monitor off. "I put the book to the side for a while. I'm working on a side project. A proposal for a potential new client."

"What project? What client?"

Brody stood and crossed the room in six steps. He took me in his arms and kissed my forehead. "Don't worry about it, sweetheart. It's a land use survey. I'll be done with it in a few weeks."

"But your deadlines . . ." I started to say. He cut

me off with another kiss on my forehead and a smack on my rear. I yelped and he laughed.

"Gem, let me worry about my deadlines. I don't question your murder investigations. Did you get any sleep?"

I nodded. "Sure, a bit. I'm going to do some work."

Brody said he'd like to go run some errands, since I'd be home for a while with the baby. We left it at that, but I was curious about his new client. Occasionally Brody picked up side projects but he (and I) had thought the book was going to take up most of his time.

A pitiful groan drew me to the kitchen. I found Seamus, scratching at the back door. He has a bladder the size of a raisin. When I opened the door, he stuck his nose out for a second, then brought it back in and turned tail and ran. I didn't blame him. Though the worst of the storm was gone, the temperatures were still well below zero.

"Don't pee in the house, old man," I shouted after him.

I grabbed a box of crackers and a couple of string cheeses from the refrigerator, then got a fire started in the living room. The fireplace was old but in good condition, and soon the flames were dancing a merry jig. I ate my snack on my knees in front of the fire, close enough to feel the heat warm my cheeks. At that moment,

I couldn't think of anything better on a cold winter's day. I sighed. I could have sat there all day, but there was work to do.

Finn answered his cell after three rings.

"I didn't wake you, did I?"

Finn said no. "I haven't slept at all, actually. I stopped by the hospital on the way home as Ravi was finishing the autopsy. I stuck around to get her thoughts. God bless caffeine. "

"Any surprises?"

Finn said, "Nah. Fuente's liver wasn't in great shape but other than that, he was healthy, although hefty, as you saw. Doc said the knife punctured the abdominal aorta; he bled to death in a matter of minutes. She said after he was stabbed, he would have lost consciousness quickly. He didn't suffer. At least, not for long."

"I can't begin to imagine," I replied. "And we're sure it's not suicide?"

Finn snorted. "Ah, well, fairly sure. She's ninety-nine percent positive. There's a very, very small chance he did it to himself but between the force of the thrust and the angle of the knife . . . the physics don't add up. He was murdered. I know it. You know it. He certainly knew it."

I moved away from the fire and curled up under a blanket on the couch.

Finn continued. "So far, the press hasn't gotten wind that Fuente's our victim, although

Matherson has called twice since you left. I've updated Chief Chavez. He's going to talk to Mayor Cabot. She'll keep her mouth shut as long as we keep her in the loop."

Mayor Betty Cabot had been in office two months. She was seventy-three, wore turquoise cowboy boots every day, and was on her fifth marriage. Whip smart, with a wit that stung worse than a hornet, she carried four things in her purse at all times: a wallet, a bottle of tequila, a pistol, and a five-pound dog-rat-creature named Dixie.

"How are they working out, the two of them?"

Finn said, "The chief and the mayor? Fine, I guess. I think this is all new territory for them both, you know? Two months in office . . . Cabot's still trying to find her way. And Chavez is just praying she's not as big a nut as she seems."

In a town our size, the chief of police and the mayor must be allies. If they're not, nothing gets done; instead, things get held up in bureaucratic meetings that drag on for weeks.

"Good. How about the school, did you call Lila Conway? Fuente's pal?"

Finn said no. I volunteered to handle that side of things and before he hung up, Finn gave me the phone number for the director of the Valley Academy, Stanley Silverstein.

Silverstein answered on the first ring. He

81

was aware of the murder; one of Chief Chavez's many calls must have been to him. Silverstein immediately went on the defense; he'd had back surgery a number of weeks ago and counted on his second-in-command, Justine Moreno, to keep things in line.

"I never would have signed off on this sort of thing," Silverstein blustered. "Of course, *of course,* we want to give our students access to incredible experiences. But Delaware Fuente, while an impressive author, was not the sort of man our children need to be listening to, not at their age. He's . . . controversial. I don't know what Justine was thinking. She told me his name was John Firestone. A lie! Do you know, I just realized, I don't think she even knew who he *really* was!"

I thought about Fuente's shaved beard, his missing eye patch. A false name . . . an altered appearance. A disguise? A man in hiding?

"Mr. Silverstein, I understand completely," I said. "We want to get to the bottom of this as soon as possible, so that everyone—your students included—can move forward. I wonder if you shouldn't consider increasing security at the campus? I met Mr. Childs last night. Does he make regular rounds of the school?"

"He's there for a few hours every day, but I think you're right. I'll talk to Kaspersky. Until this killer is caught, we can't be too cautious.

We place a premium on safety at the school; I don't have to tell you how upset this is going to make the parents," Silverstein said.

"I bet. Listen, how can I reach Lila Conway?"

"Don't bother. I'll call Justine Moreno and she can inform Ms. Conway. It will be better that way, I'm certain of it."

"Are you sure?" I asked.

Silverstein said, "Oh, yes, positive."

"Okay. Well, how about an address for Ms. Conway? I can certainly find it with my resources but you'd save me about ten minutes if you've got it handy."

Silverstein read me an address. "Before you go see her, you should know something. That woman's like her home, remote and cold."

"Excuse me?"

"It's quite sad." He sighed. "Lila suffers from extreme shyness. She doesn't do well socially. She's a loner, Detective. You'll see, if you go visit her. You'll see."

I considered Silverstein's words. "Would you call her dangerous?"

He laughed. "That's a rather absurd thought. I said she was shy, not deranged. She wouldn't hurt a fly. She's a rescuer; she saves things, damaged things like wounded baby animals and sad, friendless students. She seems to . . . communicate . . . best with things that are a little broken."

A thin glaze of bitterness coated Silverstein's

words and I wondered at the source of that resentment, whether it was professional or personal.

"Please have Ms. Moreno let Lila know that I'll be stopping by tomorrow."

Silverstein agreed and we ended the call. I stoked the fire and offered Seamus the back door again. This time, he padded out into the snow and lifted a leg. I watched as he relieved himself. What a simple life he had. If reincarnation is an option, I hope to return as a fat, spoiled basset hound with a sucker for a mother.

"I hope you know how good you have it," I whispered as he came in. Seamus looked up at me and wagged his tail as though in agreement. We smiled at each other, communicating in that special language that exists between dog and guardian. Then a rude noise erupted from his bowels, a dismal stench filled the air, and the moment was ruined.

I walked quickly back into the living room holding my nose.

I took my seat on the couch and wondered who Lila Conway was, this woman who convinced a bestselling author to come to tiny Cedar Valley and spend time with a group of private high school students. Because Conway knew Fuente intimately enough to persuade him to do something like that, she was an obvious suspect for his murder. And yet the person Silverstein described sounded like no killer I'd ever met.

A collector of broken things . . .

Plus, the anonymous caller had said there was a *man,* a suspicious man, prowling about the high school—not a woman.

There wasn't much more I could do on the Fuente case. I spent the rest of Saturday reviewing the files that Chief Chavez wanted me to get caught up on. Finn was right; it had been a quiet few months that I'd been out on leave, with the exception of the spate of robberies. Tourism was the life blood of Cedar Valley; it kept food on the townspeople's plates and paid for the next generation to go to college. But tourists don't like to travel for what they can get in the big cities, and if these crimes continued, word would get out.

In the late afternoon, I stood and went to the window. Though the shadows in the yard had grown longer, nothing else had changed since the last time I'd looked; the snow still swallowed up our patio furniture and the shrubs; it still weighed heavy on the limbs of the big pine trees. Shrouds of worry, my grandmother Julia used to say, describing the way the trees wore their winter cloaks.

"Why worry?" I asked her once. "Are the trees scared?"

She nodded and smiled sadly. "Yes, my love.

Even the trees get tired of their seasonal shrouds. Winter is the longest of the seasons, you see. It is so long, in fact, that it is quite easy to forget it will ever end. There comes a time, right around the middle of February, when all the creatures and all the trees and all the people forget that spring is right around the corner. So, we worry. And that's why they invented Valentine's Day. It's nothing to do with cherubs and love. We needed something bright and cheery to look forward to."

"But the trees don't celebrate Valentine's Day! Animals don't celebrate it, either."

Julia leaned down to look me dead in the eye, and replied, "Don't be ridiculous, of course they do. Where do you think babies come from in the spring? And new little trees?"

I wondered if she remembered telling me that; then I remembered that she didn't remember much these days. I touched the glass with the back of my hand and held it there, betting against myself that the cold wouldn't bother me. But the window was freezing and I pulled back.

It was dark out there, with the sun nearly set. Soon it would be night, and with that, nearly twenty-four hours since Fuente had been killed. Fifty years of living, ended in a moment.

I turned from the window, troubled, wondering once more what path Fuente's life had taken to culminate in such a terrible manner.

Chapter Seven

A forest, thick with dark woods and immense boulders, flanks the western slope of Cedar Valley. It is a sea of pines, aspens, and firs, and it was deep into this ocean of trees that I headed early on Sunday morning. The road was well plowed and I followed the signs for Greenback Village, a small mountain community named for the state fish.

The story of the greenback cutthroat trout is one of survival; it is the story of one creature's near extinction, followed by its slow and lengthy fight for recovery. It is also a fable, of man's attempt to right yet another wrong that he has perpetrated against nature, and of the foolhardy mistakes man makes when haste bulldozes over best intentions.

The greenback, a subspecies of the cutthroat trout, once enjoyed a healthy, thriving population in the Arkansas River. Over time, though, runoff from mining operations, water diversion for agriculture, and overfishing nearly wiped the greenbacks from the face of the planet. Luckily, we eventually came to our senses. After first destroying the greenback's natural habitat for our own selfish purposes, we decided we needed to protect it and save the fish.

Even now, though, after decades of conservation efforts, the greenback maintains a threatened status on the Endangered Species Act. Why? For years, we protected the wrong damn fish. In our haste and arrogance, we saw what we wanted to see and what we saw was the wrong subspecies. Today, the greenback trout are few and far between. Less than a thousand exist along a four-mile stretch of river southwest of Colorado Springs.

I first learned about the greenback in high school, and the story stayed with me. It seemed an appropriate lesson to keep in my mind as I conducted investigations; rarely are things as simple as they seem to be on the surface. Criminals, victims—these are easy titles to bestow but harder to justify. Given the day and the situation, we're all the victim and we're all the criminal. It's not always easy to know who truly needs protection.

Like the trout, the residents of Greenback Village were few in population. Unlike the fish, though, their numbers seemed to be by choice. As I drove, I saw homes tucked back into the woods, spaced far apart. A few of the driveways had signs indicating intruders would be shot on sight. Others had pickup trucks with rifles mounted in their rear windows and hunting stickers prominently displayed. All told of a community that valued its space and privacy.

Lila Conway was no exception; hers was the last house in the tract, at the end of the road.

I turned into the drive and slowed to a stop behind a late-model green Toyota Tundra.

I recalled Director Silverstein's words about Conway and her home: he'd said both were "remote" and "cold." But as I exited the car and stood staring at the house, my first thought was that I had wandered into the pages of an old fairy tale, the kind of story that exists apart from time and reality, the kind of story that spills over the pages with magic and possibility.

Surely Lila Conway was some kind of princess, or fairy queen, to live in a house such as this, deep in the woods, sheltered against the harsh realities of the outside world.

The stone cottage was two stories, made from smooth, polished gray river rock. Frosted leaded glass windows with beveled sections stared back at me. There was a steeply pitched gable above the front door, and a row of tidy raised garden boxes lined the edge of the driveway and continued on down a path that led toward the woods.

The forest was quiet.

I went to the front door and knocked twice, gently, with the brass boar head knocker.

After a moment, the door opened and I stifled a scream, my hand rising instinctively to my throat.

A woman stood before me, with a raised

butcher knife in one hand and a ball of twine in her other. Her hair was long and black, streaked through with silver. Her eyes were wary and red-rimmed. She wore a white apron speckled with small, bright drops of red. She sniffed as though smelling the space between us, tasting my scent on the air.

I took a step back from the woman and the knife.

The reality was that I hadn't read a fairy tale in years. I had forgotten the lay of the land. Princesses and fairy queens lived in castles perched high above the town, in fortresses where they were kept safe and secure. They lived in the light, close to the sun, where their beauty could shine down for all to see and adore from afar.

It was never the princess who lived deep in the forest, hidden, shaded by dreary woods and creeping shadows.

It was someone else who lived in the stealth of the snow, someone with dark secrets and potent spells.

The witch stared at me, expectant. Silent.

I cleared my throat, held up my badge, and introduced myself. "Lila Conway? Are you Ms. Lila Conway?"

The woman lowered the knife and beckoned me in. "Yes. Vice Principal Moreno said you would be coming by."

Inside the cottage, the fairy tale continued and

I slowly relaxed, caught up again in a spell of my own making. The walls of the front living room were lined with books, hundreds of them, stacked from the floor to the ceiling. An enormous, old-fashioned iron birdcage stood in one corner. A huge white cockatoo was inside, swaying gently back and forth on a wooden swing.

On the opposite side of the room, in the other corner, close to a crackling fire was an ottoman and a well-worn easy chair.

All that was missing was a cat curled up by the fire on a hooked rug.

Lila Conway said, "Come into the kitchen. I want to get this chicken boiling."

I followed her through the living room and into a tidy kitchen. Whatever she was cooking smelled incredible. My mouth watered when I spied a baguette peeking out of a long, narrow brown paper bag, its golden crust baked to the perfect shade of gold. I hadn't had a baguette in months.

A broken bottle lay in the kitchen sink and I read the label: cranberry juice. Not blood, then, on Conway's apron.

The chicken lay atop a large cutting board on the worn kitchen table. The woman brought the butcher knife down on the bird and a drum-stick popped loose. She caught the leg before it rolled off the table and dropped it into a pot of boiling water on the stove.

"I smell parsley, onion . . . sage. Chicken soup?"

She nodded. "Yes. I make a pot of it every weekend in the winter. My God. It is an awful task you police officers have, Ms. Monroe. I will forever link chicken soup to the loss of my friend. What was once comfort food shall now carry with it the smell of death. A broth for carrions."

I agreed with her wholeheartedly; I did have an awful job sometimes. "And for that, and your loss, I am deeply sorry, Ms. Conway."

She frowned and brought the knife down on the other leg. "I can't believe he's gone. Delaware was larger than life. I thought he'd be delivering the eulogy at my funeral one day. Let me finish this and then we can sit in the living room and talk. I have a difficult time multitasking. I don't find it comes naturally to me."

I watched quietly as she quartered the rest of the chicken, then started in on the rest of the spices and vegetables. Conway worked quickly, efficiently, not following a recipe but instead measuring everything by sight.

"Would you like some herbal tea, or coffee?"

I accepted a cup of tea. We took seats in the front living room, surrounded by the books. The cockatoo watched us from his perch, chatting quietly to himself.

Conway noticed me looking at him. "He's mad."

"Oh? Why?"

Conway shrugged. "I don't know. He's always been that way. Not angry mad, but nutty mad. He mutters to himself all day. His name is Kojak. He's a real son of a bitch but we adore each other. Del suggested the name. He was a big fan of crime television. Del, not the bird; I don't let Kojak watch television. It rots the brain."

Her eyes filled with tears again. "I just can't . . . it's shocking, isn't it? We start dying the minute we're born and yet death, every time, it shocks us."

I nodded. "We don't expect it. Somehow, we think it will skip over us; us, and our loved ones. But it never does, does it?"

I didn't want to upset Conway any more than she already was. Sipping my tea, I glanced around the room, trying to decide how to begin. Large, professionally framed black-and-white posters lined the wall. One in particular caught my eye because I recognized the woman in it.

She was a petite brunette with pouty lips, skin the color of cocoa, and a crooked nose. The nose, which I knew had been broken more than once and was what many would consider a flaw, in my opinion only served to highlight her beauty. She was a knockout, all five feet and one hundred pounds of her.

"That's Yvette Michaelson, isn't it?"

Conway, startled but pleased, nodded. Her eyes lit up. "The Daughter of Denver. That's a reproduction of the last known photograph ever taken of her. She disappeared shortly after, in 1923, on an expedition in Bolivia. There are rumors she was boiled alive by cannibalistic natives, like the chicken in my kitchen. Of course, the chicken was dead first. There are other rumors that say she was adopted by a tribe and crowned a royal princess. There's so much about her that remains unknown. You could say she's a hobby of mine."

Conway gestured to the stacks of books on the floor by her feet. "Actually, *hobby* might be inaccurate. It's probably closer to an obsession. I'm quite literally ankle-deep in research."

I asked, "What got you interested in Yvette Michaelson, Ms. Conway?"

"It's Lila. We share the same crippling pathology. We both suffered—well, to be honest, I still suffer—from crippling shyness. Social anxiety disorder, to be precise, though I've never been formally diagnosed. It's taken decades of self-discipline and practice, but I do fine in one-on-one conversations. I loathe groups. Anyway, Yvette found a way out through exploration. For me, it's reading. I've never left Colorado and I never will. My exploration is through the lives of others."

"That makes a fair amount of sense. Why was Delaware Fuente here, in Cedar Valley?"

If Lila was surprised by the sudden change in

topic, she didn't show it. She waited for me to sit down before speaking. Her eyes pooled with tears again. I saw a level of sadness and loss just below the surface that brewed like the soup in her kitchen, growing stronger with each word.

"It was all my idea. And now he's dead and I'm responsible. Del and I went to school together in Denver. We were misfits. I was terribly shy, and you know how children can be to one another, cruel and punishing. That made Del angry—he was always one to fight injustice—and his anger scared the others. He was this little runt, this poor—I mean dirt poor—little Mexican boy and the depth of his anger scared even the grown-ups. Strangely enough, he became my protector."

Lila paused to take a breath and collect herself, then continued. "We were each other's only friends. That bond took us all the way through high school. We've kept in touch over the years. A few months ago, Del mentioned he was looking for a sabbatical in the mountains somewhere. I suggested our lovely town. He agreed, and then he agreed to do a series of guest lectures at the school, incognito."

"Wouldn't the students have benefited from knowing who he really was?"

Lila shook her head. "Del didn't want that. The whole purpose of the sabbatical was to immerse himself in his memoirs. He was writing them, you see. And he felt he needed to go beyond himself, outside himself, to fully look back as almost an outsider to reflect upon his life. Does that make sense to you? It didn't make sense to me, not at first. He was fanatical, though. I was supposed to address him as John Firestone when we spoke."

"And truly no one recognized him?"

Lila shook her head again and sipped from her tea. She said, "It really is unbelievable, isn't it, that without the beard and the eye patch, no one recognized Del. And yet, someone must have recognized him because otherwise, he was simply a visiting lecturer named John. And why kill some random lecturer? Unless . . . do you think it was a horrible, random occurrence? A mugging gone wrong?"

I thought about the crime scene, the fact that Fuente's wallet had been untouched, and said no. "I think someone lured Mr. Fuente to the academy, Lila. They lured him, or drove him there, and killed him."

Lila looked out across the room. Grief, and something else, weariness perhaps, took hold in her face. Her features seemed to melt and wither. "Did he suffer?"

I told the same lie that I've told to countless others. There are some truths that carry a weight bigger than the need to know. Fuente may have died quickly but there still would have been pain, fear.

"No. He didn't suffer."

She nodded. She knew I'd lied. They always know. But I keep lying anyway.

"Lila, do you know where Mr. Fuente was staying?"

"A rental cabin up Ponderosa Lane. Please, stop calling him Mr. Fuente, he was Del, or Delaware or Big Dumb-Dumb, and I was Little Birdbrain. He was never Mr. Fuente. I have the address here."

She plucked a small notebook from the pile of journals and magazines and read me a street address. I thanked her.

"Can you think of anyone that might have wanted to hurt Mr. Fuente—Del?"

She laughed at that. "You strike me as a competent person, Gemma. I'm sure you know he, like many public figures, was equally beloved and disliked. He was such a nice man. A controversial, outspoken man, but generous to a fault. I don't know that he had enemies. Especially here in town. Although . . ."

Lila grew troubled.

"What is it?"

She said, "The last week or so, Del was . . . on edge. He thought someone was at the rental property, watching him. Maybe even following him. He talked about a large man with yellow hair, big ears, bug eyes, and a misshapen head. Del called him the Rabbit Man, because of the ears. He mentioned a truck, too. Maybe it was a large SUV, I don't remember. He saw it

97

numerous times, behind him, driving around town. He thought . . . he thought he might be imagining things, until one morning he found footprints leading to his cabin after a fresh snow. The footprints circled around the cabin, leaving deep depressions by the windows, and then trekked off into the woods. Another time, he found a dead rabbit by his car. It was torn in two, poor thing. Half-eaten by the sound of it."

"And you didn't think to mention this before?"

Lila shook her head. "No, because I didn't take it very seriously. The trouble with writers is that they have lurid imaginations. A Rabbit Man, even the name sounds ridiculous."

"Did Mr. Fuente—Del—did he take a picture of the footprints? Or report any of this to the police or the property owners? Maybe it was the caretaker or a nosy guest," I asked.

Lila shook her head. "Del was the only guest at the property. Aside from the road being plowed, he asked that even the caretaker stay offsite, at another rental owned by the company. He didn't want any distractions as he worked on his memoirs."

"This Rabbit Man, you say he scared Mr. Fuente?"

"*Scare* is a strong word. I think he made Del uneasy, on edge. I begged Del to report him to the police but Del refused. He said if the Rabbit Man escalated things, then he'd report it."

I nodded. "I'll have one of our guys put together a rough sketch."

I looked around the room, wondering if there was anything else I was missing. It struck me once again how very many books, and research materials, were in the room. "Are you a writer, too, Lila?"

She blushed. The pink stood out like a slap against her pale skin.

"Del was the one with the talent. I'm just a reader. I'm more comfortable behind the scenes. That's why I enjoy my work so much at the high school, handling paperwork and reports. No, I'm not a writer. I couldn't take something as precious as a manuscript and go out with it, into that great big world."

I nodded. "That makes sense to me. One more question, Lila, and it's one I'll be asking many people in the days to come, so please, no offense meant. Where were you on Friday night?"

"My alibi, right? The real reason you're here. The truth is, I don't have one. I stayed at work until about six o'clock, then skedaddled back here before the storm got any worse. There were a few teachers still there who I waved good-bye to. They can at least verify what time I left."

From somewhere on the wall behind me, a cuckoo clock chimed the hour, politely making it clear that I had taken enough of Lila's time. I stood, thanked her, and promised to let her know as soon as we turned up any information. She walked me to the door and I paused, taking in the lovely cottage once more.

I didn't want to leave. It was easy to see that Lila Conway had built up her own little world of magic here, a place no one ever need leave. I couldn't help but wonder, though, if there wasn't any part of her that wanted more, a bigger slice of the world, a bigger piece of the pie.

"It must have been surprising to watch Del's rise to stardom, given that you knew him when he was young and poor."

Lila stared at me. For the first time, I saw that she had two different colored eyes, one brown, and the other blue. "Surprising? No, there was nothing surprising about it. When we were thirteen years old, on a bitterly cold night in March, Del told me he was going to be famous. He didn't know how, or when, but he knew. And I swore I would do whatever I could to help him. I remember it was March because we were dressed in green for St. Patrick's Day."

"And did you?"

Lila tilted her head. "Did I what?"

"Help him become famous."

She looked out into the woods behind me, then turned back and with fresh tears in her eyes, smiled at me. "Del never needed my help, Gemma. I was always the one who needed him."

Chapter Eight

Fuente's rental cabin was eight miles west of Lila Conway's house. I called Finn from the road and he agreed to meet me there. Two sets of eyes are always better than one, and if ever there was a time to do things by the book, this was it. As soon as the world discovered Delaware Fuente was dead, the media would turn a national spotlight on Cedar Valley and the police department. The less opportunity we allowed for questions about our handling of the murder, the better.

I followed Red Ridge Road as it switched back and forth, leading me deeper into the mountains. Three or four cars passed me going the other direction, their roofs laden with skis, snowboards, and in one case, atop a thirty-year-old Ford pickup, a dead deer. I slowed as the truck passed; the driver was young, and in the front bench seat with him was an equally young woman. There were two small children between them.

They looked hungry.

We were well past deer hunting season in Colorado, and I should have called Parks and Wildlife to report the driver. But I didn't. As I watched the truck in my rearview mirror, it slowed and then took a right, onto a road that I knew dead-ended at Beaver Reservoir. There were a handful of cabins up there, and though it was illegal, I was glad the young family would have a full dinner tonight.

I kept driving, and grateful for the sunlight, however weak it was, I turned the radio louder and the heat higher. The scenery was beautiful and the drive should have felt expansive. Instead, it was oppressive. The canyon walls seemed to grow ever tighter the closer I got to Fuente's cabin. Long shadows loomed over the road.

I recalled another young family, driving on this same stretch of road five years ago, who'd had the terrible luck to round a corner just as a rockslide let loose with two tons of boulders. I'd known them in passing, having served on a volunteer board with the mother.

How do you avoid something like that, a freak accident, simply being in the wrong place at the wrong time?

I pressed on the gas and hurried past the cross that someone had placed at the scene for the family. It was small and wooden, with faded ribbons and long-dried flowers that peeked shyly out of the snow.

Finally, the canyon opened up. I followed the signs and turned left onto a rough, dirt stretch that ended abruptly in a four-foot snowdrift. Slowing down, nearly stopping, I scanned the road in front of me. Off to the right, easy to miss, there was a narrow, plowed drive that led to a single cabin on the north end of the property. A good fifty feet separated the cabin from its nearest neighbor, and the driveway leading to it was the only one that had been recently plowed.

Fuente's cabin.

I rolled down the window and turned off the radio, not yet heading down the drive. The property was silent. The grounds were deserted; the cabins empty. It was not a place most people would choose to set up a home, however temporary. In another time or another place, its isolation might have felt peaceful. Today, the remoteness of it felt dreary, with a hostile coldness.

Lila Conway's story about the Rabbit Man gained some traction in my mind. This was the perfect place to stalk someone, to watch them and get used to their patterns, their habits. You couldn't describe a more ideal hunting ground for a killer.

This is only the beginning. . . .

My engine, still running, gave a hiccup and I jumped.

"Get a grip," I whispered and put my foot gently on the gas. I stopped five feet from Fuente's front door and put the car in park, letting the engine continue to run. The cabin windows were dark, the curtains drawn fast. Fuente had stayed here for weeks, but there remained a sense of abandonment about the cabin.

There were plenty of hotels and furnished apartments in town that Fuente could have stayed in. Why had he come to this deserted compound, this ghost town of empty cabins? Why had he lived as a stranger, a man in disguise? As I thought it, though, I realized that in the most literal sense, Fuente hadn't been in disguise at all. Eye patch removed, beard shorn, hair pushed back . . . by stripping off the things that on a daily basis hid him, he wasn't in disguise but rather exposed.

Something red and shiny peeked out from behind the cabin, and it took me a minute to realize it was the front of a car, likely a Jeep or some other midsized SUV.

Seeing the Jeep only served to increase my unease.

I had counted on finding Fuente's car somewhere close to the school, maybe parked across the street in the Shady—Shaded—Acres subdivision. If I'd had any doubt, the fact that the car was instead here convinced me that Fuente knew his killer; had perhaps even been driven to his death by him. The local buses didn't pick up this far west. I supposed Fuente may have called for an Uber ride, or a taxi, but that was unlikely given the blizzard the night of his killing.

I didn't like being here, among these empty shells of homes, thinking about a dead man. Thinking about a live man, a stalker, someone known to me only as the Rabbit Man; worse, thinking about a serial killer. I took my cell from my purse and checked the reception. There was one lonely bar, and it was a good thing I'd called Finn from the road; I wouldn't be able to reach anyone now.

There were no landlines in these woods. There was hardly any cell reception. How did Fuente communicate with the outside world? Did he have to wait to make calls with his cell until he was closer to town?

I sighed, remembering Finn's words: all we had were questions right now.

I turned off the engine, got out of the car, and stood, one hand holding open the door. I stared at the small house, waiting and listening. My feet grew cold from standing in one place but still I didn't move. It was unlikely that Fuente's killer was here, now, a day and a half after the murder, and yet I knew that life's unlikely moments often turn into reality, usually when we least expect them to.

I cupped my hands to my mouth and shouted, "Hello."

Silence, then a response.

It was an owl, and he called back at me from somewhere deep in the forest. I watched the trees that lined the edge of the property to see if I could spot him, but there was nothing; not even the scurrying movements of a squirrel or the sudden flutter of wings from a crow. I closed my eyes for a few seconds against the endless white of the snow and heard another, more subtle sound. Somewhere close by, a stream glided over chunks of ice, the sound of a shaker in a quiet bar.

The thought of a cocktail made me smile and chased away my unease.

There was no one else here.

I was tired of getting spooked.

Reaching into the car, I grabbed a few things from my bag and stuffed them in my jacket pocket. Then I walked back to the edge of the driveway and peered at the other cabins. I recalled from a quick look at a map in my car before I left Lila Conway's driveway that there was a good-sized fishing pond a few hundred yards away, on an old hunting trail, that was fed from a crystal-clear lake another mile or so west. In the summer, these rentals, and others like them all over town, filled up quickly. Frugal families loved the cabins because they were cheaper than the hotels and lodges in town.

But this was winter, not summer. Canoes leaned against the outer walls of the cabins, weary old men with thick coats of snow on their shoulders and icicles hung from their bows.

Undisturbed snowdrifts ten inches high sloped against the front doors.

I walked to the back of Delaware Fuente's cabin and brushed snow from the Jeep. It was sleek and looked like a new model. I brushed more snow off, this time from the front window, and peered in. The interior was leather; a navigation system sat in the console and a stainless-steel coffee tumbler stood in the beverage holder.

At the rear of the Jeep, I checked the license plate; it was from New Jersey, and Fuente had indeed likely driven out his own car instead of flying in and renting something. Judging from the amount of snow I brushed off the Jeep, and knowing how much we'd gotten during the blizzard, I hazarded a guess that the car hadn't been driven in at least two or three days.

I continued my walk around the cabin. There was a battered silver trash can, the lid tied down with bungee cords to keep out raccoons, and in the summer, bears. I unsnapped the cords and lifted the lid. Inside the can was a single white trash bag, drawn shut with the bag's red tie. I reached in and, holding my breath in anticipation of a terrible smell, pulled open the bag. I needn't have worried; the trash consisted of empty microwave dinner boxes, wadded-up Kleenex, and a half-dozen beer bottles.

The sound of a car engine pulled my attention from the trash can. Finn met me at the front door. He looked tired. The shadows under his baby blues were dark and his normally immaculate clothes were rumpled.

"Sorry to drag you out on a Sunday," I said. "Late night?"

Finn yawned and shrugged at the same time. He ignored my question. "It's an active murder investigation. I don't want you to get all the glory. Did you go in yet?"

I shook my head. "Nope."

He tried the door; it was locked. "We should have grabbed that key we found on him. You think there's another one hidden around here somewhere?"

Finn stood on his tiptoes and ran a hand over the strip of wood above the front door. I pulled a small clear envelope out of my back pocket and held it up. I whistled to get Finn's attention. "Is this what you're looking for?"

He grinned and took it from my hand. The key he pulled out of the envelope fit the lock perfectly and after a small click, he pushed the door open. He held an arm out.

"Ladies first."

I moved past him. The smell of his aftershave was strong and I caught something else, something sweeter and more delicate, like a woman's scented body lotion.

I stepped into the cabin and fumbled against the wall until I found the light switch.

"How's Kelly? Are you two lovebirds back together?"

Finn scowled. "I haven't seen Kelly in months. This place is depressing."

Sparse might have been the word I chose. There was a small living area, with a couch, a coffee table, a fireplace, and an older model television on a wheeled stand. A stack of dated board games, dusty at the edges, sat below the television on the bottom shelf of the stand. On one end of the couch, a red-and-white quilt was neatly folded and draped over the armrest.

The walls were bare, the floor made of wood.

Finn picked up a remote control on the coffee table and aimed it at the television. Salt-and-pepper static appeared and though he pressed all the buttons, he couldn't get any clear stations.

"I hope they didn't charge him for this piece of garbage," Finn muttered.

"There's hardly any cell reception, either," I added. "At least, my phone only had one bar."

I stepped into the kitchen, just off to the right of the fireplace. There was a coffee machine with an inch of black liquid in the bottom of the carafe, and a toaster on the counter, and a sad little table in the corner with a dirty plastic glass on it, half-full of fake flowers. I opened the cabinet doors; inside was a variety of spices, oils, mostly empty cereal boxes, and a full set of plates, bowls, and mugs.

Finn came in behind me and checked the refrigerator and freezer.

"Hot dogs, a few burger patties, half a roast chicken. Milk, cheese, eggs," he said, scanning the contents. "There's about ten microwave meals in the freezer. All-American diet, if you ask me. Oh, and three gallons of ice cream. Not a fruit or vegetable in sight. Unless you count the strawberry sorbet."

"He *was* kind of pudgy. Let's check the rest of this place out."

I headed to the two closed doors on the side of the house. "Lila Conway said Fuente was working on his memoirs. I'm betting he turned one of the bedrooms into an office."

Finn followed me into the first room. He brushed a speck of something off the blue-and-white quilt, then sat on the bed and bounced up and down, testing the springs. They squawked furiously. "Pretty noisy."

"From what Fuente's agent, Choi, told me, the bed was probably used for sleeping purposes only."

"Too bad," Finn responded. He moved off the bed and smirked. "There's no one to hear a sound for miles; you could get all sorts of freaky."

He checked out the closet and bureau drawers. "There's nothing that looks out of place here. Sweaters, jeans, socks, and underwear—lots of underwear."

I went into the bathroom and called back, "There's toiletries and towels in here, and Fuente has some over-the-counter heartburn tablets and a bottle of aspirin and that's it for medicine. He's about out of toilet paper."

Not that he's going to need it anytime soon.

There was nothing unusual in the bathroom, so I moved onto the next door and opened it.

"Jesus Christ!"

I jumped backward, bumping into Finn, who'd come up behind me. He pushed me aside and put a hand toward the gun on his hip.

"What is it?"

He looked so serious that I started laughing. "I'm sorry, it's nothing. It's just, it's such a mess compared to the rest of this place."

The spare room was packed floor to ceiling: there were cardboard boxes, pieces of furniture, summer sports equipment like paddle boards and life vests, and camping gear, a half-dozen tents and sleeping bags. I'd bet this room only got cleared out in the spring, to get it ready for summer visitors. In fact, it was probably storing things that normally lived in most of the other cabins.

Disgusted, Finn pulled the door shut. "What a pigsty. I bet there's mice in there."

"Spiders, too," I added. "So where are they?"

"Where's what, the mice?"

Ignoring him, I went back to the bedroom and

fell to my knees. I peered under the bed. I pulled out dresser drawers and even pulled the dresser away from the wall and peeked behind it.

"What are you looking for?" my partner asked. He stood in the door, watching me, hands in his pockets.

"Lila Conway told me that Delaware Fuente came to the mountains to work on his memoirs. The guest lectures at the academy were a side gig. So where are the memoirs?"

Finn shrugged. "My guess is on a flash drive somewhere. What, you thought he'd have a pile of papers lying around? Forget that; you should be looking for a tiny little thing the size of your thumb."

"Okay, Mr. Smarty-Pants, where's the flash drive? Or the laptop, for that matter?"

"Let's check his car."

We went outside together. Finn tried the front door of the Jeep. It opened and a wall of snow thundered down. "He wasn't too concerned about theft, was he?"

I shook my head. "Out here? There's not a soul around. That would be like being concerned about . . ."

I almost said *murder*.

Finn read my mind and gave me a wry smile. "Yeah, exactly."

We found the laptop in a black commuter case, stowed behind the front seat. I felt around

112

in the pockets of the case and all along the interior lining. "Nothing. No papers, no flash drive, no disc. Don't you find that strange?"

Finn wasn't bothered. "They'll turn up. Maybe he emailed his work to himself, or to his agent. We'll take the laptop back with us and look at the hard drive."

Something wasn't right. Regardless of how they seem in movies and novels, mysteries are not neat little puzzles, broken apart only to be put back together. Not only are there always pieces missing, most of the time the pieces you've got don't even fit together.

"Finn, Fuente hadn't driven this car in a week, I'd bet a hundred bucks on that. And his laptop has just been sitting in it, all this time? Can't the, you know, electronic parts freeze? You don't think that's odd? What was he doing?"

He stepped back from the Jeep and assessed the snow and the lack of tire tracks. Then he looked to the sky, shielding his eyes with one hand, gauging something. I rolled my eyes and waited. I was right, and he knew it, too, but we had to do our usual dance of him at least thinking he'd had a say in our conclusions.

"A week, huh . . . yeah, that's probably about right. So we've got a writer sitting in his rented cabin, supposedly working on his memoirs. But he's left his laptop in his car, we haven't seen a single thing to support he was in fact working on said memoirs, and most importantly, his television doesn't even work. What was he doing all day? Just sitting on his butt? No wonder he was getting fat."

"I'll call his agent, Choi, again. Maybe he knows something more."

"You know, this could be motive." Finn added, "Maybe there's something in those memoirs that someone didn't want the world to see. Killing Fuente was a way to get them."

"That would be preferable to a possible serial killer. But then what about the note in Fuente's mouth?"

Finn shrugged. "Diversion?"

We finished up inside the cabin, finding nothing else that could help our case. Then we locked the place up and strung yellow crime scene tape across the front door in a large *X* pattern.

Finn said, "You watched *The Sopranos.* Fuente was from Jersey. Maybe he's mobbed up. A note like that, that feels like sort of a mob thing."

I shook my head and followed Finn back to our cars. "Fuente wasn't from Jersey; he was from Denver. He's just lived in Jersey a long time."

"Good point. So, Lila Conway. Does she have eighteen cats and a pantry full of soup?"

My stomach rumbled at the memory of Lila's kitchen. I smiled. "Yes to the soup—although it's homemade—and no to the cat. There is a bird, Kojak. Lila was upset; she and Fuente were close. I didn't want to push her too hard, but from what I could gather, she can't imagine who could do something like this."

"They never can," Finn said.

I nodded. "Well, it gets weirder. Technically speaking, Conway was the only one who knew Fuente was here in town. He was 'undercover,' clean-shaven, without the eye patch—as we saw—and going by the name John Firestone. No one knew who he really was. Which of course makes Conway the most likely suspect in his murder, but I don't buy it. I just can't see it. Although she doesn't have an alibi for Friday night. . . ."

I couldn't help but think back to the last case I'd worked before going on maternity leave. It involved another person, a young man, who had returned to town under a disguise and been killed. Makeup, disguises—they only work for so long. Sooner or later, the mask comes off and the truth comes out. It's the way of the world, it always has been.

I shivered. It was cold, standing outside, and although the skies were clear, another storm was predicted to roll through soon. It struck me again how isolated it was here, how very alone and foreboding. Even the woods felt different; the trees had grown too close together, as though a sickness had crowded them next to one another. A sickness, or a fear.

I told Finn about the Rabbit Man.

"That description doesn't ring any bells, but we should have a sketch made up and circulated," Finn said, concerned. "If Fuente had a stalker . . . that changes everything. We should check with the school, too. Maybe this guy has been hanging out there, as well. Bowie Childs may have him on his radar already."

"You can chat with our friendly neighborhood security guard; I'm keeping my distance."

"He's not that bad. Let's meet at the school tomorrow morning and start interviewing some of the people there. Maybe Fuente wasn't as incognito as he thought."

I agreed, half listening, bothered by something. "You know what else is strange, besides the missing memoirs?"

"What?"

I thrust my chin back toward the cabin. "There's not a single book in there. I've never heard of a writer who wasn't first and foremost a reader."

Finn thought on that for a minute. "I don't know, Gemma. Maybe's he's got a Kindle. I have a Kindle and I'm not exactly what you call a big reader."

"Well, I think it's strange . . . but okay, maybe he's got a Kindle. Then where is it?"

He didn't have an answer for that.

Finn decided to walk around the property and burn off some energy. He said something about needing to clear his mind, so I left him and sped down the canyon, once again feeling as though the canyon were a living, shifting thing, with the rock that made up its wall intent on closing in on me.

Chapter Nine

First thing Monday morning, I met Finn at the Valley Academy. All of the parking spots were taken, so we ended up leaving our vehicles on the street. I hadn't slept well, and in an effort to stay awake, had drunk more coffee than I was used to. I felt jittery and cranky.

The sky was a blue so pale it was nearly white. All around us, the Rockies rose like giant stone goliaths, frozen in place for all eternity. The air had a bite to it and the ground was hard with packed snow and ice. I watched as Bowie Childs, the security guard, upended a bag of ice melt near the front gate. Another man was with him; both wore jackets with the Kaspersky Security emblem and I was glad to see that Director Silverstein had increased the officer count on campus.

We walked carefully across the icy lot as a bell began to ring from somewhere deep inside McKinley Hall. On Friday night, the hall had been dark and menacing. In the light of day, though, the redbrick building felt almost cheery.

"For us or them?" Finn mused.

I didn't get it.

He said, "Come on, Monroe, you went to college. Hemingway? Who's the bell ringing for, us, or the students?"

"Ah. Well," I said, checking my watch, "I believe that particular bell is announcing first period is about to start. And yes, I did go to college. The bell is ringing for us all, according to John Donne. We'll all die in time; death diminishes mankind and so on."

Finn scowled. "John Donne, come on, what's it going to be next time, Kit Marlowe? Aristotle? You've been spending too much time with the Doc."

I started to say that Dr. Ravi Hussen almost exclusively stuck to Shakespeare when she wanted to reference great literature, and that the rest of the time her tastes ran to hard-core romance novels, but before I could finish my sentence I was roughly pushed to the side by a few panicked-looking stragglers. The bell was definitely tolling for them.

"Hey, watch it," I muttered, rubbing my elbow. Finn reached for them, a pair of boys, and I told him to let it go. We paused at the heavy front door of McKinley Hall to let one more student go ahead of us. I looked off to the east but from this angle, I couldn't see the crime scene. Fuente's body of course had been removed but the police tape would have still been there, and the crime scene technicians likely returned at some point after the storm, in the hopes of gathering more evidence.

"Come on," Finn said. I followed him into the front hall. Inside, the air was warm and ripe with Eau de Youth: heavily scented lotions, cheap drugstore cologne, unwashed gym clothes, and nasty cafeteria food. We moved down the long, narrow hallway to further smells of old sneakers, dry erase markers, and long-forgotten lunches.

"God, I'd forgotten how much school stinks."

Finn shook his head. "They need to air this place out sometime."

We walked and I decided very little had changed over the last ten years.

The year I'd spent at the academy—my freshman year of high school—was the second-worst year of my life. Kids can be cruel. I was one of a handful of students on scholarship and that, plus the loss of my parents, made me a freak in the eyes of the rich kids whose parents shelled out thousands for them to have the privilege of attending the academy.

I lasted a year before begging my grand-mother Julia to transfer me to the public school.

As Finn and I walked, our badges made us pariahs. We parted the groups of students like Moses parting the Red Sea. They moved to the side, pressed close to lockers and one another, their eyes downcast.

"You'd think they were all guilty of something," Finn said in a low voice in my ear. His breath was hot against my skin and once again, I smelled that curious blend of his strong aftershave and the sweeter, more feminine scent. He was clearly spending a lot of time in the arms of someone.

"Aren't we all?"

We reached the end of the south hall and entered a small reception area outside the administration offices. A petite, curvy black woman in a red pantsuit and ornate silver jewelry stood in the middle of the room, deep in conversation with a tall, gangly kid, all arms and legs, in a beat-up leather jacket and a pair of ripped jeans.

The look on the boy's face was one of pure anger.

The look on the woman's face was serene, almost smug.

Their talking ended as we approached and as the boy walked away, he muttered something under his breath. The woman watched him a moment, shaking her head, then set her attention on us. We introduced ourselves and she spoke, even as she was turning away and opening the door to the office. "Justine Moreno. I'm the vice principal. I believe you know Stan Silverstein is out on extended medical leave? That leaves me in charge, come hell or high water. Seems the hell reached us first. A murder, on our campus, I still can't believe it. Thank goodness it wasn't one of my students. Come in, please."

We watched as she fussed at a steel coffeepot tucked in the corner of the narrow space. Three diplomas and a number of certificates and awards lined the walls of the office. The desk itself was bare, save for a white laptop and a single, silver-framed picture of a chubby-cheeked toddler.

She finished making the coffee and offered it up. I declined; the thought of more caffeine made me feel sick. Finn took a cup and smiled his thanks.

He said, "I see a bachelor's degree in modern languages; a master's in education, and a second master's degree in business administration. You ever hear of 'overachiever syndrome'?"

Moreno laughed. "I can't help it, I crave knowledge. I tried to teach German and French at the high school level for a few years and I was bored out of my mind. It was the same material, day in, day out. Administration provides a nice mix for me. It keeps one toe in teaching and the other in learning."

Finn said, "Oh yeah? How's that?"

"Every encounter with a student is an opportunity to learn a new way of reaching them at their level. And of course there are the continuing education classes, the new trends in school administration to keep up on," Moreno replied. She stopped smiling and continued. "I never imagined having to work under such terrible circumstances, though. This is uncharted territory for me."

I asked, "Has word of the murder already spread?"

Moreno nodded. "Many of the students are aware of the tragedy. I've requested additional counselors from the public schools, in case anyone needs to talk to a professional. I will make a more formal announcement later this morning. Although very few students knew the deceased, death is always a shock, especially for the younger children. Many have never experienced it close up, so personal. It's one of the hardest lessons to learn."

Finn picked up the framed picture on Moreno's desk. "Is this your daughter? She's adorable."

"Thank you. Diana lives with her father in New Mexico. We're divorced. That's probably obvious by the fact that he lives in another state. I'm not sure when I'll feel like I can stop announcing that; it's just the divorce was recent and rather ugly. He's a good father but a terrible husband. Anyway, that one picture helps me gain tremendous perspective with the students here. When they are acting like little turds, which seems to be most of the time, I take a deep breath and look at Diana's picture. It helps me remember that each of them is someone's baby girl, someone's little guy, and that it is our responsibility to guide them, teach them, show them the correct way. How's the coffee?"

Finn said it was hot, strong, and very good.

I asked, "Ms. Moreno, how well did you know Delaware Fuente? Had you interacted much with him these last few months?"

"No, and it pisses me off that Lila went behind my back. She went completely off the reservation on this one. All the teachers and administrators know they must ask permission first rather than seek forgiveness second. Oh, but she was sly. She introduced him as John Firestone, an old friend. He and I met once, at the staff Christmas party, about six weeks ago," Moreno said. She made air quotes with her fingers and continued. " 'John' was a writer, a poet, with expansive ideas on literature, art, music. I found him charming and agreed that the senior student body would get a kick out of him. The other teachers seemed to like him, too."

Moreno took a sip of her coffee and then added, "From what I can gather, the kids really did get a kick out of him."

Finn asked, "So you had no clue John Firestone was Delaware Fuente? Really? I find that hard to believe. I recognized him after a few minutes.

You and the staff and the students interacted with him for weeks."

Moreno shrugged again. "As I said before, I only met him the one time. I never had reason to doubt Lila's honesty. You yell 'boo' at her and she'll keel over. I was thrilled to learn she had such a strong friendship with someone, anyone. She's all by herself in that house, deep in the woods . . . well, I guess I'm alone, too, now. But you know what I mean, I live in town, I have friends, I interact socially with my colleagues. I was married. I had a life. I have a life."

She took a deep breath. "Anyway, I'm not sure what else I can tell you. John Firestone was here at the school twice a week, and he spoke only to the advanced senior literature group. Harold Chapman runs that class. Firestone didn't linger or mingle; he'd arrive, check in at the front desk at ten on Wednesdays and Fridays, and go do his thing. I've double-checked our registration logs; ever since Columbine, we've required guests to sign in. There are so many strange creeps nowadays looking to inflict damage, you can't be too careful."

Finn said, "The Columbine killers were students, not strangers. In Columbine, the danger came from within."

Moreno bristled. "Are you implying that one of my students killed John Firestone? Excuse me, Delaware Fuente? We have good kids here. Yes, many of them act out of line. But we take measures to correct that behavior. We talk to our students. We give them choices, with consequences, and show them how to act accordingly. Do you remember being sixteen, seventeen years old?"

I nodded. "I do. I'm sure Finn does, too. How about that kid you were talking to as we arrived? Is he one of the students that acts out of line?"

Moreno began to twist the heavy silver bracelets on her wrist. She exhaled deeply. "That was Denny Little. He's one of our scholarship students. He's upset because I'm honoring the expulsion that Director Silverstein has recommended. Denny brought a knife to school last week. That's against our code of conduct. Unfortunately for Denny, this is the latest in a series of code violations. His time is up. Shame, too, as he could have graduated with honors. He's very smart."

Finn finished his coffee and set the mug down on the desk. Moreno set it back toward the coffeepot.

Finn asked, "What will he do now?"

Moreno moved from fiddling with her bracelets to tugging at the necklace she wore high around her neck. She thought a moment, then said, "Vo-tech school, maybe. He can earn his GED at Eagleton Community College, if he puts in the time and the sweat. If these kids don't learn about consequences here, where will they? Certainly not at home, I can tell you that. Denny's mother left when he was three. His father, Donald, works two jobs to support the family, including serving as our night janitor here at the high school. He's a good man, Donald is, but he's got his hands full. Anyway, Denny's extremely bright but very troubled. I shouldn't mention this, but he does have a juvenile record. Sealed, of course. I know a lot of it involved things like petty theft and vandalism. Graffiti, cherry bombs, that sort of thing."

It was a sad story. I agreed with Moreno to a point; in my line of work, all too often I saw the result of people not learning about consequences. And yet, as a mother, hell, as a human being, I found it difficult to think that someone like Denny Little, a kid whose life was a series of bad circumstances, could be turned out like yesterday's old news.

I stood up. "Listen, Ms. Moreno, thank you for your time. I believe Director Silverstein arranged for us to meet with Harold Chapman and some of the other English teachers? I'd also like to follow up with Lila Conway, if she's available."

The vice principal nodded. "There are three of them, Harold Chapman, Soren Baker, and Peggy Greenway. They spent the most time with

Firestone . . . Fuente. They'll be waiting for you in the conference room next door."

Finn thanked her and asked, "Besides Denny Little, is there anything else going on that we should be aware of? Other problems with students, or odd behavioral patterns that you've noticed?"

Moreno stood. "There's always something going on but that's to be expected these days. I'm sure you saw our campus safety officers out front? We went under contract with Kaspersky Security a few months back. There wasn't any single incident that prompted it but I have to tell you, it's a sad day when that becomes the norm. I miss the days when school administrators were all that was needed to stand between a thriving student body and a bunch of hoodlums. Anyway any issues would be between me and the specific student."

"And their parents, right?" Finn asked.

Moreno nodded. "Of course. Parents are always involved, sooner or later. As for Lila, she took the day off. Please, take all the time you need with Harold, Soren, and Peggy, but I do ask that you don't question any of the students. I'm sure you're more than aware that we would need parental permissions for that."

Finn and I agreed.

He tried one more time and I wondered what it was he was hoping or expecting to hear.

"So, nothing else going on? Everything is hunky-dory?"

Moreno tilted her head and peered at Finn. "I would never call a private school brimming with puberty-stricken privileged teenagers 'hunky-dory,' but yes. We run a tight ship here and so far, it seems to have kept things afloat. Denny has anger issues, but murder? I hardly think him, or any of our students, capable of that. No, everything is most certainly copacetic around here."

"Except for the death of a bestselling author on your front lawn," Finn said, unable to resist. "Sorry, the murder of a bestselling author."

Moreno scowled at him. "I'm almost certain you'll find the location of that man's death is pure coincidence and has nothing to do with my school, my students, or myself."

We left Moreno frowning in her office and moved to the room next door.

Chapter Ten

Like students in a detention hall, the three teachers were quietly waiting, absorbed in their own thoughts. Harold Chapman and Peggy Greenway sat at opposite ends of the long conference table, with Soren Baker in the middle.

Peggy Greenway looked like no high school English teacher I'd ever seen. Her hair was dark and styled in a 1940s pinup fashion. Her lips were bright with scarlet gloss and while her dress, patterned tights, and heels covered almost every inch of her skin, she still somehow managed to look sexier than if she'd been naked.

Harold Chapman, on the other hand, looked like every stereotype of an English professor. He was at least ten years older than Peggy and wore a tweed blazer and baggy corduroy pants. His hair was thin and receding, and the last time his pale skin had held a tan was likely during the Bush administration.

In terms of attire and dress, Soren Baker fell somewhere between the two. He was closer to Peggy's age, rugged in a good-looking kind of way. There was an outdoorsman quality about him, as though he'd stepped from the pages of an REI catalog. He had spiky blond hair, blue eyes, and spoke with an Australian accent.

We all shook hands and took seats at the table.

Peggy Greenway spoke first. "This is so tragic. I'm a writer, too. Well, trying to be. Delaware Fuente was a huge influence on my creative mind. To think all this time, he was here! And I had no idea. It's like the plot in a murder mystery, isn't it? Bestselling author found stabbed in the woods."

"How very unoriginal. Your creative mind has gone to mush with all the patchouli oil you breathe in, Margaret," Harold Chapman muttered. He stuck a finger in his ear and moved it to and fro. "And you wonder why your students don't take your lessons seriously."

Peggy sat up straighter. "I resent that, Hal. I have freshmen; they don't take anything seriously. You're upset because they like me better."

"Guys, please. This is no time for hostility," Soren interjected. He ran a hand through his spiky blond hair, lifting it into even more disheveled tufts. "At some point, you've got to put the past behind you."

Harold scoffed. "Says the boy wonder. It's easy for you to pay your way out of the past. What about Therese Crombie, do you think she's moved on yet?"

Peggy exclaimed, *"Hal!"* as Soren turned pale and glared at her. "You told him? Jesus Christ. You're all a bunch of fucking traitors."

I cleared my throat. "Cool it. Do you think you can put aside this family spat for a minute and answer a few questions? We've got a killer out there."

They looked at me and nodded. Finn said, "Great. So, you three are the English teachers on campus, is that correct?"

Peggy said, "Yes. I have freshmen structure and grammar, and freshmen lit. I've also got the sophomores. I have these great minds for two years and then Hal beats them over the head with Fitzgerald, Hemingway, and Baldwin."

At his end of the table, Harold snorted. "By God, woman, these kids can't survive on a diet of Shakespeare and Chaucer alone. They need the moderns! What good is it to understand the struggles of Hamlet if you can't feel the pain of Jay Gatsby?"

Soren Baker groaned. "Would you two please shut up already? Peggy and Harold here are engaged in a blood battle the likes of which I've never seen. Harold is pissed because Peggy is beloved by the students and they all try a bit harder in her classes. And Peggy is upset because Harold punishes those students when they get to his class by being a hard-ass son of a bitch on them."

Harold tilted his head to the side, considering this, then nodded. "Yup, that's about right."

"And you? What's your role in this fascinating little drama?" I asked.

Soren grinned and fished a toothpick from his shirt pocket. He stuck it in his mouth and rolled it from side to side. "Isn't it obvious? I'm the hero. I teach creative writing. No rules, no hurt feelings, just pure love."

"You can say that again. You should put in a call to Colorado Springs, detectives. Talk to Therese Crombie down at the community college. You'll see Soren's telling the truth; he's *nothing* but love."

The grin slid off Soren's face as a flush came over his cheeks. "You need to shut your mouth, old man. You think you know but you bloody don't. You're a bastard."

Peggy stepped in with a sigh. "Boys, boys. The sooner we answer the detectives' questions the sooner we'll be done. I for one can't wait to get out of this room."

My head was beginning to throb. "Three English teachers . . . isn't that a lot for a school this size?"

Peggy said, "Not at all. Our classes run about twelve or thirteen students. What do you think the parents pay for, the cafeteria food? No. It's small classes, high teacher-to-student ratios, and the privilege of attending this beautiful campus."

"Makes sense. So who worked with Fuente the most?"

Harold raised his hand. "I did. He spoke exclusively to my college prep guys and gals, in the advanced senior literature class. Twice a week he'd come in and I'd duck out and grade essays or do lesson prep. The students liked it better when I left; it was more of a treat then. Like having a substitute for the morning."

"I know exactly how they feel," Peggy said. "I, too, like it better when you're gone."

I rolled my eyes. "Okay, so, Harold. Anything weird going on that you noticed? How about any fights or disagreements between Fuente and the students, or with any of the other teachers?"

Harold shook his head. "No, the students all seemed fine. Last week, Fuente did let me know that things had gotten a little heated between himself and Denny Little, but that's to be expected. Denny tends to bring out the worst in people."

"Dennis Little? Tall guy in ripped jeans and a leather jacket? Looks like he wants to beat up the whole wide world? The same kid who's getting expelled?"

At the word *expelled,* all three of them grew sad. Soren spit his toothpick out on the table and said, "So it's going to be an expulsion, then. What a load of horse shit. All Denny needs is some guidance. He could have turned this around."

Peggy and Harold nodded. She said, "That poor boy. And his father. This will break Donald's heart. You know he works here? Nights and weekends. Janitorial stuff. He spends his days working in the meat department at the grocery store."

Finn asked, "What did Fuente and Denny fight about?"

Harold scratched at the back of his neck, uncomfortable. He finally said, "Fuente didn't elaborate and I didn't push it. He only told me that they had a different set of views on what it means to marry violence and art. The seniors had recently finished Conrad's *Heart of Darkness*, so I assumed their argument had something to do with the novel. But I'm sure Denny didn't have anything to do with Fuente's death. That's just absurd. The boy's not quite eighteen."

Peggy sighed. "Hal, you're so dense. Don't you watch the news? Kids kill, it happens all the time."

Harold sat back. "No kidding? Well, that is something. Apparently I need to start watching the talking heads. Thank you, Margaret, for once again setting me straight."

Soren smirked. I looked at him and asked, "How about you? I would have thought as the creative writing instructor it would have been you that worked with Fuente more than the others."

Soren shook his head. "No, I'm afraid not. You're forgetting, none of us knew John Firestone was Delaware Fuente. He hid it well. All we knew was that he was some friend of Lila

Conway's with a teaching background, looking to do a little community service by way of guest lectures. You see the 'family' dynamics with the three of us, Detective. We liked the idea of having someone new around for a while."

Peggy added, "The Lila Conway I know couldn't tell a lie if her life depended on it. We didn't have any reason to not believe her."

"How long have you all worked together?" Finn asked.

Peggy thought a moment, then said, "Hal and I have been peers about seven years now. Soren joined the school, what, three years ago? Four years ago? Our Aussie transplant, our man from Down Under, via the great American Southwest."

Soren nodded. "Two years come September. She's right, I'm originally from Melbourne but have spent the last ten years traveling and teaching in Arizona, New Mexico, and Colorado. On a bit of a walkabout, you might say."

"What are you hoping to find?"

Soren leaned forward and smiled at me. His teeth were charmingly crooked. "Whatever I can get my hands on, love."

I looked away, finding the sheen in his bright blue eyes discomforting.

I decided to change tactics. "Where were you all on Friday night?"

The change in the mood of the room was sudden and palpable. Soren put his head down in

136

his hands and groaned. Peggy and Harold grew agitated. They both started talking at the same time and Finn held up a hand, motioning for them to stop. He said, "One at a time, please."

Once again, Peggy spoke first. "I finished my last class of the day at three, then headed home. I have a geriatric Maltese, April, who needs medication with her dinner. She and I are on a tight schedule. I didn't want to risk getting caught in the blizzard."

Finn leaned close to me and whispered, "What's a geriatric Maltese? Is that like an elderly aunt or something?"

"No, you nut, it's a dog. A small white dog."

Finn nodded and settled back in his seat. "How about you, Hal, big date last Friday night? Do you have a small white dog, too?"

The teacher blushed again and said, "Harold, please, not Hal. And no. I, too, went home before the blizzard got nasty. I live alone and ate dinner before settling in with a good book and a bottle of Jack Daniel's."

"And Soren? What about you?" Finn prodded. At the sound of his name, the blond Australian lifted his head from his hands and shrugged. He was silent for a long moment, then finally said, "I knew this was going to come back and bite me in the butt."

"What?"

Soren leaned back and slouched down in his

chair. "I did something rather embarrassing on Friday night. I'm not proud of it. It's all part of the walkabout, see. God, but I'm a bloody idiot sometimes."

He fell silent. Peggy and Harold leaned forward and stared at him with wide, hungry eyes. It was clear this group was unable to keep many secrets.

Finn rapped a knuckle on the table. "Look, we don't have all day. What did you do?"

Soren took a deep breath. "I model sometimes for an art class."

I stared at Soren in confusion. "What's embarrassing about that? You mean, like, at the rec center or the YMCA?"

He shook his head. "It's a private class. In someone's home. And it's rather . . . um . . . scandalous."

Peggy snorted. "Are you telling us you get your Little Baker sketched? Wow. Now I have heard it all."

I sat back as Finn started laughing. Harold joined in. Soren looked miserable. He said, "Ah, come on now, guys. It's not that big a deal. A man's got to have a little spending cash."

"Well, that should be easy enough to check out," I said.

Finn leaned forward and said, "Naked modeling aside, what I find most interesting is that two of you don't have anyone who can corroborate your whereabouts on Friday night. Either of you could have killed Delaware Fuente."

"Whoa, just a second," Harold said. He stood up, then sat back down and began twisting a pen in his hands, flipping it end over end. "Now wait a damn minute. Why on earth would you think one of us killed him? We barely knew him! I thought you wanted to ask us what he was like, not see if we were suspects!"

Finn sat back and smirked. "You're not suspects, at least not yet. Don't get your panties in a twist."

"I find that expression very offensive as well as physically impossible since I never wear the things," Peggy exclaimed. She made a face at me as Finn, Soren, and Harold all stared at her, jaws agape. "Is he always like this?"

I nodded and stood. "You're catching him on a good day. Look, we'll be questioning anyone and everyone who might have interacted with Delaware Fuente during the time he was here."

We were nearly out the door when Soren cleared his throat and said the one thing that was beginning to run on repeat in my mind.

"What about the students? Clearly there's a maniac on the loose. Is it safe for them to be here?"

I turned around and looked at Soren, then at the others.

"I honestly don't know."

Chapter Eleven

Finn and I made it a few steps down the hall when a voice stopped us.

"Detectives?"

We turned around and then looked down at a slender teenage boy in a wheelchair. His dark shaggy hair was held off his face by a yellow headband. He wore black jeans and a gray hooded sweatshirt and a hopeful expression on his face.

"Yes?"

"Are you here about him?"

Finn and I looked at each other. I assumed the kid meant Fuente but thought it best to make sure. "Him who?"

The young man's face fell. "If you have to ask, you don't know."

He turned his chair around and began to wheel himself away. We watched him until he got to the end of the hall and as he turned left to head down another corridor, he looked back at us and made his hand into the shape of a gun.

"Bang, bang," he said and rolled out of sight. "See you on the other side, amigos."

Finn and I looked at each other and then took off after him.

The boy was fast. By the time we reached

the end of the hall, he was gone. There was nothing but lockers and closed doors down either corridor.

Finn said, "I hear singing. Do you hear it?"

I heard it, too. "Yes, that way."

We walked, following the sound of the music and stopped outside a classroom marked BIOLOGY LAB. I pushed on the closed door and it opened slowly, revealing an empty lab save for the boy inside and the classroom materials lying all around. The boy had a notebook on his lap and was writing something in it. Telescopes shrouded in plastic covers lined the tables, and all along the walls were shelves with glass jars, their contents floating, suspended for all time in formaldehyde.

Biology was never my favorite class. I had to be excused from the pig dissection because every time I tried to slide the sharp scalpel into the pink-gray body of the animal, I vomited. The very thought of peeling back that layer of flesh, *unzipping* the skin, was enough to push me over the edge. Ironic, wasn't it, that I ended up in a career that forces me to do just that. I peel back the outer layer and expose diseases of the heart and of the mind; I poke and prod at the secrets and lies until I can remove them, hold them in my hand, speak their truth.

I'm a dissector of human psyche, an examiner of evil.

The boy in the wheelchair looked up at us and frowned. "What do you two yahoos want?"

Finn and I looked at each other. *"Yahoos?"* I mouthed to him.

To the young man, I said, "Shouldn't you be in class? And who were you talking about, out there?"

"Ah, for fuck's sake . . . forget I said anything," he said under his breath. He continued to write and I realized that he wasn't writing at all, but drawing. A half-formed monster crept across the pages of his pad, its outstretched hands reaching for something not yet sketched.

Finn held up his hand. "Hey, watch the language, there's a lady present."

" 'That's no lady, that's my wife,' " crooned the boy and my jaw dropped, amazed. He sounded exactly like Lyle Lovett.

"Seriously?" I asked. "Who are you?"

The boy sighed and closed his notebook. "Roland Five. My mom named me after a character in a Stephen King series. She says I've been doing voices since I could talk. Give me a name, anyone, I'll mimic the hell out of them."

Finn and I looked at each other. Finn shrugged. "Marlon Brando."

Roland rolled his eyes.

"Too easy," he said, and then, " 'I'm gonna make him an offer he won't refuse.' "

I was getting a kick out of the kid. "That's amazing. What a wonderful talent. Now cut the

142

play. Who were you speaking about, back in the hallway?"

Roland shrugged. He pulled a purple bookmark out of the notebook in his lap and played with the frayed edges. "It doesn't matter. There's nothing you can do about him anyway. He's untouchable."

He was speaking in circles. Frustrated, I gave the side of his wheelchair a little tap with my boot. I was careful, though. It's always a delicate dance with teenagers. You end up putting up with a lot more from them than you would an adult. "Roland, you know we're not going to leave until you talk to us. And I think you want to talk to us, otherwise you wouldn't have gotten our attention."

Something inside him seemed to shift. "They whisper of him in the hallways."

A shiver ran down my spine. Roland Five's voice had taken on an eerie quality, as though he were speaking of a god. He began to shred the bookmark in his hand, tearing off piece by tiny, purple piece. The pieces fell to the floor in a steady drip of paper. We watched, fascinated.

Finn leaned back against one of the tables in the lab room and crossed his arms. "So who is this guy?"

Roland didn't look up. "They call him Grimm."

"Grim, like the Grim Reaper?" I asked, confused.

Roland shook his head. "No. Grimm, as in the Brothers Grimm."

"Why?"

Roland took a deep breath. He said, "Because he bullies as though he is crafting a fairy tale."

The tiny hairs on the back of my neck stood straight up.

I remembered what I first thought when I saw Lila Conway's house deep in the woods, how very like a fairy tale it all seemed.

I remembered, too, my year here at the academy, and the bullies that made my life a living hell.

Finn said, "Ah, now we are getting somewhere. Damn, kid, that was like pulling teeth. So, there's a bully? What kind of bully?"

Roland shrugged. "The bad kind?"

I tried, asking, "What does that mean, 'crafting a fairy tale'?"

Roland rolled his chair back and forth over the shredded bits of paper on the ground. "You're a smart lady. Use the library, go reeducate yourself on the classics. He puts people into a real-life fairy tale, a story."

"Hey, want to lose the attitude? You reached out to us," I said. I gestured at the wheelchair. "Did Grimm do this?"

Roland grinned, the smile of someone who once knew how to smile and who thinks his features still convey the same expression. "No.

He doesn't go after wounded creatures. He likes his prey healthy. I jumped from the roof of our house three years ago. We were watching stunt videos online and my buddy Sean paid me fifty bucks to try to make it from the roof to the trampoline. I broke my back. Sean's parents were so pissed that they threw him into a military school back east. I lost my legs and my best friend, all in the same month."

It was an awful story. I was glad when Finn changed the subject. He asked, "Do you know who Grimm is?"

"No, and I don't want to. Nobody knows who he is," Roland said.

I tried a different tactic. "What does the administration, or the teachers, do about him?"

Roland laughed again. His laugh bordered on the edge of hysterical and I began to wonder about his state of mind. "Nothing, they don't know about him. No one has come forward. That's part of the deal. Grimm puts a Grim Reaper somewhere on campus. So you know he's coming. Then you get your orders via a set of typed instructions in your locker. You burn the instructions, do your deed, and you keep your mouth shut. And that's how you survive."

I looked at Finn. "Didn't you say you got called out last week on a graffiti incident? And there's been a string of these reaper tags?"

Finn nodded, pensive. He stood and walked

closer to Roland. "If no one comes forward why are you telling us about him now?"

With the touch of a finger to the control on his chair, Roland moved away from Finn and rolled over to the window. He jutted his chin out toward the whiteness beyond. From his angle, Roland wouldn't see the trees, or the mountains, or the blue of the sky.

He'd see only the bleakness.

"Isn't it obvious? Grimm has escalated. Grimm killed your man, the author, that dude pretending to be Mr. Firestone."

I jolted. "What do you know about that?"

Roland snorted. "Please. I've read all his books. I've seen his interviews. He was here about five minutes before I began to suspect. And I wasn't even in his classes."

Finn asked, "Do you think anyone else knew his real identity?"

Roland shrugged. He waved a hand around, gesturing to the space beyond the biology lab. "I doubt it. These kids, they don't know anything about the real world. Most of them can't be bothered to think outside Cedar Valley."

I asked, "If that's true, then it sounds like this Grimm character is a step above your average high school student. Maybe he's not even a student."

"You think he's a teacher? No way, man. The teachers here are pansies. None of them could do something like this," Roland said. He stroked his hairless chin in a gesture reminiscent of a much older man. "He's skillful. Very cunning. But he's one of us. I'm sure of it. Maybe a recent grad. At least a senior."

"And you truly believe he's a killer? This run-of-the-mill high school bully murdered Delaware Fuente in cold blood?" Finn asked.

Roland stared out the window and shook his head. "You're not listening. He's not run of the mill. Underestimating him would be a grave mistake. Grimm is a collector of stories. I think in his heart, he wants to write the stories himself. And he's only getting started."

"What are you talking about?"

He shrugged. "Maybe Fuente was a practice kill. You know, kind of a first try. I don't think Grimm's going to stop with him. I think he might go after a student next."

I went to the window and waited until Roland looked me in the eye again. "I'm having a hard time believing the motivation here. I get that there's a bully on campus, maybe several. Honestly, that's pretty common at any school these days. But a murderer? Doesn't it make more sense that Fuente and his death are unrelated to Grimm?"

Roland shrugged again. "You guys are the cops. I'm just telling you what I know."

I asked, "Can you give us an example of something Grimm has done in the past?"

Roland shook his head. "Don't ask me that."

Finn asked, "Maybe you're a liar. What if this is some sick fantasy inside that smart-ass little head of yours?"

Roland looked wounded. "Okay, you want to know something Grimm's done? There's a guy, a senior, named Paul. I've known him since we were four. About a month ago, he stopped talking."

"What do you mean, he stopped talking?"

Roland rolled his head around on his neck as though he'd recently completed a workout. He said, "A few weeks ago, I got Paul alone in the gym, after class. He was white as a sheet but I wouldn't give up, I just kept hammering him about what the fuck was he doing. Finally, he pushed me into a corner and scribbled a note. He handed it to me and then took off running."

Finn and I waited. Roland was enjoying telling this story in bits and pieces. I caved first. "So what did the note say?"

Roland recited from memory, " 'Grimm took my voice. If I speak, even one word, he'll know. He knows I lied about Halloween. Now leave me the hell alone.' "

"What happened on Halloween?"

Roland eyed me and shrugged. "I can't say for sure."

"Hold on," Finn said. "Paul . . . is this Paul Runny? Are we talking about last Halloween?"

148

"Come on, man, I'm not a rat," Roland said. Beads of perspiration gathered on his forehead. Whatever else was going on, Roland was scared. "Paul is cocaptain of the football team. They initiated the freshmen players on Halloween. There were others involved, cheerleaders, the mascot, too. Things maybe got out of hand."

I thought back to the previous fall, but none of it rang a bell. "I don't remember this."

"I do," Finn said. He leaned back against the wall and crossed his arms. "I'll tell you later."

"You said he stopped talking? I don't remember a fairy tale where a man loses his voice," I mused, thinking back to the Disney movies I'd seen over the years.

Roland put his head in his hands and groaned. "You're taking it too literally, lady. Grimm doesn't, like, follow fairy tales to the letter. He just, you know, is crafty. You know in fairy tales there's, like, a sick sense of justice? That's Grimm. God, I thought you had to be smart to be a cop."

"Okay, enough with the 'lady.' You can call me Gemma or Detective," I replied. "You seem like you've been in some dark places, I'll grant you that. But I don't like your attitude. I still don't know if you're telling us the truth. If I go ask Vice Principal Moreno about him, is she going to confirm his existence?"

Roland sneered. "I told you. I'm not a liar. I'm

telling the truth. You can go talk to Moreno, or Director Silverstein, but it won't do you any good. Grimm will go underground, hide for a while, and then come back when it's least expected."

Finn spoke. "It sounds like you know him pretty well."

Roland wheeled away from the window and toward the classroom door. He looked back at us as the school bell rang. From the hallway, we heard the sounds of teenagers: slamming lockers, running feet, excited shouts. The vibrations caused the glass jars on the shelves to tremble and for a moment I believed they might come tumbling down, spilling their body parts out on to the floor in a flash flood of formaldehyde.

"Whatever. You spend enough hours sitting on your ass and you start analyzing things real deeply. I've got to go," Roland said, and he started to roll out of the room. "Ethics class. Can't miss that one."

I thought of something. "Roland, how long has Grimm been around?"

Roland stopped for a moment, then continued rolling forward. He said without looking back at us, "A couple of months, maybe."

Then he was gone, swallowed up in the sea of students flocking to classes, or bathrooms, or the cafeteria.

Chapter Twelve

We walked back down the long hallway in silence, until finally Finn blew out his breath in one long sigh and said, "What do you think?"

"I don't know what to think. The more time we spend in this school the longer our list of suspects grows. This morning we had two, neither very believable: Lila Conway or the Rabbit Man. Now we've got to add Denny Little to the list and Grimm, too. Maybe Fuente *was* Grimm. What happened last Halloween, Finn?"

"Moriarty and I caught the call. It was right as you were going out on maternity leave. You had so much going on, closing out your cases, prepping for the baby. A classic he said, she said scenario, the kind with no winners. Paul Runny pulls this cheerleader, Lacey Bolton, out of Eleanor Lake and she's been in the water for minutes. She's nearly dead. He calls an ambulance and after they revive her, and she recovers a bit, she starts pointing fingers at Paul. She says he drugged her and then tossed her in the lake when she wouldn't sleep with him. He of course is appalled. He's a straight-A student, cocaptain of the football team, Yale bound. She's got a trashy reputation, and more than one football player backed up Paul's story, that she was coming on to him, offering all sorts of drugs, trying to get him to take a swim. You get the picture."

He held the heavy front door open for me. It was snowing again, flakes as gentle as kisses, and the cool wet air felt good after the ripe heat of McKinley Hall. The snow would cover the school grounds and turn a crime scene into a forest once more.

"But you know what?" Finn continued as we walked the long hall. "Here's the thing. I never believed Paul Runny. He's a slick little bastard and if Lacey Bolton was telling the truth, then Runny got off free as a bird. It's not as though Grimm—if he exists—is punishing the innocent. It's like Roland said, there's a sense of justice about the whole thing."

"Maybe Lacey Bolton is Grimm. This could all be some kind of revenge act," I said. We reached our cars and began to brush the flakes off the windows with the sleeves of our coats. "Worse, what if Roland is right? What if Grimm killed Fuente and he's just getting started? I'm beginning to think maybe we should talk to the administration about canceling classes for a few days. At least until we can ensure that the students aren't in danger. The fact that Bowie 'Rent A Cop' Childs is on the job isn't exactly comforting."

Finn murmured something in reply that I didn't catch.

Deeply disturbed, and speaking from personal experience, I added, "These are kids, Finn. This sort of bullying leads to lasting impacts to their self-esteem. It will follow them into adulthood. It's total crap."

Finn finished his windows and came over to help me on my car. "You can take this on as a pet project, Momma. But I'm staying out of it."

I shook my head. "I'm not taking it on. All I'm saying is that we should at least consider what Roland told us, this idea that Grimm might be our killer. The flip side of course is that Fuente might have been Grimm and been killed for it. Don't you think we should talk to Moreno about this? She's the vice principal. She's got to know something is up. And if not, if she doesn't know, then we have an obligation to tell her."

Finn nodded. "Sure, great idea. I'm sure she'll be thrilled to be caught sleeping on the job."

I was about to answer when a deep voice behind me said, "Gemma?"

I turned around. Darren Chase, Cedar Valley High School's basketball coach, was two feet away, staring at me. He raised an eyebrow and grinned. Though I hadn't seen him in several months, I felt my heart skip a beat. He looked exactly the same as I remembered, a tall drink of cool, Southern water.

"Hi," I said and inwardly cringed at how loud my voice sounded. Darren had a unique way of making me feel as though I were thirteen years old, once again trying to get up the nerve to talk to my crush.

"Hi. You're beautiful," he said and immediately flushed. "Wow, I don't know where that came from. I'm sorry, I meant, you look good. Different. Something's changed."

My own cheeks heated up. "Yeah, amazing how that happens when you have a baby. It's all sorts of different. She's a girl, Grace. Three months old."

"Congratulations, that's wonderful. She's lucky to have you as a mother."

Darren Chase had played a small but pivotal role in my last case. There was something there, between us, electric and never acted upon. Truth be told, since Brody returned from Alaska, I had forgotten about him, until now. It seemed his dark eyes and Southern accent still did something to me, though.

Behind us, Finn cleared his throat.

I said, "Finn, you remember Darren Chase, don't you? Darren, Finn Nowlin, my partner."

The two shook gloved hands. Side by side, it was hard not to compare them. Darren had a few inches on Finn, but Finn was built, with broader shoulders and the lean physique of someone who spent equal time on cardio and weights. Darren looked like the tall, thin basketball coach he was.

The three of us stood there awkwardly as the snow continued to fall and the temperature started to drop. I stomped my boots on the ground and decided spring couldn't come fast enough.

"I don't have to guess what brings you here," Darren said. He gestured to the woods. "Unbelievable."

I nodded. "We were shocked to find him. What are you doing here anyway?"

"The academy offered me a job right after the holidays. Their phys ed instructor is out with a bum knee so I moonlight here a few times a week. The academy doesn't have a basketball team so there's really no conflict of interest."

I nodded. Cedar Valley was a small town. Of course I'd run into Darren Chase again. Of course he'd still be just as attractive as he was the last time I saw him.

"It's awful. I'm a huge fan of Fuente's works. All this time, he was here and I never knew it," Darren continued. "Such a wasted opportunity. I guess that sounds selfish, but it's true. Do you have any suspects?"

Finn smiled thinly and said, "You know we can't talk about that. Listen, you know a kid named Roland Five?"

Darren nodded. "Sure, everyone knows Roland. He's hard to miss. He hasn't had an easy time of it the last few years."

We waited for Darren to continue. Now he

had the power, the knowledge, and he enjoyed lording it over us. I smiled up at him and looking down, he smiled back and relented.

"I've been encouraging him to apply to colleges for early acceptance. He's only a junior but Roland is one creative kid. He's into film editing, story boarding, photography . . . music, art in general. Multitalented, very stylistic little guy. He's got a flair for the dramatic and the comic. But he doesn't want to leave his mom."

Finn scoffed. "What is he, a momma's boy?"

I whacked my partner on the arm and said, "You heard Roland in there. It sounds like it's just been him and his mother all these years. She's young. They're probably very close."

Darren Chase said, "You're right, Gemma. He's quite protective of her. And she's . . . uh, she's something else. Listen, great to see you. Let's grab a drink sometime. Or a coffee. I've got class in a few minutes. I'll catch you later."

I watched as he walked away toward the gym, and then yelped as Finn returned my whack with a pinch in the arm. "Finn! That hurt."

"Pull your jaw off the ground. Christ, woman, you've got a scientist at home and a teacher waiting in the wings. You sure like them academic types, don't you?" Finn said. He grinned. "Figures. No wonder you're always giving my poor dumb jock self a hard time. I'll see you back at the station."

I looked around to see if there were any students nearby. There was no one, so I raised my right fist and uncurled my middle finger at his retreating back.

As I got in the car and waited for the engine to warm up, I thought about how close Finn was to the truth. There had been a moment—a couple of moments, if I was honest with myself—back in the fall where had I been a little more ballsy and a little less belly, I would have jumped Darren Chase's bones.

But I hadn't, for the simple and straightforward reason that I knew what it was like to be on the other side of that equation. I'm not a vengeful type; sleeping with Darren wouldn't have made me feel like things were even with Brody. Just because Brody had been able to cheat on me with Celeste Takashima didn't mean I possessed the required tick to cheat on him. Although screwing around with Darren Chase, or some other random man, might have been a lot more enjoyable than stewing in my misery. The thing about being betrayed is, in the end, it's just not that fun to hold the moral high ground over the cheater's head.

Damn.

Even though it was four years ago, Brody's affair was a rabbit hole in my head; once I went down it, even just for a moment, it was hard to come back up for air. And that was, truly, the hardest part of our relationship. Once you've been cheated on by someone you love and trust, there remains an underlying current to the relationship. It's changed permanently.

I trusted Brody completely with my life and with Grace's life, and yet a tiny part of me would always wonder if I could trust him with my heart.

A knock at my car window saved me from my own melancholy. Soren Baker smiled and as I hit the button to lower the glass, I was struck once more by how uncomfortably piercing his bright eyes were.

"What's up?"

Soren sighed and brushed a wave of blond hair back from his forehead. "You're going to find out sooner or later that I lied, so I thought it best I come clean. I wasn't modeling on Friday night. I've never modeled in my life. I was too embarrassed for the others to hear the truth. I broke into the Seven Eagles Lodge and holed up with my camping equipment and my journal. I'm behind deadlines. My publisher is going to have an aneurysm if I ask for another delay."

"Wait, what? You're a writer, too? And you broke into the Seven Eagles?"

The lodge was a summer-only resort, boarded up for the winter to save the elderly proprietor on utility costs. It wasn't on our radar to monitor the place much during the winter; the access road was gated shut during the off-season and the hike in seemed too arduous for thieves and vandals.

Soren nodded eagerly. "Yup, I'm a writer. And I broke in to get some perspective. See, I wrote a travelogue, an autobiography, about my travels around the world when I was nineteen. It was the trip of a lifetime, all sex and drugs and rock and roll, in every country under the sky. I'm under contract for a second book, a follow-up about what happens to the guy who lived out all his dreams before his twenty-first birthday and then has to enter the real world. But I'm stuck, something terrible. I thought maybe the thrill of the break-in would spark something."

I groaned. "That has to be one of the stupidest things I've ever heard. And believe me, I've heard a lot. So how did this little plan of yours work out?"

Soren grew sheepish. "Terribly. Please don't arrest me, I'll never do it again. I learned my lesson. It took two hours to hike in. The blizzard was awful but I persevered, a modern-day George Mallory, moving forward until I summited the mighty mountain . . . uh, trail. I broke a window in the rear of the building and climbed in, then boarded it back up with some sheets I found draping the furniture. I didn't want anything to get ruined, you see. I'm not a complete asshole. I was there about an hour, hunkered down in a corner of the kitchen, my little lantern illuminating about four feet in every direction, when the noises started."

Soren shivered, then continued. His bright blue eyes took on a darker cast. "These noises, they were like nothing I'd ever heard before. I figure they must have been rats, scurrying to and fro behind the walls, maybe called out of their winter slumber by my arrival. If they were rats, they were huge. The size of house cats. I couldn't take it. I packed up and left, getting home about four in the morning."

"So you're a writer, a criminal, and you believe in ghosts? I swear to God, you can't make this stuff up," I said with a sigh. This day couldn't get any stranger. "Follow me to the station. At the very least you're going to get a ticket and a large fine. The inn's proprietor may be willing not to press charges but I wouldn't count on it."

"I've got class in forty minutes," Soren protested. "I can't just leave."

"Fine, after class. Your butt, at the station. Okay?"

Soren backed away from the car, bending at the waist in a gesture of gratitude. He turned around and trotted back to the school with a final cry of, "I'm not a bad guy!"

Right, I thought. Just a liar . . . and a burglar.

"What else are you, Mr. Baker?" I whispered into the wind as I put the window back up and left the school. "What else are you?"

Chapter Thirteen

At the police station, I pumped again and then moved into work mode. A part of me desperately missed Grace but a larger part of me was thrilled to be back in my element, diving headfirst into a case.

Finn was nowhere to be found, so I wrote him a short email explaining what Soren Baker had told me. I had just sent it when my cell phone buzzed. I checked the caller ID.

Bull Weston.

"Hi, Bull," I said as I turned on my computer and waited for it to warm up. It had been a few days since I'd last talked to my grandfather.

"Hi, sweetheart, how's your first week back at work?"

The steady sound of a running washing machine was audible in the background and I silently cursed, remembering the load of laundry I'd left in the washing machine on Saturday. I'd have to run the whole thing again, unless Brody had noticed and thrown the items in the dryer.

"Oh, peachy. We've got a murder, a bully, and a new mom who has to pump every few hours. Pretty standard stuff, really," I said. "How goes it with you? Are you in the basement?"

"Yes, Julia is upstairs working with Laura. I

161

didn't want to distract them. They are knee-deep in a quilting project. Hands-deep. You know what I mean," he said with a deep laugh. Then he turned serious. "Laura is a godsend, Gemma. I don't know where I'd be without her."

Shortly before Christmas, my grandmother's dementia had taken a turn for the worse. Bull could no longer care for her completely on his own, so we took the doctors' advice and contracted out with a healthcare firm that came highly recommended. The firm sent a health aide, Laura, to Bull and Julia's house every afternoon for a few hours. Laura and Julia worked on puzzles, reading, knitting, really whatever Julia wanted as long as it was stimulating and interesting. This gave Bull a much-needed break to get household matters attended to, such as laundry, cooking, grocery shopping, and cleaning.

"I know. I'm so glad they like each other. Who's the quilt for?"

Bull laughed. "You, it's another baby quilt. Julia's hoping for more grandkids."

I groaned. "Give me a year or two, Bull. I've not yet recovered from the last one."

Quietly, so Bull wouldn't hear me multitasking, I turned back to my computer and typed in my log-in information, already feeling antsy that I hadn't yet typed up the reports from my meeting with Lila Conway and our visits to Fuente's cabin and the high school.

"So, what's up?" I asked. I knew there had to be an ulterior motive for his call.

Bull could sense my impatience. "Nothing, Gemma, I'm checking in with my granddaughter. That's what grandfathers do. When are we going to see that adorable baby again?"

"I'll bring her by this week. Brody could use a break, I'm sure. She mostly sleeps and eats but I know it's got to be hard for him to get work done. Especially when she poops. You have to deal with that stuff immediately."

In the background, I heard the washing machine signal with a persistent ding that it was finished. Bull coughed and said, "Okay. You said you've caught a murder case?"

Bull was a former attorney and judge in Cedar Valley who hadn't yet been able to walk away from the law. It was a source of frustration for me, since I thought he should be relaxing and enjoying life. I sighed into the phone.

"What's with the attitude? You mentioned it first, Gemma. You know I'm always going to ask. And more importantly, you know I'm bound to confidentiality. Not legally, not anymore . . . but ethically and morally. You can trust me."

"Fine," I said. Bull was like his nickname, and I knew he would hound me until I relented. "This information hasn't been released to the press yet—at least, I haven't seen anything come through—but a man was murdered on Friday

night at the Valley Academy. He is—was—
a very famous man, which is going to make my
job that much harder. Delaware Fuente, you
know the name?"

"The writer? Of course I do! Are you sure it's
him?"

I nodded. "Yes. He was on a sabbatical,
working on his memoirs and doing guest
lectures at the school. He was incognito,
pretending to be a writing coach or something,
I guess. Anyway, no one knew he was here.
Fuente shaved his beard and removed his eye
patch and kept a low profile."

"Those poor students, they must be terrified.
You need to find his killer. This is awful."

"Jesus, what do you think I'm doing? Sitting
around getting a pedicure?"

I rested my cell phone on my shoulder and
held it in place with my cheek so I could free
my hands to start typing. I brought up a blank
document and gave it a file name.

"Now, there's no need to get upset and take
our Lord's name, honey," Bull said.

He and I had different views when it came to
what it meant to speak the Lord's name.

He continued. "Of course you're working
on it. I'm just in shock. Delaware Fuente was
a tremendous author. What a shame, I would
have liked to see what else he produced in his
lifetime."

"You were a fan? I would have thought he was a little too, uh, secular for your tastes."

Bull's tone was amused. "A man can both be true to his faith and be a man of the world, Gemma. Don't ever forget that. You keep up with that narrow view of yours and you'll miss everything on the sides. And that's where the good stuff is, the answers, the richness that clarifies and rounds out what the main stuff—the God stuff—just hints at."

I was about to say something witty in response when Sam Birdshead came through the door. He seemed relaxed and casually glanced around, but when he saw me, he stiffened and I could have sworn he wanted to turn around and go right back out the door.

I wasn't about to give Sam that opportunity, so I stood up and waved him over.

"Bull, I got to go. Talk to you later. Love you."

I hung up and ditched my phone on the desk. "Sam! What the hell! I've been back since Friday, and I'm only now seeing you?"

I gave him a hug, mindful of his crutches. He smelled like cigarettes and coffee. There were fine lines at the corners of his eyes that hadn't been there in the fall. I smiled at him. "It's so good to see you. I've been stuck with Finn all these long cold days."

He grinned and I saw a glimpse of the old Sam, the youthful carefree man he'd been before the accident. But the glimpse came and went. The new Sam looked hard and weary. No, not weary . . . wary. There was darkness in his eyes that reminded me of the darkness in Roland Five's eyes.

"Are you on shift?"

Sam shook his head. "Nah, it's my day off. I came in to check the schedule. Listen, do you want to grab dinner tonight? We can catch up. There's something I'd like to talk to you about. I have rehab and then some errands. Maybe meet around six?"

"Dinner would be great. Any thoughts on where you want to go?"

"How about Luigi's?"

He didn't have to sell it to me twice. Luigi's was the best Chinese food in town. The restaurant was owned by an Italian guy, Luigi Marcelo, who was married to Stephanie Tseng, a woman from Beijing ten years his senior. They served lo mein next to lasagna, merlot with sake. It was fantastic.

"Sounds great. I'll see you at six?"

Sam nodded and left. It was hard not to focus on the awkward gait, the tense shoulders, and the rigidity of his arms on the crutches as he walked out the door.

Sam was broken.

Things break, and sometimes they're made whole again. Other times, the broken pieces are put back together into something else entirely. And sometimes, what is broken can never be mended.

I wondered what kind of broken Sam was.

Focus, Gemma. You'll talk to Sam tonight at dinner. Focus, now, on the work.

I checked my email and was disappointed to see a message from the phone company. Fuente's cell was still turned off; I replied to the message, asking the rep to keep an eye on the account and to let me know the minute it was turned on.

I turned back to my report but had barely started typing when Chief of Police Angel Chavez walked through the door. He, too, gave the hanging elf a shove, much like I had done on Friday, but he pushed too hard and she flew back and kneed him in the forehead.

The chief swore. I stifled a giggle.

"Why is this goddamn doll still here? Don't you people know it is almost Valentine's Day?" Chavez yelled out into the nearly empty squad room. "Where the hell is everyone?"

"Good to see you, too, Chief."

I grabbed a pair of scissors and dragged a chair over to the middle of the room.

"Ah, let me, it's my daughter's damn doll anyway," Chavez said. He climbed up on the chair and without so much as a last rite, snipped the dirty shoelace just above Elf's head. She fell to the ground with a thump.

I picked her up. "Here you go."

Chavez took Elf and set her on my desk. She slumped to the side and he propped her up against the computer monitor. "You keep her safe. We'll bring her out again next Christmas. Welcome back, Gemma. Now catch me up. Where are we on the Delaware Fuente murder? Where's Finn?"

I suddenly realized that I hadn't seen Finn since we parted ways at the high school, after our chat with Darren Chase.

"I'm not sure where Finn is. Chief, have a seat. You look tired."

I waited until he'd removed his wool overcoat and unbuttoned his suit jacket. Chavez was an impeccable dresser; no matter the temperature, season, or occasion, he would not be seen out in public without Italian shoes of the highest quality, suits imported from Savile Row, and designer shirts and ties. If he had to, he'd wear boots outside and then quickly change shoes in his office.

"Here's what we've got. Fuente grew up in Denver. He was looking for a quiet place to write his memoirs and an old buddy of his, Lila Conway, suggested Cedar Valley. She works at the Valley Academy. He agreed to come, incognito, and do some guest lectures while he was here. Good so far?"

Chavez glared at me. "Yes, I can follow the four or five sentences you've just said quite well, thank you."

I lifted my hands. "Just checking. I've been working with Finn, remember. Sometimes I have to slow things down with him."

That got a begrudging smile from the chief. He usually wasn't such a grouch and I wondered what was bothering him.

"So, Friday night, Finn and I responded to an anonymous call about a prowler at the academy. Instead of a prowler we found Fuente, stabbed to death in the stomach with a large hunting knife. It turns out the anonymous call came in on Fuente's own phone. We didn't find the phone on his body and it has since been turned off. So, either the killer has it—maybe he's keeping it as a souvenir—or he's tossed it. We searched Fuente's rental cabin and everything there seems in order. We found a laptop—which I still need to look into—but no hard copy of the memoirs he was working on."

Chavez waved a hand impatiently. "Flash drive."

I continued. "Well, anyway, so there's that. I spoke with Lila Conway and she's obviously devastated. Fuente's agent, Brad Choi, out of New York, is also in shock. Chief, the killing, it felt . . . personal. You know, with the stabbing, the location. Fuente didn't have so much as a coat. His killer had to be someone he knew, someone who could lure or force him out there into the woods."

Chavez sat back and crossed his legs at the ankles. I noticed his socks were mismatched for the first time possibly ever. I opened my mouth to ask him about them and then thought better. I quite liked my head and I didn't need the chief to rip it off.

"What's your feel on Conway? Is she capable of murder?"

I made a face. "Sure, I suppose, aren't we all? If we get pushed hard enough. I don't like her for it, though. She's . . . I don't know, Chief, she's into birds. And explorers. Finn and I did talk to a few people at the school. Vice Principal Moreno and three teachers: Peggy Greenway, Harold Chapman, and Soren Baker. None of the teachers have alibis for Friday night and we want to look into Baker's background; Chapman alluded to some trouble down in Colorado Springs, maybe with a female student. Not only that but Baker admitted to trespassing up at the Seven Eagles Lodge, after first lying about his whereabouts. I know, I know . . . it's a long story. Also, there's a student, too, Dennis Little, who as of today has been expelled from school. It appears he and Fuente exchanged words last week."

Chavez raised an eyebrow. "I know the Littles. Dennis has had a rough go of it but so have a lot of people. His father Donald is a stand-up guy, though. So, at this point, fair to say that this is all you've got? Pretty weak."

"There's more. We found a note in Fuente's mouth; we think the killer stuffed it in there after stabbing Fuente. Chief, the note . . . it's disturbing. Taunting, almost. It said, 'This is only the beginning.' "

"My God, please don't tell me we might have a potential serial killer out there."

I shook my head. "No, not yet. After all, we only have the one body. But listen to this: Conway told me that Fuente thought someone was following him, maybe even lurking at his cabin. We haven't found anything to support this, but I can't think of a good reason why Fuente would make this up and then lie about it to Conway. Fuente called the guy the Rabbit Man."

Chavez grimaced. "Why did he call him that? Makes me think of someone skinning and eating rabbits."

I shook my head. "Fuente named him the Rabbit Man because the guy has large ears and floppy yellow hair. And Fuente found a dead rabbit near his car."

Chavez nodded. "Let's get a sketch circulating. Anything else?"

"One more thing. Finn and I met this kid at the academy, Roland Five. He thinks . . . well, he thinks the students might be in danger. There's this guy, Grimm, that's been bullying the kids up there. Roland thinks Grimm may have killed Fuente."

"Do you think there's any truth to that?" Chavez asked. He leaned forward. "Let's up our patrols of the campus. Didn't they get some security up there recently?"

"Yes, they're under contract with Kaspersky Security. The main officer is one Bowie Childs. He's . . . kind of creepy. I can't explain it, but something about him is off-putting."

"Kaspersky's decent. He wouldn't hire just anyone," Chavez said. "Let me know what else you find out about this Grimm, and the teacher, what did you say his name was? Baker? If he's got a record how the hell did he land a job at the school? Moreno would never let someone like that get through her doors."

It was a good question and I chewed on it as the chief looked around the room, distracted. "Gemma, maybe you need to have another baby and right quick. Go back on maternity leave. Things were a lot calmer while you were gone."

"Sorry, Chief, it's not like I call down the rain on purpose. Besides, it hasn't been totally quiet on the western front. You've had these hotel robberies."

Chavez groaned. "Don't remind me. Cabot is on my ass like a fly on shit. Wait, that makes me the turd, doesn't it? Scratch that, Cabot's on my ass like a bee on honey. I hope Armstrong and Moriarty bring down this group soon. You know I had to meet with all the hotel owners and Mayor Cabot for a powwow on this very topic? No one wants to think it might be their employees involved. The longer this goes on, the worse it gets. They're all fighting among themselves, more than usual."

We sat for a moment in silence.

"Do you remember high school, Chief?" I asked, then inwardly cringed when I saw the look on his face. Before he could go off on how he wasn't as old as we all thought, I quickly added, "I mean, of course you remember high school. Were you ever bullied?"

Chief leaned forward and rested his elbows on his knees. He was not a handsome man. His hair was graying and his skin was pockmarked with scars from a bout with acne as a teenager. His nose was too small for his face and his eyes too big. What Chavez had instead was an openness and air of integrity and honesty about him that was a thousand times more appealing than any typical so-called "handsome" qualities.

I knew I'd never work for someone that I admired more.

"Bullies? Is someone picking on you, Gemma?"

I laughed. "No, not me. It's this Grimm character. I'm not sure how to catch him. It's been a while since I had to deal with a high school bully."

At that, Chief Chavez stood up and patted me gently on the back. "You don't give yourself enough credit, Gemma. You never have. That's what makes you hungry on the job, successful, but I wish you'd take a little bit of Finn's goddamn ego off him for yourself. The thieves, rapists, and killers you've caught? They're nothing but bullies, just dressed up as grown-ups."

I'd never thought of it in those terms but damn if the chief didn't have a point.

"Hey, Chief?"

He was halfway out the door. "Yeah?"

I picked up Elf and drew her to my chest in a grip of rapture and grinned at him. "I hope you're our boss forever."

His shoulders slumped. "Why do you say these things to me? I should be in meetings with important people and spending my days at law enforcement conferences in Vegas. I should be dabbing spilled daiquiris off my thousand-dollar suits. Oh, and Gemma? The note in Fuente's mouth. Cases like this, they hinge on the pieces that stand out. That note was placed in Fuente's mouth for a reason. The action of doing so, or the words themselves, they mean something. Something brutal."

He walked out and once more, I was alone in the squad room, alone with the last words to come out of Delaware Fuente's mouth.

This is only the beginning. . . .

Chapter Fourteen

We sat in Luigi's at a small table in the back, next to an ancient, blackened woodstove that radiated warmth and smelled of hickory chips. Out of habit, I took the seat facing the door, and Sam Birdshead sat across from me, his back to the restaurant. A long narrow mirror hung on the wall behind me, and every few minutes, Sam lifted his head and took in the scene behind him.

"Looking for someone?"

He shook his head. "I don't like having my back to the room."

I grinned. "Me, neither."

The restaurant was quiet. A young couple sat in the middle of the room, the man in a sports coat, the woman in a tight red dress. They couldn't have been older than twenty. A family with five or six kids under the age of ten took up a long booth at the corner opposite us. The children kept climbing over one another so it was hard to get an accurate head count.

Our waiter brought us menus. I was starving. I hadn't eaten in hours. Soren Baker had shown up at the station just as I was finishing up my reports and taking his confession, and getting him in the queue for the ticket process had taken longer than I'd thought. Part of that was a lengthy phone conversation with the inn's proprietor, an elderly woman who'd declined to press charges. She wanted the window repaired and Soren to pay a fine, but that was it.

The waiter returned and we both ordered the noodles and egg drop soup. Sam asked for green tea and, deciding that sounded good, I requested it, as well.

After the waiter left, Sam spoke. "Thanks for meeting with me, Gemma. I know you're tied up with the Fuente murder."

"I've always got time for you, Sam. It's been a few months," I replied. "It's been too long. I meant to visit you more, you know, in the hospital, but after Grace came . . ."

Sam waved away my apology. "The hospital sucked. I wouldn't have wanted to visit me. I was depressed as hell."

"Did you take up smoking? I smelled cigarettes earlier."

Sam shrugged. "Sometimes. Don't worry. I'm not making it a permanent habit."

The waiter returned with our drinks and steaming bowls of egg drop soup. He leaned forward to place the food on the table. I watched as his long tie nearly skimmed the surface of my soup. Then he was gone and I took a bite. It was hot and delicious. Sam merely stirred his soup.

"Okay. You've got a bowl of the best damn soup in town cooling its heels in front of you and you're not diving into it face-first. What gives? I don't think I've ever seen you so glum."

Sam sighed. He set his spoon down and looked up. "I'm resigning."

My heart sank. "Why? If it's because of your leg, you don't have to leave. There are accommodations, changes we can make. There's still a place for you with the department."

"Gemma, here's the terrible truth: I didn't become a cop to sit behind a desk and run reports. I'm not that guy. I signed up to catch the bad dudes. This isn't the life I planned."

Unburdened, Sam stopped talking. He put a spoon in the soup and brought a mouthful to his lips. "Now, that's something good."

I leaned in and gave him my best stare-down. "Sam, life takes detours. So what, you're not chasing down criminals, full speed ahead. How often does that happen outside of Hollywood film studios? You know we get the bad guys by doing the grind work, putting in the time in the office, making calls, checking the evidence."

Sam swallowed another spoonful of soup. "I understand what you're saying. But there are wheels in motion I can't stop. I'm done."

I sat back, my soup forgotten. This wasn't just about his leg, then. "What do you mean, what wheels in motion?"

Sam started to speak but before he could, the front door of Luigi's opened with a bang and the silver wind chimes that hung above it knocked brightly against one another. The two men who walked in wore heavy black overcoats and dark hats. One of them held the door open for a third, older man, who moved in slowly.

As the door shut, one last gust of wind came in with the men, blowing something terrible, and I thought of lines from *Macbeth* that Ravi Hussen often quoted.

Something wicked this way comes . . .

Open locks, whoever knocks . . .

It was warm, suddenly too warm, and I took a shallow breath.

Sam stared at the men in the mirror and then looked back at his soup. He seemed to fold in on himself. He muttered, "Oh, hell."

I said, "What is it?"

Sam just shook his head and took another bite of soup. The men in black went to the back counter. The taller of the two removed his cap and I watched him in profile as his light eyes roved over the menu. It was posted in large print, high above the counter, in both English and Chinese. The man's hair was mussed up from his beanie and made him look younger than he probably was.

The man took a moment from reading the menu to glance around the room. Our eyes met. He slowly smiled and then looked away, back at the menu. I swallowed. The man was shockingly handsome, with a kind of Old Hollywood beauty that is rarely seen these days. He had dark, thick hair that fell just so across a wide forehead. His eyes were light, a sort of blue-green color. He looked back at me and smiled again. Something sinister crawled out of that grin and slid across my skin like a frayed scrap of silk, soft and lingering, then gone.

"Sam. Who are these guys?"

Sam whispered, "The tall man at the counter is Neil Roget. The other dude with him goes by Turtle. They'll be over in a minute, so sit tight. We're badged up. They always like to say hello to the badges. Even if we weren't, they'd be over to say hello to *you*."

Neil Roget finished ordering, then gestured to the other man who'd come in beside him. This guy was short and round and had a head that rested on shoulders that belonged to a linebacker.

"I see why they call him Turtle."

Sam sank farther down into his chair. "Shhh, Gemma. God. Whatever happens in the next few minutes, please stay cool. It's not worth it."

Sam was making me nervous. I hissed at him, "What do you mean, 'whatever happens'? And who's the third man? He's an older guy, white hair, but not too much of it."

"Is he limping? It's probably the lord of the manor himself, Alistair Campbell."

It took me a moment to place the name. Finn's

group of ex-convicts. "The construction guy? Black Dogs or something like that?"

"Black Hound Construction," Sam whispered.

Campbell hung back, close to the front door of Luigi's. He picked up a newspaper and patiently flipped through it as the two men ordered. His was a narrow face, long and lean and rugged. Campbell looked like a man who had spent much of his life in the outdoors.

Neil Roget and Turtle returned to Campbell. Roget whispered something in Campbell's ear and the older man looked up and turned around. He stared at Sam and me.

I set down my spoon.

Campbell limped over, the two Black Hounds behind him. He smelled of damp wool and a woodsy aftershave or lotion. There was a small pin affixed to the lapel of his overcoat, too small for me to see clearly what it was.

Campbell spoke first.

He spoke and I wondered what the hell this guy was doing in Cedar Valley.

"Gemma Monroe, I presume? I finally have the pleasure. How's the wee babe, does she keep you up at night? My daughter Agnes kept her mother up for weeks at a time. Made her straight mad. Literally, she spent six months in a hospital as soon as Agnes took the bottle. Samuel, good evening, how's the soup? Egg drop, if I'm not mistaken. Smells divine."

Campbell placed a hand on Sam's shoulder and squeezed. A brilliant ruby set into a wide gold band on his ring finger winked at me.

I shifted in my seat.

Sam looked up at Campbell and smiled weakly. "It really is quite good."

"I love soup," Turtle said with a grin. He moved closer to my side and stood with his pelvis a few inches from the side of my face. I resisted the urge to elbow his crotch and instead smiled at Sam.

Behind Campbell, silently watching our little meet and greet, was Neil Roget.

The three of them stood there, looking down at us, waiting for something.

I grew tired of the scrutiny. I ate another spoonful of soup, then wiped my mouth and replaced the napkin in my lap. "Can we help you with something? My friend and I are enjoying our dinner. I haven't seen Sam in a few weeks. I'd like to catch up with him."

Turtle laughed. His whole body shook with high-pitched giggles and his pelvis came dangerously close to my ear. "I don't think catching Sam is going to be a problem."

I felt my face flush. "Hey, buddy. No one asked for your opinion here."

Turtle stopped laughing. Across the table from me, Sam shook his head slightly.

Campbell motioned to Turtle and the short

man stepped back. Campbell said, "Gemma Monroe. That's a Scottish name if I've ever heard one. Tell me, are you from the old country, Gemma?"

I shook my head.

Campbell continued. "Monroe has a wonderful old Gaelic meaning, 'from the river's mouth,' if I'm not mistaken. It's a very, very common surname in Scotland. Are you sure you don't have a bit of the tartan about you?"

"Yes, I'm sure," I said. "My great-grandparents, the ones that I am familiar with, were Dutch. I don't suppose there's any chance you'll be going back to Scotland soon? Clearly you know quite a lot about me, but I don't know that much about you. And I'm really not interested in learning more."

Alistair Campbell's face darkened. The shadow came and went quickly, though. He was a man in control of his temper, and I understood that a man who has a temper that has to be controlled is a man to watch out for.

He relaxed and as he did, I did, too. There would be no showdown tonight. He would play the gentleman; in our civilized times, that role was usually so much more effective.

Campbell said, "I think I liked you better when I thought you were Scottish. Tell me, Gemma, when you were a little girl, did you spend much time playing make-believe? I didn't. I hated it.

But I had at times the occasion to be in residence with girls, foster sisters, and they all had one thing in common: they despised the impoverished homes we inevitably found ourselves in. They spent their days pretending life was something it wasn't."

Campbell continued. "Do you like Yeats, Gemma? Neil here is quite spectacular at pulling the appropriate quote from the appropriate poem for the appropriate time. It's a little trick he learned in your country's penitentiary systems. Lots of time on his hands, you see. His favorite poet is Yeats. It's quite amazing to watch. I bet he's got just the ticket for you. "

I didn't know what game we were playing but I was clearly in the thick of it now.

"Sure." I nodded. "Who doesn't like Yeats?"

Campbell gestured to Neil Roget, who thought a moment, then closed his eyes and quoted, " 'For he comes, the human child, to the waters and the wild, with a faerie, hand in hand, from a world more full of weeping than he can understand.' "

His voice was like butter melting on a hot steak; it was that smooth. Though the restaurant continued to feel too warm, I shivered. I felt feverish and cold at the same time, as though a sickness was slowly creeping into my bones. Roget's eyes never left mine. Something deep inside me froze, as though his gaze was made of ice and it had pierced my skin, my fat and my organs, and gone straight into my core.

Campbell nodded, pleased. "Ah, a classic. 'The Stolen Child.' Melancholy as hell."

"That was something," I said. "Why that particular poem?"

I waited for Roget to answer but instead Campbell said, "You ask the wrong question, Gemma. I'll bet you know all about weeping, don't you? The child weeps because he does not understand; the mother weeps because she does understand. And the people weep because once they understand, once they have seen the way of the world, they can never go back. Humanity weeps for its lost innocence."

I kept my voice steady. "What's the right question, Mr. Campbell?"

At the counter, the hostess called out, "Campbell? Order for Campbell?"

Neil Roget gave me a wink and turned away toward the counter. Turtle followed, his head and upper body moving as one unit. Only Alistair Campbell remained.

He gave us a slight bow. "I'll bet your daughter looks just like you, Ms. Monroe. Perhaps if I'm lucky, I shall one day meet her."

At the counter, Roget paid for the food and gestured to Turtle. They headed toward the door and without another word, Campbell turned and followed them out.

I sat back in my chair and stared at Sam,

shaken. "What the hell was that about? How do they know I have a daughter?"

Sam took the heels of his hands and pushed them to his eyes. He sounded miserable, and exhausted. "You're in their sights now, Gem. These guys, they know how to get in your head. They did the same thing to Finn and the chief. Probably Moriarty, too. Oh, they'd have been subtler with those guys, though. This? This was a straight-up creep show."

"But to what end? What on earth do I—or any of us—have to do with a big-shot construction company?"

Sam tore open a pair of chopsticks and stabbed them into his noodles. "These guys are sociopaths. Leeches. They go from town to town, stirring up trouble, sucking up what they can, and then they move on, having left their mark. Like dogs pissing on fire hydrants. They seem to make it a point to get to know the local PD. I'd bet they've had luck in the past with corrupt cops, cops willing to turn a blind eye to code violations and various illegal activities. They get off on rattling our cages."

I picked at my food, my appetite gone. "They seemed to know you quite well."

"It's my grandfather. He knows them from before, when he spent time in New York. I think he's done business with Campbell. They want to hire me, Gem," Sam said.

"Well, that's ridiculous. Now your grandfather makes decisions for you? You're not leaving the department, Sam, certainly not to go work for that bully and his army of goons."

Sam paused from eating to look at me. "You don't understand. I don't have much choice. My grandfather . . . you know. He's . . . persuasive. I told you, wheels are turning. Things are happening."

Gone was the Sam I'd worked with just a few months before. The Sam that sat before me was a new man, someone I didn't recognize; someone I didn't understand. The old Sam had no problem standing up to his grandfather. Wayne Bird Head was as corrupt as they come. He lived and did business on a reservation up in Wyoming.

He was called the "Godfather of the Rez," and rumor had it that he'd earned that nickname for his years of working with the Mafia. Bird Head was a big fish in a little pond—Wyoming isn't exactly mob headquarters—but his hand had a far reach and a firm grip. Like the cutthroat greenback trout, like the great white shark, Bird Head was a survivor.

The more I thought about Sam's words, the madder I got.

"Great. I've got an infant at home and a murder with no leads. And now I have to worry about you, too?" I said. Anger summoned my appetite back with a vengeance and I slurped a mouthful of noodles. But they'd lost their appeal. I checked my watch. "Damn. Now my noodles are lukewarm and I have to go pump. Thanks so much for such a lovely evening."

Sam stood up. He grabbed his crutches and stood balancing on them as he pulled a twenty out of his pocket. He tossed it on the table. "I thought you of all people would understand. You were once considered damaged goods, too, you know. Probably still are. How are *your* dreams these days?"

"What are you talking about?" I stared at him in anger and confusion. "I was considered damaged goods? By who?"

"Whom!" he shouted back over his shoulder as he left Luigi's.

I stared at my half-eaten plate of food. My breasts were aching. "Damn."

"Fortune cookie?" The slim waiter was back. He left it on the table and with a quick bow, took Sam's twenty in its place.

I unwrapped the cookie and cracked it open. The tiny fortune fell out and I picked it up off the ground. I read the message, typed in a bright red typeface against the white background.

I read it again, then stood and pulled my coat and hat on and gathered my things. I was the last customer. Outside the restaurant, the bulb in the streetlight had burned out, leaving the night black and cold, a night without light, a night without shadows.

I thought of the shadow a walking stick can make on a hot summer day, turning a hiker into an alien insect. I thought of the shadow an unpleasant man can create, a spreading darkness that eventually looms larger than the man himself, swallowing everything in its path.

This is only the beginning. . . .

I read the words from the fortune cookie again and then tossed the slip of paper into a garbage can, the words lingering like a lover's whisper, leaving me to wonder what was headed my way.

Be on the lookout for coming events; they cast their shadows beforehand.

Chapter Fifteen

The moon hid somewhere up in the great dark vastness that is the night sky.

Save for a lone truck that was behind me for the length of a few miles, I had the roads to myself. A million stars gazed down on me, seeming to outnumber the trees that flanked the canyon. The houses set along the road grew farther and farther apart. There had been one holdout, one last house with exterior holiday lights still strung, but even that family had finally given in to the changing of the season. They'd pulled down their decorations a week ago.

The merry lights lent the dark canyon good cheer; without them, I was reminded once again that we were truly in the belly of the cold season now. Cedar Valley should have felt cozy, hunkered down in that suspended dreamlike time between the holidays and the three months of snow still before us. We were on the B list for ski towns, and though we drew our fair share of tourists, we were off the beaten path. We didn't have the glitz of Aspen or the easy access of Breckenridge and Vail, nor did we have the hot springs of Steamboat. I knew that the slight edge of remoteness gave us a false sense of security.

Surrounded by the mountains, living in one

of the most beautiful parts of the world, it was easy to think Cedar Valley was immune to the nastier bits of life. Sure, we had occasional crime, even murder, and accidents, but for the most part, we were a small town, a community of hippies and skiers, families and retirees, people who had known one another all their lives.

But there were strangers here now, and the strangers that had come into our town brought with them shadows that crept into corners and darkened the edge of town.

Delaware Fuente, the Rabbit Man, Grimm, the Black Hounds and Alistair Campbell . . . I couldn't get Campbell's words out of my head. Like hell he would ever meet my daughter.

At home, I lingered over Grace, feeding her, cleaning her, holding her an extra few minutes as she slept in my arms. She smelled of bath time and baby lotion. I loved the way she fit in my arms and it nearly broke my heart to imagine the day she would not want to be held. Though that day was likely many months away, it would come.

And I had to be glad when it did, for the reward of raising a child must be the creation of an independent being. When the world spins the way it's supposed to, the parents leave first. But sometimes, the world tilts, and the parents leave too soon. I knew that all too well. And should that happen, I didn't want Grace to merely

190

survive the worst. I wanted her to thrive, to take life by the throat and give it all she could.

Choose life, little one, no matter what happens, I whispered to her.

In her crib, with her eyes closed and her face at peace, Grace was grace.

I found Brody in the study. The room was dark and I watched him for a few minutes. He was in deep concentration, a familiar scowl glowing in the reflection of the computer screen. I walked in and took a seat on his lap. He kissed the back of my neck and moved his fingers up and down my spine, but I could tell he was a thousand miles away.

"How's it coming?"

"Don't ask. Writing a textbook is trickier than I thought. I started with plate tectonics but I wonder if it would be better to begin with the principle of faunal succession. Fossils are always more accessible to young people than the asthenosphere. Sexier. What do you think, honey?"

"Hmmm . . . I think . . . I think it's best if I stick to blood and guts and you stick to earth sciences. Fossils are cool, though."

Brody laughed and his breath tickled the skin on my neck. "We're a pair, aren't we? How did you ever fall for such a geek?"

I reached around and squeezed his bicep. "It was your big muscles."

Brody stopped laughing and spun me around so I was facing him. "I'm serious, Gemma. I've accepted that I will have to spend the rest of my life proving you can trust me, and I'm fine with that. I deserve that. But I'm curious, do you remember what made you fall in love with me?"

I nodded. I could have said no, but I did remember, and there wasn't room for lies in this house, not anymore, not with Grace.

"Well?"

Brody wore reading glasses. They obscured his beautiful hazel eyes, so I pulled them off and said, "I like answers, plain and simple. It's why I became a cop. And what's more mysterious than our living, breathing, pulsing world?"

"I don't understand. Give me back my glasses, I need those to see."

It was my turn to laugh. "No way."

I put the glasses on my own head, using them as a headband. "Any question I could possibly ask you, about our world, the stars, space, you know the answer."

Confused, Brody said, "I thought you hated that about me. You once told me I sucked all the poetry and mystery out of life."

"Let's leave the poetry to the masters and the mysteries to us cops," I replied. "Speaking of poetry, can you please Google Yeats and 'The Stolen Child'?"

I moved around on his lap and together we read the poem that popped up on the computer screen.

"Hell," I said. "More fairy tales."

Brody read one of the lines aloud. "Listen to this: 'There lies a leafy island, where flapping herons wake the drowsy water rats.' Say, that's a great name for a pub, isn't it: The Drowsy Water Rat? Want to run away to Dublin with me and open a bar? I think I have a distant cousin somewhere in Ireland. I'm practically a citizen. We could live on Guinness and taters. Hunt for leprechauns."

I nodded absentmindedly and reread the lines Brody had recited. Why had Neil Roget quoted this particular poem to me? Was it intended as a threat? What interest did I hold to the Black Hounds?

"Earth to Gemma. What do you think? You, me, our little Grace, maybe a few more kids, among the emerald hills and wooly sheep of Ireland?" Brody said. "Why are we looking at this, anyway? Are you taking a literature class I don't know about?"

I shook my head. "No, someone referenced this poem today and I wanted to read it in its entirety."

I didn't tell Brody anything more about my strange encounter at Luigi's. It would only cause worry, and the last thing I needed was Brody worried about me when he should be focused on taking care of Grace and working on the textbook. If it was a success, perhaps there would be other offers to write. Besides, I was giving the meeting more weight than it deserved. The men hadn't done anything wrong. Not really.

Being a creep wasn't a crime.

"What's going on with the Fuente case?" Brody asked. "Can you talk about it?"

I shook my head. "Yes, I can talk about it, but unfortunately there's not much happening. I'm going to poke around in his laptop tonight. And shoot, just like that, I'm back in the game. I'm sorry, honey. You know I'd much rather fool around with you tonight. You and your big muscles."

Brody sighed. I sighed, too. "I have to do this."

"I know," he said. "I've always known."

Brody closed out the Google page. Behind it was an open Word document and I caught a glimpse of the page total at the bottom: sixty-five.

"Sixty-five pages. Do you have to scrap all of it to start with fossils instead of tectonics?" I asked, pleased that I remembered what the hell we'd been talking about when I entered the room. Science was never my strong suit.

Brody said no. "I can use it all in later chapters. I think I'll go with the faunal succession. Maybe structure a lot of the chapters around principles . . ."

That was my cue, so I left him in the study. On my way to the stairs, I checked the lock on the front door, persuaded Seamus to come with me, and grabbed Fuente's laptop from my tote bag. In the bedroom, I changed into flannel pajamas and then brushed my teeth and washed my face. Then I turned off all the lights except the desk lamp by my side of the bed. The room was chilly, and I pulled the covers as high as I could and still maneuver around on the laptop.

Fuente's computer was a MacBook, and for that, I was grateful. I had a hard enough time navigating between my personal Mac at home and the Dell computer at the office. I turned on Fuente's and prayed it wasn't protected by a password.

The Mac buzzed on and I closed my eyes, waited a few seconds, then peeked.

"Score," I said to myself. The laptop wasn't password protected. The desktop background picture was a black-and-white photograph of a long line of people marching down a street holding equal rights posters.

It was an interesting picture, but I didn't know if, or how, it was relevant to my case.

Delaware Fuente was organized and appeared to be tech-savvy. His desktop was clean, with no random files or shortcuts that could be lost should his computer crash.

I found Fuente's documents folder and it was

there that I ran into trouble. Every time I tried to open a file, an annoying finger popped up to wave at me. The finger blasted a silent electronic message: "Uh-oh. You didn't say the magic word!" followed by a password prompt.

I typed in "Fuente." That would have been too easy. "Del," "Delaware," "Jersey" didn't work, either. The man wasn't married and as far as I knew, didn't have any pets. I didn't have any other obvious names I could check. For fun, I tried Lila and Cedar Valley, but neither of those worked.

A few more tries and I gave up. My skills only went so far. Denver had the closest cyber unit; I'd have to ship or drive the laptop to them. They could bypass the passwords, move beyond the generic security measures, and get into Fuente's electronic world.

I left his documents folder and tried a few of the other applications. There were some nice photographs in his images file, most of which were dawn or dusk shots of what was either a pond or a small lake. The light, and the lay of the trees, made me think it was East Coast woodlands, maybe somewhere in Jersey, but I couldn't be sure.

Fuente himself was in only one of the photographs. He had his arm around a young man about fifteen or sixteen years old. They were standing on a pier that jutted out into an ocean or a very large lake; a busy boardwalk and Ferris wheel in the background completed the summer tableau. The two wore shorts, tank tops, and huge grins. Although he and Fuente didn't look related, there was something familiar about him nonetheless. I couldn't place it; maybe I was imagining things. I wondered who the photographer was. He, or she, was talented. The composition of the picture was striking, with the two men in the forefront and the chaos of a boardwalk scene behind them.

Stillness and chaos, married together in one shot.

And if that wasn't life, what was?

I took a picture of the photograph with the camera on my phone and texted it to Finn with a message. I started to shut Fuente's computer down and then realized I had forgotten to check his Excel documents. I opened the application and found one file, titled simply "Lark Co."

Lark Corporation? Lark and Company? Neither rang a bell.

I opened the document. It was a simple ledger, one side showing dates, the other side, amounts. At the top was a notation that read "Del to Lark Co." I scanned the columns and did a few quick calculations in my head. Every month for the last seventeen years, without fail, fifteen hundred dollars was moving from Del to this Lark Corporation or Company. That was over a quarter of a million dollars in total and the most recent date on the ledger was February 1 of this year.

That was a few days ago.

A few days before Fuente had been killed.

I sat back and exhaled. A quarter of a million dollars was a lot of money. Seventeen years ago, something happened. The payments started then, and they continued.

Perhaps it was the young man in the photograph with Fuente? They looked so happy together. Was he an illegitimate son, a child whose birth necessitated payments to a mother somewhere? I shook my head. This was the twenty-first century. Fuente was not one to avoid controversy. I found it hard to believe that if he had a son, he'd hide something like that.

I didn't find anything else that seemed relevant on the laptop so I turned it off and set it down gently on the floor. Something grunted and I realized I had placed the computer on Seamus's tail.

"Sorry, old buddy."

He snorted again and as I turned out the light, I heard a loud groan and then felt something heavy land on my feet. For a little guy with such short, stubby legs, he sure could gain air when he wanted to. We both shifted to this side, then that side, then settled down. We'd do the dance again when Brody joined us, but for now, we were each in good position.

I closed my eyes and took a few deep breaths of the relaxing kind, pushing the tension from my shoulders out. It was warm under the covers, and I hovered, drowsy, just on the other side of sleep.

I should have been at peace.

I wasn't.

Instead, my thoughts drifted from a dead man in the snow, to a living man quoting Yeats, to a wee child lured away by fairies, to a boy in a wheelchair, terrified of someone called Grimm. Grimm himself danced at the edges of my thoughts, a faceless man in black, all-knowing and all-powerful. Finally, like weary butterflies, my thoughts came to rest at the door of a peaceful cottage, tucked deep in the woods, a single plume of iron-gray smoke flying high from its river-rock chimney. It was there I finally found sleep.

Chapter Sixteen

I woke early on Tuesday from a dream in which enormous cranes, their wingspans twelve feet long, cavorted with drunken rats as big as dogs while fairies flew all around them. Somewhere a baby cried, hungry plaintive cries, and I woke with a start. Beside me, Brody was dead to the world. He must have come to bed late and I hoped he had figured out his fossils.

Grace stopped crying when she saw me. Her diaper was full and I changed it first and then fed her. As she nursed, I scrolled through my phone.

There was a text message waiting from Finn, a response to my text of the picture of Fuente and the unknown boy. Finn wrote, "Could be a son. I'll get started on birth certificates."

I looked at the picture again. Was there a resemblance there? It was hard to say definitively. Grace finished and I brought her into our bedroom and laid her in the bassinet we still kept next to the bed. With his eyes still closed, Brody reached over and put a hand gently on her belly and said, "I've got her."

I showered, my mind full of myths and legends.

In the far back reaches of the freezer, behind a long-forgotten frozen lasagna, I found a single microwave breakfast burrito. It took three minutes to heat, and I ate it driving into town, attempting to keep the piping hot cheese and eggs in my mouth and off my black pants.

At the station, I made myself a coffee with half-and-half and two teaspoons of sugar, then I pulled up my notes to review. I called over to the evidence lab and asked Furby, the officer in charge, if the Fuente murder weapon had been released. He said it had and agreed to drop it off later in the day. I was curious to get another look at it; the carvings on the handle of the knife had struck me as unusual, maybe even one of a kind. If I was very lucky, the knife had been purchased at a local shop.

Finn walked in at that moment with a few of our colleagues. One of them turned on the radio and Dolly Parton's voice rang true and clear, singing the song that Whitney Houston made famous in *The Bodyguard.*

"And I—E—I will always love YOU—O—U," Lucas Armstrong sang. He grabbed Finn's hand and the two of them waltzed around the room.

Behind them, Louis Moriarty growled, "What a couple of dipshits."

Lou should have retired years ago, but I was glad to see him, him and Lucas and the others. This really was home. I couldn't imagine working anywhere else. These were my people.

Finn stopped dancing. He pulled up a chair next to me, close enough to smell. And, boy oh boy, once again, did he smell delicious, like cinnamon and vanilla and hot spiced doughnuts.

"Okay, give."

He looked at me with a funny expression on his face. His beard was coming in even more full, as though he hadn't shaved in weeks. But he must have, because it wasn't gnarled and straggly but neat, trimmed.

"What?"

"Who is she?"

Finn blanched. "She who?"

"You smell way too good these days. Unless you've started wearing women's perfume and body lotion—which of course I would fully support—you are spending some serious time in the arms of a lady," I said, sniffing the air for effect. "Yummy."

Finn ignored me. I leaned forward and tapped him hard against the shoulder. "Spill."

"Ah, I don't know what you're talking about," Finn said.

Lou Moriarty overheard Finn's response and snorted. "Bull. I saw you two last week at the Tavern. Let me tell you, Gemma, this chick is one hot number. If I was twenty years younger . . ."

Finn crossed his legs and arms. "Fine. But

I'm not giving you her name. She's a nurse, she works at the hospital. We met at a bar a month ago."

"How old is she?" I asked, genuinely curious. The only other woman I'd ever known Finn to be with, in any kind of serious way, was Kelly Clambaker, and she was a certifiable nutjob.

"She's old enough to know better," Moriarty answered for Finn with a laugh. He walked over and nodded at me. "Gemma. Nice to have you back."

"Thanks, Lou, I appreciate it," I replied. I knew it took a lot for him to say that; he and I weren't the best of friends.

"How's your grandmother Julia?"

I shrugged. "Some days are better than others. You know, Bull would love to see you; you should call him, get together for a drink and some dinner. The company would do him good."

It would do both of you good, I thought to myself. At one time, my grandfather and Louis Moriarty had been thick as thieves, together with Jazzy Douglas and Frank Bellington. But Jazzy was dead, and Frank now, too. Lou's son Danny was gone and my grandmother Julia was slipping further and further away from Bull.

Old men are like sheep, I thought, not unkindly. They need to stick together.

Moriarty said he'd give Bull a call. I returned to Finn. "So, what else? Tell me more about the nurse. We're partners, Finn. I need to know everything. It might save your life one day."

"Oh, for Pete's sake," he said. "Now you're being nosy. Okay, I'll tell you one more thing and that's it. She has a kid."

I raised my eyebrows. "Oh yeah? Have you met him? Her?"

Finn shook his head. "Him. Not yet. It's only been a month. She wants to wait and see where things are going first."

"But you like her?"

Finn nodded slowly. "She's . . . nice. She's a nice lady. It's not just about the looks, not with her."

Well, bowl me over. Maybe he was a changed man.

Finn said, "Let's talk about the case."

We went over what I'd found on Fuente's laptop, both the picture of Fuente and the young man and the Excel spreadsheet. Online, we found a few references to Lark Corporations and Lark Companies but none of them made sense in the context of Fuente's death; one was an engineering firm out of Ohio, one was an escort service in Pasadena, California, and the third was an independent publishing house with no physical address, strictly an online presence.

"The publishers?" Finn asked with doubt in his voice.

"Why would a famous author pay a small independent publishing house a ton of money when he has his own publisher in New York who's much larger and more established? Plus, don't the publishers pay the authors, not the other way around?"

"I don't know; it's kind of a strange industry, isn't it?"

I shrugged. "I'll call all three companies and see if they know anything about Fuente. I think it's a dead end, though. I guess he could be sending money to an escort service every month but they appear to operate in California only. And while it's true that Fuente used to live in California, I seriously doubt he's still paying off some astronomical tab. Maybe his agent, Choi, knows more."

Finn agreed. "Why don't I call Choi and see if I can get anything from him? And then you can call the Lark businesses."

"Sure."

While Finn called Choi, I packaged Fuente's laptop up. If I overnighted it to Denver using our secure courier service, there was a small chance someone could look at it as early as the next day. I arranged for the pickup, then shot off a brief email to my contact Bucky Shepherd in Denver. There was no guarantee that DPD would prioritize examining the computer, but they might, considering Fuente's stature. Besides, Bucky owed me a favor.

Maybe this was the case to cash it in.

Finn ended his call and came back to me. "Choi said there's no way Fuente had a kid. At least, he didn't think so. He didn't sound too sure by the end of the call. Also, Choi's never heard of a Lark Company or a Lark Corporation. He's going to send over his accounting of the money Fuente's made, so we can see how big a percentage of Fuente's wealth was going out the door. There's another thing, Gemma. Choi announced Fuente's death to the press. He kept it very vague, saying Fuente passed away in Colorado under suspicious circumstances. There will be no big funeral; it turns out it was Fuente's desire for cremation. Choi's going to be in touch with Ravi Hussen; as soon as she releases the body, he'll arrange to have it shipped back to the East Coast."

"How did Choi sound?"

Finn shrugged. "Fine, I guess. He was at Fuente's house when I called, meeting with Fuente's attorneys. They have a real mess on their hands with the property. It's out on a nature preserve in New Jersey, a brownstone at the edge of protected open space, and there's a clause in Fuente's estate that the house and land reverts to the developer upon Fuente's death.

The rest of the estate goes to Fuente's as yet unrevealed heirs."

I sat back. "That is strange."

Finn nodded. "Choi is going to fax over the developers' information in a few minutes."

"Okay. By the way, I had dinner with Sam last night. He wants to quit."

"I know," Finn said. He held up a hand, then turned to the side and sneezed. "Excuse me. We've talked. His grandfather is cooking up something for Sam."

I stood and motioned for Finn to follow me into the staff lounge. I trusted the others in the squad room—Armstrong, Lou Moriarty—but I didn't want them to hear me now. We went to the coffeepot in the corner and I poured us two fresh mugs.

"It's worse than that," I whispered. "I had the pleasure of meeting Alistair Campbell last night. He and Neil Roget and Turtle came into Luigi's for dinner. Campbell wants to bring Sam on board at Black Hound Construction. Campbell and Wayne Bird Head were friendly back in the days when Wayne lived in New York. Chief Chavez is going to have a coronary when he hears."

Finn groaned and pinched the bridge of his nose. "You're kidding. Well, he's a big boy. If Sam wants to leave the department, then that is fine by me. I don't want anyone on this team who's got one foot in the room and one foot out. And stop whispering, it's creepy."

I took a sip of coffee and then added a splash of creamer. "Cedar Valley is small potatoes to a man like Campbell. He's obviously loaded; you should have seen the coat he wore last night. Maybe that's the reason Campbell is here, to recruit Sam?"

Finn raked his fingers through his hair and shook his head. "Campbell's been here two months. There's no way this is all just a big recruiting trip; no one invests that kind of time and money for one guy. Besides, what does adding someone like Sam bring to Campbell's enterprise? A bunch of ex-cons aren't going to welcome an ex-cop with open arms."

"Stranger things have happened, my friend, stranger things have happened," I replied. The coffee still tasted off; I added a spoonful of sugar. "Sam is in a bad place; I saw that last night. Maybe he's a better fit with the Black Hounds than we think. But there's no way I'm letting him go without a fight. Are you in?"

"Of course I'm *in* but I still don't think any of this explains the real reason Campbell is here, and don't tell me it's to start serious development contracts in Cedar Valley. As you said, we're small potatoes to a man like Campbell," Finn answered. He took a big sip of coffee, then burped. "Unless he knows something we don't."

Armstrong walked into the kitchen and we fell silent. He gave us a funny look, shrugged, refilled his cup of coffee, and walked back out without a word.

"What do you mean?" I whispered. I set my coffee down, unable to drink anymore. Maybe the grounds had gone bad.

Finn said, "Why are you still whispering? Campbell's smart. He's a developer. Maybe there's something here that has some value that we don't know about."

I snorted. "Like what? Gold? Silver? The last silver nugget was squeezed out of these mountains a hundred years ago."

Finn pointed across the room at a map tacked to the wall, a topographical map of the valley. "You can't be sure of that, no one can. It wouldn't be the first time in history that an area is thought to be tapped out, only to have some amateur treasure hunter hit the jackpot."

"You're serious, aren't you? Well, if that's the case, Campbell wouldn't make a red cent unless he owned the land."

Finn nodded. "True. So can we go back to our desks now? I've got work to do."

"One more thing."

I told Finn about the rest of my evening at Luigi's, the poem that Neil Roget quoted and Campbell's strange conversation. Finn's face was flushed by the time I finished.

He leaned closer, inches from my face. "He threatened you? And you're just now telling me? Gemma, sometimes you make me so mad. You're not invincible, you know. You're a hundred thirty pounds of spitfire, I'll give you that, but a badge and an attitude don't offer much protection against a man like Neil Roget. I looked into him, you know. His rap sheet is a mile thick."

I took a step back and hit the kitchen counter with the small of my spine. "Hey, cool it, okay? I didn't say he threatened me. It was a very strange, uncomfortable encounter is all. How did they know so much about me? And why? What am I to them?"

"Did you tell Brody about this? Or the chief?" Finn pressed.

I shook my head. What did it matter that I told Finn and not Brody?

Nothing, it didn't matter one bit. Partners tell each other things they'd never dream of taking home to their loved ones. Cops are good at keeping secrets, practiced at building walls around our experiences. We carry heavy burdens.

"Earth to Gemma. You dreaming again?"

"Only of a tropical beach, in a galaxy far, far away from here," I said.

Lou Moriarty stuck his head into the staff lounge. "Fax just came through for you, Finn. I left it on your desk. What are you kids doing in here? People will say you're in love."

We left the break room. Finn was back at my desk with a piece of paper in his hand before I could even sit down.

"Three guesses who the contractor was on Fuente's house."

I didn't need three guesses. I'd suspected it all along, ever since I'd heard that Campbell's home base was New York and Fuente's New Jersey.

"Black Hound Construction?"

Finn nodded. He read more and then whistled. "Fuente's house and the land are worth three million dollars. The nature preserve that backs up to the house is protected open space; the land can never be developed. Fuente bought the property fifteen years ago for a dime."

I picked up the phone. "Looks like it's time we had a formal chat with Alistair Campbell."

Chapter Seventeen

I didn't have a personal telephone number for Campbell, so I left a message for him at the Tate Lodge Inn, where Finn said he and the other Black Hounds were staying. In my desk I found a Snickers bar that took away the bitter taste of the coffee.

I called the three Lark Co's: Lark Company, the engineering firm out of Ohio; Lark Corporation, the escort service in Pasadena, California; and Lark and Company, the independent online publishing house. I left messages with receptionists at each business, asking for a call back from someone in charge.

Then I sent a request to the Victoria Police in Melbourne, Australia, asking for any records on Soren Baker. I remembered Baker had spent time in the American Southwest, as well, so I sent a similar request to Arizona and New Mexico. A search in the Colorado state criminal database returned zero hits on his name.

I took stock of where things were. It was Tuesday. Delaware Fuente was killed Friday night. Lila Conway thought she was the only person who knew Fuente's true identity, but according to Roland Five that wasn't necessarily true. And come to find out, Alistair Campbell built Fuente's home and now stood to inherit it and its three-million-dollar property value.

If that wasn't a motive for murder, what was?

Was that why he was here, to try to collect on what he was owed?

I liked Campbell for Fuente's murder. It meant there wasn't a killer out there who might target the students at the academy. But Campbell didn't strike me as dumb. If he was going to kill Fuente, he had a squad of goons available, any one of which I'm sure would be willing to kill for Campbell, and likely make it look like an accident, too. Campbell had to know that we'd find out what Fuente's will stipulated; that we'd come after him first.

Fuente's computer was on its way to Denver. I was waiting on four phone calls plus possible records from Arizona, New Mexico, and Australia. I was stuck. It was the sort of lull that hits most cases. With all the legal dramas on television these days, you'd think the life of a cop was action-packed, with action every minute.

But it rarely is.

Mostly you're pushing files, asking questions, and following leads. Then you strike a vein of yellow rock and follow that for a while, see where it goes. Sometimes there's a mother lode, sometimes there's only fool's gold.

I pushed back from the desk.

"I'm going back to the school," I called to Finn across the squad room.

"Why?"

"I want to walk the crime scene," I said. "Maybe talk to the teachers again. I'll catch up with you later. Hey, Furby from Evidence is going to drop off the murder weapon soon. Lock it up for me, if he does."

Finn waved a hand back at me, his attention already on something on his computer. The Fuente murder wasn't the only thing on his plate, I knew. There were court appearances, other pending cases. There was always something to do, it seemed, unless you'd been out of the game for three months as I had.

I was in the drive-through lane for a fast-food cheeseburger when I decided to instead stop by my grandparents' house for lunch. Though it wasn't quite noon, the skies were darkening. Another storm was coming. As I drove through town, it seemed everyone I passed was in a hurry. Mothers bustled young children from store to store, and cars barely paused at stop signs before moving through.

We'd had more blizzards this year than I could remember from previous winters, and I wondered if that was a consequence of global warming. In my mind I started to run down the list of what was in our pantry and was nearly finished before I remembered that Brody was home, and he took care of all that now.

Brody was home. I didn't have to worry.

But I did worry. I always did, when Brody was home.

I worried when he wasn't home, too.

When he was home, I worried about keeping him interested in me, in our relationship. We'd been together almost six years. Things were different now. We were parents.

And of course when he wasn't home, I worried about what he was off doing.

Who he was off doing.

At least some things don't change. As I pulled into the driveway of the house I'd grown up in, I saw the evergreen wreath hung on the front door. I knew it would stay there until spring, when Julia would replace it with a wreath more in tune with that season. I used my key and stood silently in the foyer, the way I used to when I returned to the house after a day at school.

There really is no place like home.

"Bull? Julia? Anyone home?"

A moment of silence, then happy voices trailed down from somewhere above me. I followed the voices up the stairs, past dozens of framed pictures. I was in most of them; first as a chubby baby, then a little girl with a mouth full of crooked teeth, then a young woman with braces, then with a baby of my own. There were other photographs, too, of my parents, and of Bull as a young man, years before he met and married my grandmother. I paused a moment on the stairs and realized, perhaps for the very first time, that there were hardly any pictures of Julia.

I knew they existed, I'd seen them; photographs of parties, where my grandmother was always in the middle of the room, and pictures of her on her beloved horse, Mumford.

"Sweetheart?" Bull called.

I climbed the last few stairs. "Coming."

I found them, Bull, Julia, and the home health aide, Laura, in the master bedroom and stopped dead in my tracks when I saw what they were doing. Bull lifted a finger in warning. "Not a word, Gemma. Not a single word to anyone, ever. I'm not kidding."

"What the fu—"

"Language, dear," Julia interrupted. She stepped back from Bull and smiled. "What do you think?"

"What do I think? I think . . . I think Bull's more of a peachy kind of gal, not mauve," I replied.

Laura started laughing. "I told you, Julia, didn't I? He's got those warm undertones."

My grandfather sat on the edge of the bed looking absolutely miserable. He had a towel tied around his head, turban-style, and a full face of makeup. Bright green eye shadow, black eyeliner, blusher, and pink lipstick: the whole kit and caboodle.

"Anything you want to tell me, Bull?"

He shook his head. "Nope."

Laura stopped laughing long enough to say, "Julia wanted to do a makeover on someone. She thought Bull needed it more than me. More wrinkles and all that."

I smirked. Bull Weston—combat veteran, attorney, judge, and decorated civil servant—never could say no to Julia. "Wow. It's quite a look for you. I don't know whether to throw you in the shower or take you to a show," I said, fishing out my phone. "Let me get a picture."

Bull stood up. He yanked the towel off his head and threw it to the floor. "Absolutely not. We're finished here, ladies."

Julia stepped back and straightened her shoulders. "Yes, ma'am."

"Oh, give me a break," Bull muttered. He stormed out of the room, into the adjoining bathroom, and closed the door with a resounding thud.

"Grandma, please tell me he put up a little bit of a fight before he allowed the makeup."

Julia looked at me. Her eyes flickered and a shadow of confusion passed over her face. Her voice was panic-stricken. "Gemma? Darling, what are you doing here? Who's watching the baby?"

"Brody is with her. I stopped by to say hello. I thought I'd have lunch with you."

Julia shook her head, confusion still high in her eyes. Laura took hold of her elbow. She said, "Let's go downstairs and get out the treats we made this morning. They will be perfect for dessert."

My grandmother nodded. I followed the two of them to the bedroom door, once again thanking my lucky stars that we could afford to hire such wonderful help, when Julia stopped dead in her tracks.

"Where's my husband? Bull. Bull! Drat that man, he was right here."

Laura firmly took hold of Julia's hand. "He'll come along. He's in the bathroom."

She led Julia out of the room. I picked the towel up off the floor and laid it on the bed, and then made the bed, too. The room was exactly how I remembered from my childhood: tall mirror in the corner, stack of quilts on the trunk next to the armoire, curtains always open to the view looking north, toward Mount James.

The bathroom door creaked open and Bull stuck his head out. His face was clean and red from the scrubbing.

"Are they gone?" he whispered.

"Yes. You can come out now."

He emerged and shook his head. "How do I get roped into these things?"

"Because you're a good man and a good husband. And you know you'd do it over and over, day after day, for the price of a smile from Julia." I hugged him. "How are you? I never ask that anymore. I ask after Julia, and Laura, too, and you ask after Brody, and the baby. What happened to our feelings?"

Bull shrugged. He was growing in his beard and the white hairs against his still-red skin made him look a little like a skinny Santa Claus. "Some days, heck, some years, there's just no time for our feelings. We're caretakers, Gem. Problem solvers. We give and we give until one day, we find ourselves with a face full of CoverGirl and we wonder why we never tried it before."

"Huh?"

He shook his head. "Don't mind me, sweetheart, it's nothing but the ramblings of an old man, too old for this stuff, anyway. So, what brings you to our humble abode? And without the babe, too. I should have told you, you aren't allowed to be here without her. You know how vampires can't enter a house without an invitation? Well, you can't enter our house without Grace."

He chuckled and I rolled my eyes. "I'm here for lunch but I need your help, too, Bull. It's to do with the Fuente murder."

I explained the clause in Delaware Fuente's will that allowed Alistair Campbell to inherit

Fuente's house upon his death. "Have you ever heard of something like that?"

Bull said yes. "It's not terribly common. Most developers would never agree to such a deal because they need the money up-front, to cover the costs of the project. However, if you had a wealthy developer, someone who could do a project without the cash up-front . . . it's not unheard of. And Mr. Fuente had no children?"

"We're still looking into that."

Bull nodded. "Contracts these days can be written to accommodate nearly any kind of stipulation. As long as both parties signed it, and there were witnesses, I'd say it's valid. It's certainly not the strangest will I've ever heard of. . . . That would be the heiress who left millions to her hamster."

Laura called to us that she had lunch ready. I followed Bull down the stairs and into the dining room, where we found the two women already sitting at the table, a plate of pulled pork sandwiches between them. I grabbed barbecue sauce from the kitchen, while Bull rummaged in the refrigerator for four cold cans of soda.

Very little had changed in the dining room over the years. The same three paintings hung on the walls, watercolors of gondolas and Venetian plazas. They were souvenirs from my grandparents' honeymoon; paintings they'd carefully picked out and shipped back to Colorado.

The table itself was dark wood, well oiled, with a single centerpiece—a vase of red roses.

Every Saturday, rain or shine, Bull bought Julia a dozen roses. He had them delivered; sometimes they were yellow, sometimes white. They were red at least once a month. Even now, when she could hardly remember she loved him, she remembered she loved the flowers.

I leaned forward and did a rare thing—rare for me—I stopped and smelled the roses. Laura and Bull watched in amusement, but Julia nodded, a wise look in her eyes. She smiled and said, "That's my girl. I do the same thing every day. If I don't have time to smell these beautiful flowers, well, that's not the kind of life I want to live. The flowers are the good stuff, aren't they?"

"They sure are."

After lunch, we ate the cookies that Julia and Laura had baked from scratch. They were lemon shortbread bars, dusted with powdered sugar, tart and sweet at the same time. Bull offered to pack up a dozen for me to take home to Brody.

"How are things?" he asked as he carefully wrapped the cookies in foil.

I cocked an eyebrow. "Things? Want to be more specific?"

"You know. With Brody," he said. "Since he's been home. Is he enjoying writing? I could never take to it. The law school down in Denver asked me once to write a book, a small thing, on some law or another. It took about a week of feeling mentally constipated before I threw in the towel. It wasn't my forte."

I polished off my soda and tossed the can in the recycling bin by the sink. I shrugged. "He's doing okay, I guess. He's taken on a side project. To be truthful, I think he's going a little stir-crazy."

"Already?"

I raised a hand for a high-five. Bull slapped my palm without looking up from his cookie-wrapping operation. "Exactly what I said. It's been like five days since I went back to work and I'm getting some grief. Nothing too terrible, just an occasional comment now and then. Brody and I need to sit down, when this case is over, and talk things through. There's got to be a compromise."

"That's the name of the game, honey. Compromise. You can always bring Grace here. You know that, don't you? Or I can come up there, for a few hours, every now and then. I'd be happy to spell Brody for a bit. It would be good for me, too. Laura and your grandmother have their own special bond now. There's not much room in Julia's life—I should say in her mind—for me these days."

Bull handed me the wrapped cookies. "Voilà!" Then he noticed my tears. "Oh, shoot, what is it? What did I say?"

I shook my head and grabbed a paper towel. Through big, wet tears, I managed to say, "We were so lucky to have you, Bull, in our lives. You've been more of a father figure to me than anyone else. You loved my grandma and you loved me, always, even when we were both little shits to you. And now you have to go through this. It's not fair."

"Oh, sweetheart, come here," Bull said. He pulled me in for a big bear hug. I smelled his familiar aftershave, and the laundry detergent he'd used for years, and a faint smell of pipe tobacco. "She saved me, you know that? Everything good in my life came when I met Julia. You were the best part. I always wanted a little girl, and when your parents died, Julia was so very sad. She was worried that you'd end up with distant relatives, far away. Then you came to live with us, and it was like this little firecracker was going off every day. I couldn't wait to see what you did with all that energy. I knew you could light up the whole world, if you wanted."

"But you two should be traveling, enjoying life. Instead she's sick. It sucks," I said. I wiped my nose against his sleeve, like I used to do as a kid, and pushed back out of his arms. "It just sucks."

Bull nodded. "Of course it sucks. But the Lord works in mysterious ways and you know what I've learned these last few months? There's a lot to be said for living in the moment. I never did that before; neither did your grandma. Now, we can't help it. The moment is all we've got."

"How did you get so wise?"

"Old age. Now, you want to talk about something that truly sucks, try that on. When you're young, all you've got is time without wisdom. And when you're old, all you've got is wisdom without time. In my opinion, the whole thing is backward, but there you have it," Bull said. He handed me another paper towel. "It's a mystery. Now, what other problems can I solve for you?"

I smiled. "I think I'm good for today. You guys should come up this weekend. I'll make a lasagna."

"Sold. Don't let your grandmother see how many cookies you're leaving with. She's developed a sweet tooth like you wouldn't believe," Bull said. He pulled me in for one more hug and kissed the top of my head. "We're proud of you, darling. You're doing right by Grace, already, every day. And you know this is only the beginning, right?"

My breath caught in my chest and I pushed back from him slowly. "What did you say?"

Bull looked startled at my reaction. "I said, this is just the beginning, Gemma. For you, for Grace, for Brody. As a family. You've got years ahead of you to figure out all the details."

Nodding, I took a deep breath. He was right, of course. We had plenty of time.

Chapter Eighteen

At the academy, I had the grounds to myself. Class was in session and every so often I caught a glimpse, through a window, of students going about the business of learning.

I walked, a solitary figure in a long black overcoat, my only companion a lone crow in matching garb. The bird cackled from a tree, a laugh that somehow both mocked and commiserated. I wondered how much it had seen in its short lifetime. I made a shooing motion but the crow refused to leave. It kept watch over me as I moved around the crime scene, skirting the edge of the police tape, imagining the brutal killing on that cold night.

I felt haunted by the starkness of the scene: naked aspens, virgin snow, yellow tape, and black crow. Around and around I went, hoping with each step that I'd fall into some rhythm of understanding.

It was day four of our investigation.

Why the school? Was it significant or random that the killing occurred here? We'd found Fuente's Jeep back at his cabin. There was a terrible storm that night, so how had he gotten here? What was he doing?

I stopped walking and stared back at McKinley

Hall. There was someone in there who might be able to answer some of those questions. I could have gone inside but the brisk air was refreshing. I called the main switchboard and asked for Lila Conway in the administration office. She answered on the first ring.

"Lila, hi, Gemma Monroe. Listen, we found Delaware's Jeep at his cabin and it looked like it hadn't been driven in a few days. Do you know how he was getting around town? How he got to the school on that Friday?"

"I picked him up that morning," Lila said. "He told me the Jeep was making a funny noise and he was worried about driving it too far. I offered to take him home at lunch, after his class, but he said he'd take the bus into town and putter around. If I didn't hear from him, that meant he got a ride home, too. It was a good thing, since he criticized my driving so much that I told him he could transport himself the next time. Talk about a backseat driver. Only, there was no next time."

She sniffled into the phone and I heard her hold back the tears.

"Okay," I said, thinking aloud. "That makes sense. So where did he spend the rest of that day? If he had finished class by noon, and wasn't killed until late that night, well, that's a lot of hours unaccounted for."

"I don't know. The storm didn't pick up until

late afternoon. He may have gone into town and come back. He had a work space in McKinley, barely more than a crawl space up in the attic. I don't know why I didn't think to mention it before. Maybe he stayed up there?"

"But again, why? Why not go home? You, or maybe it was one of the other teachers, said most everyone had left for the day by five, six o'clock," I said, kicking myself for not asking about an office space. There could be more evidence there, maybe even Fuente's cell phone.

Lila sighed. "I really don't know. Del could be quirky that way. Maybe he had a date. Maybe he arranged for a ride from someone else. He had this ability to make friends very easily."

She sounded terribly sad.

"How are you holding up?" I asked. Above me, the black crow jumped from one branch to another, sending down a gentle drift of snow.

Lila said, "I'm sad. It's starting to feel more real. That he's not coming back. That he won't be calling."

She sounded tired, hesitant, coughing a few times. Her voice was a little hoarse, as though she'd been coughing all day. Coughing and crying, likely.

"What did you talk about when he called, if you don't mind my asking?"

"Well, the writing. Always the writing, really, that was the basis of our talks. Del loved to pick my little birdbrain when he got stuck on a certain chapter or a scene. He got a kick out of my suggestions, any ideas I threw his way. I think they were so ridiculous they somehow broke his writer's block, inspired him."

"Birdbrain" reminded me of something else. "Lila, did Del ever mention something called the Lark Corporation, or the Lark Company? Does that ring a bell?"

Lila coughed into the phone. She coughed again and then asked me to hold on while she took some water. I heard her move away from the phone and then she was back. "No. No, that doesn't ring a bell. I'll consult my diary—I write in my journal every day—but offhand, no," she said. "A lark is a bird, you know."

"Yes, I know."

We were silent a moment and I looked at McKinley Hall, trying to picture where her office window might be. I wondered if she was staring back at me. I thought about the other things that had come up in the past few days, the picture I'd found on Fuente's computer, the strange clause in his will. I supposed it was worth a shot to ask Lila about these things, too.

"Did Delaware ever talk to you about his house in New Jersey?"

A pause, then, "Well, some. Mostly how beautiful it was, on the edge of a protected nature preserve, with no one around for miles. Oh, but he liked to brag how he'd gotten it for a song. He called it the 'house that words built' or something like that. The 'house of story,' maybe."

"Did he ever talk about the developer, the contractor who built it?"

"Hmm, no, not that I recall. You need to understand, we only spoke a few times a year, to be truthful. And it was rarely over anything as banal as a contractor," Lila said. I could hear the grief in her voice and it struck me that she must be realizing that she'd have three or four fewer phone calls to look forward to in any given year. I decided that when this case was over, I'd make it a point to reach out to Lila on a regular basis and check in on her.

I heard a door open and close and then a new voice in the background of Lila's office.

"Anything else, Gemma?" Lila asked. "I've got a student here."

"Yes, just one more thing. Was Del a father? Did he have any children?"

She laughed but it turned into another coughing fit. I waited again for her to recover. "A father? Ha! No kids, period. You tell me Del had a child, and I'd tell you that you'd just bought some oceanfront property in Arizona. That's from a George Strait song. He's one of my favorites. I always loved that line."

I did, too, actually. We ended the call and I glanced up at the crow.

"Well, what do you think?"

The bird cocked his head and stared at me with an inquisitive eye.

"Thanks a lot, you've been a big help," I muttered.

In response, the crow flapped its wings once and rose. For a second, it hovered in the air, suspended, waiting. My twin. We stared at each other, the black bird and I, and then it was gone.

The words from the nursery rhyme "Sing a Song of Sixpence" drifted across my mind. My stomach turned as I thought of the line where the young woman has her nose pecked off by a blackbird. If we hadn't found Fuente when we did, that very likely would have been his fate, as well, maybe even from this same crow.

Winter has a way of keeping creatures both small and large constantly on the edge of hunger. And for a body, outside in the elements—well, the nose, ears, and eyes go first.

My cell phone rang, startling me out of the morbid visions running on repeat through my head. It was dispatch, letting me know that Alistair Campbell had received my message and would meet me at the Tate Lodge Inn at three o'clock.

I checked my watch; I had enough time to swing by the station and get a few things done before my meeting with Campbell.

I headed back to my car. I was halfway there when a voice stopped me in my tracks.

"Different jacket today, huh?"

I slowly turned around. Bowie Childs stood behind me, leaning on a shovel he'd stuck into the snow. He smiled and pulled a Tootsie Pop from his pocket. "Candy?"

I shook my head. "No, thank you. How are things going on campus? Where are the rest of you?"

Childs cocked his head and unwrapped the lollipop. "Rest of us? You mean the other security officers? Oh, they're around somewhere. Mr. Kaspersky's got two of us working at a time. Long shifts but the pay is worth it. I saw you walking around the crime scene. You got any leads on a perp yet?"

He stuck the candy in his mouth as I again shook my head. I said, "No, not really. How did you end up in private security?"

Childs spoke around the candy. "My daddy was a cop in Missouri. That's where I was born. I tried to join the force, too, but they said I had 'anger issues.' I still can't figure out what they were talking about. So, I came out here. Mr. Kaspersky didn't even ask if I had 'anger issues.' In fact, he didn't ask many questions at all."

Uh-huh.

"Were you working that night? Friday, when Mr. Fuente was killed?"

Childs bit down on the Tootsie Pop with a crack and then swallowed. He shoved the lollipop stick in his pocket and said, "Nope. I had the day off. The only reason I got called that night to come let you and that other guy in was because Mr. Kaspersky couldn't get a hold of Teddy. That's who works Friday; Teddy Renter."

"Has anyone been in touch with Teddy since then?"

Childs nodded. He picked up his shovel and brushed past me. I smelled sugar and sweat and shampoo, all rolled into one powerful stench. "He was passed out at a bar in town Friday night. Never even heard his phone ring. I need to get back to work."

Unsettled, I watched Childs walk away. I was about to follow him and ask more questions when my phone beeped.

I read Finn's message, then broke into a run. I reached my car as his second message came through. A quick turn against traffic and I was on my way back to the station, Finn's words running on repeat in my mind.

Soren Baker is missing. Blood at his apartment.

The words from the note in Fuente's mouth raced in behind Finn's words and I pushed down the gas pedal, urging the car to go faster.

This is only the beginning. . . .

Chapter Nineteen

"What happened?"

Finn leaned back in his chair and pinched the bridge of his nose. "You got any Tylenol? This migraine is killing me. I got a message from Baker's attorney an hour ago. He was due at court this afternoon, you know, to answer for the Seven Eagles Lodge break-in and pay his ticket. Well, Baker never showed. He's not answering any of our calls. After I spoke with the attorney, I talked to the school. He missed his classes this morning. So I sent a patrol officer to Baker's apartment. There's a fairly significant amount of blood in the foyer and the place has been jacked up. I'm talking drawers pulled out, clothes everywhere, broken dishes."

"What about his car, phone, wallet? Keys?" I rummaged around in my desk drawer and found a bottle of aspirin. I tossed it to Finn and he caught it one-handed. "And what's a fairly significant amount of blood look like?"

"Like someone would be having a lot of trouble moving around after losing that much." Finn shook his head. "His car and wallet are missing. I've put out a bulletin on the vehicle and so far, zilch. Did you ever get any information from Australia on him? Or Arizona or New Mexico?"

"Let me see," I said, already pulling up my email.

I read for a minute, my heart sinking. "Shit. We had him and we let him go. Check this out."

Finn came to my desk and read over my shoulder. When he was finished, he let loose a low whistle. "Arizona's been looking for him for a while. Assaults, misdemeanors. Violent streak . . . unpredictable behavior. How did this guy get hired to teach at a private school like the academy?"

"Look at the name he was using. Simon Cook. A different social security number, a few faked references, and he would have passed a background check with flying colors."

Finn said, "Even at the school? They've got the strictest background checks I've ever seen."

I shrugged. "They also have been hurting for qualified teachers for years, Finn. All those budget cuts, and the cost of living in town . . . we can't compete with the Denver metro area. And seriously—read this stuff. This guy is a top-tier con artist. He sure knows how to pull a fast one."

I read more, then continued. "Finn, this is just Arizona. Baker moved on to New Mexico after he left Tucson; I haven't heard anything from NMPD yet. I should have brought him in for more questioning as soon as I heard about Seven Eagles Lodge. Instead I took him at his word and had him fill out a short confession. I'm a sucker."

"What's the connection? First Fuente, then Baker? Do we have a killer with a grudge against writers?"

"Maybe it's not against writers but teachers. Something is going on at that school," I said, standing. I started to tick things off on my fingers, pacing as I talked. "First, Fuente arrives right before Christmas. Sometime right around there—and we can't overlook this timing—Grimm starts leaving Reaper drawings and terrorizing the students. Now a teacher—a violent, unpredictable man—has gone missing. Given the amount of blood in his apartment, he's at least injured, if not dead. Finn, that note in Fuente's mouth was right; this is only the beginning."

Finn rubbed a hand over his dark beard. "Hold up, sister. We don't know that any of these things are connected. I mean, they're connected, obviously, but not necessarily in the way that you mean. There's no body. Where's Baker's body? If he has been killed—by the same person who killed Fuente—where's the next note? Where's the anonymous call in to us, summoning us to the crime scene?"

I had a chilling thought and stopped pacing. "Finn, what if Baker is both our killer and Grimm? And he's staged his disappearance? We had the bastard. We had him, right here, and we let him go with a slap on the wrist for breaking and entering. He had to know we'd look into his background. After that, it would only be a matter of time before we'd come for him."

Finn went back to his computer. "I'm going to put a bulletin out on Soren Baker, too, not just his car but him."

"His cell phone, too. See if they can locate him by cell."

Nodding, Finn picked up his phone and dialed. He put it to his ear, talking and typing on his computer at the same time. I sat back and cursed again. And tried to think of a single motive that made sense for Soren Baker killing Delaware Fuente or bullying students.

A commotion at the front of the station interrupted my thoughts. Finn looked over at me and motioned for me to go check it out. I was already on it, and when I reached the lobby, I had to do a double take. Two young women, no more than sixteen or seventeen, stood on either side of a middle-aged man. I didn't recognize any of them; the women wore coats and hats and the man had on a pair of worn corduroy pants and a thick leather jacket. All three were talking at the same time and the receptionist, a temp, looked frazzled.

I interrupted the group. "Linda, I can take this.

Please, would you all be quiet for a moment? Thank you. Let's go somewhere a bit more private and you can tell me what's going on."

I ushered the three of them into our conference room. "I'm Gemma Monroe with the Cedar Valley Police Department. And you are?"

The man spoke first. As he introduced himself, I wondered, not for the first time in my career, at the threads that bind this town together, threads that link individuals, couples, and families.

Threads that ultimately link stranger to stranger.

"I'm Donald Little. I work at the Valley Academy, usually at night, doing janitorial work. Sometimes handyman stuff. I work days at the grocery store. Today, though, I had the day off, so I thought I'd go for a hike up on that elk hunting trail, you know the one I mean? Up behind the old recreation center?"

I nodded and he continued. "Well, who should I find but these two clowns. Star dates my son, Denny. I parked in the lot and had just started walking when I heard yelling. I found them on the ground, in the picnic area. At first I didn't know what I was seeing. Then I realized Becky Hamilton here was pinning down Star and cutting off her hair. Well, I came up on them and started hollering and they broke apart and started sobbing. And that's all I know."

I looked at the girls. "Which one of you is Star and which one is Becky?"

"I'm Star Knudsen," the taller of the two girls said in a flat, emotionless voice. She removed her wool hat and I gasped when I saw her scalp; ugly patches of chopped, bushy brown hair stood out like tufts of fur on skin.

Donald Little spoke again. "They're best friends, or at least they were, until Becky decided to take a machete to Star's head."

"It wasn't a machete. It was a pair of scissors," Becky corrected. She wrapped a fistful of her own long red hair in her fist and began to twist it to and fro.

"I don't care if it was a machete or scissors or a kitchen knife, Becky," Little said. "Look what you did to Star!"

I held up a hand. "Please, let's all have a seat. Star, are you bleeding? Do you need anything?"

Star put her hands to her head and felt around. Fresh tears bloomed in her eyes and she said, "No, I'm not bleeding. Yes, I need something! My beautiful hair."

"Star," Becky started to say. "Star, I had to—"

"Bitch, shut your ugly face. Look what you did to me!" Star yelled. Becky recoiled as though she'd been slapped, and I saw Little slump down in his chair.

"Enough. Mr. Little, I'm a bit out of my element here. Shouldn't you have taken the girls to the school? Clearly they were cutting class."

"Nope." Little shook his head. "They insisted they couldn't go back to the academy. Star begged me not to take her there. I told them I had to take them somewhere and in the end, this was the only place I could think of. I'm trying to do the right thing here."

"Thank you, it's fine, we can contact the school," I said, biting my lip, thinking. I had bigger matters to deal with than some spat between two high school girls. I was itching to get back to my desk and see what I could do to help track down Soren Baker. "Mr. Little, do you mind if I talk to the girls alone for a moment?"

Little looked unsure. "I don't know, shouldn't they have their parents here? Do they need a lawyer? Like I said, Star dates my boy, Dennis. I'm practically family."

Out of his line of sight, I saw Star roll her eyes. Becky continued to twist her hair to and fro, tying it in a knot, then undoing it.

"I just want to talk," I said, taking Donald Little by the shoulder and gently urging him up and out of his seat. He moved slowly, reluctantly. "Don't worry, it's only a conversation."

At the open door, I pointed down the hallway and explained where he could find a cup of coffee and a waiting area with some magazines and newspapers. Then I returned to the girls. I remained standing, arms crossed over my chest, the sternest expression I could muster on my face. "What happened? One of you needs to start talking, now."

Becky paled but spoke first. "I can't tell you."

"Can't? Or won't?"

She shrugged. "Same difference, you don't get an answer either way. If I tell you why, it will have all been for nothing. If I don't tell you why, at least one good thing might still come out of this."

"How old are you, Becky?"

She unwrapped her hand from her hair and leaned forward. "Eighteen as of a month ago."

I thought a moment, then turned to Star. "Star, you can press charges against Becky. Third-degree assault. That's a class-one misdemeanor. Depending on who's sitting in court, she could see some jail time. Yes, jail time. She's an adult."

Becky blanched as Star turned to her and slowly grinned. Star said, "Did you hear that? Good-bye, Stanford."

"I didn't know I could go to jail. My mother is going to kill me," Becky moaned. "I didn't have a choice! Hurting you is the last thing I ever wanted to do. You're like a sister to me. But I didn't have a choice."

Anger and confusion twisted Star's features. "I don't understand."

Becky put her head down on the table and

mumbled, "If I didn't cut your hair off by three this afternoon, my future was ruined. Stanford, medical school, all of it gone, just like that. But I see now I was screwed either way. I never really had a choice."

"Quit talking in circles, Rebecca! I don't understand the words coming out of your mouth," Star yelled. She slammed a hand down on the table and Becky jumped up, her face a mess of snot and tears. "Look. At. My. Head."

Becky stared at Star. She bit her lip, peered into Star's eyes, and whispered something.

Star gasped and sat back. "No!"

I had missed it.

"Becky, what did you just say?"

She said it again, and this time, I heard her, clear as day.

Grimm.

Chapter Twenty

An hour later, I sat at my desk, grateful once more that my high school days were far behind me. Finn was wrapping up an update to Chief Chavez on the Fuente case, including the latest news about Soren Baker. When they were finished, Chavez turned to me.

"What was that all about with Donald Little and those girls?"

"Grimm struck again," I said. A thin layer of sweat had dried on my skin, clammy and sticky under my clothes. "He left instructions in Becky Hamilton's locker yesterday. He gave her an ultimatum: chop off her best friend's hair or be exposed as a cheater. Apparently she's not exactly the golden child she pretends to be. She's smart, but lazy. She gets her homework and test answers from a few guys on the debate team. In exchange for, um, favors. She's also got some inside connection with a student aide who has access to old copies of final exams that are still used."

Chavez grimaced. "And no one has any idea who Grimm is? How is that possible? By the way, I'm now officially sending my daughters to Catholic school."

I nodded. "Me, too. Anyway, Donald Little

was the one that found the girls, up behind the old rec center. He brought them here. I called the academy and spoke to Vice Principal Moreno. She was shocked and said this was the first she'd heard of Grimm. Moreno promised to launch an internal investigation right away. There will also be disciplinary action taken against Becky Hamilton for the cheating. Chief, Becky could have really hurt Star. One slip of those scissors . . ."

The chief nodded. "It's a good thing Donald found them before it got any more heated."

I added, "I have to say, in a way I'm almost happy this happened. It means Roland Five is wrong and Grimm hasn't escalated; he's still tormenting these kids by bullying them. He's not killing them."

Finn asked, "What I don't understand is, what does Grimm get out of it?"

"I don't know. Maybe nothing, other than seeing pain, and misery, and knowing he created it. Or maybe he's out for justice," I said. "Although both girls walk out of this damaged, broken. Grimm didn't just punish Becky, he punished Star, too."

Chief Chavez said, "And how does this kid, Roland, how does he know so much about Grimm? Have you considered the possibility that he *is* Grimm?"

I shook my head and checked my watch. "Not

yet. I think Finn and I should pay him a visit tomorrow, though."

My stomach gave a mighty rumble and I realized that I was starving. The lunch I'd eaten earlier had long since run its course. I rummaged in my desk and found an old energy bar. It had three ingredients and was terrible but I scarfed it down with the help of the Coke I found next to it.

Finn watched me with a disgusted look on his face. "I don't know how you can eat that crap. By the way, check your bottom drawer. Furby dropped off the murder weapon."

I retrieved the knife that Ravi had pulled from Fuente's body. It was in a clear plastic evidence bag and I held it up to the light. The blade length was about nine inches long, and the handle added another three inches. Fuente's blood stained the blade, scarlet on silver. "Look at these carvings. I've never seen a knife like this."

The chief took it from out of my hands. "The handle is bone. I'm surprised you haven't come across these. They sell them at the general store, the sporting goods shop, hell, even the hunting lodges sell them. I bet the welcome center carries them in their gift shop. They're carved up in Wyoming, at one of the reservations, and sold all over this region. It'll be hard to track down the sale of this specific one."

"Wyoming . . . Wayne Bird Head?"

Chavez rubbed at the back of his neck. "He's not that stupid, Gemma. He would never kill someone with a weapon that could be traced back to him. The knife's probably a dead end. You could ask around, but I wouldn't waste too much time on it."

He stood and left. I checked my watch. It was after six.

Finn reached over and took my shoulder in his right hand. He gave it a shake, then another. "Don't look so dejected, Gemma. Go home, get some dinner, and play with your kid. Play with your dog. Play with your husband. Play with your handcuffs and your husband at the same time, if you're into that kind of kinky thing. We'll start fresh in the morning. After all, you know what they say about tomorrow."

"That it is going to be cold as heck?"

Finn stood up and looked down at me, very serious. He said in a high falsetto, "Tomorrow is another day."

I groaned. "When did you get to be such an optimist? It must correlate with getting laid on a regular basis."

Finn walked away. He called over his shoulder, "I'm not going to dignify that with a response."

Chapter Twenty-one

The sky was dark as I drove home. I was bone-tired, of the snow, and the cold, and the way the scar on my neck ached all season long.

I used to love winter.

I found great solace in the snow, how it made Cedar Valley look like one of those pretty little towns in a globe, perfect and charming. Safe. And in a strange way, I suppose, the arrival of winter forced me to think about my mother and father in ways that I typically tried not to. It was impossible to drive along a slick road, hemmed in on both sides by enormous banks of snow, and not relive that terrible day.

I remembered the way the old station wagon slid sideways, and the awful noises of the car crashing and the bones snapping. What was worse than the noise, though, was the silence that settled over the scene. Gasps of pain gave way to ragged breaths that slowly gave way to silence.

Dead silence.

For a long time, I appreciated the forced nature of the remembering. It meant that for a few months out of every year, I was never too far from my parents. But winter, for me, was now too much about death; first my parents, then the

McKenzie boys, whose graves I'd discovered on a backcountry ski trip. I could add Delaware Fuente to the tally, too.

I turned up the steep and narrow road to our house and allowed myself a small smile. I wasn't quite thirty and melancholy was already an old friend. It was important to keep perspective; without tragedy, there is no recognition of grace. And after all, it was winter that had brought me Grace, on a cold stormy night a few months ago.

It wasn't until I'd parked, gotten out of the car, and pulled up my windshield wipers to prevent them from freezing that I noticed the dark truck parked behind Brody's car. It had rental stickers on the back window and I paused, racking my brain to think who might visit us in a rental car, at this time of day, at this time of year.

Inside, the house was quiet and gloomy. A few lights had been turned on but they did little to chase the shadows from the dark corners. Seamus plodded out to greet me, then turned around and trudged back toward the kitchen and his dog bed.

"Brody? Hello?"

I hung my coat and traded my heavy snow boots for a pair of house slippers. Keys and purse went to their normal spot. I took a few steps forward and called again.

This time, Brody answered. "We're in the study!"

We . . . we who?

Brody's friends weren't the type to pop over for a beer, especially now that we had a child, and I wondered again at the rental tags. Then, for one heartbreaking and absurd moment, my insides turned to ice.

What if it was Celeste Takashima, Brody's colleague and former lover? The woman who was preventing me from saying yes to a man I loved?

No. There was no way Brody would do that. He would never invite Celeste into our home, our sanctuary.

He had done a cruel, cruel thing, but *he* wasn't cruel.

I went to the study and stopped dead in my tracks. Brody sat at his desk, pointing at something on his computer screen that looked like an EKG reading, all spikes and valleys, jagged peaks and sheer descents.

Standing behind him, peering at the screen over a pair of rimless eyeglasses, holding my daughter, Grace, and bopping her up and down like a trusted old uncle, was Alistair Campbell.

As soon as I saw him, I remembered my three o'clock meeting with him. I'd missed it, completely forgotten about it, and now the man was here, in my house.

Campbell noticed me first. He smiled and nodded a hello. "Gemma."

Brody looked to his right. "Hey, sweetheart, you know Al, right?"

Al?

"Um, yes."

In three steps, I was in the middle of the room, taking Grace from Campbell. "Brody, can I talk to you for a moment, please?"

Brody nodded, engrossed in the screen before him. "Sure, what's up?"

I cleared my throat and waited. Brody didn't get it but Campbell stepped to the side. He said, "Is there a restroom I might use?"

I jerked my chin forward. "Down the hall, last door on your right. You have to hold down the handle until it flushes all the way."

"Thank you, Gemma. By the way, your husband makes the most delicious coffee," Campbell said and left the room.

I waited until I heard the bathroom door close, then let loose.

"Jesus, Brody, what the hell is going on? Don't you know who that is?" I hissed. I pulled back from Grace and held her up, looking for . . . something, anything, some mark of the devil I was sure Campbell had left on her.

She looked fine. She smelled stinky but that was poop, of her own doing.

Brody picked up on my tone. It was one

he'd heard before. He pushed off the desk and swiveled in his chair to face me. I was shocked at the tone in his own voice when he spoke.

"Yes, it's Alistair Campbell and he's offered me a job. A side gig, really, to supplement the textbook and get me out of the house. I'm going stir-crazy, Gem. I'm here, all day, with the baby and I love it—I love her—but it's not natural. I need to be outside, you know that. You've always known that. It's what I do. You haven't noticed but this has been really hard on me."

I stared at Brody's put-out expression and felt anger begin to boil, moving up from my chest to my neck. My face grew warm. There were about a hundred things I wanted to scream in that moment but I was aware Campbell would be back any second and I didn't want him to experience one more personal thing in my life.

I hissed at Brody, "Who's going to watch Grace? I have to be at work. I don't have the luxury of working from home. You do."

He shrugged. I could tell he hadn't thought that through and it bothered him. Brody grew sulky, like a child. "Bull would love to watch her. Laura's there with Julia; he's got more free time now. He's always griping about how he doesn't get to spend any time with his great-granddaughter."

The bathroom door opened and closed again.

"We'll talk about this later," I whispered. Grace gave me a gummy smile and I kissed her cheek, bouncing her gently in my arms. "She's got a dirty diaper."

"So change it," Brody said in a low voice. I stared at him, waiting for an apology that didn't seem to be coming.

Campbell's footsteps beat a steady rhythm on our old wood floors as he returned to the study. He stopped in the doorway and smiled at us.

"It's getting late and I should get back down that dark canyon. Gemma, a minute of your time before I go?"

I wordlessly handed Grace to Brody and brushed past Campbell. He'd used the hand lotion we keep in the guest bathroom, a cinnamon-scented balm, and I decided to toss the lotion the moment he left.

Campbell followed me into the kitchen. I saw two coffee cups and two plates on the table, the remnants of apple pie on each plate. There was even a can of whipped cream sitting on the counter. I wondered how long Campbell had been in my house; how darkly his presence would shadow my sanctuary.

I leaned against the counter and crossed my arms in front of my chest.

He stared at me, waiting.

"Well?" I asked.

Campbell cocked his head. "Gemma, it's no secret that you despise me. To be honest, I'm not exactly sure why. Were I a lesser man, I'd wither like a flower in the heat of that glare of yours. Somehow, it impresses me very much that I have better manners than you. You quite clearly grew up in a loving environment; I had only the experiences of spending my youth in foster homes to learn how *not* to behave to guide me through life. A simple apology is all I'm looking for. You may not view my time as valuable, but it is, quite. I'm old, you see. I've got less sand at the top of the hourglass than you."

The last bit of energy I had left went out the window and I went into polite mode, on overdrive. "I'm sorry for standing you up, Mr. Campbell. It wasn't my intention to do so. Something came up. Something that needed my immediate attention. A few things, actually."

Brody walked past the kitchen. Grace was squirming in his arms, starting to fuss. Campbell waited for Brody to make his way up the stairs before speaking again.

"That's understandable. It was an hour that I won't get back, but I appreciate the apology. I am curious, though, what it was you wanted to discuss in the first place?"

"Delaware Fuente. Surely you've heard?"

Campbell nodded. "I had a call from my

attorneys this morning. Then, of course, I saw the news at the café where I waited for you. I had a lot of time to watch the television. Terrible business. Any suspects?"

I ignored the question. "Were you aware Fuente was in town? He arrived before you and your crew."

Campbell smiled. "Your department has kept great tabs on me, haven't you? I wonder why. In my heart of hearts, I'm a simple contractor with a soft spot for those in society who've gotten a raw deal."

"You call spending well-deserved time in prison after committing a crime a 'raw deal'?"

Campbell shook his head. "You misunderstand me. Of course there must be consequences to poor decisions, society simply could not go on without consequences. Man is not a species that finds peace and harmony in nature easily. The life of man is 'solitary, poor, nasty, brutish, and short.' Hobbes."

"Yeah, I took freshman philosophy, too. You didn't answer my question; did you know Delaware Fuente was in town?"

Campbell stuck his hands in the pockets of his pants and rocked back and forth on his heels. "You didn't answer my question, either. Do you have a suspect in sight yet?"

He held up a hand as I started to sputter about doing this the easy way or the hard way.

"Spare me your *Dirty Harry* tactics, Gemma Monroe. You are much too smart to believe that route effective on me. Yes, I was aware Fuente was here. You see, we haven't spoken in years. I had hoped to change that. When I reached out to his agent to set up a meeting, I was disappointed to learn Fuente had left town. Imagine my surprise when I learned where he was. Cedar Valley has been on my radar for a number of years. I've been watching the political climate, gauging the tolerance for new development. When Mayor Cabot took office I decided the time was right; it seemed like fate that Fuente was here, too."

"Why hadn't the two of you spoken in years?"

"He never paid me after I built him his damn castle on the edge of that nature preserve. Hence, the will that decreed I get it all after his death. Had I died first, then the estate would go to my heirs."

"Surely he was paying you as the project progressed? No one would build something—not on that scale—without seeing money along the way. Not even you."

Campbell stopped rocking and tilted his head. "What can I say? I'm a trusting old soul, it was a fascinating project, and Fuente is a world-famous novelist. How could I know he was broke?"

"But he wasn't broke. We've looked into his

accounts. He had plenty of money," I protested. "None of this makes any sense, except the fact that you stood to gain a great deal of money upon his passing. And only upon his passing."

Campbell walked over to the kitchen table and retrieved his coat from a chair where he'd draped it. He put it on slowly, the movements of a man with joint trouble in his shoulders. I watched him, studied the contrast between his pale hair and face and his dark overcoat. Darkness and light . . . black and white. He was winter personified.

Campbell came back to me.

"It's time I go now, Gemma. I've got more money than I'll spend in this lifetime. Fuente's house—The House of Story, as he called it— is nothing more than a pittance in my pocket. In fact, I don't want anything to do with it, and I've instructed my attorneys to sell it and donate the proceeds to a charity of my choosing. It should have been called Bleak House."

A chill ran down my spine. "Why do you say that?"

Campbell shot me a knowing look. "On the inside, I believe Fuente was an unhappy man, and his house was an unhappy house. A drearier place would be hard to find. It was littered with the corpses of unwritten thoughts. Does that make sense to you? Do you understand? I'll put it another way. Fuente's words have done more harm than good. Look to his words, Gemma. You want to find a motive for murder? Look to his words."

With that, Campbell walked past me and out the front door. After a moment, I followed and stopped in the foyer. I watched him climb into the dark truck. He turned the engine on and then he sat there, watching me, as I watched him from the front window. Finally, he threw the engine in reverse and backed out of our long driveway and into the night, leaving a chill in my house that had nothing to do with the cold, bitter air outside.

Chapter Twenty-two

I woke Wednesday morning with a stale taste in my mouth and heavy, tired eyes. I'd gotten little sleep. Brody and I had talked for hours. Campbell had approached him two weeks ago, reaching out through the university that was funding Brody's textbook work. Campbell was looking for a local geologist, someone who could do some survey work in the hills, someone who could be discreet.

"He used that word? *Discreet?*" I'd asked.

"Yes," Brody had answered.

Brody showed interest in the offer but asked to meet Campbell in person to get more details. That was the visit last night, Campbell laying out more of his plan.

"Surely there are other people who could do the job," I'd said. "I wonder if this is all some ploy to worm his way into my life."

Brody had gotten upset. Not everything was about me, he'd said. He was a talented geologist, one of the best in the state if not the country, he'd shouted. Why was I so suspicious of everything?

He calmed down after the baby woke crying. I asked for more information about Campbell's plan. Brody couldn't tell me. Not because he didn't want to, but because Campbell was cagey, giving only enough details for Brody to understand the scope of what he was being asked to do.

The rest of the time we'd talked about what Brody had said, his unhappiness at being home all the time, stuck inside. I made Brody a promise that after the Fuente case was wrapped up, we would talk more, about how we could better structure our lives around Grace's care. It wasn't a bad idea to ask Bull if he would watch the baby one or two days a week; at the same time, though, he was going through his own struggles with Julia. I felt terrible adding anything to his plate.

We didn't even discuss the possibility of me becoming a stay-at-home mom. There was no way we could live on Brody's salary alone, and besides, I would go crazy cooped up all day with a baby. It wasn't in my nature. I'd been positively twitching by the time my maternity leave was over; like an addict, only my fix wasn't alcohol or cigarettes but the chase, the hunt.

After a hot shower and a quick bowl of cereal, I headed down the canyon to the public library. It was a place I'd come to know well during my last case—but it was not a place I especially enjoyed visiting. There was someone there I trusted, though, someone who I knew could help us.

Campbell's parting advice had danced through my dreams all night: look to Fuente's words for a motive for his murder. I didn't understand what he meant but it was as good a lead as anything else at this point.

Finn greeted me in the lobby with a cappuccino. "You look exhausted. Long night? What are we doing here?"

I accepted the coffee gratefully. We stood under a bulletin board peppered with colorful fliers and cards for local businesses and I caught him up to speed on my conversation with Alistair Campbell. "It's a long shot, but I'd like to see what all Fuente's written."

Finn gulped. "All of it? Novels, and . . . other stuff?"

I nodded. "All of it. Novels, short stories, interviews. Campbell talked about the power to hurt with words. It's worth looking into."

"So now you're taking advice from Campbell? He's got the clearest motive for murder out of anyone we've looked at," Finn said. He held up his right hand and rubbed his fingers together. "It always comes down to the dineros."

"I know. I meant to ask him where he was last Friday night but I was just so thrown off, finding him in my house. In fact, let me call him right now."

He wasn't in, though, so I left another message for him at the Tate Lodge Inn.

"Any updates on Soren Baker?"

Finn shook his head. "Nothing. Well, not nothing. We got the blood results back and they're a match for his type. Doesn't mean he didn't stage the whole thing, though. The more I think about it, the more I like him for Fuente's murder. But he could be on either coast by now. If he got on a plane . . . he could be back in Australia."

"He'll turn up. One way or another."

We walked to the reference station in the middle of the library. A young woman passed us, pushing a cart heavy with books. She whispered, "There's no food or beverage allowed in the library."

Finn pulled his coat to one side like a flasher and showed her his badge. "It's okay, sweetheart, we're not going to touch any books."

She scowled in response and hurried past us, muttering something about the lack of respect these days for the printed word.

"Jesus," I muttered under my breath. "Come on."

We found Tilly Jane Krinkle sitting behind the massive reference desk. Her hair was dyed a deeper shade of orange than I remembered. It still stood up in tufts, like ducks' bottoms, and today she wore a black sweater and faded blue jeans.

"Tilly. How are you?" I asked. It made me happy to see her looking well.

She scowled up at me. "The hemorrhoids are back but that can't be helped. Hello, young man."

Finn somehow managed to turn his grimace into an awkward smile. "Hello, Ms. Krinkle. Lovely weather we're having, isn't it?"

She glared at Finn, then at me. "Next time leave the buffoon at home, Gemma. What do you need?"

"Everything you can find on Delaware Fuente. Not biographical information, but his actual writings, his novels, short stories, interviews, all of it; a complete literature review. Think you can get that for me in, say, a day or two?"

Tilly stood up. She was hunched at the shoulders and it appeared she'd lost weight she didn't have to lose over the last few months. "This isn't my first time at the dang rodeo, Gemma. I knew you'd stop by sooner or later. When I saw the paper this morning, I said, 'Now there's a man who knows how to die.' I've already started pulling some information together for you."

She sat back down and took some notes. Finn leaned in and whispered in my ear, "Where's her parrot? Pauley?"

"Petey," I mouthed back at him. I shrugged. I wasn't about to ask where the stuffed parrot was that she always wore on her shoulder.

Instead, I asked, "Tilly? Is everything all right? You seem . . . different."

She waved a hand in the air. "I'm fine. I had a double mastectomy right after Christmas. Don't miss the tits one bit, but I swear, I've never felt so tired in my life. 'Chemo brain,' they call it. More like 'no brain.' "

"I can ask one of the other librarians. . . ."

Tilly shook her head. "No way, Jose. I loved Fuente's stories. If this helps you catch his killer, I'm all in. Just give me a little patience and time. Couple of hours, I'll have something for you."

We thanked her and headed back out. On our way we passed the young woman with the cart of books again. Finn slowly lifted his coffee cup and then quickly flipped it upside down. The young woman gasped, having no way of knowing the cup was empty.

Finn smiled and she stormed off.

"You're such a dick sometimes," I said.

He held the heavy front door open and we stood on the front steps. Finn shrugged. "Get a sense of humor, Gemma. It's fine. It's a library. They need to join this century. It's like they think this is a monastery."

"We need to talk to Roland Five again."

"The kid on wheels? Why?"

The air was cold and I shivered. Finn noticed and hustled me over to his car. We got in and he cranked the heat. I'd worn long underwear under my clothes but it hadn't been enough.

"All of this: Fuente, Baker, Grimm, even Campbell to a lesser extent . . . they all tie back to the Valley Academy. And so far, Roland Five is the only one who seems to know anything about anything. Maybe there are other questions we should be asking him."

Finn lowered the heat from full blast to a toasty temperature in the middle. "I'm so tired of this weather," he muttered. He fiddled with the radio until he found the weather station. We listened as they updated the forecast.

"Another eight to ten inches by this time tomorrow. We're going to be pulling double duty," Finn said. He rubbed his eyes. "Okay, fine, you want to talk to Roland? We can go talk to Roland. Then it's back to the station."

I nodded. "Of course. One conversation with Roland."

While Finn drove toward the academy, I phoned ahead, then told him to change direction. Roland Five had called in sick and was home. The school gave me his mother's phone number.

"Mrs. Five?" I asked when a woman's voice came on the line.

A pause, then, "No, this is Cassie Gunther. I haven't gone by Mrs. Five in years, not since my divorce. Who is this?"

"My name is Gemma Monroe, and I'm with the

Cedar Valley Police Department. I was hoping to stop by in a few minutes and speak to Roland. I understand he stayed home today from school. By any chance are you there with him?"

Finn slowed down to let a bicyclist cross ahead of us. I hadn't even seen the guy; he'd come out of nowhere on the right side of the Suburban and then whizzed by, his studded bike tires kicking up all sorts of slush and snow.

"I don't understand, is Roland in trouble? What's he done?" Cassie Gunther asked. She sounded young, and I remembered Roland explaining that she had only been fifteen or sixteen when she had him, which put her right around thirty. About my age, give or take a year.

"No, Roland is not in any trouble. It will be easier to talk about in person. Can we come by?"

Cassie sighed. "Sure. I just got home from a night shift at the hospital, though, and I'm exhausted."

I promised that we wouldn't take up too much of her time, and she gave me the address. I recited it back to Finn and he nodded. We were there in ten minutes. Cassie and her son lived at the southern tip of what we consider the north end of town. Solid middle class, not too ritzy but certainly more attractive than the trailer homes that were all too common on the true south side of town.

As we pulled into the driveway of the modest ranch house, Finn craned his neck to the left, staring at something.

"What is it?"

He parked and jerked a thumb back toward a white Toyota 4Runner parked along the curb. It had a bumper sticker with the numbers "26.2" on it and a vanity license plate that read "Brn2Run."

"You know the car?"

Finn nodded. He looked puzzled. "Yeah, I know it."

I waited for him to say more but his mouth was shut and his face had taken on a grim look of determination. We walked to the front door and I knocked. From somewhere inside, I heard footsteps.

Finn wiped at his forehead.

"Are you sweating?" I whispered incredulously. "Are you nervous?"

Finn shook his head at the same time the front door opened. A woman stood before us, slack-jawed. "Phineas?"

Finn blew out all the air in his chest in one big exhalation. "Hi, Cass."

Phineas?

I stared at him, then back at her. She was tiny, and stunning, like a doll come to life. I was a giant next to her. She wore scrubs and I groaned. Not only was she gorgeous, she was also a do-gooder. What had she said, she'd just come off a night shift at the hospital?

Then understanding hit me like a Mack truck. No wonder Finn was smelling so good these days; he was in love with Florence Fucking Nightingale.

I didn't have time to register what felt like prickles of jealousy on my skin. Finn was leaning forward to give Cassie a kiss on the cheek at the same time she was outstretching a hand to me for a handshake.

It was awkward.

"Oh, hi. Yes, Cassie, I'm Gemma Monroe, and this is my partner. Uh, obviously you two already know each other, don't you, *Phineas*."

Cassie smiled. "Yes, we sure do. But I don't understand, you said y'all wanted to talk to my son?"

Finn stepped in. "Cass, why didn't you tell me? About Roland, his . . . condition?"

In my mind, I reached over and slapped Finn upside the head. He wasn't the most tactful of guys. But Cassie didn't seem to notice. To my utter shock, I realized she was head over heels for him as he seemed to be for her.

"Finn, I didn't want to scare you off! Too many men I've dated have split after they meet Roland. They think, 'Oh, poor little Cassie and her handicapped son,' and they can't take it. I was so worried you'd think the same thing,"

Cassie said. "And I couldn't allow that. We're having too much fun."

She beckoned us in. The house smelled like chocolate chip cookies and fresh coffee. On the white walls were brightly colored drawings and paintings in black frames, arranged in groups of threes and fours. I stepped closer to them and saw the lower-case letter *r,* followed by the number five, in the bottom right corner.

Cassie noticed me looking. She smiled and whispered, "I've been framing his art since he was four. He's so talented."

I looked at the picture more closely; it was a sketch of a centipede-type creature with a scantily clad woman on its back and a man's hairy arm hanging out of its mouth.

It was the stuff of nightmares, I decided.

"He did that one when he was eight," she said. "He's been sleeping on and off. I think it's a little flu bug; something's going around. Our beds at the hospital are all full. So, please, tell me why you need to talk to Roland."

I briefly explained what had happened between Becky Hamilton and Star Knudsen. I left out any mention of Grimm. Cassie looked bewildered. Her dark eyes grew even wider and she chewed at the corner of her lip. "Those poor, poor girls, of course I know them both. It's a small school. But what on earth does this have to do with Roland?"

"We'd like to ask him a few questions, about the girls," I answered, deliberately vague. "Where is he?"

Cassie said he was in the basement. I followed her, Finn lagging a few steps behind me. He wasn't exactly angry, but I could tell he wasn't happy, either. Not so much about Roland being Cassie's son, but I think the fact that I was with him when he found out.

She led us down a flight of stairs to a finished basement. Roland lay on the middle of the L-shaped couch, his wheelchair up against an ottoman. The room was dim, all the better to watch a movie: *Home Alone.*

Cassie turned on a side lamp. "Roland, honey, I think you've met these two?"

The young man hit the pause button on the remote control and groaned when he saw us.

"Hi there." I waved. "Remember us?"

Roland nodded. "Unfortunately, yes. Why are you here? Mom, turn off that light and go to bed. You look beat."

Cassie nodded. "Thanks, sweetheart, for the ever encouraging words. I'll go to bed soon. I think I should stay right here; I want to hear what the police have to say. They have a few questions about Becky Hamilton and Star Knudsen."

When you work long enough with a partner, under stressful situations and over long hours, you develop a sort of telepathy. It's similar to the way that married couples can finish each other's sentences. Finn and I both knew that Roland wasn't going to say a word with his mother in the room, and we both knew that Cassie wasn't going to leave her son alone with two cops.

Finn put a hand on Cassie's lower back. I was watching Roland, so I saw the look that crossed his face. He recognized the level of intimacy in that simple gesture.

It displeased him.

"Cass, let's go upstairs," Finn said. He gently pushed Cassie toward the basement door and the stairs beyond. "It's fine."

Finn's words (or maybe his hand on her back) did the trick. Cassie shot Roland a look over her shoulder. "I'll make you some tea, sweetie."

I watched them leave, wondering how Roland got down those stairs.

"I slide down, on my ass. My mom follows with my chair; there's a bathroom down here. Even a mini-fridge," Roland said, reading my mind, pointing to a waist-high refrigerator in the corner. He shrugged. "It's nice and cold. I'm always hot, even in the middle of the winter. Ever since I fell. Jumped. Whatever."

The basement was cool, chilly almost.

I nodded. "Good movie."

" 'You know, Kevin, you're what the French

call *les incompetents*,' " Roland quoted with a smirk.

I put my hands on either side of my face and did the silent scream that Macaulay Culkin does in the movie, after he splashes on the aftershave. That got a giggle out of Roland.

Then he stopped laughing. "Why are you here? What happened to Star and Becky?"

I took a seat on the couch, facing Roland. "Grimm happened. He made Becky cut off Star's hair. He threatened to expose her cheating, her 'arrangements' with some of your classmates."

Roland took a deep breath. "Wow. That's . . . pretty sick, actually. I told you, he's escalating."

"Yes, you did. Tell me again, what did you mean by that?"

Roland was silent, deep in thought. He started to speak, then stopped, rephrasing his words.

"Everything he's done to this point has been out of the public eye. Private. I mean, the kids all talk about him and share stories. But the teachers, the grown-ups, they had no idea," Roland said. "Hand me that Coke, will you?"

I gave him the half-empty can of soda and he took a deep swallow, then let loose with a truly disgusting burp. He followed the burp with, "But this . . . This is the first time he's made a student hurt another student. This is going to go public. Everyone will see Star's hair."

"Yes, they will. I've already talked to Vice Principal Moreno; she's opening an investigation. Why do you think he's escalating? This latest incident, the hair cutting . . . there's a sense of violence to it."

Roland shrugged. He had on a black T-shirt and pajama pants and big red fuzzy slippers. A blanket was halfway on his lap and half on the floor. For the first time I noticed the walls down here were covered in framed art, too, just like upstairs. I wondered what my daughter would be like as a teenager. I wondered if she would have a brother someday, and if he would be anything like Roland.

"Did you draw all these, too?"

Roland rolled his eyes. "Yup. No matter what I draw, my mom feels the need to frame it and hang it. One of these days, there's going to be so much art on the walls that the whole house will come tumbling down from the weight of my mom's love."

To my surprise, a knot formed in my throat. I swallowed it and blinked back sudden tears. "You're lucky, kid, to have a mother who loves you that much, who is that proud of you."

Roland burped again. "I guess. Don't you have a mom?"

"No, she died when I was little, she and my dad. It was a bad car accident," I said. "My grandmother raised me."

Roland didn't know what to say to that, so he kept his mouth shut.

I tried again. "So, why now? Why doesn't Grimm care if the grown-ups know about him?"

Roland hit play on the remote control, then paused it again a second later. He sighed and looked at me as though he were about to spill the very secrets of the universe. "I told you. I think he killed Fuente. I don't know how this latest thing with Star and Becky plays into it. Maybe he planned that before he killed Fuente. But the reason he doesn't care about the grown-ups is because even if they know, they won't believe. That's what makes a grown-up, Gemma. It's someone who's stopped believing in fairy tales."

Did I still believe in fairy tales?

"Are you Grimm, Roland?" I asked.

He laughed. "Hell to the no. You saw my mom; it would kill her if I pulled any shit like that. I'm not a complete jerk; I don't want to kill my mom."

"Then how do you know so much about him? Why are you, out of everyone, coming forward and talking to me?"

Roland shrugged again. "I hear a lot, okay. Like I said, the kids all talk. I really don't know more about Grimm than anyone else, I'm just the only one talking to a cop about him. I don't know why. I guess . . ."

"Go on."

Roland struggled to get the words out and I sensed I was hearing something he'd never told anyone before. "I guess going through this, my accident, it makes me sad when I see other people hurt. Getting hurt. God. I sound like such a pussy."

"No, you don't. You sound like someone with a lot of empathy. Do you know Soren Baker?"

Roland nodded. "Yeah . . . what does he have to do with this?"

"He's missing. We can't reach him and there's blood in his apartment."

"No shit? But that doesn't make any sense," Roland said. He moved around on the couch and tucked the blanket in under his legs. "Why would Grimm kill Baker? Unless . . . maybe Grimm is going after teachers now. Maybe he's killing teachers and bullying students!"

"There might be another possibility."

I waited a beat until Roland figured it out. He looked truly spooked. "Holy hell, you think Mr. Baker is Grimm? Maybe he killed someone else in his apartment!"

"We're not certain of anything at this point. Do you think he could be Grimm?"

Roland slumped back on the couch, perplexed. "I guess. If he's not, then I think Grimm killed Fuente and Mr. Baker."

"Okay. Let's pretend Grimm is not Mr. Baker

or Fuente or anyone else we know. How do I catch him?"

I didn't know if Roland could answer that particular question. But I hoped he had an idea.

The young man closed his eyes. He was so still and quiet for so long I thought maybe he had fallen asleep. When he spoke again, it was in a voice that was very sad.

"I don't know if you can. I don't know if anyone can stop him. I think Grimm's going to keep on hurting people for a long time. I think he's just getting started."

Chapter Twenty-three

On the drive back to the station, we didn't talk about Cassie, or Roland, or even Grimm. As soon as we got in the car, Finn had turned on the radio, loud, and the look on his face said I should cool it on the conversation. I wondered what was going through his mind; after all, he had known that Cassie had a child.

Once inside the station, we went our separate ways, me to my desk and email, Finn to his desk and a stack of messages. I had a courtesy update from the phone company; Fuente's phone still had not been turned on, so that was a bust. I did have an email from Tilly at the library, with a large attachment. Before I opened it, I called over to Moriarty.

"Hey, Lou. When's Sam next on shift?"

Moriarty grunted something.

"What?"

He turned around. "I said he's on tomorrow afternoon. He can't trade with you, he's already working. Everyone's trying to get out of work. It's like you people have never lived through a blizzard before."

"I'm not asking because I want a trade," I mumbled to myself. "I just want to talk to the man."

"What?"

"Nothing," I shouted back to Moriarty. "Don't worry about it."

I opened Tilly's email and read through the terse introductory sentence that she'd included as a preface to the attachment. She said to expect more in the next day or two but that this should be enough to get me started. I took a deep breath and opened the attachment. There was a lot to read. I rummaged in my desk drawer for a pair of reading glasses and stealthily slid them on. The saleslady at one of the local gift shops had recommended I try them for long periods of reading, after I struggled to read the tiny sales price on the bottom of a cheap ornament. I didn't buy the trinket but the saleslady was good, and sold me the reading glasses before I knew what was going on.

I slowly looked up again. No one seemed to have noticed the glasses. I settled in and began reading. Tilly had sent a list of the titles of Fuente's novels, and links to his short stories and flash fiction, the ones that were available online. I made a note of what wasn't available, then saw that Tilly had already gone ahead and put some books on hold for me. They'd be ready to pick up at the library in a few days.

Three hours later, I'd read six short stories and was finishing my seventh. I scanned the last few sentences and went to close out of the story, when I saw a familiar name in the footnote.

Lila Conway.

I read through the footnote, and then leaned back, thumbnail in my mouth. The piece was well written but spooky as hell. A young boy and girl, Eddie and Alana, come up together in a poor neighborhood, friendless but for each other, with parents mostly out of the picture. On Eddie's tenth birthday, they find an abandoned suitcase in an alley behind their elementary school. In the suitcase are three things: a passport, of which the face on the photograph is scratched out; a leather-bound notebook, filled with unlined, blank pages; and a slim, battered volume of Chinese fairy tales, translated into English.

Engrossed, Eddie and Alana begin to read the fairy tales. Each tale is a few pages, and as they read, Alana starts to feel strange. Her skin tightens, her bones ache, her eyeballs water from a strange pressure. Halfway through the collection of fairy tales, Eddie looks to his side, and Alana has disappeared. He shrugs—she is an impetuous child, after all—and starts the next tale. To his horror, Alana is right there, in the story. Scared, she waves to him from the pages of the book, mouthing "help me," but there is nothing he can do. Frantically, he reads to the end, and when he turns the last page, he sees she's gone.

She's simply gone.

Eddie goes on to become an author himself, and he spends the rest of his days trying to write Alana back into his life. By the end of the story, he can't remember if she was ever real in the first place.

Another fairy tale; I couldn't get away from them.

The footnote referenced an article written by Lila Conway. It said she was a friend of Fuente's and the inspiration for the little girl in the story. Tilly was even better than I thought because she'd included the article that Lila had written, too.

I read through the article and when I was finished, I had a throbbing headache. I went into the staff lounge and chugged a glass of cool water with a side of Advil. In the fridge I found a lone slice of strawberry cheesecake, the last remainder of someone's birthday cake. I scarfed it down and then immediately wished I hadn't. The sugar made me feel queasy and nauseous.

Lila's article was a piece for a Denver newspaper that had gone out of print years ago. The content was an impassioned plea for the state to bestow on Yvette Michaelson—the "Daughter of Denver"—the Colorado State Honor Medallion. The award recognized historic achievements of native Coloradans and was given every five years as part of a special ceremony at the state capital. In its sixty-year history, it had never before been given to a woman, or for that matter, anyone of color.

Yvette Michaelson was not only a woman; she was half black, as well.

Lila's article laid out Yvette's early beginnings and her struggle with social anxieties. Then Lila moved on to Yvette's explorations, her voyages and travels with her beloved companion, Louise Ruse, and finally her solo explorations in South America after Ruse's death from cancer. The article ended with: *Michaelson never did return from her last brave adventure; most presume that she did indeed die at the hands of a native tribe deep in the Bolivian jungle. But let us no longer wallow in the focus on her death. I implore you to instead rejoice in this grand woman's life and grant her the immortality she deserves and do side with me and bestow upon her the Colorado State Honor Medallion.*

The closing paragraph, while touching, was similar to the rest of the article: poorly written, with strange grammatical sentence structures and run-on sentences. Lila may have been a crackerjack researcher but her writing skills left much to be desired.

I thought back to the school project I'd done on Michaelson; to my knowledge, she'd never received any kind of formal award or recognition of her achievements other than the nickname of "The Daughter of Denver"—which in its own strange way, still implied a patriarchal sense of ownership over her accomplishments. She wasn't the daughter of Denver, she *was* Denver: pioneer, explorer, frontierswoman, brave, unique. A true force of nature.

I left the staff lounge and went back to my desk and wrote a few more notes, recapping what I'd learned while it was still fresh in my mind. The article was fifteen years old; yet when I'd visited her, Conway was ankle-deep in her research on Michaelson.

Fuente wrote novels, short stories, and more. One of his stories featured a girl—inspired by his own childhood friend Lila—who disappears into a story and her pal Eddie spends the rest of his life trying to write her back into existence.

What the hell did it all mean?

I reminded myself as I packed up to leave for the day that it could mean nothing. Investigations routinely turn up a tremendous amount of information, much of which ultimately means little and exists as mere clutter and distraction from the real meat of the issue.

Brody texted me as I was about to turn up the canyon; we were out of Seamus's dog food. I headed to the grocery store, knowing it would likely be a madhouse. Storms have a way of sending everyone shopping.

I was right; the place was packed. I found

a spot around back and trampled across the parking lot, groaning as each step brought another puddle of dirty, oily snow splashing up against my pant legs. Inside was a nightmare; pushy shoppers cut one another off with loaded carts, desperate to get at the last bottle of milk or the lone loaf of bread. I gritted my teeth and bypassed the shopping carts, intent on one purchase and one purchase only. Seamus's dog food came in a heavy bag, but with both hands around it, I could manage it.

I headed to the single self-checkout machine and waited patiently behind four other women, each holding one or two purchases in their hands. They were women after my own heart, and we gave each other smug, knowing smiles while rolling our eyes in the direction of the long lines at the other checkout stations.

I scanned the crowd. There was Peggy Greenway, the English teacher, in line, dressed to the nines in a fur-trimmed navy blue vintage coat, complete with black gloves and a small, feathered black cap. She was almost at the checkout, waiting behind a large woman with an even larger purse.

Two aisles down from her were Harold Chapman and Vice Principal Justine Moreno, engrossed in a conversation. The whole damn academy was at the grocery store and I casually brushed the hair from my forehead and looked around, wondering if Darren Chase was somewhere nearby.

A small shriek called my attention back to Peggy Greenway. I watched as she shrank back, dangerously close to melting into the stone-faced man behind her. She said, "Please, please, get it away from me. I can't stand them."

I stood on tiptoe but couldn't see who Peggy was talking to. She sounded terrified. The woman in front of me noticed my curiosity. She leaned back and said over her shoulder, "Betty Page over there is pleading with the gal in front of her. There's a small terrier in the lady's purse. It's scaring the crap out of that poor girl."

The woman behind me chimed in, "That's Ms. Greenway; my daughter is in her English class. I know her well. She's deathly afraid of dogs, even the tiny little suckers like that rat-faced creation."

I watched as the larger woman with the purse and the dog moved away, ignoring the checkout attendant's calls that dogs were never allowed in the grocery store. Peggy looked pale and both Vice Principal Moreno and Harold Chapman, though appearing concerned at the commotion, made no move to comfort her or even speak to her.

My line moved quickly after that and I was able to catch up to Peggy in the parking lot.

She was slamming the trunk door of her Toyota Corolla when I took her by the elbow.

"Oh, Gemma, you startled me," she said. Her eyes were wide and her pale face had taken on a flush from the cold air.

"I'm sorry, I wanted to make sure you were okay," I replied. I let go of her elbow and frowned. "You seemed terrified back there."

Peggy Greenway nodded vigorously and her little black cap with the feathers and netting slipped down an inch. "I was bitten as a child. Dogs have terrified me ever since. Big ones, small ones, it doesn't matter."

I nodded, thinking. "And yet you told my partner and I that you had to get home early last Friday to feed your dog, April? The elderly Maltese?"

I watched as she realized she'd been caught in a lie. Her gaze fell to the ground and the flush in her cheeks deepened.

First Soren Baker, now Peggy. I was tired of being lied to.

"How about you tell me the truth? Lying during the course of a murder investigation is a serious offense."

"Oh, God, you can't seriously think I had anything to do with that man's death? I just went home, that's all. By myself. And, yes, it was to an empty house. I . . . I don't know why I lied. I guess I didn't want to seem as pathetic as Hal Chapman. Isn't that insane? I thought a dog would make me seem like less of a loser. At least it's something. The truth is I, too, had a microwave dinner and curled up with a stiff drink and a hardcover novel," Peggy said. She looked up at me and attempted a weak smile. "I don't like people thinking I'm a loser. Does that make sense?"

"Of course it makes sense, no one wants to be thought of as a loser. Although truth be told, Peggy, there's nothing loser-like about going home to an empty house. The problem now is that you've broken my trust. How do I know if I can believe you? Did you talk to anyone? Chat with a neighbor? Call the police on a loud party upstairs?"

Peggy shook her head. "No, no, and no. Please, Gemma, I'm telling you the truth. I wish someone could confirm my story, but there's no one who can."

I knew she was lying, but I didn't know about what. Going straight home or being alone all night? She was an attractive girl and if there was one thing this town had plenty of it was equally attractive and available men. And Delaware Fuente, while not necessarily attractive (at least to me), would have possessed just the sort of worldly experience and charm that a young lady like Peggy Greenway might have fallen prey to.

Had they been together that night? Was Fuente a mentor, helping her with her own writing? Was his death the result of a lover's quarrel?

Before we said good-bye, I asked her if she had any idea of Soren Baker's whereabouts. Peggy looked bewildered and said she wasn't aware that he was missing.

"I bet Harold Chapman is covering for him," she added. "Soren and Hal have an arrangement; they teach each other's classes from time to time when either of them feels like playing hooky. Of course, they never asked me, not that I would partake. Director Silverstein turns a blind eye. Moreno would freak out if she knew but it's not worth the angst for me to tell her."

"Why would they get in trouble for that?" I asked, curious.

"Because they're supposed to use their general leave. It's administrative policy. If they just cover for each other, no one's the wiser," Peggy said. She shook her head. "Men."

I watched as she pulled out of the crowded parking lot, her brake lights barely flashing as she turned back toward the school and presumably her home.

I've encountered a lot of liars in my line of work and what still surprised me are the ones you never see coming. Their reasons for lying are almost always equally as shocking.

By the time I arrived home, Brody was nearly done preparing dinner so instead of helping him, I played with Grace. Play is an exaggeration; she sat in my arms, nursed, then snoozed while I stared deeply at her features. She really was a beautiful baby. I put her down in her crib when Brody called that it was time to eat. Then, for the first time in weeks it seemed, we sat at the dining table and enjoyed a real supper, together: spaghetti, a simple green salad, toasted French bread, and wine.

After, we played a game of cribbage and then put a movie on. Brody started a fire and poured us each a second glass of red wine. The pinot noir was light and tasted of summer cherries. The movie was a predictable legal thriller but still enjoyable, especially after the second glass of wine. It felt good to take a break from work. The room grew warm from the fire and the wine. I closed my eyes for a moment, relaxing.

I woke with a crick in my neck and the television still going, albeit the screen was a salt-and-pepper mess of static. Brody was slumped to the side, fast asleep. Curled in his lap was Seamus, who woke as I stretched out my neck and shoulders. He gave me the sad basset hound face he does so well.

"Sorry, buddy, we can't sleep down here all night," I whispered. I shook Brody awake. He sat straight up and said, "What is it? What's wrong?"

"Nothing's wrong, sweetheart. We're old. Two glasses of pinot and we were both out. I don't think I saw thirty minutes of the movie. Let's go up to bed."

We trooped up the stairs in a single file line, me, then Brody, then Seamus. I checked on Grace in the nursery and remembered Bull's words, how this was only the beginning of our lives together as a family. How we had all the time in the world to figure things out.

She stayed asleep the whole time I watched her, until my eyes were so heavy I couldn't keep them open one minute longer. I left her, wondering if that was true, that we had all the time in the world.

I hoped it was true but I knew that hoping for something and getting it were two very different things.

In the bedroom, I peered out the window, wondering if I'd be able to see the storm moving in. It hadn't come yet, though, and so I crawled into bed and pressed myself against Brody's warm, bare back. But he didn't move and after a moment, I rolled over and a minute after that, I was dead to the world.

Chapter Twenty-four

The storm arrived early. I stood on the front porch, wrapped in a heavy plaid blanket, and drank a cup of hot chocolate as the sky brightened from an inky black to an indigo blue and finally to an angry gray. The air grew icy and then came the snow, first in small, gentle flakes, then in big, bold pellets. By the time I dressed and left the house, there were two inches already on the roads.

As I drove, I thought about the ways that winter changes people. When the cold hits, the drinks seem to flow a little more freely. When the sun has been out of sight for days, it's easier for depression to slide in and take hold. The forecast was calling for an additional ten to twelve inches of snow over the next day and a half. There would be drunks to get off the road, homeless to get into shelters, and fighting spouses to separate from each other.

I was almost to work when I thought of something. Rather, someone . . . someone who would never dream of calling in, of working from home. Someone who could perhaps shed some light on one or more of the mysteries that seemed to be piling up. I checked my rearview mirror and when I saw it was clear behind me, and in front of me, I hit the brakes and took a sharp right, away from the station.

It had been months, maybe six, since I'd last seen Dr. Dean Pabst. I pulled into the parking lot of his office and sat there, my eyes closed, reliving the awful dreams that had led me to him in the first place. Dark, terrible dreams about the Woodsman and the McKenzie boys. For a moment, I was afraid. What if seeing the doctor triggered a flashback, a retroactive return to that dark place? I had worked so hard to crawl out of those dreams, and the thought of them returning was enough to slow my heart and then speed it up in triple time.

"Stop it," I whispered to myself. I grabbed my purse. "Stop it."

I went through the front doors of the office building and retraced the route I'd walked dozens of times. When I entered Pabst's office, though, everything was different, and for a moment I thought perhaps I had chosen the wrong door.

In the past, we—patients—were instructed to wait in the tiny anteroom and Pabst would retrieve us at our appointment time. Back then there were two plastic chairs, a dusty old coffee table, and that day's newspaper. Sometimes there was a water cooler in the corner; other times, if Pabst hadn't paid the bill, there was a small tree with drying, dying leaves instead.

Now, there was a receptionist, and colorful art on the wall, and armchairs with slipcovers. The coffee table was the same, but it was sparkling clean, and there were a few more reading options besides the day's paper. It made me happy to know Pabst was doing so well, and I wondered what turn of events in the last six months had brought on this good fortune.

The receptionist was kind and efficient. She pulled up the doctor's calendar on her computer, smiled triumphantly, and said he could spare some time to talk, if I could wait about ten minutes. I took a seat and picked up the paper. On the front, in a column that took up a fourth of the page, was an article by Missy Matherson.

I started reading it and groaned.

"Are you all right?" From behind her computer, the receptionist leaned out to the side and looked at me over her glasses. "Can I get you something?"

I shook my head. "I'm fine. Ignore me, please."

The article was titled "Our Right to Know" and was all about how the Cedar Valley Police Department had withheld vital information from the press—and by extension the public—regarding the recent murder of famous novelist Delaware Fuente. Matherson went on to question the handling of several recent cases, including the murders last fall.

I tossed the paper on the table. Matherson had

no idea what she was talking about. She was a two-bit reporter who skimmed the surface, trying to spin gold out of scum. She wasn't worth my anger and I took a few deep breaths to cool off.

The receptionist leaned out again. "We have coffee?"

"No, thank you."

Another minute, then she said, "Dr. Pabst can see you now."

His office wasn't the only thing that had changed. Dr. Pabst had lost fifty pounds and his bad toupee. Though still heavily overweight, without the hair and the extra weight in his face Dr. Pabst looked like a different person.

I took my customary seat in the armchair across from his desk, facing him. From his chair, he nodded at me and laced his fingers together.

"Dean," I said. "You look great."

He smiled at that. "Thank you, my dear. You exaggerate; I've lost a few pounds but I hardly look great. But I *am* trying. I'll celebrate my seventieth birthday in April. I hope I'm around to see my eightieth, but my doctors and my trainer tell me I won't be, unless I make these changes."

He gestured to his head, then his body. "It's a funny thing, cresting the hill and sliding head-first into senior living. I don't feel old, but I am. It's a young man's world, I fear. Well, at least a brave man's world. Tell me, Gemma, have you seen the Woodsman lately? Does he visit you in your darkest dreams?"

Chilled at the mention of the Woodsman, I shook my head. "It's been months. I think he's gone for good. At least, I hope he's gone."

Pabst removed his too-small eyeglasses and pinched the bridge of his nose. "Be careful, my dear. You look tired. You're undoubtedly on the hunt again, distracted. No, no, don't bother protesting. I can see it in your eyes. You're chasing a monster again. But you must remember, our enemies have a way of sneaking up on us when we least expect it. Stay vigilant. Are you journaling?"

I laughed at that. "Dean, I have a three-month-old baby at home; a boyfriend who's not sure what he wants; a grandmother rapidly slipping down into the grips of dementia; a dead author; a missing schoolteacher; a Rabbit Man in the woods; and a high school bully terrorizing his peers. And everyone I meet seems determined to lie to my face. When exactly do you think I should be journaling? Oh, just a moment, Chief, while I have a spot of tea and write in my diary."

The psychiatrist replaced his eyeglasses and gave me a stern look. "You mock me. You shouldn't do that. Tell me about the bully."

I found it curious that Dr. Pabst had gone

straight for Grimm, and not the Fuente case, but that was the doctor for you.

And in all honesty, it was Grimm I wanted to discuss.

"He calls himself Grimm, with two *m*'s, like the Brothers Grimm, the Germans. He's also an author of sorts. He bullies the other students by creating these elaborate sorts of situations that have some basis in a fairy tale," I said. I told him about Paul Runny, and Becky and Star, and how there were others whose stories I hadn't heard yet. Pabst's brow grew more and more furrowed.

"Are you sure he works alone? No accomplice, no partner in crime?"

Soren Baker and Delaware Fuente?

I slowly shook my head. "Why would you ask that?"

Dr. Pabst waved a hand in the air, dismissing my worry. "No reason, other than the original Grimm was a pair of brothers. Blood brothers, bound to each other, very, very close. Did you know they were both librarians for a time? Yes, that's where their interest in collecting and modifying folk tales began. But we call them fairy tales, which implies a bit of fantasy, doesn't it? A folk tale somehow feels sturdy, rooted in truth. Society likes to run from truth; truth often bores us. And so we call a folk tale a fairy tale and no one is the wiser."

I shrugged. "I didn't know any of that. A brother, or a partner, is certainly something to think about. Dean, what about the pathology of someone like this? Why does he do what he does?"

The doctor leaned back in his chair, closed his eyes, and folded his hands over his ample belly. He wore a white dress shirt under red suspenders and a matching bow tie. He was brilliant, and as I waited for him to speak, I wondered what horrors of his own the doctor had lived through. I knew he'd seen things, terrible things, in his many travels. He'd spent time doing pro bono work in Africa and Europe in the nineties; he went to places like Rwanda and Kosovo, working with survivors of genocide.

He went silent so long that I'd thought he'd fallen asleep. I shifted in my seat, and with that small squeak of fabric against fabric, he began to speak. "Well, there are control issues here, of course. By creating these situations—stories, if you will, Grimm becomes Master of the Universe. He controls the play, the actions. It appears that he gives his characters free will through choice, but he doesn't, not really. He knows what choice they will make before he even involves them. It's not fun for him if there's wiggle room. He has to know the ending."

I nodded. Becky Hamilton was always going to cut Star's hair, because the alternative—be exposed as a cheater—was, in her mind, so much worse . . . and yet, that's exactly what happened.

Pabst continued. "There are feelings of insecurity, but they may be very deeply rooted. On the surface, Grimm would appear confident, strong. He's intelligent, of course, and well versed in a number of subjects. Hmmm . . . you say this is at a school?"

"Yes. The Valley Academy. Why?"

"Because Grimm is quite clever. Clearly he's studied the classic tales and understands the nature of the folk tale, what it's meant to do. Have you considered the possibility that Grimm is a teacher?" Pabst asked quietly. He leaned forward. "This . . . game that he plays, it's very sophisticated. I would actually be quite surprised if it's a young person perpetrating these crimes."

I blew air through my lips. "To be honest, yes. I suppose I've thought about that but it seems so violent, so very dark. If Grimm is a teacher, he must be schizophrenic; pleasant enough during the day, scheming at night. Have you heard of a teacher doing something like this before? I guess all the teachers I knew were schoolmarm types or bookish science guys. It makes me furious to think of someone in a position of trust doing this to the kids."

Pabst nodded vigorously. "Oh heavens, yes. It's much more common than you'd think, unfortunately. It's referred to as 'teacher bullying' in the field. Think of the power, the influence a teacher wields in his or her day-to-day activities. Most teachers, I'd say the vast majority in fact, are gentle with that power. They use it to effectively guide their pupils toward positive outcomes. However, imagine one of these same teachers going over to the dark side, for lack of better imagery. Imagine that same power used as a punishment, meant to disparage or coerce a student."

"Why? To what end?"

Pabst smiled gently. "That, my dear, is your realm. Perhaps the teacher was bullied as a child, or is in an abusive relationship. He may have severe insecurities, or narcissism. I'd wager money that Grimm thinks he knows what's best for people, for the students. His students. *He* is the only one who can help, *he* knows all the answers. If he is working with a partner, they may be playing off each other, or playing the students like pawns in a chess game."

I thought about that for a moment. "So, Grimm thinks he's helping the very students he's terrorizing?"

Pabst nodded. "Absolutely. My guess is the Grimm persona allows him to secretly do what he wishes he could do in plain sight. This is a determined monster you are chasing. He, or they, have very rigid ideas about how the world should operate. Again, I wouldn't at all be surprised if there are two of them working together."

Soren Baker and Delaware Fuente? Baker and Peggy Greenway?

"Do you think someone like Grimm could also kill?"

Pabst looked disturbed. "Yes. Yes, I'm fairly certain he—or again, they—could kill. Of course, given the right circumstances, any one of us can kill."

I nodded. "If there are two of them, could one of them kill the other? A partnership gone bad?"

Instead of answering, Pabst asked, "You said there is a teacher missing?"

"Yes, an English teacher named Soren Baker," I replied. "He's crooked, a con man, and we found blood in his apartment. He's nowhere to be found."

"And Delaware Fuente is dead," Pabst said slowly. "I would wonder how the two of them concocted this game. To your knowledge, the two didn't know each other? Before Fuente arrived in town, I mean."

"No, not to my knowledge," I said.

Pabst said, "It's not that far-fetched, Gemma. Occam's razor. It's a much cleaner and simpler explanation if this Soren Baker is both Fuente's killer and Grimm. Because if he's not, then you're left with at least three monsters to chase: Fuente's killer; Grimm; and Soren Baker."

I leaned forward. "There's one more thing, Dean. Fuente's killer left a note in his mouth. It was a crumpled piece of paper, with the words 'This is only the beginning' printed on them. What does that make you think of?"

"Arrogance," Pabst answered without hesitation. "And strangely enough, someone quite clever. Again, much like your Grimm. Stories have beginnings; Fuente in dying has literally eaten his own beginning. There's a taunt, too, a promise if you will. If Soren Baker has been murdered, as well . . ."

Pabst grew pale. He took a breath, then continued. "If Soren Baker has been murdered, well, I don't have to tell you. I'd say you may eventually be looking for a serial killer. And if that's the case, then it's not a beginning at all, but a terrible, terrible end. The tourists will leave, the money will dry up, and Cedar Valley will die. I'd keep a very close eye on that school, Gemma. Those students may be in grave danger."

Chapter Twenty-five

I drove back to the station with Pabst's words as my passenger. The roads weren't as deserted as I'd like to see in such a storm but at least the cars that were out were driven slowly, shuffling along like great hulking dinosaurs. As I parked, the radio offered another reminder that schools in the valley would be closed for the day and possibly Friday, too.

I got out of the car and looked again at the Victorian houses across the alley from the parking lot. They were beautiful, like something out of a Norman Rockwell painting, with the deep snow on their roofs and front lawns, and the lights twinkling at me from the front windows. I paused and took a moment to quietly acknowledge the blessing that I lived in such a spectacular place.

"The cat lady's trying to get a hold of you," Finn said by way of greeting. Moriarty, at his desk in the corner, threw a hand up in a half wave. The other desks were empty and the room was quiet.

I made a face at him. "Cat lady?"

Finn nodded and took a bite of his granola bar. There was a large smear of melted chocolate at the corner of his mouth. I wondered how long Moriarty and I could get away with not telling him about it.

"You know, Lila Conway from the school? Why are you smiling?"

I pulled my lips in, trying to lose the smirk. "No reason. I told you, she's not a cat lady. She's got a bird, not cats. Not even a cat calendar."

Finn shrugged. "Birds, cats, they're all the same. She's called twice this morning. She won't talk to anyone but you. She was upset."

I dropped my bags at my desk and hung my coat over the back of the chair. "Where is everybody?"

Moriarty leaned back in his chair. He hooked his ankles behind the chair legs and tipped back precariously, daring me to comment. He was going to fall but I kept my mouth shut.

Moriarty made a wiping motion at his mouth and I tried to keep a straight face.

After a moment, he said, "We have a skeleton crew today. You better pray everyone stays home and off the roads. I don't want to freeze my ass off responding to some moron who gets his shitty Escalade stuck in a drift."

"Aren't you in a lovely mood?"

Moriarty smirked and righted his chair with a heavy thud. "I should have called in sick. Everyone else did."

I rolled my neck from side to side and sighed. It was going to be one of those days, then. I turned on my computer and made a cup of tea before returning Lila Conway's call.

Her phone rang just once before she answered. She was breathless, as though she'd been running. She gasped when I said my name.

"Oh, thank goodness. I've been waiting for your call!" Lila cried. "Where have you been?"

I sat up straighter when I heard the tone of her voice. "I just arrived at work. What's wrong? You sound upset."

She took a deep breath. "He was here. The Rabbit Man, I'm sure of it. He was here."

"Fuente's Rabbit Man? Are you sure?" I grabbed a pen and my notebook. "Tell me what happened."

Lila exhaled again. "Of course I'm sure, he matched Delaware's description perfectly. The man had yellow hair and big ears. He was here last night. I was sitting in the front living room, reading, when I heard a noise outside."

"What kind of noise?"

"I'm . . . I'm not sure how to describe it. You're going to think I'm crazy," Lila said. "It was as though a heavy animal were moving through the forest, but gracefully. Deliberately. Steady, unafraid. Does that even make sense? Listen to me, I'm rambling like an old poet."

I paused and stopped writing. "Could it have been a bear? Or a mountain lion?"

"Mountain lions don't make noise. Not the

ones that live very long, at least. And I've never seen a bear out of hibernation this early. Besides, I told you. I saw him. After I heard the noise, I went to the window. It was late, dark outside, so I turned down my lights and stood there, at the window, watching. At first, there was nothing. Only the moonlight reflecting off the white snow, flooding my front drive with a bright, clear light," Lila said. I heard her swallow. "Then, from out of the woods, came a man."

"And you're sure it wasn't a neighbor?"

Lila was frustrated. "No, it wasn't a neighbor! I've lived here twenty years and you better believe I know what my neighbors look like. I've never seen this man before in my life, I'd swear to it. He was . . . ugly. Thick, yellow hair—not blond—yellow. It hung under his hat in long strings. And his ears were enormous."

"The hat didn't cover his ears?"

"No," Lila responded. "The hat looked too small for his head, like maybe it was a child's hat. His ears stuck up and out like an elephant's. Enormous. And his eyes . . . he turned at one point and looked straight in my window. I could swear he was looking right at me. He wasn't more than fifteen feet away. And then he stood there! For ten minutes, at least."

"Why didn't you call the police? We could have had a patrol car there quickly."

"I couldn't leave my post! I was scared to death to take my eyes off him. I thought if I did, he might get to the window or a side door and get inside. Stupid, I know. It's like the boogeyman," Lila said. She took a deep breath and laughed shakily. "Listen to me, I sound like a certifiable nut."

"While you watched him, did he do anything? Make any kind of threatening gesture? Was he armed?"

"No, he just stood there. I don't think he was armed. He stood there and stared right at me. And then he walked away, right back into the woods. He practically melted into the trees. Like Sasquatch. Bigfoot."

I thought a moment. "What's behind your house, in the woods? Is there a trail?"

Lila snorted with frustration. "No. For years, I've written to the city's Parks Department, begging them to put in a trail connection between Big Dirt Hill and the Greenback community. They say it would cost too much. So the woods just sit there, inaccessible. It's a waste of our natural resources."

"How about the road, can you get to the main road from those woods?"

Lila thought a moment. "Sure, in the summer or fall, I suppose if you bushwhacked far enough south, you could traverse the creek and you would hit the road soon enough. But in winter, you'd have to know your way around. There are pockets of snow five feet deep in places. One wrong step and you'd break your leg. No one would hear your cries for help and you'd freeze to death in a matter of hours."

"Do you want me to come out there and take a look?"

Lila said, "Heavens no, not in this weather. Besides, the fresh snow will have obliterated any trace he was ever here. My, but there's something comforting about that, isn't there? The way the snow covers over what has happened, and prepares the earth for what will be. A fresh slate, if you will, after every storm."

"That's a lovely thought. And you haven't seen this man anywhere else? Hanging around the school or maybe at the grocery store?"

"Yes, I'm quite sure. I've never laid eyes on him. I'd remember."

Lila Conway lived alone in a remote part of town. She was tall and sturdy but I wouldn't bet on her having any kind of significant physical strength. Should someone try to attack her or enter the house . . . I didn't want to think about that.

I tried to sound calm but I was worried. "Okay. Keep your doors and windows locked and your phone close to you. Do you have a generator if your power goes out tonight?"

"No, but I've got a wood-burning stove and

enough kindling to get me through the next month. I have a gun, should I get it out? What if this man, the Rabbit Man, what if he really did kill Del?"

"I don't know, Lila. What connection could he have to Fuente? What reason would he have to kill him? And if he did stalk and then kill your friend, why would he be after you now? It doesn't make sense. Unless . . ."

I stopped talking, trying to follow a thought that refused to move in a straight line.

"Unless what, Gemma? You're worrying me," Lila said.

I rubbed at my right eye with my free hand. It felt as though there was a lash trapped at the edge of my contact lens. At the window above my desk, I heard the storm push the tree limbs from an old evergreen against the glass.

"Gemma?"

"Is there anything in your past, you know, your shared past with Fuente, that someone might be seeking revenge for?" I said.

Across the aisle, Finn watched me. He'd been listening to my side of the conversation and now he nodded, encouraging me to go on.

Lila said, "I'm a high school administrator with crippling social anxieties. My life is a footnote in the annals of history. Delaware's life did not involve physical harm or hurt to others."

I asked, "What about emotional? Or verbal?"

"What do you mean?"

"You said Fuente never physically hurt anyone. What about emotional abuse or verbal harm?"

Lila was silent a few moments. "Maybe. He could have. I mean, my God, when I think about it, I sometimes feel like I didn't even know the man. Our lives barely intersected after he left Colorado. Truly. He left the day after we graduated high school, and over the years we kept in touch, sure, but we never *did* anything together."

Maybe Fuente's killer didn't know that.

We ended the call with Lila promising to call me the next day and check in, or sooner, if anything further happened.

"What was that all about?" Finn asked.

"You heard the call. The Rabbit Man is on the prowl. I'm worried about Lila. There's some connection there, between her and Fuente and his death. We just can't see it yet."

"I'm telling you, the Crazy Cat Lady did it, with the hunting knife, in the woods," Finn said. "How does Baker fit in? And Grimm?"

"I don't know." I called across the room to Moriarty. "Hey, Lou, you ever run across a big man in the woods, yellow hair, large ears, kind of rabbit-like? Maybe up by Greenback Village?"

Moriarty thought a moment, then shook his head. "Doesn't sound like anyone I've ever met. Greenback Village, huh? You know, there are some real wackos living back in those woods, survivalists, apocalyptical types. One of these days we're going to have a Ruby Ridge on our hands, I can promise you that. Guarantee it's a day I'm supposed to be off."

I thought about the young family I'd seen driving in the canyon, with the dead deer. Fuente's rental cabin was in the same sprawling tract of forest that backed up to Lila Conway's house. There were hundreds of miles of trails and networks—some hidden, some known—that existed back there.

Finn stood and went to the window. He tapped the glass with his fingertip, a twin reflection mirroring the actions of the branch on the other side of the pane. "I ran into a few of those guys a couple of years ago. I was camping up by Bride's Veil, half a mile or so from the waterfall. It was near dark, and I'd started a fire. From out of nowhere these two men come out of the woods. At first I thought they were day hikers, but they didn't have water bottles on them, or packs. One of them had a big machete strapped to his leg. They were in good shape, fit, heavily bearded and dressed in faded army gear, you know, camouflage shirts and black pants. They walked right by me without a word. They didn't even make eye contact. At first I thought I dreamt the whole thing."

Moriarty swiveled his desk chair back and forth. The squeaking of the rusty screws was the only noise in the room. I've often thought the station had the feel of a church but today it felt like a tomb.

"What did you do?" Moriarty asked. He swiveled again and the noise this time was like fingernails on a chalkboard.

Finn scowled. "Get some WD-40 on that thing, Lou. It sounds like a cat in heat. I waited a few minutes, then followed them up the trail. I stayed far enough behind so they couldn't see or hear me. They weren't trying to be quiet. They weren't talking but they were rustling around, cracking twigs and disturbing leaves. It was late fall and the leaves were drier than dry. One of the guys must have hit a rock at one point, because I heard a low thud and one of them cussed. Then, after about ten minutes, the noises stopped."

I pulled a can of grapefruit soda from my pack and cracked it open. The carbonation sizzled and the bright smell of citrus filled the air.

"What do you mean, the noises stopped?"

Finn left the window and returned to his seat. He shrugged. "They simply stopped. I hiked another ten minutes, thinking maybe I'd been too slow and they had gotten too far ahead, but those guys were gone. Like they'd never been there at all. Just . . . vanished."

"Like they melted into the woods?" I asked, remembering Lila's description of the Rabbit Man's disappearance.

Finn looked thoughtful. "Exactly."

"Baloney," Moriarty coughed. "Bullshit you hiked twenty minutes, in the dark, in those woods. It would have been pitch-black up there, in what, September? October?"

"If I'm lying I'm dying," Finn said. "Swear to God, it was the first weekend in October and there was a full moon. There's plenty of light, once your eyes adjust."

"How do you know you weren't spotted? Maybe the men ducked behind a tree and hid until you were gone," I asked, also faintly suspicious of Finn's story. It had the air of an *X-Files* episode. "Were you hitting the peppermint schnapps?"

"You two can believe whatever you want to, it makes no difference to me," Finn said. "I was stone-cold sober and I know what I saw. One minute they were there, the next they weren't."

He grinned and added, "I will tell you this, though. I don't go up there without a gun anymore."

"Seriously? I think that's so sad," I said. "That's the one place we should be able to go and leave our guns at home."

Moriarty shook his head, his face flushed. His skin was always red these days. Maybe all that white hair made it look redder than it actually was. "You're naïve if you think there's any safe place left anymore. When the shit hits the fan, Finn and I'll be ready. And you'll be the one calling for the cavalry. A little pussy cat in a world of wolves."

I stood and stretched. "Now who sounds like a survivalist? This is going to be a long day. Don't you think we should save the city some ducats? I could go home early."

Moriarty said, "No way. If anyone's going home it's me. I've got thirty years' seniority on you kids. That might not count for much, but it should count for something."

Snow days are good for catching up on old reports, writing notes, organizing files, and in general tidying up the office. I had three messages in my voice mail, each from the different Lark Companies we'd found. I returned the calls and spoke with a CEO, a CIO, and at the escort company in California, a principal planner, whatever that meant. I knew it didn't have anything to do with urban design, that's for sure. By the time my conversations ended, I was convinced none of the companies had anything to do with Delaware Fuente.

"Lark Co is a dead end, Finn," I groaned. "It must be code for something else. We need to get a warrant and have a look at Fuente's bank accounts. Maybe we'll get lucky and we can see who was getting the money."

Finn shook his head. "I doubt it's going to be that simple. When I talked to Choi on Tuesday, he said he'd pull together what he could on Fuente's accounting. But he said it might take some time. Fuente had funds all over the place, including some that Choi suspected were in offshore accounts."

"Great."

Moriarty bugged out sometime before lunch. I pumped, called Brody and checked in, and then made a peanut butter and jelly sandwich and ate it at my desk. I sat in silence, watching through the window as the snow fell heavily outside.

I thought about Lila's words, how the snow covers everything that has happened and prepares the ground for what is to come.

But what is coming?

I told Finn about the reading I'd done the day before; the review of Fuente's literature and the inclusion of Lila Conway's article. I finished with, "So I've got Alistair Campbell telling me to look to Fuente's words and there's nothing there, at least that I can see, that would provoke someone to murder. I've still got a lot of reading to do, though."

"Maybe that's Campbell's way of distracting

you, throwing a bone in one direction so you don't look his way. 'Look to his words'? That sounds incredibly melodramatic. I don't trust the guy," Finn said. He blew his nose on a tissue, then wadded it up into a ball and tossed it into a trash can eight feet away, easily nailing the shot. "Why are you letting Campbell dictate your moves, anyway?"

I shook my head. "I'm not. We'd have had to do the reading anyway, Finn. It helps us get inside Fuente's head."

"I guess. I think your time might be better spent looking into Campbell's background, his, and Neil Roget's, and Turtle's."

I started to respond but before I could, Sam Birdshead walked in the room. I hadn't seen him since our fight—if you could call it that— at the restaurant. He gave us a half-hearted smile and set his crutches against the edge of his desk, then sat down.

"What's happening?" Finn asked.

Sam shrugged and turned on his computer. "Not too much. The roads are crap and the city plows can't keep up. Hey, have you been down to Frank's new bar yet? Jenna and I hit it last night, it was packed. He's talking about turning the place into a real brewery. Imagine that, Cedar Valley's first brewery."

Finn perked up at that. "Oh yeah? He's going to have some competition. I hear a permit just got issued for a distillery on the east end of town in the old schoolhouse. How is Jenna? She's a sweetheart."

Sam tipped his head to the side and scratched at his shoulder. "She's good but she's getting restless. I don't think she'll stay in town much longer. Once the season's over, she'll quit the resort and go to New York to get her master's degree. Jenna's too smart to stick around here. I told her, this valley sucks you in if you stay too long."

Finn murmured agreement.

I sat back, listening to the two of them, feeling like a third wheel. I had been gone a long time; their friendship had deepened in the last few months.

"Are you going to go with her?"

"To New York?" Sam scoffed at that. "Hell no. What would I do there? This is my home, the mountains, the dirt and the plains. This land is in my blood. It's been in my family's blood for hundreds of years."

I was relieved to hear that Sam would be staying although a part of me wanted to scream that he *should* run, far away from his grandfather and Alistair Campbell.

I spoke up. "Are you still thinking about leaving the force?"

Finn gave me a dirty look.

Sam turned around and with his back squarely

to me, faced his computer and started typing. He called back over his shoulder, "I told you, Gemma, this is a done deal. It's out of my hands. A few more weeks and I'm out of here."

"Just like that, huh. It must be pretty easy for you."

Sam spun around. "What exactly is easy for me?"

I shrugged. "Leaving. You've got a voice, Sam. Use it. You don't have to go do this thing. You never had to. Stay here, with us. Work with us. You belong here."

"I don't belong here. This isn't my home; not my real home, anyway. Being a cop was an idiot's dream. My whole life has been preparing me to work with my grandfather. The accident only proved that," Sam said. He grinned and it broke my heart to see that old, easy familiar smile. "You're only making this harder on yourself, Gemma. Finn's okay with it, aren't you, Finn?"

Finn lifted his hands in an "I'm not touching this one" kind of gesture. Then he said, "A man's gotta do what a man's gotta do."

"That's so typical," I muttered. A ping sounded from my computer and I turned back to my screen, curious to see what new email had arrived. I read it and before I was done, I was out of my seat and pulling on my jacket.

"Finn," I said urgently. "Finn, it's Fuente's

phone. It was turned on, just for a few minutes, but it was enough for the phone company to get an address. It's local, ten minutes away. Come on. We have to go, now."

Finn wasted no time grabbing his own jacket and phone and keys. He checked his service weapon while I pulled mine from the desk drawer and slid it into the holster on my belt.

"What's the address?" Sam called. I read it to him, already buttoning my coat and tucking my long hair up into my hat.

Sam typed the address into his computer and read out the name of the person who owned the property.

I froze and stared at Finn. He looked as worried as I felt.

"Say it again," I whispered.

Sam swiveled around again on his chair and looked at the two of us. "Donald Little. You know this guy?"

Chapter Twenty-six

"Something is not right here, Finn. Why was the phone turned on? I met Donald Little, he didn't strike me as a stone-cold killer," I said, holding on to the door handle as Finn took a corner a little too sharply. "And slow down. We're of no help to anyone if we get in a wreck."

"I'm not going to crash," Finn muttered through gritted teeth. "I'm trying to concentrate here. The roads are awful. I can't see shit in this snowstorm. You want to drive? Be my guest."

I shook my head. "No, no, you're doing great."

We pulled up to the front of a modest two-story house with green trim and white shutters. Planters full of snow lined the windows and in the driveway an old black Mustang sat next to a newer red pickup truck.

"Looks like someone is home," I said. We hurried from the Suburban to the front stoop and stood there a moment, shaking the snow from our coats. "How do you want to play this? Guns blazing or cool and collected?"

Finn thought a moment. "Let's go in ready but cool. Be prepared, be sharp."

He pounded on the door until it was opened. Donald Little stood there, in sweatpants and a wool sweater, a beer in one hand and a surprised expression on his face. The surprise turned to panic when he saw who we were.

"What's going on? Is it my kids? They were both here a few minutes ago. Denny! Joy?" he called over his shoulder, up the stairs. "Kids!"

I stepped into the house and laid a hand on his arm. "Mr. Little, it's not your kids. Do you remember me? Gemma Monroe, and this is my partner, Finn Nowlin."

Donald Little nodded, the beer beginning to shake in his hand. "Are you sure my kids are all right?"

I nodded. "I'm sorry if we frightened you. Can you please call your kids and get them down here? Is there anyone else in the house, a girlfriend perhaps? Or another family member?"

Little shook his head. "It's just the three of us. Denny and Joy are probably upstairs watching TV in their rooms. Hang on, I'll be right back."

Finn intercepted him. "I'm going to need you to stay within our sight, sir. Call them from the stairs."

"What is this all about? Do you two have a warrant?" Little asked. He set the beer down on a small console table in the foyer and rubbed his hands together. The color was returning to his cheeks. "Well? Let's see it."

I swallowed. *Shit.* "We don't have a warrant, Mr. Little. I'm afraid there wasn't time to get one. We're investigating the murder of Delaware Fuente. His phone has been missing and tonight, I got word from the phone company that it was turned on, for a few minutes. They traced it to this address."

"That's impossible, what would I be doing with that man's phone?" Little sputtered. But the color had gone out of his face again and the shakes returned to his hands. Above us, on the second floor, two doors opened simultaneously and a minute later, Denny Little and a girl, a few years younger but with the same features, only more feminine, appeared at the top of the steps.

Donald Little looked up at the two of them and started crying.

"Dad? Dad! What's going on?" the girl said. She started down the stairs, a worried look on her face. Denny seemed confused.

Little looked at his son and said, "I'm sorry, Dennis. I'm so sorry. I tried to protect you."

Denny followed his sister down the stairs and we moved from the foyer to the adjoining living room, where there was more room. Donald Little collapsed on a sofa and brought his hands to his face. "Oh, my son. My beautiful boy. I'm so sorry."

Denny looked freaked out. "Dad, stop crying. What's going on?"

Little paused in his sobbing to ask, "Why did you turn the phone on, son? Why?"

Out of the corner of my eye, I saw Joy open her mouth, then shut it quickly. She gently sat down in an armchair in the corner and pulled her knees up to her chest.

Denny cried, "What phone? What are you talking about?"

Donald Little sobbed harder, unable to speak.

I sighed and said, "Delaware Fuente's phone. His cell phone. It was turned on, here, in this house, within the last hour."

"The dead guy? I don't have his phone. Why would I have his phone?" Denny gasped. "I barely knew the guy. Jesus, Dad, what the hell is going on?"

In her chair, Joy drew a hand to her mouth and started chewing on a fingernail.

Donald Little wiped his eyes and took a few deep, calming breaths. When he finally got himself under control, he stood up and gripped his son by the shoulders. "Tell the truth now, Dennis. It will feel much better than these lies."

Denny wrenched himself from his father's grip and reached a hand into his back pocket. Finn moved more quickly than I did and was at Denny's side in a heartbeat. "Slow down, kid. What do you have back there?"

Denny shook his head. "Damn it, I haven't done jack shit. It's my phone, see? The only phone I've got." He held up a black iPhone and waved it in the air.

"How about you, Joy? Do you have a phone?" I asked gently. The girl uncurled herself from the armchair and launched into her father's arms. He caught her, surprised.

"Joy?"

She started crying. "I didn't mean to do something bad. My phone is broken. I dropped it on the bathroom floor and the stupid tile cracked it. I found the blue phone in your room, Dad. I just wanted to borrow it for a minute and text Stacy. But then I got scared so I turned it off and hid it back in your drawer where I found it."

"My God," Finn said under his breath.

Little straightened his daughter up in his lap and took her by the chin. "Joy, you must never, ever look through my drawers again. Those are private. There are things in there that belonged to your mother, things you can have when you're older. And there are dangerous things there, too, from my time in the Army."

"I'm sorry, Daddy. I promise I won't do it again."

"Well, I for one am glad we cleared that up, but Donald, that still doesn't answer the question of why you have a dead man's phone in your possession," Finn said.

Little sighed. "My son killed Delaware Fuente."

"Dad! What the hell? Are you out of your damn mind? I never killed anyone. How could you think that?" Denny screamed at his father.

Joy started crying again and Finn and I, by an unspoken decision, each took a step toward the father and son.

"I saw you! I saw you and Fuente fight, on Friday afternoon, in the parking lot at the academy. I'd just arrived to start my shift and you two were yelling at each other, next to your car. You didn't see me, and I was reluctant to intervene. You've been in so much trouble, Denny, over the years. I thought if I tried to say anything, it might make the situation worse. But I did see you and worse, I heard what you said to that man," Little spoke through a fresh round of tears.

"We were having an argument, Dad, not a fight. There's a difference. What did you hear me say?" Denny asked. His anger had once more been replaced by confusion.

"You said, and I quote, 'Come around Star again and I'll gut you like a fucking fish,' " Donald said. "And then Fuente went back into the school and you got in your car and sat there, smoking."

Denny exhaled and brought his hands to his eyes. He rubbed them and shook his head. "Yeah, okay, I said that. Fuente wouldn't leave Star alone. He kept thinking if he got to her, he could somehow save me."

I asked, "What do you mean, 'got to her'?"

Denny said, "He kept hassling her, telling her

I was lost if I didn't change my ways. The guy thought I was some tough guy putting on an act. He was horrified at the thought of me, God forbid, actually getting expelled. Star was sick of it, sick of him, sick of me, sick of the whole thing. Anyway, she likes my dark side. It turns her on."

From her seat on the couch, Joy watched us with wide eyes. She was probably seeing more than she should, and we really ought to have taken them all down to the station, but we were in the thick of it now and it was too late for that.

"Mr. Little—Donald—it's a far cry from a parking lot disagreement to murder. That can't have been all you saw or heard," Finn prodded.

Little shook his head. "It wasn't. Later that night, much later, I was cleaning one of the labs on the second floor. I saw flashlights outside, bobbing along the trail. I thought it was kids, messing around. I got worried; with the storm, someone could get hurt. Then I thought maybe it was the guys spray-painting the graffiti all over the school and I got mad. So I took my coat and gloves and hat and headed outside. After a few minutes, I came upon Fuente, dead. He'd been stabbed with a hunting knife, just like the one you got for Christmas last year, son. I remembered your threat, and I panicked. I didn't have my cell phone on me, so I took Fuente's, called 911, and then got the hell out of there."

"Why make the call?"

Little shook his head. "I'm a religious man, Detective. I couldn't leave the poor man out there like that all weekend. And I also couldn't let my son spend the rest of his life in jail."

"But, Dad, I did not kill Fuente. I swear to you. That knife is in my car in the glove compartment. Star and I use it for wood carving. I make little squirrels with it, not kill people. What kind of psycho do you think I am?" Dennis said.

He took a seat next to his sister on the couch and slumped back, emotionally drained. Above them, a framed picture of Jesus Christ smiled down beatifically and I wondered, not for the first time, at the contradictions that religion can inspire in some people.

Donald Little, in the middle of the living room, fell to his knees, relief in his eyes. "You didn't kill that man? Oh, thank you, Lord. Thank you, Jesus. I've been living with the pain of this false belief for days. You have no idea how it's been tearing me up inside."

Joy and Dennis stared at their father. Dennis spoke first, "I can't believe you thought I killed him. I'm out of here. As soon as this storm breaks, I'm moving in with Star. Her folks said I could live there, as long as I get a job and pay my own way. They've got an extra room in the basement."

"Don't get her pregnant, Denny," Joy

whispered. "Dad will really lose his shit if you knock her up."

"Joy! Language," Donald Little said. He struggled to his feet and turned to us, realizing we were still in the room. "I'll go get the phone."

"Why don't I come with you?" Finn suggested. Donald nodded and the two of them went up the stairs.

The kids stared at me and I stared back at them. The girl asked, "What's going to happen to my dad now? Is he in trouble? Our mom doesn't live here anymore. Please don't take my dad away."

I exhaled through my nose, unsure how to respond. Dennis put his arm around his little sister and said, "It's going to be fine, Joy. I bet Dad gets in a little trouble. He shouldn't have taken that phone. But Dad, unlike me, doesn't have a record. He'll probably be okay. They won't throw him in the slammer."

I nodded. It was true, most of it. There would be consequences to Donald's actions, that was a given. But . . . could I blame the man for what he did?

Would I have done the same if it was my child I thought I was protecting?

"We're going to need to see that knife, the one in your car, Denny."

He stood and grabbed a coat from the closet in the foyer. I watched through the window as he went to the car, ready to run after him if it looked like he was going to bolt. In the meantime, Finn and Donald came down the stairs. Finn held up a blue cell phone. "Got it."

"And Denny's getting the knife," I replied. A minute later, the boy pushed open the front door and like a wet dog, shook the snow off his coat.

"Here you go," he said. He handed me the knife. It was similar to the murder weapon, but not identical. "Do you have to keep it?"

"Nah," I said, handing it back. "Sounds like you've got more use for it than we do. Squirrels, huh?"

Denny grinned. "Star likes them. She's got a whole collection. I found her a squirrel hat to wear while her hair grows out."

"Is she doing okay?"

He nodded. "She looks like a badass, like Charlize Theron in the new *Mad Max*. She's still upset, though. I think it's going to be a while before she and Becky are on speaking terms again."

"I don't blame her. It was a terrible thing that happened," I said. Finn and Donald moved farther down the hallway, out of earshot, and I knew Finn would be explaining to Donald what would come next. There would be charges; how serious they were remained to be seen.

I felt sorry for the man.

While I had Denny's ear, I might as well make the most of it. "Listen, Denny, what do you know about Grimm?"

Denny shrugged. "He's a piece of shit. If I knew for certain who he was, I'd kick his ass. Not just for Star, but for the others, too."

"What do you mean, if you knew for certain? Does that mean you have some idea?"

Denny moved the knife from one hand to the other. "I have some ideas. Nothing I can prove yet."

I decided I might not have this opportunity again. "It's a teacher, isn't it? Is it Soren Baker? He has access to the students and would know things."

A surprised look fell across Denny's face. "Mr. Baker? You're kidding, right? It's not a teacher, there's no way. Some of the stuff Grimm knows . . . no, you're wrong."

Confused, I said, "Then who do you think Grimm is? Come on, you've been expelled. You don't have any reason to protect anyone at school."

He looked at Joy, still in her seat on the couch, still wide-eyed at all that was happening in her house. Then he leaned in close to me, close enough I could smell his fruity aftershave and cinnamon gum. The knife was dangerously close to my face and I took a step back. Denny didn't seem to notice my sudden wariness.

He said, "I'm not protecting anyone. Do you like riddles? What has two wheels, likes to draw, and spends his time moving around the school, seeing everything but unnoticed by everyone?"

He leaned back and crossed his arms. "Answer that and you've got your Grimm."

Chapter Twenty-seven

I reached for the phone in the dark, missing and knocking it to the ground. I swore and leaned out of the bed, sweeping my hands across the floor until I touched it.

I didn't recognize the number.

"Hello?"

"Gemma?" Her voice was familiar but I couldn't place it. "Gemma Monroe? I'm sorry to call so late . . . so early. I've been working nights; my schedule is all screwy. I'm sorry."

"Who is it, honey?" Brody mumbled from his side of the bed. "It's the middle of the night."

The room was cold and I whispered, "Hang on a second" into the phone, then hurried into slippers and a robe. I walked downstairs, Seamus at my heels. He flopped next to me on the couch and I struggled to clear my mind. I'd gone to bed at midnight after an emotional evening of booking Donald Little on charges of obstructing justice and then sending Denny and Joy off to stay with a relative in Vail.

I rubbed my eyes and peered at my phone. It was four o'clock in the morning. This couldn't be good.

"Who is this?"

"Gemma, it's Cassie. Cassie Gunther. Roland's mom?"

Calling *me?* At four in the morning?

She spoke again. She was scared. "Gemma? Are you still there?"

"Yes, hi. I'm here. Cassie, what is it? What's wrong?"

"It's Roland. He's . . . done something," she said.

"What's going on, what happened?"

A pause, then, "Well, it would be a lot easier to show you. Can you come over? I know it's incredibly early. I'll have coffee, eggs. I've got bacon, too. Please come?"

I thought a moment. "Why not call Finn? He lives in town and could be there in fifteen minutes."

"No, Roland asked for you. He's . . . not a fan of Finn, it seems," Cassie replied. She sounded sad. "So, will you come?"

Next to me, Seamus shifted. He threw a paw across my thigh, imploring me to stay. Upstairs, there was a room with a warm bed, and in the room next to it, there was a baby who needed her mother.

It seemed everyone needed me these days.

"Yes, I'll come. Give me thirty, forty minutes. I need extra-crispy bacon and coffee, very strong coffee."

My headlights cut a narrow swatch through the predawn darkness, exposing a world of white snow and dark morning, light and shadow. I hadn't been up and out on the road so early in a long time. Even the deejays were still sleeping; the local radio stations played drowsy canned music. I switched over to the disc player and let Dire Straits keep me awake all the way to Cassie Gunther's house.

"Some blizzard, huh?"

She met me at the door, a cup of coffee in one hand. In black scrubs, with a pink long-sleeved shirt under them, she looked tired and scared at the same time.

I nodded and took the offered coffee. "Some blizzard. I'm ready for summer. Are you from here originally?"

Cassie shook her head. "New York, by way of Germany, Japan, and South Carolina. I was an Army brat. My dad was a judge advocate, you know, a military lawyer? I moved out here with my ex-husband."

"Roland's dad?"

"No. Roland's dad is somewhere in Texas, last I heard. Fred was a soldier on one of the bases. I was sixteen. He was eighteen. It wasn't a great situation," Cassie said. "My ex-husband, Harry, he adopted Roland. He was a good man. Is a good man, I mean. It just wasn't a good marriage. He lives in Denver and sees Roland a few times a month. He's the one who is paying for Roland to attend the academy. There's no way I could afford that school on my income."

"I see. So, why am I here?"

Cassie asked me to follow her. She led me to a room at the back of the house. It was Roland's bedroom. He sat at a desk in the corner of the room, in his wheelchair, staring out a window that had no curtains. His face was caught in the faint reflection in the glass, a face with no substance, a ghost.

I thought of what Denny Little had told me the day before, and I wondered why so much of an investigation comes down to who's lying and who's not.

Had I been blind? Had Grimm been in front of me all along?

Roland wore blue sweatpants and a yellow T-shirt. His hair was mussed up and he looked like he hadn't slept all night. He must have taken after his birth father, for I saw very little of Cassie's perfect, doll-like features in his face. He was young—young and tired.

"Roland?"

I stepped into the room. He swiveled his neck and smiled. "I took your advice."

"What advice?"

He looked to Cassie. "Mom, can you make breakfast now? You've already seen all of it. I got this."

Cassie's eyes welled up with tears, which she slowly brushed away. "I'm proud of you, son. Always."

Then she left, closing the door behind her, and it was just Roland and me.

He said, "Fairy tales are grounded in morals, in lessons. I started thinking, what if all this time Grimm has been trying to teach us all a lesson? And then I thought, who else teaches lessons? So, I did something that I've done a bunch of times before, but this time, I went further than I've ever gone."

He pointed at his computer. The screen was turned on, but all I saw was a black window with a series of command prompts in white.

"What am I looking at, Roland?"

Roland grinned. He typed something into the computer and the high school's website popped up. Another burst of typing and then another page appeared on screen.

"I hacked the academy's network. Don't ask me the details, you wouldn't understand the coding, the language. Don't bother lecturing me, either. I know it's illegal, that's why I never go this far. But like I said, I started thinking, and I did some messing around, behind the scenes. I wanted to see who had access to what, what files were saved where, that sort of thing."

There was a chair in the corner of the room, covered with dirty clothes and schoolbooks. I shoved them to the floor and dragged the chair over to the computer.

The magic workings of the internet were

beyond my skill level and Roland was showing me a secret world. I put the chair next to his wheelchair and took a seat, a captive audience of one.

"Is this the 'dark web'?"

Roland rolled his eyes. "God, no. Just be quiet, hold on a sec."

"The suspense is killing me. What did you find? And after you show me, I don't want you to ever do this again. This is bad, very bad. Can you manipulate records and grades from here?" I asked. The whole thing was making me nervous.

Roland shook his head but then nodded sheepishly. "I guess I could but that would require more work. I'd have to figure out a way to hide my trail if I actually changed anything. Right now, I'm only looking around. Someone could tell I'd been here, if they were really looking, but the IT guy at school is a douchebag. He'd never work that hard. His system was a joke to bypass in the first place."

"Okay. So?"

"Almost there," Roland said. "Got it. There, do you see it?"

I stared at the computer screen. There were a number of files and folders. Nothing jumped out at me as unusual. "I don't know what I'm supposed to be looking for, Roland."

He pointed to a file saved as Wilhelm, Jacob. It

was one of a series of files under the subheading "Senior Class."

I shrugged. "There's a senior named Jacob Wilhelm?"

Roland shook his head. "No. There's not. However, there were two brothers named Jacob Grimm and Wilhelm Grimm that lived about two hundred years ago. You know, in Germany? And they wrote some stories?"

"Open the file."

"I can't. It's password-protected. I've tried getting around it but nothing I do seems to get me access."

I sat back and exhaled. "So, what? What does this tell us?"

Roland sat back, too. He wheeled around so he could face me.

"I'm at the admin level. There are about ten people who have access to these files," he said. He started ticking names off his fingers: "The systems administrator, the director, the vice principal, the administrative coordinators, and maybe three or four very senior teachers. All the other personnel, the other teachers, the English teachers, they don't have this kind of access, not to this level. At least, I'm pretty sure they don't. There's something else. Someone named Kaspersky has access, too. I've never heard of him."

"Kaspersky Security is the private security firm that supplies the safety officers on campus. Why would he have access to these files?" I asked. "Could this Wilhelm file be anything else? Would Grimm be stupid enough to save something incriminating on the school network? I can't believe that. Maybe the file is one of those, what do you call it, a Trojan horse? A virus? Maybe Grimm put it there as a trap."

Roland hung his head and groaned. "Please, please. Go take a class on Internet security. You sound like my mom. Just don't talk about this stuff, okay? It's not a virus. It's a file, and it's sitting there, and someone at a high level in the school put it there."

"Okay. Say Grimm is Director Silverstein. Couldn't then, say, the vice principal open that file? And see, what? A list of victims? Grimm's next dastardly plan?"

Roland said no. "It's the password. Even though the file is saved there, the password protects it."

"But the IT guy, the systems administrator, he could bypass the password, right?"

Roland looked skeptical. "Maybe. I mean, yes. In theory and in practice, that's usually how these things are set up. But I'm willing to bet the owner of the file has to provide some kind of key for even the systems guy to open it, like a security deposit box at the bank. Because of the confidentiality of these student records."

"That makes sense. Well, shit. So Grimm is probably a teacher."

Roland nodded. He was upset. "I think so. I didn't want to believe it. They're all pretty nice. I mean, some of them are tough, and they come down hard on you, but Grimm is so mean. And even worse, that means a teacher might have killed Fuente. Maybe even Mr. Baker, too."

I told Roland about my conversation with Dr. Pabst. He grew excited. "Yeah, yeah. I can see that. Grimm is thinking he's righting the wrongs of the world. But in reality, he's probably real scared inside, and insecure, and this is his way of controlling his environment."

"Exactly." I nodded.

Roland leaned to the side and switched off his computer. "Man, I'm going to be so happy when we get this guy. So, I told my mom about Grimm. I had to. She wouldn't call you until I told her everything. She's pretty upset. Wait until she finds out he's a teacher. Hang on, I've got to take a leak."

He rolled himself out of the bedroom. I stood up and yawned. Roland's room was about what I expected from a typical teenage American boy. There were posters on the wall of famous bands—Coldplay, Pearl Jam, Nirvana. I hummed a few lines of "Smells Like Teen Spirit" and smiled. A skateboard hung above his bed and I ran a finger along the length of it, pulling away a layer of dust that made me sneeze. It was a skateboard that wouldn't be ridden again, at least not by Roland Five.

On the far wall were built-in bookshelves. I walked over and perused the titles, curious to see where Roland's tastes ran. Stephen King . . . the Harry Potter series . . . *Divergent.* No teenage vampire love stories, I was happy to note. A thick volume caught my eye, mostly because it looked old, while the other books were new. This particular book was bound in rich navy blue leather. There was no title on the spine. I pulled the volume from the shelf and opened it to the title page.

I felt the breath catch in my throat.

Collected Fairy Tales from the Brothers Grimm.

Down the hall, I heard the toilet flush.

It's a coincidence, I told myself. Most kids had some kind of nursery rhyme or fairy-tale storybook in their house. My hands shook as I flipped through the volume. Narrow pink sticky notes marked various chapters.

More sounds from the hallway: a creaking tap turned on, running water, then a door opening and wheels rolling down the wooden floors. I slid the book back on the shelf and returned to my seat. When Roland entered the room, I was on my cell phone, checking my email.

"All set?" he asked, just as Cassie called from the kitchen, "Breakfast's ready! Come and get it."

I nodded and put a bright smile on my face. I'd lost my appetite.

Chapter Twenty-eight

It was eight in the morning when I arrived at the station, tired, feeling like I'd already put in a full day of work. Before I left Cassie and Roland, I'd managed to choke down a few slices of bacon and a fried egg. Somehow my mouth went on autopilot while my mind was a million miles away. Cassie was a talker and didn't notice, or didn't care, that my side of the conversation was banal and trite.

Just ask him, I told myself. He's probably doing research into the Grimm fairy tales, just as he's doing research into the academy's website. But I couldn't bring myself to form the words. Maybe I was afraid of his answer. Maybe I was afraid of what asking the question might do. This was sticky territory; my partner was dating Roland's mom.

There was something else, too. I didn't know why, but the kid trusted me and he was sweet in his own quirky way. But he was smart, too. Was Denny Little right? Could Roland have been playing me all this time? Stringing me along in some kind of a sick game? And what were the implications if Grimm was indeed Fuente's killer? I didn't know that Roland could physically have done the murder. But if he had a partner . . .

Why was I so reluctant to believe Denny?

I knew why but I was loath to admit it. I felt sorry for Roland; he was destined to spend the rest of his life in a wheelchair. He was broken, like Sam Birdshead. And like Sam, I wanted to protect Roland instead of approaching him with the same basic distrust that I approached everyone because of my line of work.

The station was warm and noisy. I threw my coat and bag on my desk and went in search of the party. Chavez intercepted me between the break room and the conference room, a cup of coffee in one hand and a clipboard in the other. He stopped when he saw me and said, "Where have you been?"

"Home. I'm here now. I'm early, in fact. What's going on?"

Chavez jerked his head to the side, motioning for me to join him. "There's been another killing."

My God. *This is only the beginning. . . .*

I followed the chief into the conference room. Finn and a few others were there, gathered around a series of color photographs spread out on the table. I pulled one to me and then pushed it away, gasping.

"Probably a baseball bat," Finn muttered. "If he wasn't found in his own car, it might have taken weeks to identify him."

I made myself take another look at the picture. The man's head was a battered mess of blood, flesh, and bone. He lay curled up in the trunk of a sedan, his hands and legs bound, a single word carved into his bare chest.

"Lobos," I whispered under my breath. "Wolf."

I'd seen wolves before, not here in Colorado, but up north, in Yellowstone, during a back-country ski trip. I was alone; Brody was a few hundred yards behind me, fixing a loose binding on his ski. He'd told me to keep going and he'd catch up. I skied a few minutes, then stopped and waited in a particularly dense thicket of trees near the trailhead. There was a fork up ahead and I wasn't sure if Brody wanted to go back the way we'd come or try the other trail.

It was near dusk when the first wolf appeared. Later, I would say he must have been the alpha, for he was nearly twice as large as his brethren. His fur was darker than black, and indeed I thought he was merely a shadow at first. He was long-legged and silent in the snow, moving with the dignity and grace of a creature that has no firsthand knowledge of fear.

The wolf strolled out of the woods, crossed the trail with one long glance at me, and slipped into the woods again without a sound. His eyes were lit with an inner glow that left them yellow and fathomless. Those eyes held a secret world of knowledge in them, a shared existence with all his forefathers stretching back for hundreds of thousands of years.

This was his land, those eyes told me. I was a short-timer here.

Then the rest of his pack appeared, eight more in total. They paid me no attention, though I could have sworn the sound of my racing heart was louder than anything else in that moment. I didn't start shaking until Brody appeared. We measured the prints of the alpha and Brody estimated he was likely a hundred, a hundred twenty pounds. The park was flush with elk that year; these wolves were eating well.

Finn nudged my shoulder. The chief was staring at me.

"What? I'm here. Who is he?"

Finn said, "It's Soren Baker, Gemma. It's his car. His driver's license is in the wallet and his cell phone in his pocket."

"Oh no," I breathed. "Oh, that poor man."

"Yeah. An early-rising dog walker reported the car at a trailhead in Avondale. It was parked off the lot, practically in the trees, and it spooked the lady enough to call APD. They saw the car was a match for the bulletin I put out on Soren and, well, you know the rest of that story. They called us an hour ago," Finn said.

Chief Chavez added, "That 'Lobos' carving, that's an Arizona biker gang calling card. The

Crazy Wolves. I think Baker's past has finally caught up with him."

"Retaliation? A hit?" I asked. "Why here, why now?"

Finn said, "You saw those records; he's been living under an assumed name. Maybe it's taken this long for the Wolves to find him. They've probably never stopped looking for him. Men like the Wolves don't take too kindly to being scammed out of thousands of dollars."

Chief Chavez picked up one of the photographs and then set it back, disgusted. "What is the world coming to? There's always been violence but this . . . this doesn't happen here. Not in the valley. Listen, Avondale's running the investigation. We'll help as needed but they've got total authority on this. You all focus on the Fuente case. I suppose we can eliminate Baker as a suspect."

"I don't know," I said. "Baker could still be Fuente's killer. It might all be a terrible coincidence that he's now been killed, too."

"Where's the evidence? You've got nothing on Baker for the Fuente case," Chavez said.

"Well, what if this wasn't a gang hit? What if Baker's been murdered by the same person as Fuente?" Finn asked. He raised his hands, placating, when he saw Chavez's expression. "Just playing devil's advocate here, Chief. I know, it's a different M.O. There's no note that we know of. This was an incredibly personal, brutal—as you said—killing. This wasn't one or two death strikes. This was over, and over, and over again. It's rage, pure rage."

"Fuente's killing was different. It was a single strike, calculated. He walked into those woods with someone. Donald Little confirmed that," I added. "We know from the blood in his apartment that Soren Baker was attacked there, and likely taken elsewhere and killed."

"As you said, completely different M.O. Everything tells me you're dealing with two different killers; not one schizophrenic killer," Chief Chavez said. He walked to the front of the room and listed the differences between the killings on the whiteboard.

"Campbell."

Chavez and Finn looked at me strangely. Finn said, "Come again?"

"Campbell," I said again insistently. "What if Campbell and Baker had dealings together? Campbell's got a whole crew of goons. One of them kills Fuente for the inheritance on the New Jersey property and another one kills Baker, for some reason we don't know about yet."

"And the 'Lobos' carving?" Finn asked skeptically.

"Oh, come on! Black Hound Construction? Hounds? Wolves? Practically the same animal?"

Finn spoke. "You know my Nan was from

Ireland. She raised first my mother, then me, on Celtic mythology. Some of it is pretty fucking gruesome, gave me nightmares for weeks. The black hound is often associated with the devil. It's considered a harbinger, or a portent, of death. Seems right on, when you consider some of Campbell's men. Wolves, hounds . . . ex-convicts . . . in their hearts, they're all predators, one and the same."

"Yeah? And sometimes a black hound is just a damn dog. You two have gone and lost your minds. While I don't agree with Alistair Campbell's choice of employees, the man's done nothing illegal. Whatever happened to innocent until proven guilty?" Chavez asked. He added a few more words to the whiteboard, other differences between the killings. The locations of the bodies; the lack of a note in Baker's case; the anonymous call tipping us off to Fuente's death.

"Don't forget, Chief, the anonymous call only came in because Donald Little, among other things, has a conscience. If he hadn't come across Fuente's body, it wouldn't have been found until Monday. Maybe not even Tuesday, if no one took the footpath to get to class. Just like Soren Baker, Fuente was tucked away in the woods," I said. "He was never meant to be found so early."

"And like Fuente, Soren Baker has a tie to the

academy," Finn added. "Hell. We can't get away from that school."

I told Finn and Chavez about my early morning with Roland Five and his mom, Cassie. If Finn was upset that she had called me, and not him, he didn't show it. I told them about finding the Grimm Brothers' book in Roland's bedroom, and Dennis Little's suspicion that Roland was in fact Grimm.

"So bring him in for formal questioning, Gemma. Why haven't you done that yet?" Chavez asked. He straightened his tie and adjusted his belt. "You more than anyone else in this department have a way with the teens."

I nodded. The chief was right; it was time to bring Roland in and ask him some hard questions. "I will, I promise. In the meantime, I think Finn and I should go have that conversation with Campbell now. And after, I'll let Vice Principal Moreno know about Baker's death. What a week that woman's having."

As we left the room, Chavez offered one final piece of advice. "Be careful, you two. If the Crazy Wolves have come to town, we're in for a world of hurt."

Chapter Twenty-nine

The Tate Lodge was a sprawling estate, listed on the National Register of Historic Places. In the 1930s, before the residence was bought by a Japanese businessman and turned into a hotel, it was the private home of one of Cedar Valley's last living silver barons. While the place was in his hands, there'd been a number of unusual deaths; one woman had fallen from a fourth-floor turret, another had drowned in a near-empty bathtub. An arborist bled out after an unwieldy chainsaw took off his arm, and a gardener with severe allergies stumbled into a hornet's nest. There were other, more mundane deaths, whose details hadn't lived on in such morbid retellings.

Over the years, enough visitors had experienced ghostly encounters—strange visions of figures in white, heartbreaking moans that seemed to seep from the walls—that a popular television show, *Seekers of the Dead*, had filmed an episode there. Alas, the dead proved shy that particular night and the television host, a brash and cocky man from Hollywood, proclaimed Tate Lodge free of any ghosts. He offered faulty electrical wiring and too-strong evening cocktails as the likely explanation for the sightings.

Slowly, though, the dead began to appear again. The rumors and whispers continued of strange sightings and awful noises in the darkest hours of the night. It was a spooky place to visit, no matter the time of the day or the strength of the sun.

We paused in the massive lobby to remove our coats. A smiling, attractive concierge took them and told us that ten minutes earlier, she'd seen Alistair Campbell come down from his room and head to the bar.

"The restaurant food is just so-so, but the bartender makes a mean espresso. Sometimes he's got biscotti," she whispered with a wink. "Mr. Campbell likes to start his mornings there."

Finn and I thanked her and walked past the grand staircase. Over the years, the touch of thousands of hands had polished the banister to a high gleam.

"Do you believe in ghosts?"

I said yes.

Finn looked surprised. "I wouldn't have thought that."

"Why not?" I shrugged. "I think the fool is the man that believes he knows what's out there. We live in a mysterious world, Finn. We're nothing but atoms and molecules, walking around like we own the place. Who's to say there's not spirits around us? What happens to all that energy after death?"

He looked at me sideways, a hint of laughter in his voice. "I guess it's a matter of opinion. Get it? Matter?"

I groaned. "I get it. You forget I share my bed with a scientist. I'm impervious to nerd jokes."

We found Campbell sitting alone at the Tate's bar, sipping an espresso and scanning a newspaper. In the fireplace on the opposite wall, red and yellow flames danced merrily to a tune of their own hearing. Turkish rugs embroidered with rich scarlet and deep indigo threads lay on wooden floors that shone with fresh polish. The room was warm and cozy; on the wall, the eyes of men whose names I did not know watched us from somber portraits, their faces frozen for the ages.

"This is a treat. To what do I owe the honor?" Campbell asked. He folded his newspaper and used it to gesture toward the window. "It's early, on a bastard of a day. Please tell me this snow does eventually stop."

I nodded. "Five, maybe six more weeks. We'll get about a week of sunshine. Then the snow will return. This is nothing. Wait until early April, when we get spring snow like a wet wool blanket, heavy and stubborn, and your soul is so desperate for warmth that you'd do just about anything for a little heat."

Campbell pursed his lips and set his paper

down on the bar. "Have you ever spent much time in the north, say, Canada or Alaska?"

Finn and I both said no.

Campbell continued. "I spent six months in Fairbanks, Alaska, in the late eighties. There's a misconception that it is dark up there for twenty-four hours a day in winter. That's not true; even on the winter solstice, we'd still see about four hours of true daylight. No, what really got me, and what no one talks about, is the ice fog. When the temperature drops to thirty degrees below zero, a sea of tiny ice crystals frozen in the air begins to roll in. The trees become ghosts. The town is obscured. You don't know the meaning of the word *cold* until you've stood in an ice fog and turned in a circle with not a damn idea of which way is up or down. That's a terrible feeling, not knowing your way home."

Finn said, "We didn't come to talk about the weather."

"Please, I'm all ears," Campbell said. He stared at us, a pleasant smile on his face. His eyes, though, were cold and sharp.

"There's been another death. Soren Baker. He was an English teacher at the high school, originally from Australia. Did you know him? He also went by Simon Cook in a previous life," Finn said.

"Baker, Baker . . . I don't believe I ever had

the pleasure. You say he was a teacher at the school, too? I'm surprised you're not there right now, questioning people who knew him. Why are you wasting your time here?" Campbell asked.

"Because so far, Mr. Campbell, you've got the strongest motive of anyone to kill Delaware Fuente," I said.

"I don't need the money. I told you once, I'm selling the property as soon as it's in my hands," Campbell replied. He took another sip of espresso and a displeased pucker took over his mouth. "Damn, the coffee has gone cold."

"Why do you hire ex-convicts? You don't strike me as a bleeding heart liberal," Finn said.

Campbell pushed his coffee to the side and wiped his mouth with the napkin. "You don't understand my concern for these people. You see thugs and criminals when you look at my men. I see broken beings that have been devoid of love and care for so long they physically react to it when they finally experience it, in rashes and hives. It takes a lifetime to build up trust and a moment to destroy it. I spent my youth in foster homes and orphanages, seeing the worst that people will do to one another in the name of discipline. Spare me your judgment and save it for those who need it. Now, is there anything else?"

"Did you kill Fuente?"

"I did not," Campbell said. He scratched his chin. Something like regret journeyed across his face and then it was gone, moving as quickly and silently as the wolf I'd seen in Yellowstone. "I spent Friday night in the company of Mayor Cabot and a few of her cronies. Lovely bunch of rotten apples. She won't be mayor very long, I predict. I was with them from about seven o'clock until midnight, here, in the bar. There are a dozen people who can vouch for that."

"Why didn't you tell me before?" I asked. "Why didn't you tell me when you were in my house?"

Campbell smiled. "You never asked me, Ms. Monroe. Tell me, did you look to Fuente's words as I suggested?"

"Yes. So far I've found nothing of note."

"Well, perhaps I was wrong then," Campbell said. He spread his arms open and added, "Forgive me."

"You must have meant something by that."

Campbell shook his head slowly. "Only a clearly mistaken belief that the best writers leave something of their soul in their works. I assumed if a man is murdered, there lies an answer to it somewhere."

Finn spoke. "Do you know who killed Fuente?"

A pause. "No, I don't believe so."

Finn and I glanced at each other. Campbell noticed, and smiled sadly. "Your list of suspects is my list, I'm afraid. I'm not completely naïve nor am I especially stupid. I know my men are capable of great violence. I know a few of them—Roget, Turtle—they were aware of the deal I'd made with Fuente. These men tremble against their urges and wage silent, internal battles that we can only imagine in our worst dreams. They're here now, upstairs, in their rooms, available to answer your questions. But understand this—your actions will rip scabs off old wounds, wounds I've tended to and brought nearly to healing. Do you know what happens when you tear a scab? You expose raw, vulnerable tissue."

"What's your point? If I want pop psychology I can watch Dr. Phil," Finn said. He walked to the fireplace and fanned his hands before the dancing flames. "You're boring, Mr. Campbell. I believe you consider yourself a savior among these men. But you're nothing more than a ringleader. You surround yourself with followers, troubled men that pick up the scent of your cold heart and fall in place, tails wagging, to trail in your line of bullshit."

Campbell finished his drink and carefully tucked a ten-dollar bill under the porcelain dish. He stood and as he walked to the door of the bar, he slowed and leaned close to me. His breath tickled the fine, downy hair near my ear. "I like you, Ms. Monroe. You possess an inner strength that I've not come across before in someone so young. I'm not a bad person. You want to believe that I am, because it's easier for you, in your line of employment, but you're struggling. Lose the boorish fool the next time you visit me."

Chapter Thirty

There were threads connecting these cases—Fuente, Baker, Grimm, the Rabbit Man—but they were as invisible to me as radio waves, naked to the human eye. The fortune cookie at Luigi's had given me clear and simple instructions: *Be on the lookout for coming events; they cast their shadows beforehand.*

What shadow was I missing? What event was barreling toward me unseen, unnoticed?

I left Finn at the Tate Lodge to question the Black Hounds while I headed to the academy to let Vice Principal Moreno know of Soren Baker's murder.

I found Moreno in her office. She looked surprised to see me but said her calendar was free and she'd be happy to meet. As before, she brewed coffee and offered me a seat. She'd curled her hair, and it was short and chic, and I complimented her on it. She thanked me and mentioned something about the season leaving her feeling restless.

Surprised, I said, "I feel quite the opposite in winter. I think the snow and the cold are so grounding. For me, the restlessness hits at the end of the summer, as the nights grow colder and the days shorter. I always get the urge to pack it in and move to Hawaii. I'd chase the sunshine west, all year round."

She nodded. "I understand that feeling, too. My restlessness is not so much weather related as holiday related, I think. That stretch between Christmas and Easter can be so bleak and long. And don't get me started on Valentine's Day or St. Patty's Day. I'm talking about the real holidays, the ones you build family traditions around."

"You're on to something there. That was quite a storm we had, wasn't it?"

She nodded. "Director Silverstein and I discussed closing the school again today, but yesterday was the fifth snow day these kids have had since school started in September. Every day we close is another day's worth of curriculum we then have to squeeze in. What would you have done?"

Surprised to be asked, I shrugged. "I'm not sure. Probably closed. I guess I would have weighed the risks of a car accident against another day of algebra and frog dissections. It's not really my area of expertise."

"Of course it is," Moreno said. Behind her, the coffeepot chimed. "Excuse me."

She poured us each a cup of coffee and then handed mine to me. "You're a reasonable, afety-conscious person, and a new parent. Don't you want your child to be safe *and* be educated?"

"Well, sure. I just meant . . . I've been out of school a long time, Ms. Moreno. I see the kids here, and in town, and they're a completely different species than the kids I grew up with. So I don't feel qualified to gauge the tempo of their learning."

"Fair enough, I suppose."

She straightened the framed picture of her daughter on her desk and then looked at me. "What is it you wish to talk about?"

I took a deep breath. "Soren Baker is dead. He was killed sometime in the last day or two, his body left in Avondale. I'm so sorry."

Moreno gasped, her fingers moving to her mouth and then back to her lap. She stared at me, shocked, reaching for words that struggled to come.

"I know this is awful news. Ms. Moreno, I also need to tell you that Baker had a very dark past. He was wanted in Arizona on a number of charges, some of which were quite violent. We believe he passed your background check using a false name and social security number. We also believe that his past may have caught up with him; it appears he may have been murdered by a motorcycle gang," I said. "Did he have a list of kin, of emergency contact numbers, on file here at the school?"

"Oh, I can't believe it," Moreno said slowly,

her eyes filling with tears. "I think he has a mother or an aunt in Melbourne. This is terrible. It's going to be devastating for the children. Fuente was bad enough, but Soren? Soren's been here for quite a while. He's beloved."

"We'll help you however we can. Ms. Moreno, there's another matter I need to discuss with you. It's regarding Grimm. Have you made any progress with your internal investigation?"

She took a deep breath and shook her head. "No, to be truthful, I haven't gotten around to launching it yet. I know a school bully like this should be our first priority, but with Fuente's murder, and now this . . . we'll get to it when we can."

As gently as I could, I said, "I spoke with a psychologist. He worked up a rough psychological profile on Grimm. He used words like *clever, advanced,* and *sophisticated.* Now, does that sound like a high school student to you?"

The implication of my words was clear. Moreno stood and straightened her jacket. She wiped away the tears in her eyes. "What are you saying?"

"Grimm might be a teacher."

She shook her head. "I don't believe it. Not one of my teachers. There's no way any of them would or could do something like that, behind my back."

"Please, sit. Do you have that much control over their actions and behavior?"

Moreno sat back down. "I'd like to think so. What else did this psychologist say about Grimm?"

I thought back to Dr. Pabst's words. "Grimm is rigid, controlling, but hides it well. He's insecure and likes to control his environment. He actually probably thinks he is helping the kids by his bullying—of course he doesn't see it as 'bullying'—because Grimm thinks he knows best. Grimm thinks he is teaching the students about consequences. He's preparing them for the real world."

From the small reception area next to Moreno's office, I heard someone enter and start opening drawers. A young woman appeared in Moreno's doorway, then apologized when she saw me. Moreno waved away the apology and told the young woman that she'd be there in a minute.

The vice principal bit her lip and checked her watch. "I'll be right back, Detective, I need to pass on a few messages to my secretary. She came in late today on account of the weather."

Moreno stepped out. I heard Moreno mention "suspension" and "final reports." Checking my own watch, I sighed deeply, feeling the air fill my lungs. I held it a moment and then slowly released, exhaling out tension and stress. It was a move I'd learned in a long-ago yoga class.

Moreno and the secretary continued to chat.

Bouncing my crossed legs, I glanced around the office. Moreno had rearranged the diplomas on her wall. They hung perfectly straight, the edges of the frames mere centimeters from one another. There was the undergraduate degree in modern languages and two graduate degrees in education and business administration.

Modern languages . . . I pulled my phone from my purse and did a quick internet search. It turns out the degree usually required at least two foreign language proficiencies and time spent abroad.

Foreign languages. Time abroad.

From behind me, Moreno came into the office. She paused a moment, as though taking the temperature of the room, then gently closed the door. "I'm sorry about that. Annette is wonderful but scatterbrained at times. But we got it all straightened out."

I tilted my chin toward her office wall. "Did you spend time out of the country?"

Moreno smiled. "Yes, I spent my sophomore year in Italy and my junior year in Germany. Those were my languages, Italian and German. I dabbled in French but I could never perfect the accent. *C'est la vie.*"

"It's you, isn't it?"

Moreno looked at me curiously. "What are you talking about?"

"Grimm. You're Grimm. The Jacob Wilhelm file is yours."

"How the hell do you know about . . ." Moreno trailed off. She took a seat at her desk and sipped her coffee. I watched her hands tremble as they held the cup. "As I said, I'll speak to the faculty members about this matter. We'll get to the bottom of it."

I shook my head. "You're an abuser. You've been entrusted with these kids' lives, their futures, and you sit here and play God. You write the kids into these twisted fairy tales and then you pull the puppet strings. How could you?"

Moreno paled at my words.

She whispered, "I never meant for it to get so out of control. I thought . . . I thought I was helping them. You have no idea what it's like to be with these kids, day after day, and know that no matter what you do, they could walk out the door and be the next Aurora theater shooter, or the next Charles Manson. You want to talk about responsibility? You have no idea of the meaning of the word."

"You aren't their parent. You hurt people in the process. Star, Becky—they are scarred. Paul Runny doesn't speak anymore. Who knows how many others you have brutalized? Don't give me some bullshit about how it's your job to do that to people," I said, pointing to the framed picture of Moreno's daughter. "What's her name—Diane? Diana? Would you want someone bullying Diana?"

"Of course not. But if she was misbehaving, making the wrong kinds of decisions . . . then yes, I think I would want someone to step in. Someone who cared and was smart enough to realize their role in life might just be to get these kids turned around!" Moreno said. She threw up her hands. "We are turning into a society of self-centered, cell phone–obsessed, brainless twits. Moments, events—they don't matter unless they're posted for the whole world to see and 'like.' These kids barely know how to carry on a conversation. I'm scared for the future."

"I am, too, but that doesn't give you the right to do this."

"Then who is going to help them? You? Their parents? I don't think so. These kids, they post their exploits on Instagram and Facebook like they are things to be proud of. Just try to punish them, I dare you. These helicopter parents . . . if little Johnny doesn't get a participation medal or Susie comes home crying because God forbid a teacher held her accountable . . . do you know how many calls I field in a single day? Dozens. In these parents' eyes, their kids' *feelings* are more important than their actions," she said.

"And the Grim Reaper drawings? That was your work, too?"

She nodded and rubbed her eyes. "Yes. I wanted a calling card, something sinister."

"So what do you do, troll Facebook and figure out who to punish?"

Moreno shook her head. "I have students who bring concerns to me. I look into them and if there is any validity, then I follow up. It's that simple."

"Wouldn't the consequences be more effective if they were actually real-life, adult consequences? You could have turned in evidence of Becky's cheating to Stanford and she'd have been rejected. Why make her cut Star's hair?" I asked.

"Why should Becky be the only one who gets a life lesson? If ten or twenty or fifty other kids can take something away from it, why not?" Moreno replied.

I shook my head, blown away by the sheer ridiculousness of her argument. She was delusional. Moreno saw the look in my eyes and hung her head. "So what happens now?"

"To start, you're finished here. You're going to turn in your resignation within the hour to Director Silverstein, effective immediately. Then you're going to drive to the police station and turn yourself in for abuse of power and likely a host of other charges. I won't damage these kids any further by escorting you out in handcuffs. On the way there, you may wish to get in touch with a therapist."

Fresh tears streamed down Moreno's face. They softened the bluntness of her power suit, and the sharp edges of her office, but they had no effect on me.

"What will I do? I've dedicated my life to these children. They are my whole world."

I stood and took hold of the framed picture of her daughter. I slid it closer to Moreno and tapped on it. "I'd start by thinking long and hard about this kid. You and I, we're nearly halfway done with our time here on Earth. What kind of a mother do you want Diana to know? You want to leave a meaningful legacy? Start with her. You owe her. You owe all these kids."

Chapter Thirty-one

Before I left the high school parking lot, I sent Roland a text message: *Grimm's done. You don't have to worry anymore.*

His reply was immediate. *"Who?"*

I shook my head and typed back, *"Doesn't matter. It's over."*

Back at the station, I had a number of notes and messages waiting for me, including one from Bucky Shepherd, my contact with the Denver Police Department's cyber-crimes unit. As promised, they had prioritized Fuente's laptop and Bucky had bypassed Fuente's passwords, then taken a good, hard, long look at the documents; or rather, the lack of documents. Bucky's message was short and to the point—there weren't any files or documents stored in the laptop that I hadn't already seen.

In other words, there wasn't a trace of a memoir or any other work in progress.

Not only that, but aside from my powering the machine on and off, the laptop hadn't been turned on in weeks. If Fuente was writing and saving his work to a flash drive, or even just emailing it to himself, he wasn't doing it from this computer.

I sat back and considered that.

I thought about a writer who doesn't write.

Fuente had come to Cedar Valley for a respite from his day-to-day life on the East Coast. He came intending to work on his memoirs and give a few guest lectures. Instead, he'd written nothing and been killed at the very school at which he taught.

And how did we know that was Fuente's purpose in coming to town? I reviewed my notes and found that it was Lila Conway who first mentioned the memoirs. Had Brad Choi, Fuente's agent, said anything about them? I thought back. I didn't think so.

Moriarty walked over and dropped a file folder on my desk. "From the doc. It's the final report on the Fuente autopsy. She stopped by but you weren't in."

"Thanks."

I read through Dr. Ravi Hussen's report. She took her duties as the town's medical examiner seriously and considered herself a final care-taker to the dead. I'd already made her swear to do my postmortem, should I have the unfortunate luck to expire early in an unnatural manner.

The details of his death hadn't changed. Fuente was stabbed in the abdomen with a hunting knife. But as I read the report, I was once again struck by a number of things that seemed out of place. The man wore no hat, no gloves, and no jacket. To me, that suggested a man who didn't think he would be out *in* the blizzard in the first place.

I called Lila Conway's home number, then remembered she was likely at work, at the school. An administrative secretary answered and said Lila had taken another sick day. I asked if I could speak to someone who might be aware of office space in the high school. The secretary sounded confused about my request, but she said she could forward my call to someone who might be able to help me. I waited patiently while the phone *beep-beep-beep*ed at me.

"This is Darren Chase. Can I help you?"

I closed my eyes. The basketball coach's voice was like molasses, his thick Southern accent softening his words and making me think of palmetto trees swaying gently in a tropical breeze. I could practically smell the salty air and feel the damp breeze on my suddenly warm cheeks.

"Hello?" he asked again, and in my mind, I gave my cheek a nice, hard slap.

"Darren, hi, it's Gemma. Gemma Monroe. Did they put you in charge of offices, as well, at the academy?"

He laughed. "I'm not. Jeff, the instructor I'm replacing, has been leading up a committee that's doing a space study. I offered to sit in and help keep things moving along. We're looking at everything from ergonomics to feng shui. Are you in the market for a new workspace?"

"No, not at the moment. Listen, I heard that Delaware Fuente—John Firestone—had some sort of office space there at the school? Is that right?"

I crossed my fingers that he might be able to provide me with some information.

I was in luck.

"Yup, sure. John found a little nook for himself up in the attic storage area. It's hardly more than a crawlspace but there's a small desk and a great view of the fields."

"Thanks, Darren. I'll swing by and check it out this evening. What time do the front doors lock?"

He said, "Well, hold on just a minute. I'm a three-minute walk away. I'll go see if there's anything there. For all I know, he cleared it out or took things home with him when he left for the day. I'll call you right back."

Before I could protest, or ask him not to disturb a possible crime scene, Darren Chase had hung up. I slowly did the same and bit my lip. Okay, then. I'd sit tight and wait. I tackled my in-box and the rest of my messages, setting aside the one from Bucky Shepherd in Denver to follow up on the missing memoirs. Most of my emails were routine; among other things, there was a reminder my certifications were coming due in a few months and a thank-you note for a small donation I'd made to a charity organization.

There were also three voice mails from Missy Matherson, each sounding more heated than the last. The third message referenced "intentional withholding of information by the Cedar Valley Police Department," and I felt my blood begin to boil. Balancing the public's right to know with the discretion an active investigation requires is always a delicate dance, and Missy Matherson was getting too fresh for my taste.

The phone rang twice before she picked up.

"Missy, hi, Gemma Monroe. Do you have a pickle up your ass or what?"

"No, I do not, and that's a disgusting image. I'm simply hoping for an update, same as everyone else," Missy said. "Are the Soren Baker and Delaware Fuente murders connected? Is a serial killer targeting teachers? Or is this just the start? Are the children safe?"

"No comment. Missy, you know you can call the department's public information office directly, right? Did they teach you that in school?"

"Funny, a comedian and a cop. You should go on tour. People are getting scared, Gemma. There have been two murders in less than a week and your cute little 'no comment' leads me to believe you all don't know jack shit. There's talk that Mayor Cabot will be holding a town hall meeting soon. Want to know how much business the gun shops have seen in the last day?"

I heard steady typing in the background and wondered what she was writing. "And I'm sure none of the panic has anything to do with your articles. You're a fearmonger, Missy. Soren Baker was killed in Avondale, not Cedar Valley. Call them if you want information."

"Fearmonger? Oh, honey, I've been called a lot worse." Missy laughed. "All right, you don't want to play nice? That's fine. I've got a number of other people more than willing to give me what I'm looking for. This was a courtesy call, Gemma. Nothing more."

She hung up and almost immediately my phone rang.

"This is Gemma."

"Hi, it's me. Darren. I checked out the cubby and there's a heavy parka with what look like gloves sticking out of the pockets. I think I remember Fuente wearing the same jacket, so I'm fairly certain that it's his. There's also an umbrella and some snow boots tucked under the desk. There's nothing else, no papers, no calendar, not even a pencil. I didn't touch anything."

I exhaled a breath I hadn't realized I was holding. "Darren, you're a godsend. I'll head over there in a few minutes."

"Perfect," he said. "I'll meet you outside McKinley Hall and let you into the attic. We keep it locked up most of the time. So, did I do good?"

"Yes, you did good."

"What do I get?"

I paused, my face feeling warm. "What do you mean?"

"You know, do I get a reward or something? Like, dinner with my favorite officer?" Darren asked. He laughed at my silence, then turned serious. "I never got a chance to thank you for what you did last fall. You closed a painful chapter in a lot of people's lives. A drink and some grub is the least I can do."

It was a sweet gesture, and I told him as much. I took a rain check but promised to reach out once things settled down on my end. It was the sort of promise you make hoping you never have to fulfill it.

Darren Chase was trouble through and through.

I headed back to the school, feeling fatigue creep into my bones and muscles. I'd been up since the crack of dawn with Cassie's early morning phone call. I felt as though I'd driven across town fifteen times in the last ten hours. I decided that after feeding Grace and giving Brody a kiss hello, the very next thing I'd do when I got home was a face-plant, straight into bed.

The academy's parking lot had cleared out; only a handful of cars remained and a few students stood by them, talking in loud voices, laughing. I parked close to the entrance and pulled an evidence kit from the trunk of my car.

Darren was as good as his word, and he was waiting for me on the steps of McKinley Hall, leaning against the railing, watching the afternoon fade into dusk. He wasn't alone; Bowie Childs stood nearby, cleaning his fingernails with a pocketknife.

"Well, if it isn't the girl wonder," Childs said. "Back for more clues, Nancy Drew?"

Darren shifted uncomfortably and then pushed off the railing. "Gemma, I think you know Bowie."

I nodded. "Yes, I've had the pleasure."

Childs folded his pocketknife and slipped it into his jacket. "You know, you're supposed to check in with me every time you come on campus. Those are the new rules. That comes straight from Kaspersky. This is a private academy, after all. Private property."

"I'm just here on a social call," I replied, straightening my shoulders and looking Childs directly in the eye. "Visiting an old friend."

"Ah, I'm just teasing. The police are always welcome here. Don't be a stranger, ma'am, all right?" Childs said. He backed away from us with a grin and then turned around and headed down the footpath.

"Sorry about that," Darren said. "Bowie has

an odd way of turning up when you least expect it. He's done some work at Cedar Valley High, too, odd jobs here and there. I think he may have been fired, though. Listen, follow me. It's not often I can help fight real crime in this good town of ours. Most of the time, I'm just trying to keep my basketball players from beating up on one another."

He led me down the hall to a staircase near the administration offices. The lights were off and I wondered if Justine Moreno had left immediately after our conversation or if she'd sat in there a while, thinking on her actions, wondering how she found herself doing such terrible things.

Darren and I walked up the stairs to the second floor, then he pointed at a locked door with a sign on it that read "Restricted Access." I raised an eyebrow at him and he grinned.

"I've got the key, don't worry. Fuente must have had one, too. This is the only way in and out. We've got a ton of crap up there in the attic, old gym mats and broken chairs and desks, blackboards that haven't been used since the seventies. You'll see, somehow he managed to hobble together this little cubby. It's more like a hidey-hole," Darren said. He unlocked the door and held it open. "Ladies first."

I headed up the narrow stairs, aware that my rear was still carrying the last five pounds of pregnancy weight and equally aware that Darren had a first-row seat to those same five pounds as he walked behind me. "Does Bowie Childs patrol inside the school, too? Or just the exterior?"

Darren said, "He comes inside, too. He likes to check in on the classes and sneak snacks from the cafeteria. I get the sense he always wanted to be a cop. All he can talk about these days is the murder. Fuente this, Fuente that. It's like he's trying to solve the case himself but the poor guy is short a few lightbulbs if you know what I mean."

"I know exactly what you mean." We were halfway up the stairs when I paused. Darren stopped, too, nearly running into me. "What is it?"

"I heard something." I took another step then stopped.

"There," I whispered. "Did you hear it?"

From somewhere above us, deep in the attic space, came the noise again: a low moan, followed by a quiet cry.

I pointed up and whispered, "Someone's crying up there."

Darren nodded. He said, "Maybe a student? Whoever it is shouldn't be there. It's not safe; you could practically get tetanus just by breathing in the air."

"Darren, two of your peers have been killed

in the last week. Tetanus is the last thing I'm worried about at this school."

We moved quickly up the last few stairs, pausing to stop and listen at the top. The noise came again, only this time the cry was louder, more intense, that of someone in great pain, and I followed the sound of it past what appeared to be Fuente's cubby and around the corner of a large stage prop of a windmill.

The room was dim; only the faintest bit of daylight entered the space through the dormer windows set in high near the ceiling. It took me a minute to register what I was seeing, between the pale writhing bodies, each emitting sharp cries, and the undulating blue gym mat, sending dust up everywhere.

"Oh, shit," I said as a man and woman scrambled to cover themselves with their clothes. I saw their faces and gasped, half laughing with relief that we hadn't stumbled upon a murder in the making. "Well, hi. You're not exactly who I expected to find here."

"What the hell," Darren breathed. He put a hand on my shoulder and pulled me back, allowing the couple some modicum of privacy. "Jesus Christ."

"No kidding. Did you have any idea?"

Darren shook his head. "No, and I almost asked her out last year. I'll never get that image out of my head. For both good and bad."

"Her or him?"

Darren thought a moment. "Both." Then he started laughing and soon was struggling to stand up right. Finally he gave up and collapsed into a chair that was too small for him. It fell over under the weight of his body and he lay there, on the floor, crying with laughter.

"Shut up, this is mortifying. For us and them," I said. "Seriously, get a grip."

From behind us came a hushed, female voice. "Excuse me, but was that Coach Chase and Gemma Monroe? What are you two doing up here?"

A man's voice added, "You can come back. We're dressed now. And Darren, we can hear you laughing. Do you mind? I'm going to get a complex."

Darren picked himself off the floor and wiped at his eyes. He whispered an apology and took a moment to compose himself. Then we joined Harold Chapman and Peggy Greenway on the other side of the blackboard.

"We started dating two months ago. It was such a surprising turn of events. We've always hated each other, you see. Hal is such a modernist, and I can't see the point, once you get past the classics," Peggy Greenway explained.

Harold Chapman said, "Neither of us expected this. It started at the holiday party. One minute we were standing at the bar, and the next, it was as though someone had cast us in a fairy tale. The lights seemed to grow dim, the music receded, and our hands brushed against each other."

"Hal has the most masculine hands," Peggy said with a nod, taking his hands in hers. Her makeup had rubbed off, and she looked softer, less intense, than she had in our previous meetings.

"And now, we can't keep our hands off each other. I proposed last week. This is the best relationship I've ever been in. And Margaret's the most beautiful woman I've ever known," Harold said. "But we've had to keep it a secret. Silverstein and Moreno don't approve of office romances. They would never allow us to both continue working here."

"And I take it you were together last Friday night? When Fuente was killed?" I asked gently. Watching the two of them, how sweet they were together, was almost enough to forgive any lies they might have told to protect the secret.

They both nodded. Peggy said, "My mother has the geriatric Maltese. As you saw the other day, I can't stand dogs. I'm so sorry we lied; we each said the first thing that came to mind. We couldn't tell you we were together. We couldn't risk it. We've had to keep up this charade of hating each other. And to tell you the truth, it's been like foreplay. We'll probably pretend we hate each other for the next twenty years!"

I nodded. "I understand. I think Coach Chase does, too, right, Coach?"

From across the room, Darren bobbed his head up and down.

"At some point, though, sooner rather than later, you need to tell Director Silverstein about this," I said. "I'm serious. Better he hear it from you two than he finds out on his own. Maybe, since you're getting married, he'll let you stay teaching here."

Peggy and Harold nodded. After they left, and Darren finished another fit of giggles, we looked over Fuente's cubbyhole. There was a jacket, gloves, a pair of boots, and an umbrella. Tucked behind some dusty old textbooks, we found a half-empty pint of whiskey, a few cans of ginger ale, and a copy of *Time* magazine with a recent publication date. There was also a plastic wrapper from a sandwich, the kind you buy from a vending machine.

I held up the wrapper and Darren nodded. He said, "They sell them down in the cafeteria. Nasty but they'll do in a pinch."

I thought out loud. "Lila Conway drops you off in the morning. You teach your class and then you finish by lunchtime. If you leave the school, you're dressed in your winter gear because your plan is to head home after. Isn't it? Or do you come up here and wile away the afternoon? Why? Are you meeting someone?"

"Fuente wasn't killed until late, is that right?" Darren asked. He squatted down and picked up Fuente's boots and looked at the bottom of them.

"Correct. What are you doing?"

Darren shrugged. "I don't know, looking for clues. That's a long time to sit up here, drinking and reading one crappy issue of *Time*."

"You're right about that. Okay, I'm going to take this stuff with me and then you're going to get the locks changed on that access door. Lord help us if some poor student stumbles up here and finds Hal and Margaret re-creating *Romeo and Juliet*."

"That's morbid."

I smacked him gently on the back. "The sex, not the dying."

We parted ways at the parking lot. I expected to see Childs's truck or another one of Kaspersky's security vehicles but the lot was empty. I wondered if Kaspersky was staggering his men, having them do the bulk of their shifts when the students were in session.

It made me nervous, knowing there was a killer out there on the loose and possibly the only thing standing between him and the students was Bowie Childs.

Then I decided that Childs was better than

nothing, and we were doing all we could on our end to catch Fuente's killer.

I headed up the canyon, weary to the bone and trying to stay positive.

I listened to two voice messages from Finn as I drove. The first was that two men had been arrested in Utah in connection with Soren Baker's murder. They turned on each other, each blaming the other, but both giving enough details to convince Avondale PD the killers had been caught. I was pleased to hear that another loose end had been wrapped up.

Soren Baker's death was unrelated to Fuente's killing.

Alistair Campbell had an alibi for the night of Fuente's murder. Finn had confirmed it with the bartender at the Tate Lodge and with Mayor Cabot's staff.

And Justine Moreno was Grimm.

The question was, was she also Fuente's killer? For the life of me I couldn't establish a motive. Perhaps she had discovered his real identity and the anger of being lied to propelled her to murder him?

It was Lila who had lied, though. It was Lila who had protected Fuente's true identity.

Moreno had fallen apart when I confronted her about Grimm. I've been wrong before but I just couldn't wrap my head around Moreno killing Fuente.

Something else occurred to me: as sweet as Peggy and Hal were, the fact remained that they'd both lied to me.

Peggy and Hal.

Partners with a secret they were desperate to protect. Partners who cavorted in the very space Fuente used as an office.

This is only the beginning. . . .

The note left in Fuente's mouth haunted me. It seemed to hold the promise of a killer . . . and yet there'd been no further killings.

Peggy was a would-be writer and the first time we'd met her, she had specifically referred to Fuente's murder as something out of a mystery novel. If she and possibly Hal had conspired to kill Fuente *because* he'd discovered their secret, it made sense there hadn't been any more deaths. His murder had been for a very specific reason.

I shook myself. There were too many things wrong with that theory. Peggy and Hal were lovers. Their secret, while scandalous, was hardly earth-shattering. To kill to protect it took things to a whole new level of psychotic.

I listened to Finn's second message. He had spoken to all of the Black Hounds and most of them had alibis for the night of Fuente's killing. All except Neil Roget and Turtle. Both claimed they had turned in for an early night of television and room service. The hotel confirmed the room service deliveries but both men had their dinners dropped off by six p.m. That still left plenty of time for either or both of them to have left the Tate Lodge, killed Fuente, and returned with no one the wiser.

I wanted to turn around and head back to the station and dive into Roget and Turtle's backgrounds. I wanted to see their criminal histories and understand if these were simply bad men or if they were killers.

That's what I wanted to do, but I kept my car pointed toward home. I needed sleep. Sleep and time with my family. If there's one thing I've learned, it's that sometimes all you need is a fresh perspective. Step away from something worrisome for a few hours, or a few days, and your mind starts working in all sorts of crazy ways. Images sharpen, puzzle pieces fall into place, and answers fall like manna from heaven. Things that seem overly complicated are revealed to be much, much simpler than you ever imagined.

At least, that's what I hoped would happen.

Chapter Thirty-two

The sun was shining when we woke on Saturday and while the snow was nowhere near melting, the blue skies and crisp air propelled us out of the house. We arranged to meet Bull and Julia for a midmorning coffee and pie at the Four and Twenty Blackbirds Café.

I dressed Grace in her panda bear ski hat, bundled up so all that showed were her chubby pink cheeks, perfect little nose, and eyes the color of ripe blueberries. I kissed her on the tip of her nose and she smiled in return.

"Let's go, sweetheart!" Brody called up the stairs. "There's a piece of spiced apple pie with my name on it. Should we take Seamus?"

"Sure," I replied, balancing Grace on one hip and a diaper bag on the other. "He'll enjoy the outing. And he loves Chaos."

We piled in Brody's SUV after I noticed that the air in one of my tires was getting low. Once everyone was strapped in and secured, we headed down the mountain, singing along to an old John Denver album. I sang in a low voice, remembering Finn's words comparing me to a cat in heat. From the corner of my eye, I watched Brody for a reaction that he felt the same about my singing, but he looked blissful, happy to be out of the house, enjoying the ride. From the backseat, Grace babbled to herself.

Not wanting to miss out on the musical party, Seamus released a few notes himself, although they were from the wrong end of his body. His impromptu concert had Brody and I immediately cracking the windows.

"Sorry, Gracie," I muttered to the backseat. The poor baby was next to Seamus and would get the brunt of this particular foul wind.

"Jesus, what are you feeding that dog, Gem?"

"Nothing. You're the one feeding him most days."

We found a parking spot in the little lot adjacent to Four and Twenty Blackbirds. Brody took Grace while I slipped Seamus's halter over his shoulders and under his chest. We were lucky; it was still early, and the café was half-empty.

Brody spotted Bull and Julia near the back, close to a roaring fireplace, each with a magazine on the table in front of them.

Seamus had a dog to greet, though, before we could join the rest of our family, and I knew he would whine until he got to say hello. So I detoured and stopped at the edge of the pastry display case, one eye on the lone slice of flaky pear pie, the other eye on Chaos.

"Here, Chaos. C'mon, old boy, come say hi," I crooned. Seamus stopped, then crouched down onto his belly and crept forward, inch by inch, until he was nose to nose with the five-pound Chihuahua. Seamus knew the drill. He knew that going much farther into the café without a blessing from the owners' dog was rude.

From his tiny leopard-printed dog bed, Chaos curled his upper lip and bared three scraggly teeth. Seamus mewled like a kitten, then slid backward on his belly. When he was back in line with my feet, he stood and pulled me toward Brody and my grandparents. I chanced one last glance at Chaos, who stood up and rearranged himself on his dog bed with hardly a glance at me.

At the table, I kissed Bull and Julia. Julia looked beautiful, dressed to the nines, and Bull was dapper in a tweed blazer and dark jeans.

"We ordered cappuccinos for the table and a water for Seamus," Julia said grandly. "Now, what kind of dessert would you like? Brody wants the spiced apple pie."

"I was eyeballing that last piece of flaky pear pie, but if one of you wants it . . ." I said as graciously as I could, "I'm happy to get something else. . . ."

Bull grinned and chucked Grace under the chin, making a clucking noise with his tongue. "You were always a terrible liar, Gemma. I am going for a slice of the chocolate cream pie, and I think your grandmother is having cake. I know, shocking. But she's been craving pineapple upside-down cake something fierce."

Debbie Carol took our order. Together with her husband, Ron, they ran the Four and Twenty Blackbirds Café as well as the adjacent booktore, No Rhyme or Reason. They were a sweet couple, in their early sixties, who in previous lives had been emergency room doctors in New York City. Ron baked the pies in the back kitchen, and Debbie managed the front of the restaurant.

We chatted with Debbie a few minutes, then she left and Brody and I took turns telling Bull and Julia all about Grace's latest developments.

"I tell you, she's a genius. Smartest baby I ever saw," Bull said. He added, "No offense, Gemma. I didn't know you as a baby, and of course you're pretty smart . . . you, too, Brody. But this one is special. You can see it already, watch the way she tracks my face. Watch out, Mensa."

"Stop babbling, darling. Tell the kids about that strange man we met at the grocery store yesterday," Julia said. She patted my grandfather on the arm. "He was such a strange man. So good-looking, though."

"What man?" I asked, distracted as Debbie set four plates of delicious-looking dessert down in front of us. I'd gotten fresh whipped cream with my slice of flaky pear pie, while Bull and Brody had opted for homemade vanilla bean ice cream. I tried to subtly snag a corner of Bull's pie. I was too slow, though, and he sharply rapped my spoon with his.

"Get away, you no-good low-down dirty pie-stealing brat. We were at Whole Foods yesterday, picking up some salmon. Your grandmother thinks the fish at the market tastes off. So we pay ten dollars more to get it at Whole Foods. Anyway, we were standing in line and this man behind us started humming. Of course I recognize the tune, it's from *Evita*, which I've only seen about a dozen times. So, we turned around and started chatting with him. I showed him a picture of Grace, after he asked," Bull said. He took a bite of chocolate cream pie. "That is amazing pie."

"Why would he ask to see a picture of Grace?" I asked. "That's weird."

Julia, her mouth full of food, shook her head and said, "No, it was within context. We were talking about kids, the man said he missed his daughter."

"Oh."

Bull continued. "Then the most unusual thing happened. The man held up Grace's picture and quoted Shelley."

My blood froze, another bite of pie halfway to my mouth. "What do you mean, he *quoted* Shelley?"

Bull shrugged. "Just that. The man held her picture up, grinned, and said, 'The image of thy mother's loveliness.' And then he walked away."

"What did he look like? Julia, you said he was handsome?"

"Oh yes. He looked like a movie star from the olden days, like Clark Gable, or Rock Hudson. But there was something terrible about him, too. I wished Bull hadn't let him hold Grace's picture," Julia said. "I must have wiped that picture on my sweater ten times trying to remove his touch."

Neil Roget.

"This was yesterday?" I asked.

Bull and Julia nodded, both looking worried now. "What is it? Do you know him?"

I said yes.

I was debating how much to tell them when I noticed Brody had gone white as a sheet. He stared at me and said in a low voice, "I think the same man was at the house yesterday. He said he was with a real estate company and they were canvassing the neighborhood, trying to get a sense of who might be selling or buying soon. I let him use our bathroom. What is going on, Gemma?"

He watched as I considered lying and he turned away, disappointed. I sighed. "His name is Neil Roget. He's an ex-convict who works for Alistair Campbell. Remember how I talked you out of working for Campbell? Well, there you go. It's because his whole crew is filled with guys like Roget. He's a Black Hound."

"An ex-con, is that right?" Bull asked. "Sounds like a man in need of a second chance."

"That's baloney, Bull, and you know it," I said.

I sat back, my appetite gone. Had Campbell put Roget on me, my family, as payback for Brody not accepting his job? Or was something else going on?

"You don't think a man can change?" Bull asked. "I don't buy that. You can't possibly believe that."

"Of course I think a man—or woman—can change. Prison reform is the real deal, *sometimes*. I couldn't survive in this line of work if I didn't keep a little faith and hope in my back pocket, along with my handcuffs and weapon, of course. But these guys—guys like Neil Roget and Turtle, another lovely one of Campbell's henchmen—they are born with something wrong in their heads and something missing in their hearts. You can't sit there and tell me that a few years under the tutelage of a man like Alistair Campbell is going to turn a hardened thug into Pollyanna. I tell you, the first time I met Campbell, I felt like I had worms crawling under my skin."

"Gemma, if anyone knows anything about guys like this, it's me," Bull replied. "And, yes, the fact is most parolees in this state are back in jail within a year. Colorado has a high recidivism rate and nothing is going to change that except better parenting, education, and putting the fear of prison in people's hearts."

"And prayer, right?" I said with a smile.

"Darn right. Prayer, too."

Julia finished her cake and sat back. "Where's Laura? I want to go home. What kind of a place allows dogs inside?"

Bull took another sip of his cappuccino. "We'll leave in a few minutes. Gemma, I don't like this one bit. This Neil Roget character is targeting your family. It was no coincidence that he showed up in your home or at the store the same time as Julia and I. What's even more disturbing is that he's doing it in a way that makes it clear he wants you to know about it."

The plate hit the floor with a sharp crack and Julia stood up. We all jumped, Seamus included, and Grace puckered her face. Julia said, "I said, I want to go home *now*. Take. Me. Home."

Bull stood and shoveled the last bite of his pie into his mouth, his mustache twitching at the corner. "Sorry, kids, I've got to get this lady home. Julia, put your coat on."

My grandmother stood and saluted him. "Aye, aye, captain." Then she slid on her coat, grabbed her purse, and walked to the front door of the café. Bull followed behind her, waving a good-bye at us.

Brody and I looked at each other. "Well, that was fun."

I nodded. "At least the pie is delicious."

Grace dropped a stuffed toy and I leaned over and picked it up.

Brody asked, "Do I need to be worried?"

"I don't know. Roget does Campbell's biding. I don't believe he's an actual threat to us. I get the feeling that for whatever reason, though, Roget's latched on to this idea of making me uncomfortable," I responded. "Maybe it's his way of flirting. I'll talk to him."

"Not alone."

I shook my head. "No, I'll take Finn." Grace started to fuss in her chair. "Should we head home?"

Brody said yes. "I'll make a roast chicken for dinner. Does that sound good?"

"Good God, yes. Do we have potatoes and stuff for salad?"

"I think so. If not, we'll pull something out of the freezer," Brody replied. He hoisted Grace up and took her to the counter to settle our bill. I led Seamus back to Chaos so the two could say good-bye.

Brody had accepted my words without further discussion and that was one of the things I respected most about him. He trusted that I knew how to do my job and keep our family safe. There was no part of him that questioned my abilities just because I was female, no part of him that felt he should go find Neil Roget and tell him what was what.

The truth was, though, I was disturbed. Roget took time to discover who my grandparents were and where I lived, although Campbell could have told him that. Not only that, but he'd followed Bull and Julia, tracking them, waiting for the perfect opportunity to intercept them and make contact.

How long had he watched them? How long had he watched my house? Was he there now? The more I thought about it, the angrier I got . . . but I kept that anger inside, out of sight from Brody, not daring to let it enter the air near Grace.

Roget and I were due for a conversation. But it could wait until Monday. The weekend was for my family.

On Sunday, we went for a long hike along the edge of the woods. The weather was warm enough to bundle Grace up in a baby wrap and hold her against my chest. We let Seamus off leash, and he was a good boy, not straying too far from us. All around us, the sound of the snow melting, accompanied by birds singing, made it seem as though spring could be just around the corner. The glare off the snow was bright and Brody and I both wore sunglasses.

Back at the house, we put Grace down for a nap, then peeled out of our sweaty clothes and bathed, enjoying the double-shower head and each other. After, dressed in sweats and slippers, we had a picnic-style lunch of apples, crackers, and cheese in front of a roaring fire. Brody cracked open a bottle of Cabernet and his laptop, while I curled up with the new James Lee Burke novel and drifted away to southern Louisiana.

It felt indulgent to drink at noon on a Sunday, indulgent and long overdue. The exercise—outside, and in the shower—worked with the wine to cause a profound drowsiness. I fell into a deep sleep in which I dreamed about a puzzle. The puzzle pieces were white and gray, with sharp edges, like shards of an ice fog. They moved, oily, sliding about on the table and slipping to the floor, one by one. It was a frustrating dream.

When I woke, crusty-eyed and confused, it was twilight. The weekend had come and gone like a dream itself.

"You were out cold, honey," Brody said. He leaned over and kissed me. "Dinner's about ready, if you're hungry."

I stood and stretched. "I'm starving. I had the strangest dream. I was doing a puzzle. When was the last time you saw me do a puzzle? The pieces kept slipping to the floor, just out of my reach."

Brody shrugged. "Honestly, I think sometimes we read more into dreams than we really should. Why make things more complicated than they are? It's just a dream."

He kissed me, long and slow, then slapped me on the rear and told me to clean up for dinner.

I went to the bathroom and as I washed my hands, I stared into the mirror. "Is that what you're doing, Gemma? Are you so busy making things more complicated than they need to be that you can't see the forest for the trees? You have all the pieces. Put them together and see what kind of a picture you get. Talk to me, please."

But the woman in the mirror stared back silently, unable to answer.

Chapter Thirty-three

First thing Monday morning, I called the Tate Lodge and asked to be transferred to Neil Roget's room. I prayed he hadn't left for the day already and for once, luck was on my side. He answered on the third ring.

"Mr. Roget? This is Gemma Monroe, with the Cedar Valley Police Department."

He was slow to speak and by the pitch of his voice, I imagined he was still in bed. "Good morning, beautiful."

"Knock it off. This isn't a social call and you can address me as Detective. I don't know what kind of game you're playing but I want you to stop it immediately. If I hear you've gone near my family again, I'll arrest you for harassment. Is that clear?" I asked, my voice low, my words measured.

He laughed into the phone and I heard bedsheets rustling and a television being turned on. "Have you seen the news? More snow tonight. We like this town, Detective. You've got a lot of . . . virgin land here. Mr. Campbell sees a great deal of potential," Roget said. He yawned. "Yes, we really do like this town."

"You didn't answer my question, Mr. Roget," I said. "Did I make myself clear?"

Now he sounded bored. "Yes, *Detective* Monroe. You made yourself very clear. I can picture you right now, you're so clear. I'm not playing any sort of *game.* I simply find you intriguing. I just want to get to know the local scenery. I'm not trying to scare you. But it sounds like I have."

"I'm not scared. More like pissed off. Did Campbell put you up to this? Stalking my grandparents, coming into my house?"

Roget laughed again. "We're not a bunch of dogs taking orders from our master. Try to remember this, sweetheart, I make my own decisions just like any other big boy."

I hung up without another word. I didn't know if Roget was lying and Campbell had in fact sent him after me and my family, or if Roget had gone rogue. In the end, the why didn't matter much. I'd make good on my promise if he came near us again.

Roget's words stayed with me, that they "liked this town."

Sure, we had a great deal of undeveloped land but the bulk of it was protected open space, national forest, or state park. There was only so much development that could be built out. Everyone in town knew that; that was why most of the big contractors stayed away or were content to build massive homes on private property for the wealthy and leave the town itself as is.

Campbell was wasting time here. There was money, lots of money, to be made elsewhere. And no matter what he said, Campbell was a businessman, a smart businessman, through and through.

Businessmen don't take money lightly.

"What are you doing here, Campbell? What are you and your Black Hounds really doing here?" I whispered. Whatever the reason, Campbell had tried to drag Brody into it, and Sam, too.

There was something there, but what it was, I couldn't yet say.

Finn and I spent the rest of the day poring over the financial records that Brad Choi, Fuente's agent, had sent us. It was another dead end. Fuente had accounts all over and by the looks of it, the money he was sending to Lark Co was but a drop in the hat compared to the royalties he earned on his books.

At some point, we decided to call it a day. I opened my desk drawer for a snack, hoping to see a bag of hickory-smoked almonds or a tin of olives, but instead I saw a receipt from our evidence room.

Fuente's phone.

The receipt reminded me that I'd meant to take a good look at the phone when I had some free time. I went to Evidence and handed in the receipt to Furby and he gave me Fuente's phone in return.

Back at my desk, I put on gloves.

I turned the phone on and after a long moment, the screen lit up. I found the call log and skimmed through it. Lila's number popped up frequently, as both caller and called. A few other numbers appeared that I recognized, like the high school and Brad Choi's cell phone. The rest were a variety of Colorado, New York, New Jersey, and California area codes. On a whim, I scrolled down his contact list, stopping in the middle of the alphabet but finding no references to Lark Co. Another dead end.

"Finn, don't you feel like we're waiting for a killer that's not going to strike again?"

He looked over at me from the doorway, where he'd been stretching out his legs. "Elaborate, please."

"This whole time we've been thinking the note in Fuente's mouth was from a serial killer. We've been waiting for the killer to strike again, only . . . only it seems to me that maybe we'll be waiting a long time," I said. Standing, I stretched my own legs, pulling each one up behind me, one at a time, feeling the tight muscles relax. I needed to get back in shape; three months on maternity leave hadn't done much for my strength or stamina.

"Still not following," Finn said. He finished and joined me at my desk.

"What I'm saying is that maybe the note was a diversion. Remember our first thought when we saw the body? How personal it was, and how random the location seemed?"

Finn nodded. "Uh-huh."

"Does that jibe with any serial killer you've ever heard of? It's been over a week and there's been nothing. No killings—other than Baker and that doesn't count, it doesn't seem related at all—no threats, no one missing or attacked. Either we have a very patient serial killer on our hands or we don't have a serial killer at all. And we've been chasing up the wrong tree," I said.

"Barking up the wrong tree."

"Whatever. We've been going down a rabbit hole. We need to go back to the reason why Fuente was in Cedar Valley in the first place: to write his memoirs, to put to paper his own story."

"And you think someone didn't like his story. And that's why we can't find the memoirs," Finn said. He moved to his desk, looking for something. Finding it, he held up a piece of paper with some chicken scratches on it.

"My notes," he said. "This Rabbit Man . . . what if he grew up with Lila Conway and Fuente? You said she saw the Rabbit Man outside her house. Maybe he's cleaning up loose ends from something that happened years ago. Maybe Lila wasn't always shy or Fuente wasn't always a teddy bear. You just saw what we went through with Grimm; maybe they bullied the Rabbit Man."

"I'm going to call her." I tried Lila's home and work numbers, twice, but she didn't pick up. I grew uneasy, thinking about Finn's words.

"I'm going there, to her house. Want to come?"

Finn checked his watch. "It's after six. I told Cassie I'd come by for meat loaf. I can cancel. . . ."

I shook my head. "No, don't cancel. I'm sure everything is fine. I want to push her on the Rabbit Man, and the school years she and Fuente shared. You could be onto something there."

"Are you sure? Meat loaf is not my favorite."

"Even more reason you should go. It will make Cassie happy. Just ask for ketchup and douse that thing with it."

It was cold and dark by the time I pulled into Lila's drive. I shut off the engine and stared at the cottage, once again enchanted by its lovely storybook quality. As before, a plume of gray smoke drifted toward the sky from the chimney. Her truck was parked where I'd seen it before, but judging from the snow piled high on it, it hadn't been driven in a few days.

Watching the house, I waited to see if Lila

would come out, if the noise of my engine or the grind of my tires had caught her attention. No one came to the door, though, and it struck me again how truly isolated was the life that Lila had created for herself.

Not isolated, I corrected myself. Peaceful.

The woods were quiet and still as I walked to the house.

There was a new floor mat at the front door. It was tan with rough-looking fibers meant to catch dirt and mud. Two cardinals were laid into the middle of the mat, their red feathers bright and cheery. When I was a child, I once watched a cardinal attack its own image in the reflection of a window. The bird was obsessed, mad with rage, and it terrified me. My grandmother Julia explained that in springtime, the cardinals are highly defensive of their breeding territories. This bird had mistaken his own reflection for a competitor.

I thought that seemed accurate. It takes both bravery and a bit of madness to emerge from winter, into spring, to step forward and face the sun again after months of cold. You see it in the animals when they emerge from hibernation; their caution and trepidation. Of course, by summer, everyone is bonkers. But that first step is fraught with both danger and possibility.

I was wrong; Lila had heard me pull up after all. She opened the door and roused me from my melancholy thoughts before I'd had time to knock. She was surprised to see me. "Good evening, Gemma. What are you doing here?"

"I have a few more questions about Delaware Fuente; do you have a minute? I tried calling but I didn't get an answer. I got a little worried."

She nodded. Her hair was pulled back and her face free of makeup. Her eyes shone bright in the front porch light. "I'm so sorry, I must have the ringer turned off. I'm fine. Come in, please. I was reading by the fire, an early Agatha Christie mystery novel. Have you read much of her?"

I said no.

"The thing about mysteries, unlike life, is that they are never about the killer, or the victim, or even the detective, really. In the end, they're all about the puzzle. And the joy of reading a mystery comes from the riddle within the riddle, you see. If you solve the puzzle before the detective, it's much more fun," she continued. "Tea?"

"Sure."

She hummed as she poured me a cup of tea in the kitchen and then we adjourned to the front living room. Kojak swung gently in his cage, muttering away. The great white bird's yellow crest moved in tandem to his head bobbing. Behind him, on the wall, were the prints of birds that I remembered seeing before, and the posters of the various explorers and adventurers.

After we were settled, she asked, "So what questions did you have for me?"

I began to ask about the memoirs and the Rabbit Man but thought of something else that I still didn't have an answer for. I pulled out my phone and scrolled through it until I found the picture I'd taken of the photograph on Fuente's computer, with him and the young man.

"Do you know who this is?" I asked her, holding the phone so that she could see the image.

She stared at it for a long minute, then slowly shook her head. "I've never seen him before in my life. Whoever he is, he's making Del very happy. You know, now that I think of it, I know he did some work with a local youth group out there, in Jersey. It was a YMCA or a Big Brothers camp. Maybe this kid is one of his boys?"

I nodded. Could it be that simple?

"He liked kids, didn't he?"

Lila nodded. "Yes, I think so. I think he liked their innocence and their openness to life. Not in a pervert kind of way. You have to say that, you know, nowadays. We're immediately suspect of any older male who takes too strong an interest in kids. Sad days we live in."

"Lila, I think you mentioned that Delaware Fuente initially contacted you because he was looking for a quiet place to work on his memoirs," I said.

She nodded again. "Yes, that's right. He said his life at the moment was too noisy back east. He remembered the quiet of a Colorado winter and wondered if I had any ideas of a peaceful place he could spend some time writing. And I of course suggested he come to Cedar Valley. He thought that sounded like a grand idea. He was also intrigued by the idea of doing this series of guest lectures at the school."

"In disguise, though," I said.

She nodded again. "Yes, he didn't want to be recognized. He said it would distract from his 'mission.' He was adamant about that."

I set my cup of tea down. "The thing is, Lila, we can't find any evidence that Fuente was working on any project, let alone something as important as his memoirs."

The smile fell from Lila's face and was replaced with one of confusion. "I don't understand."

"Neither do I, to be honest. We even sent his laptop down to a special unit in Denver and they found nothing," I replied. I leaned forward, placing my elbows on my knees. "I can't find any handwritten documents, either, or notes, or research. Don't you find that strange?"

Lila stood and paced the room. "Every time I talked to Del, he was so enthusiastic about his progress, he kept telling me all these stories that he remembered from our childhood and his early years in New York. He was lying to me?"

"Could he have been working on his memoirs in long hand, writing them out?"

"I suppose," Lila said.

"Lila, the Rabbit Man, are you sure you've never seen him before? The reason I ask is that maybe he, or someone else, took Fuente's memoirs. They could be the motive for his death. There might be something in them that the killer didn't want exposed."

"I told you, I've never seen that man before in my life." Her face darkened. "Maybe Del was counting on someone else to write his memoirs for him."

"What do you mean?"

Lila shook her head. "I'm not sure. Del was always more interested in outcome than process. I'm tired, Gemma."

I was tired, too, and uneasy. It wasn't that I thought Lila was lying to me, but there was something in her eyes that had changed since my last visit.

I stood. "May I use your restroom?"

"Of course. It's down the hall, last door on the right."

I walked down the hall, then stopped and listened. From the sound of the pots and pans banging together, I guessed Lila had returned to the kitchen. I peeked in the last door on the right and saw a toilet and a sink and a tub, nothing unusual. I quietly opened a few more doors and found a closet, a door into the garage, and a small guest bedroom. Everything looked in order, but I stepped into the guest room and closed the door behind me and turned on the light.

I didn't know what I was looking for, but a small, framed sketch resting on the dresser caught my eye. I crossed the room and picked it up. It was a pencil drawing, with an inscription from Del to Lila and the caption, "Hide your carrots."

I swallowed hard. The picture was of a large man, with huge ears and sparse hair and over-size buckteeth. The man leered down at a couple of small rabbits. They were in a garden box and the man was oversize compared to the bunnies and the vegetables.

The Rabbit Man . . .

Chapter Thirty-four

The house was quiet, too quiet, and I'd already been gone too long. I set the drawing down and slipped out of the room and quickly crossed the hall and entered the bathroom. I flushed the toilet and let the sink run a minute, then patted my clammy forehead with a hand towel.

"Everything okay?" Lila asked when I reentered the living room.

I nodded.

I needed a minute that I didn't have.

Lila had a sketch of the very man she'd said had been stalking Fuente and had been at her house. I walked around the living room, trying to gather my thoughts. Lila watched me, a peculiar look on her face. Kojak muttered in his cage.

A small, intricate bird sculpture caught my eye on the mantel and I walked to it, buying more time.

"This is beautiful," I said, holding up the bird sculpture. It was only a few inches high, ceramic, and hand-painted. The little thing was speckled, with a bright yellow breast and distinctive black *V* below its throat. "What is it, a yellow-breasted chat?"

Lila was impressed. "Not a bad guess. You know your birds."

I shook my head and smiled. "Not really, but my grandmother did. Does. Some of what she imparted has stuck."

"Well, I'm not surprised you don't recognize this fellow. We hear them much more than we see them," Lila said, taking the bird from my hands. She whistled the bird's familiar tune, then turned it over and showed me the bottom. The base was unpainted and the initials "J.C." were scratched into the bare ceramic finish.

She continued. "My grandmother Jocelyn Conway was an artist. She made this for me when I was a little girl. It's a meadowlark. By then, my shyness and anxiety were obvious, and she made it, and gave it to me, and told me that I should aspire to be a little lark, flying high above all my cares."

I swallowed hard and took a step back.

Lila didn't notice my unease. She said, "And from that day forward, I was Lark to my family." She smiled sadly. "I told Del my nickname once, and he loved it. He took to calling me Lark, too."

I had been so stupid.

I'd been distracted by Soren Baker, and Alistair Campbell and his Black Hounds, and by Roland Five and Grimm. Once again, I'd forgotten who truly lived in the woods, deep in the shadows, closed up in her cottage. Lila set the little meadowlark back on the mantel and looked at me. There must have been something telling in my eyes because the color suddenly drained from her face.

"How did you know?"

I casually took a step to the side, moving away from the heavy stone mantel with its array of objects and the iron fire pokers.

"It wasn't any one thing, Lila. You've got a sketch of the Rabbit Man in your guest bedroom. Fuente has a file called Lark Co on his computer. I kept thinking it meant Lark Company, or Lark Corporation, but it refers to you, doesn't it? Lark, Colorado?"

She nodded.

"Why was Fuente paying you every month, Lila? What did you have on him?"

She moved to the birdcage and stuck a finger through the iron bars. Kojak gently touched his beak to her.

Lila looked up with a sly smile. "Maybe he was simply helping an old friend. Did you know my salary has been frozen for the last three years? Budget cuts. Justine Moreno promised to keep fighting for raises but she doesn't always get her way."

"These payments go back a lot longer than three years, Lila," I responded. "Is it the boy in the picture? Did you lie about that? Did you and Delaware Fuente have a child together?"

At that, she laughed and the laugh was the worst thing of all because it was the laugh of someone who was truly well on her way to becoming unhinged.

"I guess you could say we had a child together, Gemma. Or rather, many children together," Lila said.

She laughed harder.

"Where are they?"

She laughed again, shaking her head. "Oh, we keep our children bound up, unable to grow or change once we've spawned them."

She pointed behind me, and I remembered seeing a closed door there. Cold horror ran down my spine. Did the door lead to a set of stairs, down to a basement or up to an attic? Was this truly a witch's house, with children locked away?

Then I turned, and I saw, and understanding bloomed in my head.

On a bookshelf, in tidy alphabetical order, was row after row of Delaware Fuente's novels. They were bound, just as Lila had described. Words and sentences that were unchanging, that would remain forever frozen on the page.

I turned back to Lila. "You helped him write these?"

"No," she said. "I didn't help him."

"What, then?"

Lila smiled. "I didn't help him, I wrote them myself. All of them, every single word."

"I don't understand."

"Del couldn't write for nothing. But his dreams were so big and mine were so small. He read my first story, a throwaway piece, really, and he fell in love with it. Del begged me to publish but I couldn't. I was frozen with fear. Behind my back, he submitted it, under his own name, to an agent. The rest is history. Oh, I was furious when I found out, furious and giddy and prideful, all at the same time. Del was clever, he fed that small slice of pride, fed it until it grew bigger than the fury. I wrote and he published. I was the words and he was the face and it worked quite well for a number of years," Lila said.

"But I've read your writing! An article you wrote a number of years ago, pleading for Yvette Michaelson to receive an award. Your writing . . . it was awful."

"Staged, all of it. Del was terrified that someone might catch on if they ever saw my real writing," Lila said.

She moved away from Kojak and picked up her cup of tea. She sipped from it, then set it down again.

I was in shock. "How did you get away with it? How did no one figure out that Fuente wasn't a real author?"

Lila waved her hands in the air. "Magic. People see what they want to believe. Del never gave them any reason to doubt his story. Over the years, he learned enough about the craft of writing to successfully talk about it, write about it. Not only did people not doubt it, they ate it up with a spoon. Interviews, articles, social media . . . Del did it all and the fans loved it. Son of poverty-stricken immigrants makes dreams come true. They thought he was the real deal. If they'd only known."

It was incredible. If true, it would shake the literary world at its core. Fuente's legend would die. Conway would become famous overnight.

"Did he decide to stop paying you? Is that why you killed him, over the money?"

Lila looked hurt. "I thought you understood me, Gemma. How can you think that?"

"Well, you did kill him. You must have had a reason. What happened?"

She thought a moment and nodded. "I'll tell you, so that you understand why I did what I did. You'll see I had to."

I waited.

The room grew cold; the fire, dying. Lila picked up the iron poker and stoked it. The coals and embers woke, burning red again, and the flames picked up their heat. Lila kept the poker in her hand, and I kept an eye on her, wary.

"Del was going to take away the one thing that

means more to me than anything else. I asked for five minutes to stand in the sun and he refused me that, after everything I had done for him. Can you imagine how that felt?"

"I don't understand. . . ."

Lila finished her tea and struck the ground with the iron poker. I jumped at the deep thud it made when it struck the wood floor.

"It was my masterpiece. Yvette Michaelson's biography, told through the eyes of the woman who loves and understands her. Writing her story made me feel alive, powerful, in a way that writing those stupid novels never made me feel. Del saw my power and it scared him. He said the book would never be published under my name. He said it was of such magnitude, such beauty, that no one would believe I had written it, and it would be dismissed. Del insisted only he could publish it," Lila said, her words coming fast and furious. "I was in total and utter shock. He sat there, right there in that armchair, and said those words to me and I literally felt the blood begin to boil in my body."

"You must have been very angry."

Lila began to pace the room, tapping the wood floor with the iron poker with each step as though it were an ornate cane. "Anger doesn't begin to cover what I felt. My whole life, the overriding feeling I've experienced is anxiety.

It touches everything I've ever done; where I live, where I work. I don't have friends or dates. I find solace in solitude. Out here, in my own private corner of the world, I find peace. I had accepted that I would be alone, until Yvette changed something in me."

I hated to point out the obvious. "Lila, Yvette is dead. You know her only through stories, tales, legends."

Lila smiled at that. "Haven't you ever fallen in love with a painting, or a song, or a novel?"

I thought about that. "I suppose I've loved pieces of art, but I've never been in love with one."

"Then I pity you. It's the most absolute, pure form of love. Yvette Michaelson is perfection. For her, I was willing to step out of the shadows and let the world see—let the world understand—my love. My adoration," Lila said. "She was my twin, my inspiration, my hero, my North Star."

I had to take a moment.

I was in a cottage, deep in the woods, having a philosophical conversation on the nature of love with a murderer.

"So you two fought and you killed him, just like that?"

Lila grimaced. "It wasn't planned. Nor was it easy. We spent weeks having the same conversation, talking in circles. Del truly did come to town with the intent of writing his memoirs, and doing the guest lectures. That first night, when he arrived and came over for a drink, I was so . . . I was glowing. I'd finished the manuscript and Del could always tell when I had finished a project. He knew there was a fresh story, and I refused to share it with him. I told him I was working on a novel for him, to publish on his expected schedule, but that this other particular project was all mine."

She took a deep breath, then continued. "He was relentless. I came home one night and he was here, sitting in my damn living room, cool as a cucumber. He'd torn apart my desk and found my manuscript and was nearly finished reading it. He was enthralled and instantly jealous. He wanted it for himself. Del said it would be an awakening for his career, a chance to show the world he could not only write fiction but nonfiction, as well."

Lila closed her eyes, remembering. "I was furious and in pain; it felt as though I'd been assaulted in my own home. I hid it well, though, never letting on how much he'd hurt me. I asked to meet him the next evening, after classes, at the school. I had no idea the blizzard would be as bad as it was. I told him I had a diary, a secret diary that I'd discovered during the course of my research. I said he could tell her story if he agreed to read the diary and see what I saw in her. I told him only then would he fully understand her."

"Why the high school? Why not meet here, or at Fuente's cabin?"

She opened her eyes and I saw tears. "I couldn't stand the thought of him in this house ever again, among my things, in my most sacred corner of the world. Our friendship had turned into a disease. The high school was the logical place to meet. We'd both already be there, of course."

"Killing someone is not an easy thing, Lila."

Lila said in a flat voice, "As I said, it wasn't planned nor was it easy. We were in my office when I gave him the diary to read. He read the sections I'd earmarked and then laughed. He laughed in my face. He laughed at me and said it was now his story, to tell as he wanted. I lost my mind, I was so angry. I grabbed the diary from him and took off running. He chased me, that stupid man, not even bothering to go get his coat or hat. I took a flashlight on my way out; I knew I needed to get out of the building, away from him. He must have grabbed a second one from another office, because the next thing I knew there he was, chasing me, with a flashlight in his hand and a look on his face like he was going to kill me."

She stopped and took a shaky breath, then continued. "I knew the area better than him and so I decided to surprise him on the footpath. I turned off my light and pulled my old hunting knife out of my purse. I meant to scare him, make him promise to leave me alone forever. But he lunged and the knife ended up in his belly. He died quickly. I was in shock and was convinced no one would believe that it was all a terrible, terrible accident. So I tore a blank page from the diary and wrote the note you found stuffed in his mouth. I hoped it might be enough to keep the suspicion off me."

She was right, of course. That's exactly what the note had accomplished. "What about the Rabbit Man? Did you make him up, too? Base him off of Fuente's sketch?"

Lila nodded. "There's no Rabbit Man. At least, no real Rabbit Man. He was an imaginary friend of Delaware's when he was quite young. Del liked to say the Rabbit Man saved him from a childhood of loneliness. After Del and I met and became friends, the Rabbit Man wasn't needed anymore. He faded away, living only in tales Del told. He came back to life when I needed a supposed stalker for Del."

"You killed your only friend," I said. "Your best friend."

Lila shook her head. "No, Gemma. I killed my worst enemy."

She stepped toward me with the poker, raising it as she advanced. I told her to stop and moved to pull my weapon. But I was too slow, and Lila brought the poker down on my right arm, with the sharp edge first. I cried out as it cut through my skin and left my dominant hand numb. I struggled to yank my weapon from my belt with my left hand.

"Stop it," I yelled. "Stop or I'll shoot, Lila, I swear to God."

But she didn't stop, and with her next move, she lifted the poker up over her shoulder and brought it down hard on my head.

Darkness fell all around me.

When I came to, the first thing I noticed was the smell of something burning. I tried to sit up and groaned as a wave of nausea hit me. Then panic as I realized the room was slowly filling with thick gray smoke. Pushing through the pain, I rolled over and got to my knees. The smoke was increasing and I began coughing. The smoke made my eyes water and that was when the real panic set in.

Think, think. You were in the living room. The front door is right there.

From somewhere in the house, maybe upstairs, a window popped. Jesus, the whole thing must have been on fire. Did Lila start it? Did she knock me out and then set fire to her own house to cover the crime?

I had to get out.

Blindly, I crawled forward, one arm outstretched. My hand touched a leg, wooden and tall. I felt around and realized it was the kitchen table.

She dragged you into the kitchen.

I pictured the room; the table was in the back rear, behind the island and the appliances.

Damn it, I was going the wrong way. Another coughing spell overtook me and I wept from the pain in my head, the rising panic in my chest, and the fumes.

I was going to die here.

The thought took what little wind remained in my lungs right out and my forehead fell to the floor. There was nothing left to do. Behind me, a beam crashed down and I heard more glass explode. I tried to lift my head but it felt as though it were made of lead and my neck made of feathers and try as I might, I couldn't find the strength to move.

I wasn't ready to die but I accepted that there was little in my control now. A strange peace descended on me and I thought of Grace, and Brody, and my grandparents. They weren't here with me, and that meant they were safe, and that was all that mattered.

I prayed that I would fall unconscious soon, before the flames reached me.

Maybe it was cowardly, but I didn't want to suffer.

The next thing I knew, someone was tugging at my waist and then I was being carried. My eyes felt heavy, difficult to keep open, but I caught glimpses of blackened walls and fiery flames. The wallpaper curled as it burned, peeling down from the walls in great strips.

Then I was outside, and the icy air burned my lungs and face in a whole new way. Over the tremendous noise of the cottage burning, a high tinny pitch of sirens filled the air.

My rescuer laid me gently on the snow and for the briefest of moments, a face hovered over mine. The face was fuzzy, like the edges of a dream; his gold hair appeared as a halo.

Then he was gone and I slipped away once more.

Chapter Thirty-five

"We miss you," Brody said simply. I missed him, too, and Grace, and Seamus.

I missed my home.

The baby was asleep and I longed to hold her. The doctors said it would be another few days before they would release me, though, and I was too shaky to trust myself with her in my arms.

All in all, my injuries could have been a lot worse. I'd suffered a concussion from the blow to the back of my head, and there was some minor damage done to my throat from the smoke inhalation; luckily, the fire itself hadn't touched me. My hands were bruised from the fight with Lila and I had a new scar to add to my collection, a straight narrow slice down my forearm from her attack with the fire poker. I also had a black eye and a few scrapes on my cheek.

"I can't wait to get out of here."

After their visit, I slept a while. A knock woke me, and when I opened my eyes, I saw Finn in the doorway with a bouquet of flowers and a stack of magazines.

"Hey, kid."

"Hey yourself. You shouldn't have."

Finn smirked. "Don't worry, I didn't. The

flowers are from the chief and the magazines are from the guys."

He walked in and nodded, impressed. "That's quite a shiner, Gem. You look like a badass."

I thanked Finn for the flowers, and the magazines, and the compliment. He looked uncomfortable and I knew this wasn't a social visit.

"Lila?"

"They found her this morning. She had gone into the basement—that's where she started the fire—and then either stayed down there or was trapped. There's not very much left of her."

I remembered the passion in her eyes when she talked about Yvette Michaelson, and the fury when she spoke about Delaware Fuente.

"I don't think she wanted to die."

Finn lifted a shoulder. "I didn't know her well enough to say one way or another."

I closed my eyes. "I don't think anyone really knew her."

"We went to see the house this morning, Chief Chavez and I. It's a pile of rubble, Gemma, there's hardly anything left but a few pictures, odds and ends. You were incredibly lucky to crawl out of there when you did." Finn continued. "It looks like the whole thing came down right after you got out."

My eyes opened. "But I didn't crawl out of there. The Rabbit Man saved me."

Finn looked at me warily. He sat down on the edge of the hospital bed and placed a hand on my shin. Through the thin hospital blanket, I felt the heat of his touch and I was grateful for the human contact. It was further evidence I *had* survived.

Once again, I'd survived.

He said softly, "There was no one else there, Gemma. The doctors said this might happen. Concussions can play tricks on your memory. You got yourself out of that house. The fire department found you in the snow, you and no one else. You made it to the front door, then crawled back on your hands and knees to open the door on a birdcage in the living room and let the damn bird fly out, and then you crawled far enough away from the house to be out of harm's way before you fainted."

"But . . ."

I remembered lying down on the stone tile in the kitchen, gasping for air, struggling to find the energy to get up and *move,* and get the hell out of there. I had given up, putting my fate into the universe's hands.

Or had I?

Had I found the strength within me to move and fight for my life?

I didn't think I had. I didn't think I possessed that kind of strength.

Someone carried me out of Lila Conway's

burning cottage. He laid me in the snow, safe from the flames and spitting embers. He vanished into the woods like someone who knows them intimately, knows their secret trails and hidden caves.

"You said Kojak was saved, too? The bird?"

Finn nodded. "The cage is a big twisted heap of metal but the door was definitely open and we haven't found any barbecued chicken yet."

I leaned back. "Lila said she made up the Rabbit Man. She has—had, I guess it probably went up in the fire—a sketch that Fuente drew years ago of a rabbit-looking man with a funny saying on it. She based this fake man that stalked Fuente at his cabin on that drawing. She admitted it."

"Well, there you go," Finn replied. "You'd been talking about this guy with Lila, and you imagined him as your savior. But it was all you, Gemma. You saved yourself."

I knew what happened. I knew someday, I'd see the Rabbit Man again. If he were really up there, in the woods, I'd see him again. The Rabbit Man was real. I didn't know how Fuente knew to sketch him, and I didn't know how he came to be my rescuer, but there it was nonetheless.

More magic, more mystery in a world already brimming with it.

I owed the Rabbit Man my life.

Finn fidgeted in his seat.

"What?"

"You're not going to like it."

"Tell me anyway," I said.

"Sam's gone," Finn said. He shook his head slowly. "This morning."

"What do you mean, he's gone?"

Finn removed his hand from my shin, stood, and went to the window. "I hate hospitals. The view is always terrible. And no one's ever in here for anything good. Sam cleaned out his desk and turned in his resignation letter to Chavez. Effective immediately. I talked to him for about a minute before he left; poor kid looked like he was going to start bawling."

I couldn't believe it. "What's he going to do?"

"Just as he said, he's going to work for Campbell. Sam's a Black Hound now. His grandfather's got him all tangled up in both the family business and Campbell's business," Finn said. "Sam never really had a chance."

I groaned. "Jesus. Get me out of this room. I'll talk some sense into him."

Finn turned from the window and stared at me. "We already tried, all of us, even Moriarty. But Sam is in a bad way. He's messed up. I don't know if we'd even want him working with us, the shape he's in."

The full implication of Finn's words sunk in.

"So Campbell is putting in stakes here? I hoped

he would realize Cedar Valley wasn't the place for him and his crew after all."

Finn nodded. "They're here to stay. Campbell put an offer in yesterday on a house on the north side of town. There are rumors in town that Campbell's on to something in the mountains. Maybe it's an untapped gold vein. Maybe silver. The Black Hounds are going to try to piss all over this valley. But we're not going to let them do that, are we?"

He came back to the bed. To my surprise, he leaned down and gently kissed my cheek. He didn't smell of Cassie Gunther's scented lotions; he smelled of aftershave and coffee.

He smelled of Finn. What that meant, I didn't know.

I watched him walk out of the room. As he passed through the door, he said over his shoulder, without looking back, "We need you home soon, Gemma. I have a feeling that this is going to be a long spring."

Chapter Thirty-six

Fresh snow dusted the ruins of Lila Conway's home like powdered sugar on a broke-down gingerbread house. The air smelled of charred wood and burnt insulation materials. I'd checked in with the city; a crew was scheduled to begin clearing away the rubble in a few weeks. They planned to fill in the basement and lay dirt and sod over the remains of the foundation.

By springtime, the scene of Lila's death would be nothing more than a large patch of bare dirt, with the tiniest signs of life struggling to break through. By summer, enough grass would have grown to give the place a sense of hope, and by fall it would appear as if no one had ever lived here. There was good soil and strong light. The land would return to the woods and the forest would creep ever closer, reclaiming what was once its own.

It was an unsettling thought, how easily and quickly all the moments of one's life can be wiped away. If we're not remembered after we're gone, were we really ever here? I thought about Lila's comments about the snow, how it wipes the world clean.

Maybe in the end it wipes away too much.

I carefully walked the edge of the rubble,

avoiding any flooring that looked burned through or ready to collapse. From my jacket pocket, I withdrew a small plastic bag of birdseed and chopped fruit. Kojak hadn't seemed like a picky eater, but I wanted to give him some options, if he was still alive. I hoped he was but he was a bird forged in the tropics, in a place of heat and humidity, and this was a cold, dry land.

The same snow that I found solace in would be certain death to a creature like Kojak.

The woods were silent and more than once, I paused in my walking, gazing toward the thick, dark tangle of trees, hoping to see the Rabbit Man.

I felt a debt to him.

But he didn't come and I paced the rubble, searching for what, I didn't know. Lila Conway had killed Delaware Fuente and tried to kill me. I should have hated her. Instead, I felt only sorrow. It seemed to me that her life was made up of great loneliness and fear and lies.

Lila Conway was one of the world's most celebrated authors and no one would ever know. She and Delaware Fuente were the only two people who knew the truth and any evidence there might have been had burned to the ground with Lila. They both took their secrets to the grave.

"What a tragedy," I whispered and kicked at a

piece of broken and burnt pottery. It crumbled with my touch and tears sprang to my eyes. "What a waste."

In the rubble, I saw something twinkle back at me. I bent down and brushed away soot and debris. It was the framed poster of Yvette Michaelson. Save for a burnt corner and some broken glass, it was unscathed. I'm not normally superstitious but I took that as a sign.

I pulled the poster out of the frame and the shards of glass fell away. I held the picture at arm's length and looked into Yvette's eyes. Could I have fallen in love with this woman?

In another life, perhaps.

I looked into her eyes and saw a deep restlessness. There was something else there, too, the hint of even deeper secrets and mysteries. I felt myself falling under her spell, beginning to wonder if I couldn't try to find out just a little bit more about her. . . .

I rolled the poster up and tucked it under my arm. It seemed important that I should find a new home for her. Lila's biography of Yvette may have gone up in flames, but Yvette's story was not complete. The rest of it, the unanswered questions about her life and death, were out there somewhere, and there was something peaceful about thinking she had found what she was looking for, thousands of miles from home, in the jungles of South America.

It's a brave thing, leaving all that you know to find what you might become.

I decided the poster would go on the wall above my desk at the station. If Finn was right, and it was going to be a long spring, then I needed all the guardian angels I could find.

As I walked to my car, something broke through the tops of the trees with a great deal of noise and took flight in the woods behind me. I turned and saw a large white bird rise up into the sky, its yellow crest shining like a crown of gold-dipped feathers. I rubbed my eyes, sure I was imagining things, but the bird continued to soar. I watched it in wonder until it was no more than a speck in the distance. Kojak followed some primal, migratory map imbedded deep in his psyche, urging him on to a warmer, more southern destination.

"Phoenix rising," I whispered. A great peace settled on my shoulders and I thought to myself that there truly is a season for everything. I hoped the bird would continue south. There was a home for him somewhere, among his kind and kindred.

In the end, that's what really matters, isn't it?

Find your home, and you find yourself.

Center Point Large Print
600 Brooks Road / PO Box 1
Thorndike, ME 04986-0001 USA

(207) 568-3717

US & Canada:
1 800 929-9108
www.centerpointlargeprint.com